"F. Paul Wilson is one of the finest storytellers of our time"
– Rocky Mountain News

"Ghoulish and macabre"
– Publishers Weekly

"What comes through most clearly...is the author's unconscious
enthusiasm of the craft of storytelling"
– San Francisco Chronicle

"Wilson is a master of the theme story and even a more master of
letting subject matter generate emotional force"
– Booklist

"A wonderful smorgasbord sure to please any reader of genre fiction"
– CNN.com

"Sharp social satire"
– Kirkus Reviews

"Reminiscent of T.V.'s Twilight Zone"
– Publishers Weekly

THE
COMPENDIUM OF
F
VOLUME ONE

By F. Paul Wilson

CONTENTS

INTRODUCTION

S o many ways I could have gone with the title:

50 F-ing Years
50 Years of F
50 Years of F-ing Around
Fortunately, wiser heads prevailed.

Fifty years…1971 to 2021…half a century since my first story saw print.

Sixty-plus books, nearly 100 short stories, novelettes and novellas.

Can't believe I've had that many ideas.

Can't believe I've typed all those millions and millions of words (with two fingers, no less).

Can't believe I've fooled you all for so long.

Because, really, I'm not a writer. Don't look to me for luminous or evocative prose. Don't expect enlightenment or insights into the mysteries of existence, the intricacies of the human condition.

I'm just a storyteller. I make up stuff I think is cool—stuff *I'd* like to read—and I put it down on paper. I'm not sure why I've written so much, or why I keep on writing. It's become some kind of obsessive-compulsive disorder. I am not writing for myself or out of a need for self-expression or a quest for immortality (as Woody Allen said, I'd prefer to achieve immortality through not dying). I am writing because I don't seem to have a choice. I am writing to entertain, which means I am writing for *you*, and if you are not entertained, if you are not turning those pages, then I am not doing my job.

I am not writing to make you smarter, although I'm happy if you learn something from my research. I am writing because I want to be read. I want to control you. That is what a storyteller does. Like the voice on *Outer Limits*, when you pick up one of my stories I want to control the transmission, all that you see and hear—the horizontal and the vertical, sharp or soft images, the volume—making sounds louder or softer—tickling your tear ducts, squeezing your adrenals, pushing your buttons.

In pure, boiled-down essence, I'm a romance writer. I write *chansons de geste* (literally: songs of heroic deeds) which became the romances—a term coined in the renaissance to distinguish popular tales in vernacular from scholarly and ecclesiastical writings in Latin. Early romances were *Beowulf,* the *Nibelungenlied,* and the Arthurian tales.

I don't write mimetic fiction—fiction that mimics reality—because I believe it's a betrayal of the promise of fiction.

We love stories because they impose a symmetry on the capricious chaos of reality. Whether we know it or not, we're looking for symmetry. The ubiquity of religion throughout human history is an excellent example of the search for symmetry. What is religion but a collection of stories we started telling each other to make sense of reality? Religion and fiction impose a sort of symmetry on reality, and that feels *good.* Not every loose end needs tying up, just enough to allow the reader to infer some sort of order to existence.

As a rule, this is when some yahoo pipes up and says, "But real life's not like that!"

No kidding, pal. That's why we call it *fiction.* Because the promise of fiction is that it's *better* than real life. It looks beyond or reshapes reality. It lets you experience events and situations real life doesn't offer. It takes you places you can't go because they're too far or life's too short or because those places exist only in the writer's head (and now they exist in yours).

Mark Twain summed it up very nicely: "The difference between reality and fiction? Fiction has to make sense."

I've ordered this look back by the dates of the stories' trade publication, even if they'd been written years before or were first published by a small press. Obviously the novels had to be excluded; also missing are the shorter pieces I've incorporated or expanded into those novels. I've excluded stage plays, teleplays, and comic scripts.

The Repairman Jack short stories are all collected in *Quick Fixes,* but Jack demands strong representation in any overview of my work, so I've allowed some overlap. The missing stories have either been incorporated into novels or included in the recent collection, *Other Sandboxes*:

"The Last Rakosh" (included in *All the Rage*)

"Home Repairs" (included in *Conspiracies*)
"The Wringer" (included in *Fatal Error*)
"Infernal Night" (*Other Sandboxes*)
"Recalled" (*Other Sandboxes*)

I recently collected all my pastiches in *Other Sandboxes*, so, again, no reason to reprint them here. I made an exception for "The Barrens" because it nails my H. P. Lovecraft connection. The missing pastiches are:

"Definitive Therapy"
"Rockabilly"
"Dreams"
"The November Game"
"Recalled"
"The Dead World"
"The Widow Lindley"
"Fix"
"Sex Slaves of the Dragon Tong"
"Part of the Game"
"Dragon Tongue"
"Infernal Night"
"The Adventure of the Abu Qir Sapphire"

Also missing are the dozens and dozens of introductions and forewords and afterwords and appreciations and scads of miscellaneous pieces I've penned through the years. These are already collected in a fat tome titled *Ephemerata*. (Available on Amazon.)

Summing up: Damn near every word I've written or co-written can be found in the novels and in the following:

Quick Fixes
Other Sandboxes
Ephemerata
The Compendium of F—Volumes 1-2-3

THE SEVENTIES

Most genre writers of my generation got their start writing short stories for the magazine market. The vast majority went through years of frustration trying to cajole editors into simply looking at their work. If you make a sale it's a bonanza, no matter how low the word rate.

I was no exception. I wrote my first story in second grade (about a haunted house, natch). Actually I wrote only half of it. We had a reading circle in class and we took turns reading aloud. When it came my turn I told the teacher I had written a story myself. She asked me if I wanted to read it to the circle. Yeah, it was unfinished, but I couldn't resist. So I read the part I had written, and then I started adlibbing. Within a few sentences it became obvious that I'd run out of text. The teacher was very nice, and she said when you finish it, you can come back and read the rest of it to us.

I was a little embarrassed that I'd got caught, but as we were pulling our chairs away from the reading circle, kids came up to me and said, "Well, what happened? What happened next? What about that guy with the bow and arrow? Was there really a ghost?" Somewhere inside of me, something came alive at that moment and said, *You've got them.* I really liked that feeling. I'd made contact. They were mine. They really wanted to know. They would have sat down right there and listened to the rest of the story. That's what we storytellers are after. To someone else it might have meant nothing, but to me—I was stoned. I wanted to do it again.

I poked at fiction in a desultory fashion during high school and college, making passes at stories here and there, but during my senior year at Georgetown I got real about it and started writing with the serious intent of selling. If I could sell just one story, I'd be a *writer*—well, at least I could call myself one—and after that I'd take a dilettantish approach and sell a story every now and again when inspiration struck.

But man, that first sale eluded me for years. As it should have. Here I was, a pre-med Biology major with not a single writing course to my credit, and I was going out there to compete with the pros. But I'd always been a voracious reader. I knew what I liked, so the only thing to do was to write something I'd want to read.

No market existed for my first love, horror fiction, so I pursued my number-two fave, SF. But every paying (and nonpaying) market I knew rejected every submission with Pavlovian regularity. I even kept track of editorial changes, so that as soon as a new editor took the helm of a magazine, I could resubmit the stories rejected by his or her predecessor. It got so confusing after a while that I had to design a flow chart to keep things straight: a grid with the magazines listed along the horizontal axis and the stories listed along the vertical. When a story came back from *Analog* it immediately went into an envelope addressed to *Amazing* and sent off in the next day's mail. A check mark was placed in the *Amazing* box next to that story, and the *Analog* box earned a big black "X." When it came back from *Amazing* it went off to *Fantasy & Science Fiction* and the *F&SF* box was checked. Ad nauseam. I burned up a *lot* of postage in those days and, quite literally, can paper a wall with all the rejection slips I collected. ("Thank you for your submission. Unfortunately, this does not suit out editorial needs at this time.") I've saved every single one, and someday I may do just that.

After graduating from Georgetown, I took a year off from school and went into psychopharmaceutical research at CIBA in Summit, NJ. I was convinced the human brain was where the action was—the future of medicine. Despite the parade of printed rejection slips, I kept writing. Then, finally, in the spring of 1969, John Campbell wrote a personal note telling me *why* he was rejecting my story. (More on that when you get to "The Cleaning Machine.")

After I finally broke into *Analog* with "Ratman," I began selling regularly to various other mags (even sold comic scripts to Archie Goodwin at *Creepy* and *Eerie*).

THE NOVELS AND NOVELLAS

The Accidental Patriot

A political novel written during my year doing psychopharmaceutical research at CIBA. I recall it being rather short and little more than a bunch of vaguely connected snippets. It has a libertarian protagonist who happens to save the country while pursuing a personal goal.

That's about all I remember of the story. Like the rest of my output at the time, I couldn't give it away. So I stuck it in a drawer and forgot about it. Skimmed through it years later and found it perfectly awful. I decided that no one must ever read it. No one. Ever. So I sat before my parents' fireplace and burned every page of the only copy.

Healer

Officially my first novel.

First novels are unpredictable.

Sometimes it's the best thing a writer will do in his career, something into which he empties so much of his heart and talent and experience that he's left with too little fuel to light much of a fire under future work.

For another it sets the course for an entire career: He's found the key in which his voice is most comfortable and he sticks to it.

Sometimes that first novel gives no hint as to what is to come—the restless been-there-done-that school where every new work is a departure from the last.

And then there's that first novel, not terribly uncommon in the science fiction field during the seventies, in which the writer is learning his craft in public.

Healer is one of those.

I wrote it in 1975, using "Pard," an *Analog* novelette, as a springboard. All of my published science fiction to that point had been set in a cohesive future I was slowly piecing together (à la Heinlein's Future History). And piecing together was precisely the process. I hadn't sat down and worked out a firm timeline for this future; I had an idea as to how it had begun but not where it was going, all I knew was that somewhere along the way the freedom movement had won and something called the LaNague Federation (LaNague—rhymes with the Hague—was chosen for no reason other than I liked the way it rolls off the tongue) was overseeing the far-flung colonized worlds in a very laissez-faire fashion. Only coercion was illegal. Beyond that, do what thy wilt was the whole of the law.

At that point the historical underpinnings of my future didn't matter to me; the *issues* were my burning concern, and the issues were timeless ones, all boiling down to the endless struggle between the individual and the collective. The good guys had won, but the bad guys—the never-ending stream of men and women with the monstrous self-assurance that they know best how other people should live and work and play—hadn't gone away. Fueled by either religion or long-discredited philosophies of social engineering, they were slinking around as always, chipping away at our hard-won freedoms.

I'd written and sold "Pard" in medical school—at a nickel a word it paid a fair number of bills—and had always intended to continue the story of Steven Dalt, a man who shares his brain with an alien. The alien, Pard, was conscious down to the cellular level, making Dalt potentially immortal. However, I had no room in my life for writing during my fourth year of med school and my rotating internship. But after joining a five-doc family practice group in 1974 I found I again had time to scratch the writing itch.

Starting with "Pard" as the opening section, I picked up Dalt's story a few decades after the end of the novelette and tracked him through the centuries as he becomes a mythical figure known as "The Healer." But I needed a publisher. With my short stories, I'd submitted to the top markets first, then worked my way down. I did the same here. Agentless, I sent off the novelette plus an outline of the rest of the book to Doubleday, the folks who published Isaac Asimov. A couple of months later I heard back from Sharon Jarvis, Doubleday's SF editor at that time, with a whopping $2,000 offer for world rights—$1,800 if I had an agent. Well, I didn't, so I signed the contract and sent it back.

Wow. I was officially a novelist. My first book proposal, accepted by the first publisher I'd sent it to. As the saying goes: How long has this been going on and why didn't anybody tell me about it? Looking back later I realized that *Healer* had a significant advantage in that the anchoring novelette previously had been purchased and published by John W. Campbell, Jr., the Zeus of modern science fiction. That pedigree gave it a definite leg up on the average over-the-transom proposal in Sharon's office. (How many people these days know what a transom is?)

Published in June of 1976, *Healer* garnered decent reviews, with paperback rights picked up almost immediately by Jim Frenkel at Dell. But I wasn't satisfied. Month after month I scanned the *New York Times Book Review,* waiting for the full-page ad that would announce to the world the existence of this epochal novel. Every Sunday I checked the Bestseller List for the magic word *Healer* (told you I was naïve). I haunted the science fiction sections of bookstores but only rarely was I rewarded with the sight of *Healer* in the "W" section. Finally I gathered the courage to ask the manager of the Doubleday Bookstore on Fifth Avenue—owned by Doubleday, my publisher—why he of all people wasn't carrying my book. He looked up *Healer* and informed me it was out of print.

Out of print? It was published in June and this was only November! There had to be some mistake!

I staggered home and called Sharon Jarvis who patiently explained that as soon as the libraries have their copies and paperback rights have been sold, Doubleday remainders most of its science fiction books. I'd be getting a letter soon allowing me to buy leftover copies for pennies on the dollar.

Welcome to the wonderful world of big-time publishing.

Healer was the first fiction wherein I dealt with the Miracle Cure. Keep watching, because it becomes a recurrent theme I'll hit on again and again.

I'm older and (somewhat) wiser now, but I've always known that *Healer* is not really a novel. Oh, the dust jacket labeled it a "novel" and reviews called it "a picaresque novel" or "an episodic novel," but in my heart I knew it wasn't. Not really. Because I wasn't a novelist then. I was a short-form writer, completely daunted by the task of sustaining a novel-length narrative. So I'd copped out by putting together a novel-length collection of interconnected short stories and novelettes following one character through twelve-hundred years of future history.

Healer did snag me an agent, however. In 1977 I got a letter from Al Zuckerman who had just started a literary agency called Writers House. He'd been selling foreign rights for *Healer* and said he was impressed with my ability to "sustain a narrative" (go figure). He asked if I had an agent and, if not, he'd like to represent me. We met, we clicked, and he remained my agent until his retirement in 2020.

In 2019 I rewrote *Healer* as a contemporary novel titled *Double Threat*. But more on that in Volume 3.

Wheels within Wheels

Wheels Within Wheels is listed as my second novel. And it almost is—a novel, that is.

It's rooted in the high point of my writing career to that time: Campbell gave the original "Wheels Within Wheels" novelette the cover of the September 1971 *Analog* with a fabulous (not a word I use very often) cover by John Schoenherr that perfectly captured the menacing elements of the story. Talk about a thrill. To a newbie SF writer in those days it was equivalent of your garage band making the cover of *Rolling Stone*. I didn't have it made, but I felt I'd made it.

Healer had more than earned out for Doubleday, so they wanted another novel. I decided to follow the same process that sparked the first book: Take one of my *Analog* stories and use it as a springboard. "Wheels Within Wheels" begged for expansion, and so it got the nod.

Al Z negotiated a fifty-percent increase in my advance (up to a whopping $3000), and Jim Frenkel again took paperback rights for his SF line at Dell.

I was cruising.

WWW the novel is less episodic than *Healer*, and certainly hangs together better, but it still strikes me as not quite as cohesive as a novel should be.

Perhaps I'm being too tough on it. The important thing is that, after forty-plus years, it still works on many levels. But not all. Its main failings are those suffered by any science fiction novel written in the seventies—we were working before the microchip revolution: Computers you can hold in your palm? Get out. The stories also predate the communications revolution: Word Wide Web—are we talking giant spiders? Email—what's that? And then there's the nascent genetics revolution. (Whatever I say here on that subject won't come even close to the imminent reality, so why set myself up for a fall?)

That aside, I think the plot is still strong and engaging, and the mysteries fairly presented.

As for style, well, I recall upon rereading it for the Stealth reprint edition that I kept running into spots where I step in and out of point of view, a carelessness I now find infuriating. And exclamation points—sheesh. It contains more than any ten of my recent novels. Make that twenty. Same for adverbs.

The good news is that all this tells me I've learned a lot about writing through the intervening years.

Also, it's a bit didactic on the economics front. But you have to realize what was going on in the world at the time. *Wheels* was written through 1976, sold in 1977, and pubbed in 1978. People these days don't realize (or have forgotten) that talk radio, as it is today, didn't exist. Today you hear hosts discussing economics and market forces and such all the time. Not something you'd hear about from Long John Nebel or Jean Shepherd in the mid-'70s, even though we'd just come off years of Nixon's price controls and his disallowing further conversion of dollars into gold. Inflation in 1974 was 11% (!) and 9% in '75, all from the government screwing with the economy.

When Al Z sent me the new Doubleday contract, I noticed he'd crossed out all sorts of paragraphs.

I called him. "You can do that?"

He said, "That's what you're paying me for. We'll handle foreign rights for you, and you'll do a lot better."

Now I knew why Doubleday had offered me the lower sum for *Healer* if I had an agent: I'd signed everything over to them and they were cleaning up on my foreign rights. It took me a long time to get them back.

Taking stock of my writing career, I realized that I'd spent three years writing two novels which I'd sold for the grand advance of $5000. I was glad I had a day job.

But wait—there's more. The novel was about to pay a dividend…

WWW became a milestone in my career when the Libertarian Futurist Society selected it for the first Prometheus Award. I had never heard of LFS and was delighted to learn I was a winner, but bowled over when they told me the award consisted of a certificate (no surprise there) and 7.5 ounces of gold in bullion coin. (Yes!) Gold at that time was running around $200 per ounce, so the award's value equaled half the novel's advance from Doubleday. At the current price of over $1,500 per ounce, it's many multiples of the advance.

I was an award-winning author at age 32. Cool. I still have the coins… somewhere.

The Tery

The Tery had a long strange trip. My science fiction beauty-and-the-beast tale got its start in 1971 as a novelette called "He Shall Be John" published in an off-beat little magazine in 1973 and promptly forgotten.

Years later, I'm in practice, and Jim Frenkel, the science fiction editor for Dell who'd bought paperback rights to both *Healer* and *Wheels Within Wheels*, approaches me at the 1978 Lunacon about a series of books he's putting together called *Binary Stars*. Each volume would consist of two novellas, much like the venerable Ace Doubles; the books would have interior illustrations and each novella would be introduced by the author of the companion piece.

At that time I was breaking ground on a new house and needed all the cash I could lay my hands on. I signed on and went to work. I'd always thought "He Shall Be John" was under-developed and so it became the basis of the first ten chapters of the novella; I continued the

story of Jon the tery from there. I added a new character named Tlad
who linked the story to my LaNague Federation future history. I also
tried my hand at overt horror for the first time.

I called the resultant novella *The Tery*. It doubled the length of the
novelette and ended with a satisfying catharsis. A bit thin in spots, I
thought, but I'd reached the word limit and the submission deadline
was upon me, so I had to let it go as was.

The Tery appeared in *Binary Stars* #2 in 1979 and was graced with
five wonderful Steve Fabian illustrations. Unfortunately, only those
who have seen the originals know how wonderful they are. Everyone
else was subjected to the muddied, almost indecipherable reproduc-
tions on the cheap paper Dell used. Fabian's delicate half tones were
lost, reducing his illos to elaborate smudges.

An Enemy of the State

The year was 1979. I had written and sold *Healer* and *Wheels Within
Wheels*, both patchwork novels extrapolated and expanded from shorter
works previously published in *Analog*. Now I was ready to write a novel
from scratch. I decided to stick with the LaNague Federation future history, but this time I'd write about the roots of the Federation, about its
founder, the reluctant revolutionary Peter LaNague.

I saw LaNague as a non-violent man trying to bring down a repres-
sive government without bloodshed—or at least very little. But how to
go about that?

At the time I was pursuing a personal radicalism based on the anar-
chocapitalist writings of Lysander Spooner, Ludwig von Mises, Murray
Rothbard, and others. They contend that the soul of a free society is a
free economy: If individuals are not allowed to deal freely with each
other, then they are not free. I became fascinated with the Weimar
hyperinflation during the early 1920s (a well into which I'd dip again
decades later for *Aryans and Absinthe*). I began to wonder: If a government can manipulate the economy to further its own ends via fiat cur-
rency, why couldn't a clever revolutionary do the same to bring down
a government?

And when I realized that Peter LaNague's target and weapon could
be one and the same, the story clattered into place.

All this dovetailed perfectly with my long-term disdain for that
hoary SF cliché, the galactic empire. Really, even with a faster-than-
light drive, the idea of an ironfisted centralized power micromanaging

a collection of worlds spanning dozens of light years is absurd. My concept was a little more practical: a loose confederation of colonized worlds left pretty much to their own devices with a centralized Big Stick hanging over them to dampen any aggressive or acquisitive tendencies. In other words: Hands Off. Laissez Faire.

What a concept. It's now called libertarianism. Today there's a libertarian movement and a Libertarian Party, but back in the late sixties when I first arrived at my—for want of a better word—*Weltanschauung*, it didn't have a name. I spent the years 1964-68 at Georgetown University in Washington, DC. I made the peace marches, mixing with the gathered hordes around the Lincoln Memorial that trooped en masse across the Potomac toward the Pentagon. It was a happening, a huge party, and sure I wanted the war ended, but I was alone in that crowd, a political and philosophical orphan.

My problem was an inability to perceive much functional difference between fascism and state socialism/communism. The rhetorical window dressing was certainly different, but the result either way was central control of business, industry, media, and education, all at the expense of the individual. It didn't matter to me whether the state or the collective slipped the cuffs around my wrists, I was shackled either way.

So I struck out in a different direction, away from the Left-Right axis, and let me tell you, it was lonely out there. I turned off the Lefties with my espousal of a free-market economy (one woman at an antiwar rally cried, "You must have been frozen for a hundred years!") and Young Republican types all but held up crosses when I suggested legalizing drugs and prostitution.

From the outset I wanted my science fiction to incorporate this odd but fundamentally consistent view of the world. It felt right. Lots of SF concerns aliens, and this nameless philosophy seemed pretty damn alien to just about everyone I knew.

When I finally got around to writing *An Enemy of the State*, I decided to make it a manifesto of sorts. But I didn't want it too deadly serious, so I had some fun with the quotes that opened the chapters, using a wide array of sources ranging from Thomas Jefferson to Roger Ramjet. And when I couldn't find something that suited the mood, I fabricated a quote and attributed it to *The Second Book of Kyfho (Revised Eastern Sect Edition)*.

Kyfho is my word (an anagram that's explained in the novel) but it seems to have taken on a life of its own. A moment ago I did a DuckDuckGo search for the word and got almost 9K hits. I've seen a

Kyfho license plate; newsgroup participants have incorporated quotes from *The Second Book of Kyfho* into their sig files; I've had readers contact me asking me where they can buy a copy of the book (sorry, you can't); someone wrote and suggested that I should write the book and sell it, and if I didn't have time, he'd do it for me (sorry, you can't).

A number of people wrote to tell me that *An Enemy of the State* changed their lives. Now that's scary. If you change someone's life, aren't you responsible for what they do with it?

An even more unsettling result of the success of *An Enemy of the State* (and my receiving the first Prometheus Award for *Wheels Within Wheels*) was that I began to hear myself referred to as "that libertarian sci-fi guy." Not wanting to be stuck in that or any other pigeonhole, I decided to take a vacation from SF. My next novel was *The Keep*, but that's a whole other story.

The '70s non-novel fiction excluded in Volume One are the three comic scripts ("The Sound of Wings" and "With Silver Bells and Cockle Shells..." and "The Anarchist") which aren't available anyway—they vanished long ago along with the "Pard" and "Wheels Within Wheels" novelettes I incorporated into novels.

STORIES FROM THE '70s

I'm starting off with "The Cleaning Machine" (now *there's* a gripping title) because, although not my first sale (it sold second but became my first published story), it turned things around for me.

I wrote it in 1969 while working in pharmaceutical research at CIBA. I thought of it as a science-fiction horror story. I mean, it had a weird machine, so that made it sf, right? And weird things happened to people, so that made it horror, sort of. Plus it had an unreliable narrator. Whatever the genre, it was the best thing I'd written so far.

And like all my stories before it, I couldn't *give* it away.

It earned form-letter rejections from every sf, fantasy, and mystery periodical I could find. Only John W. Campbell (Yes! I sent a horror story to *Analog*! What was I thinking?) had the courtesy to tell me why it did not suit his editorial needs at that time. (From then on he would tell me why he was rejecting my stories, and I always will revere him for that. When he'd accept one, however, he sent only a check.)

Here are Campbell's exact comments:

> *April 10, 1969*
> *Dear Mr. Wilson:*
> *Sorry---but it's not a story, because it doesn't go any-where. (The tenants did, but the story doesn't!)*
> *It's a vignette, because it states a situation---then doesn't use it.*

Cool. I'd written a vignette, whatever that was—sounded like those sugary things they serve at Café Du Monde in the French Quarter. But I still didn't have a sale.

And Campbell was right, as usual. "The Cleaning Machine" didn't work as science fiction, but I had faith in it. Vignette or not, I felt it was a decent piece of quiet horror. Trouble was, hardly anyone was publishing horror in 1969. I'd tried Joseph Payne Brennan's *Macabre*—he liked it but wrote back that he was overstocked and not accepting new material.

But then in 1970, as a first-year med student, I stumbled on a pair of magazines edited by Robert A. W. Lowndes: *The Magazine of Horror* and *Startling Mystery Stories*. Lowndes wrote informative editorials which he followed with reprints of hoary yarns from *Weird Tales, Strange Tales, Argosy,* and other Depression-era pulps. But he also published one new story per issue by newcomers with names like Stephen King and Greg Bear. Hey, if those nobodies could sell to Lowndes, so could I.

So I sent him "The Cleaning Machine"...and a few months later he wrote back to say he was taking it for *Startling Mystery Stories*. This was my second sale in a month (a few weeks earlier John Campbell had bought "Ratman" for *Analog*). The big difference was that Campbell had sent a check on acceptance. Lowndes's company paid on publication.

So I waited. Despite being my second sale, "The Cleaning Machine" became my first published story, appearing March 1971 in *Startling Mystery Stories* #18—with my name on the cover, no less.

I had arrived!

Unfortunately, the check never did. The publisher folded *Startling Mystery Stories* with that issue. I contend that this was pure synchronicity. "The Cleaning Machine" had nothing to do with the failure of the magazine. Nothing.

But that's not the end of the story. Fifteen years later I'm signing books at a convention and here comes a reader with the August 1971 issue of an illustrated sf magazine called *Strange Galaxy*. I ask him what he wants me to do with it. He says a signature on the title page of my story would be greatly appreciated. What story? I've never even heard of *Strange Galaxy*, let alone sold to it. So he opens to the only text piece in the issue, and there's "The Cleaning Machine" (as "The Machine") under my byline.

The story I initially couldn't give away had been pirated and reprinted within months of its first publication, and I still hadn't seen a penny for it.

And people wonder why so many writers die drunk or go mad.

Nowadays I like to think of the mysterious device in the story as one of the Seven Infernals. (Yes, I've retconned it into the Secret History.) *The Compendium of Srem* lists seven Infernals, strange devices of unknown origin left over from the First Age.

This one is the Kislival—"the Cleaner"—but there's also the Phedro, the Kaiilu Èntgab, the Cidsev Nelesso, the Bagaq, the Lilitongue of Gefreda, and one more... to be revealed in the future.

The Cleaning Machine

D *r. Edward Parker reached across his desk and flipped the power switch on his recorder to the "on" position.*

"Listen if you like, Burke," he said. "But remember: She has classic paranoid symptoms; I wouldn't put much faith in anything she says."

Detective Ronald Burke, an old acquaintance on the city police force, sat across from the doctor.

"She's all we've got," he replied with ill-concealed exasperation. "Over a hundred people disappear from an apartment house and the only person who might be able to tell us anything is a nut."

Parker glanced at the recorder and noticed the glowing warm-up light. He pressed the start button.

"Listen."

...and I guess I'm the one who's responsible for it but it was really the people who lived there in my apartment who drove me to it—they were jealous of me.

The children were the worst. Every day as I'd walk to the store they'd spit at me behind my back and call me names. They even recruited other little brats from all over town and would wait for me on corners and doorsteps. They called me terrible names and said that I carried awful diseases. Their parents put them up to it, I know it! All those people in my apartment building laughed at me. They thought they could hide it but I heard it. They hated me because they were jealous of my poetry. They knew I was famous and they couldn't stand it.

Why, just the other night I almost caught three of them rummaging through my desk. They thought I was asleep and so they sneaked in and tried to steal some of my latest works, figuring they could palm them off as their own. But I was awake. I could hear them laughing at me as they searched. I grabbed the butcher knife that I always keep under my pillow and ran out into the study. I must have made some noise when I got out of bed because they ran out into the hall and closed the door just before I got there. I heard one of them on the other side say, "Boy, you sure can't fool that old lady!"

They were fiends, all of them! But the very worst was that John Hendricks fellow next door who was trying to kill me with an ultra-frequency sonicator. He used to turn it on me and try to boil my brains while I was writing. But I was too smart for him. I kept an ice pack on my head at all hours of the day. But even that didn't keep me from getting those awful headaches that plague me constantly. He was to blame.

But the thing I want to tell you about is the machine in the cellar. I found it when I went downstairs to the boiler room to see who was calling me filthy names through the ventilator system. I met the janitor on my way down and told him about it. He just laughed and said that there hadn't been anyone down in the boiler room for two years, not since we started getting our heat piped in from the building next door. But I *knew* someone was down there—hadn't I heard those voices through the vent? I simply turned and went my way.

Everything in the cellar was covered with at least half an inch of dust—everything, that is, except the machine. I didn't know it was a machine at that time because it hadn't done anything yet. It didn't have any lights or dials and it didn't make any noise. Just a metal box with sides that ran at all sorts of odd angles, some of which didn't seem to meet properly.

It just sat there being clean.

I also noticed that the floor around it was immaculately clean for about five foot in all directions. Everywhere else was filth. It looked so strange, being clean. I ran and got George, the janitor.

He was angry at having to go downstairs but I kept pestering him until he did. He was mighty surprised.

"What is that thing?" he said, walking toward the machine.

Then he was gone! One moment he had been there, and then he was gone. No blinding flash or puff of smoke . . . just gone! And it happened just as he crossed into that circle of clean floor around the machine.

I immediately knew who was responsible: John Hendricks! So I went right upstairs and brought him down. I didn't bother to tell him what the machine had done to George since I was sure he knew all about it. But he surprised me by walking right into the circle and disappearing, just like George.

Well, at least I wouldn't be bothered by that ultra-frequency sonicator of his anymore. It was a good thing I had been too careful to go anywhere near that thing.

I began to get an idea about that machine—it was a *cleaning* machine!

That's why the floor around it was so clean. Any dust or *anything* that came within the circle was either stored away somewhere or destroyed.

A thought struck me: Why not "clean out" all of my jealous neighbors this way? A wonderful idea!

I started with the children.

I went outside and, as usual, they started in with their name-calling. (They always made sure to do it very softly but I could read their lips.) About twenty of them were playing in the street. I called them together and told them I was forming a club in the cellar and they all followed me down in a group. I pointed to the machine and told them that there was a gallon of chocolate ice cream behind it and that the first one to reach it could have it all. Their greedy little faces lighted up and they scrambled away in a mob.

Three seconds later I was alone in the cellar.

I then went around to all the other apartments in the building and told all those hateful people that their sweet little darlings were playing in the old boiler room and that I thought it was dangerous. I waited for one to go downstairs before I went to the next door. Then I met the husbands as they came home from work and told them the same thing. And if anyone came looking for someone, I sent him down to the cellar. So simple: In searching the cellar they had to cross into the circle sooner or later.

That night I was alone in the building. It was wonderful—no laughing, no name-calling, and no one sneaking into my study. Wonderful!

A policeman came the next day. He knocked on my door and looked very surprised when I opened it. He said he was investigating a number of missing-persons reports. I told him that everyone was down in the cellar. He gave me a strange look but went to check. I followed him.

The machine was gone! Nothing left but the circle of clean floor. I told the officer all about it, about what horrible people they were and how they deserved to disappear. He just smiled and brought me down to the station where I had to tell my story again. Then they sent me here to see you.

They're still looking for my neighbors, aren't they? Won't listen when I tell them that they'll never find them. They don't believe there ever *was* a machine. But they can't find my neighbors, can they? Well, it serves them right! I told them I'm the one responsible for "cleaning out" my apartment building but they don't believe me. Serves them *all* right!

"See what I mean?" said Dr. Parker with the slightest trace of a smile as he turned off the recorder. "She's no help at all."

"Yeah, I know," Burke sighed. "As looney as they come. But how can you

explain that circle of clean floor in the boiler room with all those footprints around it?"

"Well, I can't be sure, but the 'infernal machine' is not uncommon in the paranoid's delusional system. You found no trace of this 'ultra-frequency soni-cator' in the Hendricks apartment, I trust?"

Burke shook his head. "No. From what we can gather, Hendricks knew nothing about electronics. He was a short-order cook in a greasy spoon downtown."

"I figured as much. She probably found everybody gone and went looking for them. She went down to the boiler room as a last resort and, finding it deserted, concluded that everybody had been 'cleaned out' of the building. She was glad but wanted to give herself the credit. She saw the circle of clean floor—probably left there by a round table top that had been recently moved—and started fabricating. By now she believes every word of her fantastic story. We'll never really know what happened until we find those missing tenants."

"I guess not," Burke said as he rose to go, "but I'd still like to know why we can find over a hundred sets of footprints approaching the circle but none leaving it."

Dr. Parker didn't have an answer for that one.

Although it worked out as my fourth published story, "Ratman" was my first professional sale. After years of detailed rejection slips from John W. Campbell, editor *of Analog*, I finally broke the barrier: On June 8, 1970, a check for $375 arrived in the mail from Conde Nast. A nickel a word.

I was a first-year medical student at the time, with a wife, no job, no money, and a baby on the way. You can't imagine how $375 looked to us, especially since its buying power (according to online inflation calculators) was equivalent to almost $2,500 in present-day dollars.

The only rain on my parade was the lack of comment from Campbell. He'd been telling me why he'd rejected everything else; I kind of wanted a "Good job, Wilson. You made it." Some tiny comment. But no, just a check. I later realized he had nothing to do with the check itself. He sent a payment requisition through and accounting took it from there. Kind of fitting in a way. Campbell liked to argue. If he disagreed with you, he could go on for pages. If he agreed, he had nothing to say. So I figured the check said it all.

The story grew out of the psychopharmacological research I did at CIBA between pre-med and med school. Day in, day out, we dosed white rats with new drugs and placed them in Skinner boxes. I grew fond of rats.

(Please forgive the size of the computers mentioned here. "Ratman" was written in 1970, years before Steve Jobs began playing with microchips.)

Ratman

Since its purpose was neither to load nor unload cargo, his converted tramp freighter was directed to a landing pad at the far end of the field where it wouldn't get in the way. Orz, red-haired and of average height and build though somewhat stoop-shouldered, didn't mind. As long as he was in the general area his efficiency would be unimpaired.

When the viewscreen picked up an approaching ground car, Orz snapped his fingers and a half-kilo space rat leaped from the control console to his shoulder.

"Let's go, 62," he said to his favorite employee.

The space rat grasped the fabric of his master's shirt tightly in his tiny paws and lashed his tail about nervously. He didn't like meeting strangers, but it was part of his job; his master had found that there was a definite psychological advantage in appearing with a space rat on his shoulder.

Orz and 62 reached the hatch just as the ground car pulled up alongside. They scrutinized the two occupants as the freighter's loading ramp descended.

The first to debark was a portly little man wearing a stylish orange tunic that should have been two sizes larger. His companion probably weighed as much but was taller and better proportioned.

Orz's long legs carried him swiftly down the ramp after it had settled and the portly one came forward to meet him.

"Mr. Samuel Orzechowski?" he asked, mangling the pronunciation.

Orz smiled. "That's right, but you can call me Sam, or Orz, or, as some people prefer, Ratman." *And being a client,* he thought, *you'll no doubt choose the last one.*

"Well," the little man replied, "I guess 'Ratman' will do. I'm Aaron Lesno, president of the Traders League, and this is Evan Rabb, our treasurer," he said, indicating the man beside him.

"Welcome to Neeka," said Lesno.

"Could I ask you something, Ratman?" Rabb hastily interjected. He couldn't take his eyes off 62. "Is that a space rat?"

"A small one," Orz nodded. "A baby, really."

"Aren't you afraid of...?"

"Of losing my ear?" he grinned. "Not at all. I imagine you two and the rest of the League are somewhat in the dark as to my methods, and you've probably got a lot of questions. I've found it best in the past to get everyone together and explain things to everybody at once. It saves me time and you money."

"An excellent idea!" Lesno agreed. "We've all been anxiously awaiting your arrival... Well," he corrected himself with a glance at Rabb, "almost all... but I'm sure there would be no problem in getting everyone together."

"What did you mean by 'almost all'?" Orz asked.

Rabb spoke up. "One of our more influential members was vehemently opposed to the idea of retaining you."

"Oh, really? Why?"

"Have no fear, Ratman," Lesno assured him with a smile, "he'll let you know why at the meeting tonight."

"Fair enough," Orz said. "Can someone come back and pick me up in a few hours for the meeting?"

"Why not come with us now and let us show you around a bit?" Lesno offered.

Orz shook his head and gestured over his shoulder to the ship. "Sorry... feeding time."

Rabb and Lesno stiffened and glanced nervously from 62 to the open hatch. "Yes, quite," Lesno muttered. "Very well, then, we'll have someone call for you in, say, three hours."

"That'll be fine." This settled, the two-man welcoming committee lost little time in putting some distance between themselves and the squat little freighter.

"Seem like pretty decent fellows," Orz told 62 as he made his way up the ramp and down the central corridor. As they approached the rat room, 62 began to prance excitedly on his master's shoulder and was literally doing a dance by the time Orz hit the door release.

His several hundred fellow employees inside took up the same excited dance at the sound of the door sliding open. The cages were arranged five high along the walls of the long, narrow room. They were simple, steel-sided boxes with front doors of quarter-inch steel mesh; each was self-cleaning, had its own water supply, and was equipped with an automatic feeder.

But Orz had never trusted automatic feeders, so now he went from cage to cage and shoved food pellets through the tiny feeding hole in the front of each. He had to be nimble, for the rats were greedy and anxious and a fingertip could easily be mistaken for a pellet. His practiced eye decided how much each rat should get. This was important: A rat became fat and lazy if overfed and would gnaw his way out of the cage if underfed. A rat in either condition was of little use to Ratman.

Fifty cages stood open and empty and Orz placed a few pellets in each. 62 was frantic by now so he decided to give the little fellow something before he jumped off his shoulder and into one of the empty cages. The rat rose up on his hind legs, snatched the pellet from Orz's proffering fingers with his tiny, handlike paws, and began to gnaw noisily and voraciously.

Three hours later, Orz flipped a particular switch on the console, checked to make sure the door to the rat room was open, then headed for the hatch. There, after casting an eye through the dusk at the approaching ground car, he secured the hatch, but opened a small panel at its bottom. With 62 perched watchfully upon his shoulder, he was waiting at the bottom of the ramp when the car arrived.

Lesno was alone inside. "Well, Ratman," he said with a smile, "everybody's waiting, so—" then he spotted 62 and his face fell. "Does he have to come along? I mean, he won't get too excited, will he?"

"Don't worry," Orz replied, sliding into his seat, "he won't bite you." To lessen the man's anxiety he made a point of keeping 62 on his far shoulder.

"Your advertising literature was quite timely," Lesno remarked as they got under way, hoping conversation would take his mind off those two beady eyes peering at him around the back of his passenger's head. "The rat problem was reaching its peak when we received it. I trust that wasn't just coincidence."

"No coincidence at all. I keep my ear to the ground and word got around that there was a space rat plague on Neeka. I figured you could use my services."

Lesno nodded. "We had heard a few stories about you but didn't know whether to believe them or not. Your advertising claims were quite impressive. I just hope you can live up to them."

About twenty exporters and importers were waiting in the conference room on the second floor of the Traders League office complex. It was a motley group of discordant colors, shapes, sizes, and ages. Lesno entered ahead of Orz and lost no time in bringing the meeting to order.

"We all know why we're here," he said, tapping the gavel twice, "so there's really no use in wasting time with introductions." He pointed to Orz. "The creature on this man's shoulder is introduction enough: Ratman has arrived and he's going to tell us something about himself and about space rats." So saying, he relinquished the podium.

Nothing like a businesslike business, Orz thought as he stood up and received a slight spattering of applause. They knew of his claim to be able to control space rats with space rats and were frankly dubious. But this was nothing new to Orz.

Without even a glance at the audience, he nonchalantly snapped his fingers and tapped the top of the podium. 62 immediately leaped from his shoulder to the podium and began to sniff the wood curiously.

"This," he began, "although a specimen of *Rattus interstellus*, is not a true 'space rat' in the full sense of the word; but his parents were.

Lab-raised space rats—such as 62, here—can turn out to be quite friendly, but they are no less cunning, no less intelligent, and certainly no less vicious when cornered. These are the rats I 'employ,' so to speak.

"But first let's puncture a few of the myths that have grown up around the space rat. First of all, no matter what the spacers tell you, space rats have no psi powers; they don't know what you're going to do next… it's just that their reflexes are developed to such a high degree that it almost seems that way when you take pot shots at one with a blaster. They will respond to ultra-frequency tones but by no means do they have a language… they're intelligent, all right, but they're a long way from a language."

His eyes flicked over the audience. These were traders, barterers; they recognized a man who knew what he was talking about, and they were all listening intently.

He continued. "But just what is it that distinguishes the space rat from other rats?" To dramatize his point, he allowed 62 to crawl onto the back of his hand and then held the fidgety creature aloft.

"This is the product of centuries in the pressurized but unshielded holds of interstellar cargo ships. Wild genetic mutation and the law of survival of the fittest combined to produce a most adaptable, ferocious, and intelligent creature.

"Everyone knew of the space rat's existence, but no one paid much attention to him until an ensign aboard the freighter *Clinton* was kept awake one night by the continuous opening and closing of the compartment door outside his cabin. The ship was in port, and, under normal circumstances, he would have spent the night in town, but for one reason or another he had returned to his quarters.

"Now, these doors which divide the corridors into compartments open automatically when you touch the release panel, and remain open as long as a simple electric eye beam is broken; when the beam makes contact again, the door closes. The doors naturally make some noise when they operate, and this is what was disturbing the ensign. But, every time he checked to see who was wandering up and down the corridor, he found no one. Checking with the guard detail he found that he was the only person authorized to be in that area of the ship.

"So he set up watch. Opening his door a crack, he peeked through to the corridor and waited. But no one came and he was about to give up when he spotted this large space rat come running down the corridor. As it approached the door it leaped over a meter into the air and threw itself against the release panel. The door slid open as the creature landed on the floor and it scurried through before the door closed again."

The traders were smiling and shaking their heads in wonder as Orz paused and placed 62 back on the podium. "Since it is doubtful that the rat could have accidentally leaped against the release panel, it must be assumed that he learned by watching. That would make him a highly unusual rat... they thought. Then they discovered that the whole colony aboard the *Clinton* knew how to operate the doors! Then other spacers on other ships began watching for space rats while their ships were in port—that's when their movements are the greatest; they stick pretty much to the cargo holds in transit—and it was discovered that the *Clinton* rats were not so extraordinary. These reports fired the interest of researchers who figured they would go out and catch themselves a few space rats and put them through some tests."

The audience broke into laughter at this point. They were all well familiar with the elusiveness of the space rat.

"Another characteristic of the space rat was soon discovered: viciousness. It took quite a while, but after much effort and many scars a number of space rats were caught. And, as expected, they proved virtually untrainable. We hoped to do better with their offspring.

"I was working with the offspring when I heard about a rat problem in the nearby spaceport. Traps, poison, even variable frequency sonic repellers had failed to control them. I went to investigate and found that a good many space rats were jumping ship and setting up residence in the warehouses which ring every spaceport. Another factor was added: In the warehouses they meet other strains of space rat from other ships and the resultant cross-breeding produces a strain more intelligent and more ferocious than even the cargo-ship rat. I managed to catch half a dozen in as many months, mated them and began to go to work on the offspring. Through a mixture of imprinting and operant conditioning, second-generation space rats proved quite tractable.

"But I needed more wild rats and tried the wild idea of training my lab rats to help catch other rats. It worked out so well that I decided to go into the business of space-rat control."

He paused and glanced around the room. "Any questions?"

An elderly trader in the front row raised a bony hand. "Just how does one rat go about catching another?" he asked in a raspy voice.

"I'll demonstrate that tomorrow," Orz replied. "It'll be easier to understand once you see the equipment."

A huge, balding man with a grizzled beard stood up without waiting to be recognized. "I've got a question, Ratman," he said belligerently. "If all you've got are a few trained rats, why do you charge so much?"

This elicited a few concurring mutters from other members of the audience. Here, no doubt, was the man Lesno had referred to earlier that day.

"You have me at a disadvantage, sir," Orz replied with a smile.

"I'm Malcomb Houghton and I guess I rank third, or fourth, around here in cubic feet of warehouse space."

Orz nodded. "Very glad to meet you, sir. But let me answer your question with another question: Do you have any idea what it costs to operate a privately owned freighter, even a small one such as mine? My overhead is staggering."

Being a businessman, this argument seemed to make sense to Houghton, but he remained standing. "I just wonder," he began slowly. "If you can train rats to catch other rats, how do we know you didn't land some special trouble-making rats here on Neeka a few months ago to aggravate the situation to the point where we had to call you in?"

The audience went silent and waited for Ratman's reply. Orz cursed as he felt his face flushing. This man was dangerously close to the truth. He hesitated, then cracked a grin.

"How'd you like to go into partnership with me?" he quipped.

The tension suddenly vanished as the audience laughed and applauded. Orz gathered up 62 and left the podium before Houghton could zero in on him again. He couldn't tell whether the man was stabbing in the dark, or whether he really knew something.

Lesno escorted him out the door. "Wonderful!" he beamed. "I think you're the man to solve our problems. But time is of the essence! The port residents have been on our necks for months; their pets are being killed, they're afraid for their children and they're afraid for themselves. And since the rats are based in the warehouse district, we might be held liable if we don't do something soon. And"—he put his hand on Orz's shoulder and lowered his voice—"we've been keeping it quiet, but a man went after a few of the rats with a blaster the other night. They turned on him and chewed him up pretty badly."

"I'll start as early as possible," Orz assured him. "You just send somebody around tomorrow with a good-sized truck and I'll be waiting."

Rabb must have overheard them as he approached. "That won't be necessary," he said. "We're placing a truck at your disposal immediately. I'll drive it over to your ship and Lesno will bring me back after dropping you off."

Orz said that would be fine and he arranged a time and place of meeting with Lesno for early the next morning on the way back to the ship. A few minutes later he and 62 were standing next to the borrowed truck watching the two League officers drive away.

"*Ratman!*" whispered a voice from the deep shadows under the ramp.

Orz spun around. "Who's there?" he asked guardedly.

"I'm your contact."

"You'd better come out and identify yourself," he said.

Muttering and brushing off the knees of her coveralls, a tall, statuesque brunette stepped out of the shadows. "Where have you been for the past hour? We were supposed to meet as soon as it was dark!"

"Just who are you, miss?" Orz asked.

She straightened up and stared at him. "You don't take any chances, do you?" she said as a wry smile played about her lips. "O.K. I'm Jessica Maffey, Federation agent NE97. I'm the one who received a smuggled shipment of fifty of your best harassing rats, drove them into town, and let them go in the warehouse district. Satisfied, Ratman?"

Orz grinned at her annoyance. "You're Maffey, all right… I've got a picture of you inside, but you can't be too careful." He glanced around. "Let's get inside where we can talk."

"Speaking of going inside," she said, "there's been a steady stream of rats going through that little opening in the hatch."

He nodded. "Good. I activated a high-frequency call before I left. All the harassers you loosed should be snug in their cages by now."

He unlocked the hatch and led her to the rat room. As he busied himself with transferring 62 to a cage and checking on the harassing rats, Jessica looked around. From the darkened recess of each cage shone two gleaming points of light, and all those several hundred points of light seemed to be fixed upon her. She shuddered.

"Three missing," Orz was saying. "That's not too bad… accidents do happen." He pressed a button on the wall and the open doors on the cages of the harassing rats swung shut with a loud and simultaneous clang.

"How about a drink?" he offered his guest.

"As a matter of fact, I'd love one," she replied, sighing with relief as they stepped back into the corridor. Orz looked at her curiously. "It gets a little dry and dusty sitting under a loading ramp," she explained with a tight smile.

With Jessica seated in his spartan, fastidiously neat living quarters with her hand around a cold gin and tonic, Orz began to talk business. "Federation Intelligence only gave me a sketchy idea of what's going on here. You were to fill me in on the rest, so why don't I tell you what I know and you take it from there."

"Go ahead," she told him.

Drink in hand, Orz paced the room as he spoke. "Let's start with this planet. Neeka is a fiercely independent, sparsely populated world which exports a lot of food and imports a lot of hardware. Formerly a splinter world, it agreed to trade with the Federation but refused to join it. They were asked to join the Restructurists in their revolt against the Federation but turned them down. They want absolutely no part of the war... and I can't say as I blame them.

"*However:* The Haas Warp Gate is right outside this star system and the convoys stack up in this area before being shot through to the battle zones. Fed agents discovered a turncoat feeding information on the size and destinations of the convoys to someone on this planet. That someone, in turn, was transmitting the info to the Restructurists via subspace radio. He's been stopped temporarily, but as soon as he makes another contact, he'll be in business again. I was told to meet you here and stop him. That's all I know."

Jessica nodded and drained her drink. "Right. But subspace transmissions can't be traced so we had to depend on deductive reasoning. First of all, you're allowed to be pro-Federation, or pro-Restructurist on Neeka, and you're allowed to talk all you want about either cause. Nobody minds. But try to do something to aid either cause and you wind up in prison. Strict neutrality is enforced to the letter on Neeka. Therefore, partisan natives, such as myself and the man we're after, have to go underground.

"Now, it would be as easy to smuggle in a subspace transmitter as it was to smuggle in your rats, but hiding it would be an entirely different matter. It's a huge piece of hardware and it needs a large power supply."

"So the man we're after," Orz broke in, "is someone with easy access to an off-planet source of information, and a place big enough to hide a subspace transmitter without arousing suspicion."

"And a warehouse right here in port has the size and access to the necessary power," Jessica concluded. "Since the members of the Traders League own all the warehouses, they are the obvious target for investigation."

"But which one?"

She shrugged. "Their security is too tight for me to do much snooping. The only way to get into those warehouses is to be invited in. That's where Ratman comes in."

Orz was thoughtful. "It really shouldn't be too difficult. I was informed by the Traders League when they retained me that their warehouses are fully automated and computer-operated."

"With a population density as low as Neeka's," Jessica added, "labor is anything but cheap."

"Right," he continued. "And, if I wanted to hide a subspace radio in one of those warehouses, I'd disguise it as part of the automation works and no one would ever be the wiser. All I've got to do tomorrow when I go into the warehouses is keep my eyes open for an unusually large computer-automation rig. When I find it I'll just 'accidentally' expose it as a subspace transmitter. The Neekan authorities will take care of our spy after that."

He suddenly halted his pacing and snapped his fingers. "Forgot to turn off the call signal for the rats... I'll be right back."

"Mind if I come along?" Jessica asked.

"Not at all."

She watched Orz's back as he led her down the narrow corridor to the bridge. "Can I call you something other than 'Ratman'?"

He grinned over his shoulder. "Sam will do fine."

"O.K., Sam: How did you get started in all this?"

"Well, I got the idea a few years ago and thought I was a genius until I started looking for backers. Everyone I approached thought I was either a swindler or a nut. As a last desperate hope I went to IBA."

"What's IBA?"

"Interstellar Business Advisors. It's a private company with some pretty canny people working for them. They dug up somebody who promised to back me halfway, then they approached the Federation with this undercover idea. Since I'd be able to get on otherwise unfriendly planets, the Federation put up the rest of the money. So now I'm a full-time Ratman and a part-time Fed man. And when my reputation spreads, IBA has got some ideas for starting a corporation and selling franchises."

They entered the bridge as he was speaking and Jessica noticed that it was as meticulously ordered as his quarters. Two additions to the standard console caught her eye immediately.

"Improvements?" she asked, pointing to a brace of toggle switches.

Orz flipped one of the toggles to "off" and turned to her. "Those are the high-frequency signals for my rats. They've got an effective range of about two kilometers and when a rat hears the proper tone, he makes a beeline for this ship."

"And what's that?" She indicated a bright red lever with three safety catches and "Danger" written in white letters along its length.

The lightness left his voice. "For the direst of emergencies only," he replied.

Feminine curiosity aroused, Jessica went to touch it. "What does it do?"

"That's my secret," Orz replied with a tight smile and snatched her wrist away from the lever. "I've yet to use it and I hope the day never comes when I do." To draw her attention elsewhere he pointed to the far wall. "See that inconspicuous little switch over there by the intercom speaker? When that's in the down position—like now—the controls are locked."

"You're just full of tricks, aren't you?" she said, trying to hide a smile. He was like a little boy showing off a new toy.

"Can't be too careful."

Lesno, Rabb, Houghton, and a few others were ready and waiting when Orz pulled up in front of the Traders League offices with the truck.

"Straight ahead," said Lesno as he hopped in beside Orz. "We'll start with Rabb's places first since they're the closest." Two left turns brought them up before a huge structure with a "Rabb & Co." sign above the sliding doors. Orz waited until the others had arrived, then addressed the group.

"First of all," he told them, "you must keep all humans away from any warehouse where my rats are at work, so give whatever employees you have the day off. Next, let me explain that space rats set up a close-knit community within a warehouse—one community per warehouse—and that each community has a leader who achieved his position by being the most cunning and the most ferocious in the community."

He reached into the back of the truck and brought out a simple cage. Inside was a very large and very vicious-looking space rat. "This is one of my Judas rats. I've selectively bred them for ferocity and any one of these is a match for any three ordinary space rats. Within hours after his release, my Judas rat will have established himself at the top of the community's pecking order."

Once again Orz reached into the back of the truck and brought out a cage, but this one was larger and empty.

"Normally a space rat wouldn't go near a trap like this, but he'll follow the Judas if the Judas is the community leader. And once the community has followed him inside and is busy at the bait, the Judas hops outside, releases this catch and a spring closes and locks the door. He then returns to the ship. The cage is made of a lightweight titanium alloy that not even a space rat's teeth can dent." He held up the cage. "Tomorrow morning this should be filled with a community of very angry space rats."

"Is that all there is to it?" Houghton blurted incredulously. Orz could imagine the man's mind tallying and totaling, and deciding that no matter what his overhead, Ratman charged too much. "This is outrageous! I'll have nothing to do with such nonsense! We're being hoodwinked!"

Somebody doesn't want me in his warehouse, Orz thought and was about to say something when Rabb beat him to it.

"The League has already retained Ratman, Malcomb, and we voted to use the treasury to do so... remember? So you have, in effect, already paid for his services, and it would be foolish of you not to take advantage of them."

Houghton paused, considering Rabb's words, then he glanced at the cage and shrugged. "I guess I don't have much choice," he said sullenly and turned toward his car. "Let me know when you get around to my places."

———

It was late in the day when they finally did get around to Houghton's warehouses, but Orz had preferred it that way. He had his suspicions and wanted to see as many of the other warehouses as possible before confronting Houghton. There had been nothing suspect in the others, although Lesno's computer setups had been somewhat larger than most, but nowhere near big enough to house a subspace radio.

Houghton met them outside.

"I've only got a few cages left," Orz told him, "so we'll do as many as we can and I'll get the rest tomorrow after I collect the cages I've set out today."

"Might as well start with the main house," Houghton replied and led them toward the largest building of his complex. The doors slid open to reveal a huge expanse of concrete floor with crates and boxes stacked almost to the ceiling. Huge cranes—controlled by a computer that knew the exact location of every item in storage—swung from above. Looming against the far wall was a large, metal-paneled structure.

Orz pointed to it. "Is that your computer?"

"Yes," the bearded man replied absently, "now let's get on with this... I haven't got all day."

"Mind if I take a look at it?" Orz asked and started walking toward it. This was what he had been looking for; it was big enough to house two subspace transmitters. "Rats love to nest in those things, you know."

"I assure you there are no rats in there so stay away from it!" Houghton almost shouted. He began to follow Orz, and Lesno and Rabb trailed along.

Orz went to the nearest inspection plate and began loosening the screws which held it in place.

"Get away from there!" Houghton yelled as he came up. "You don't know what you're doing. You could mess up my whole operation!"

"Look, if I'm going to do my job right, I've got to check this out!" The inspection plate came off in his hands then and he stuck his head inside. Nothing unusual. He replaced it and went to the next plate with the same result. Four more inspection plates later he was sure there was no subspace transmitter hidden within.

Houghton was standing behind him and tugging angrily on his beard as Orz replaced the last screw. "Are you quite through, Ratman?"

Orz stood and faced him. "Awful big computer you've got there, Mr. Houghton," he said matter-of-factly. He was chagrined, but refused to show it.

"That's the computer for my whole operation. I found it easier to centralize the system: Instead of installing new units all the time, I just add to the central unit and feed it into the new buildings as they are built. It's much more convenient."

"More economical, too, I'll bet," Orz added laconically.

"Why, yes," Houghton replied. "How did you know?"

"Lucky guess."

Jessica was waiting for him back at the ship. "Don't bother telling me you didn't find anything," she said as he collapsed in a chair. "That look on your face tells me the whole story."

"I was so sure it was Houghton! The way he objected to the League retaining me, the way he tried to rake me over the coals at the meeting last night, the way he blew up this morning, I was sure he had something to hide. Turns out he's only a cheapskate with a centralized computer."

"What makes you so sure he hasn't got it stashed somewhere else?" Jessica asked, coming over and handing him a drink.

He accepted it gratefully and took a long slow swallow before answering. "I'm not sure of anything right now. But, if that transmitter's here—and we know it is—it's got to be in one of those warehouses. Which reminds me…" He got to his feet slowly and trudged to the rat room.

Jessica didn't follow, but glanced out into the corridor when she heard the clang of cage doors. Furry gray and brown shapes were scurrying toward the hatch.

"What are you up to?" she asked as Orz reappeared.

"I had a brainstorm on my way back to the ship. We'll find out if it worked tomorrow."

Orz noticed Jessica in the crowd outside Rabb's main warehouse. She smiled and winked mischievously, knowing he couldn't acknowledge her. The crowd was waiting to see if Ratman could live up to his claims and watched intently as he and Rabb disappeared inside. An uncertain cheer began and died as he reappeared dragging—with little help from Rabb—a cageful of clawing, squealing, snarling, snapping space rats. Having retreated to what it considered a safer distance, the crowd applauded.

Lesno strode forward, beaming. "Well, Ratman, I knew you could do it. But what are you going to do with the little monsters now that you've caught them?"

"Most of them will have to be gassed and killed, but I'll save a few of the best for breeding purposes… I like to keep my working stock as strong as possible."

They completed the rounds of Rabb's buildings, then moved on to Lesno's. The novelty had worn off and the crowd was beginning to thin by the time they got around to Lesno's third warehouse, but interest was renewed at the sound of Orz's voice calling from within.

"Mr. Lesno! There's something you ought to see in here."

Lesno went in. Rabb, Houghton, and some of the braver members of the crowd—Jessica among them—followed him.

It looked as if a bomb had gone off inside. Every crate, every package had been torn open. Even some of the computer paneling had been torn away.

"What happened?" Lesno cried, staggered by the destruction.

Orz shrugged and pointed to the full cage. "I don't know. There's your community, caged and ready to go. But I've never seen anything like this before."

Houghton was looking over the ravaged computer. "Never seen a computer that looked like this," he muttered. "Is this some new model, Aaron?" he asked Lesno.

Rabb came up. "Looks like part of a subspace radio!"

"Ridiculous!" Lesno sputtered. "What would I be doing with—?"

"You're a spy!" Houghton declared. "A Federation spy!"

A blaster suddenly appeared in Lesno's hand. "Don't insult me by linking me to the Federation!"

Houghton shrugged. "So you're a Restructurist spy, then. Just as bad. You get twenty years either way."

"I'm not going to argue with you, Malcomb. Just stay where you are."

"You can't escape, Aaron!" Rabb warned.

Lesno smiled. "Of course I can," he said and pointed the blaster at Orz. "Ratman is going to volunteer the use of his ship. He's even going to come along for the ride to make sure no one gets trigger-happy."

Orz caught Jessica's eye. She was readying to make a move, but he shook his head. They had succeeded in destroying Lesno's effectiveness as a spy. It didn't matter if he escaped. And so, with a blaster at the back of his head, Orz preceded the little man to the truck.

"You work for the Federation, don't you?" Lesno said as Orz drove them toward the spaceport.

"I'm afraid I don't have time to work for anyone other than Sam Orzechowski."

"Come now, Ratman. I was suspicious yesterday when I saw the way you gave Houghton's computer a going over and this morning's revelation confirmed it. Why deny it?"

Orz shrugged. "O.K., I occasionally do some snooping for the Federation."

"How did you get on to me?" Lesno asked earnestly. "I thought I had a foolproof arrangement."

"Well, I wasn't sure, but Houghton's centralized setup started me on a new approach. I figured that if one man could centralize his computers, another could decentralize a subspace transmitter. Then it struck me that you'd have to take the transmitter apart in order to sneak it into town. And since it was already in pieces, why not leave it that way? At least that's what I would have done. So the next thing to do was to look for the man with the *slightly* larger computers. You fit the bill."

"But how did you manage to tear the place apart?"

"That was easy. If you could go back to that warehouse now, you'd find a tiny, high-frequency *labeler* attached to the door. I have a number of vandal rats trained to be specialists in making a mess out of a building. The *labeler* told them where to go to work."

Shaking his head in admiration, Lesno remarked, "You should be working for us."

"But I don't want a restructured Federation," Orz replied. "I sort of like it the way it is."

"But there are such inequalities in the galaxy! Some planets are drowning in their surpluses while other planets are starving, and the Federation does nothing."

"The Federation doesn't think such matters are within its scope."

"They will be when we win," he replied righteously.

Orz knew argument was futile and allowed a shrug to be his only reply. Once on the ship, it was evident to Orz that Lesno knew his way around freighters. He retracted the ramp, secured the hatch, and then followed Orz to the bridge.

He gestured to the extra seat. "You just sit there and keep out of the way, Mr. Ratman, and you won't get hurt. I'm not a murderer. If all goes well, I'll drop you off at the first neutral port we reach. But I won't hesitate to shoot you if you try anything."

"Don't worry," Orz told him. "My mission was to stop you, not capture you. I really don't care if you get away."

Lesno's eyes narrowed. This lack of chauvinism did not fit his conception of a Fed man. Something was up. His suspicions were reinforced when he found the console inoperable.

"Where's the lock?" he demanded.

Orz pointed across the room. "By the speaker." But Lesno made no move. Instead his eyes roved the room until they came to rest on the red lever. His face creased into a smile.

"You didn't think anyone would be fooled by that, did you?"

Orz nearly leaped from his seat as the Restructurist reached for the lever. "Don't touch that!"

"Sit down!" Lesno warned, pointing the gun at Orz's chest. "I told you before, I'm not a killer but—"

"I know you're not." Orz said frantically. "Neither am I. That's why you've got to leave that lever alone!"

Lesno merely smiled and kept him covered while he released the first two safety catches. "Listen to me, Lesno! That lever sets off a special tone stimulus and releases every one of my rats! They've all been trained to attack anyone and everyone but me when they hear that tone... I installed it for use in a situation when it was either kill or be killed! This is not one of those situations!"

Lesno was having some trouble with the third catch, but it finally yielded. "A good try, Ratman," he said and, ignoring Orz's cry of protest, pulled the lever.

Faintly, from far down the corridor, came a metallic clang. A loud, wailing tone filled the ship. Lesno paled and turned anxiously toward his captive.

"Why didn't you listen to me, you fool!" Orz yelled.

Lesno suddenly believed. Horror-stricken, he began to push and pull the lever back and forth but with no effect. He was still working at it when the squealing, gray-brown carpet swept through the door.

Orz turned away and tried unsuccessfully to block out the screams and sickening sounds of carnage that filled the bridge. He had trained the rats too well... there would be no stopping them.

And when all was quiet again, Orz congratulated himself on having kept his stomach in place. But then 62 leaped up to his accustomed spot on his shoulder and began with great contentment to clean his reddened claws and jowls.

Only Jessica came to see him off. Orz had cleaned up the rat problem and the people were appreciative, but they had either seen the corpse that had been removed from his ship, or they had heard about it. It hadn't been easy to identify it as Aaron Lesno.

"I see the red lever's been removed," Jessica remarked. She hadn't been near the ship since the incident.

Orz avoided her gaze. "Yeah. I took it out... can't quite look at it." He changed the subject abruptly. "Well, now that this thing's been cleared up, what'll you be doing with yourself?"

"I've no intention of settling down and becoming a good Neekan citizen, you can be sure of that," she replied. "I'm putting in for an assignment as soon as possible. There's too much going on out there for me to get tucked away on this rock."

Orz smiled for the first time in several days. "That's funny. I was thinking of taking on an assistant. This business is getting a little too complicated for me to handle alone."

He paused as Jessica waited eagerly.

"You like rats?" he asked.

I could have included this and "The Man with the Anteater" in my first story collection, *Soft and Others*, but decided against it for a simple reason: I'm not crazy about them.

Yes, they follow my continuing theme of the individual versus the system, but they're preachy, didactic, pedantic... I could go on, but you'll see for yourself. Back in those days I was learning my craft in public. These stories were written in 1970 (equivalent to the late Jurassic Period for some of you) and occupy the lower-left end of my learning curve.

I still like what I said, just not so much how I said it.

"Higher Centers" (Analog, April 1971) is a parable of Big Brother versus local/market control. (Guess which side I come down on.) It has a clever MacGuffin, but it's as subtle as a dropped anvil.

Higher Centers

He didn't know how long he had been sitting there, looking out through the dirty window without seeing anything, when a movement caught his eye. A small dog, a mongrel with a limp, rounded a corner and loped down the near-deserted street. Something about the dog made him lean forward in his chair and stare intently. And while his eyes were riveted on the animal, his mind reviewed the events of the past few weeks in an effort to make a connection between the dog and the catastrophe that threatened Morgan City and the rest of the planet.

Decker Eiselt gnawed at a stubborn cuticle as he gazed from the flitter window. He was short, very dark and had an intelligent, fine-featured face. He was presently engaged in marveling at Morgan City which lay spread out below him. This was hardly the first time he had seen it from the air but the perfect harmony of its layout never failed to stir him. This was a city as cities should be—a planned city, a city that knew where it was going, a city with a purpose.

Discounting a few large islands, Kamedon had only one continent and Morgan City occupied its center, a fitting capital for a world that had become one of the centers of Restructurist ideology and the pride of the Restructurist movement.

Yes, Morgan City was beautiful as cities go, but Decker Eiselt preferred the coast. The university was there and the years spent near the sea in study and research had instilled a narcoticlike dependency in his system... without the continual dull roar of the surf and a certain, subtle tang in the air, he could not feel quite at ease, could never relax and feel at home.

And then there were the fishermen. During his stay in Morgan City he would miss rising early with the sun glaring on the water and watching the fishermen head out the harbor as he and Sally ate breakfast. Most of the men on those slow, ponderous boats were salaried by the government fisheries but a few diehards still insisted on freelancing and trying to earn more by catching more. Eiselt detested their stubbornness but their spirit struck a resonance somewhere within him and he was forced to admit a grudging admiration for them—until they got out of hand, of course.

He idly wondered if there could possibly be any connection between the disorder at the local fishery the other day and his being called to Morgan City, but promptly dismissed the thought. He was a research physician and had nothing to do with fisheries. And besides, the incident had been minor by any standard, just some pushing and shoving at the pay window. Some of the local fishermen—the free lancers especially—had become angry when the pay authorizations were delayed. Nothing to get excited about, really; this was the first time such a delay had ever occurred and would no doubt be the last. The Department of Sea Industries was far too efficient to allow such an oversight to happen a second time.

They were coming in for a landing, now. The roof of the Department of Medicine and Research's administration building grew large beneath them as Eiselt's darting brown eyes strained to recognize the figure waiting below. It was Dr. Caelen, no doubt. Eiselt hadn't liked being called away from his work for some mysterious reason that would not be explained until he arrived in Morgan City, but an unmistakable note of urgency had filtered through the message.

And so Decker Eiselt chewed a cuticle as he did whenever he was puzzled. What was the urgent need for a research physician? And why the mystery? He smiled grimly. No use in getting worked up about it; he'd know soon enough. He didn't have much choice in the matter, anyway: when Dr. Alton Caelen summons you to the capital, you go to the capital. Immediately.

The flitter touched down with a jolt and Eiselt, the only passenger, hopped out as soon as the engines were cut. A lean, graying man in his fifties stepped forward to meet him.

"Decker!" he said, shaking his hand. "Good to see you!"

Eiselt couldn't reply. Was it...

Yes, it was Dr. Caelen and he looked terrible! Bright eyes gleamed from sockets deep-sunk in a lined and haggard face.

"Dr. Caelen!" he stammered. "I..."

"I know," the older man said quickly. "You're about to say I look like death warmed over and you're right. But we'll talk about it downstairs."

Caelen led him to the elevator and kept up an incessant flow of trivia on the way down, punctuating each phrase with quick, nervous gestures.

"How's the wife? Very pregnant and very happy, I suppose. Lovely girl, Sally. Dr. Bain's taking care of her, I suppose. Good, good. How about that little disturbance out your way? Unfortunate, very unfortunate. But things may get worse before they get better. Yes, they may well get worse."

Stimulants? Eiselt asked himself. Dr. Caelen was definitely hyper. He had never seen the man so worked up. After reaching his office, however, he visibly sagged and Eiselt could no longer contain himself.

"My God, Doctor! What's happened to you?"

"I'm not sleeping very well," he replied simply and calmly.

Under normal circumstances, Eiselt would have waited for an invitation before sitting down but these weren't normal circumstances. He grabbed the nearest chair and, without taking his eyes off Caelen, slowly sank into it.

"There must be more to it than that. A sedative will cure insomnia."

Caelen followed Eiselt's lead and fell into the chair behind his desk before answering. "There's not much more to tell, really," he said, putting his hands over his temples and resting his elbows on the desk top. "I just can't seem to get enough air at night. When I doze off, I wake up a few minutes later, gasping frantically. And it's getting worse."

Eiselt repressed an audible sigh. Pulmonary diseases had been his field of research for the past ten years and he felt as if he were on firm ground again. His muscles relaxed somewhat and he settled more comfortably into the chair.

"Was the onset of symptoms slow, or abrupt?"

"Slow. So slow that I didn't become concerned until recently. But I can trace it pretty clearly in retrospect. The symptoms started showing up during my daily exercises—"

"You mean you have respiratory troubles during periods of exertion, too?"

"Yes...sorry if I gave you the impression that I'm only bothered when I'm trying to sleep. The problem isn't that simple. You see, about nine months ago I started noticing little irregularities in my breathing rhythm as I exercised. I didn't pay too much attention to it at the time but it's got to the point where short, simple exercises, that I formerly performed with ease, leave me gasping for air. Two or three months ago I started having sleeping problems. Nothing much at first: restlessness, insomnia, inability to sleep for more than an hour at a time. Things have progressed to the present stage where I can hardly sleep at all. And, unless I concentrate fully on my breathing, I can't exert myself in the slightest."

"Are you having any difficulty right now, just sitting and talking?"

"Only a little, but I find myself out of breath at the oddest times."

Eiselt mused a moment. "The syndrome, as you've related it, doesn't ring a bell. I'd like to make some tests, if I may."

"I figured you would," Caelen said and managed a smile. "The lab downstairs will be at your disposal."

"Good. But one question: Why me? There are plenty of others in Morgan City who could handle this, many of them right in this building. Of course I'm honored that you thought of me but I am, after all, a research physician."

"I wanted you here for a number of reasons," Caelen stated. "Central among them was the fact that there isn't much you don't know about respiratory pathology. The others I'll explain to you after you've made your tests."

Eiselt nodded. "Okay, but one other question, if you don't mind: What psychological symptoms? If you're losing REM sleep..."

"I'm as irritable as hell, if that's what you mean. It's only with the greatest exercise of will that I keep myself from biting off the head of anyone I meet, including you. So stop quizzing me and get on with your tests!"

"Well, then," Eiselt said, rising and smiling, "let's go."

He didn't know what was plaguing Caelen but was confident he could come up with an answer in a short while. No doubt it was a variation on another familiar syndrome.

———

Later in the day he wasn't so sure. All his tests for pathology had come up negative. Strange, a man with Caelen's symptoms should certainly show some pathology. Feeling not a little embarrassed, Eiselt took the grav chute to the upper levels. Dr. Caelen had taught at the university before the Department of Medicine and Research decided to move him into Administration. He now headed that department and Eiselt, one of his former students, had wanted to look good for the old man.

Dr. Caelen awaited him in his office. "Well, Decker, what have you found?"

"Frankly, I'm a little at a loss," he admitted. "Your lungs are in great shape. You shouldn't have the symptoms you do."

He paused, but Caelen waited for him to go on.

Obviously crestfallen, he concluded: "I'm afraid I'll need some more data before I can even guess which way to go."

"Don't feel too badly about it," Caelen told him. "Nobody else knows what's going on around here, either—and we've had the best working on it. I knew you'd want to make those tests yourself and draw your own conclusions so I let you."

"Thanks. That makes me feel a little better. But now I'd like to know those 'other reasons' for sending for me."

Caelen nodded. "Okay. Tell me: have you noticed anything unusual about our personnel?"

"To tell the truth, the building seems almost deserted."

"True, that's part of the problem. But what about those you have seen?"

"They all look pretty beat," he replied after a pause, "almost like... Doctor, is there an epidemic of this syndrome?"

"Yes, I'm afraid so," Caelen said.

"Why haven't I heard anything about it?"

Caelen sighed. "Because we've been doing our best to keep the lid on it until we find out just what it is we're dealing with."

"Does it seem to be spreading?"

"Most suburban hospitals are packed with cases, but they're not as bad off as the city proper. It seems as if the entire population of the capital has come down with this... this syndrome. And we've also had reports of isolated cases from coast to coast. Figure that one out!"

Eiselt's teeth found a cuticle and went to work on it. "I have an instinctive feeling that this isn't the work of any pathogenic organism, known or unknown. Yet, an epidemic usually means contagion..." His voice drifted off into thought.

"Speaking of contagion," Caelen said, "I must apologize for exposing you to whatever it is that's plaguing us but we needed someone who was uninfected to work on it. The rest of us are so exhausted that we can't think straight about any subject other than sleep. We don't trust our own judgment. I hope I haven't endangered you, but you must understand that we're getting desperate. None of the departments can get anything done because no one can concentrate anymore. That's why the Department of Sea Industries made that error with the pay authorizations. And there have been a number of other, similar cases. The Department of Public Information has been keeping it quiet but little things have a way of piling up. We may have a very frightened planet on our hands if we don't come up with something soon. I tried to handle it myself but my stamina has been completely sapped."

"Could it possibly be a Federation plot?"

Caelen repressed a smile. Decker Eiselt hadn't changed much. He had been an adamant Restructurist during his college years and had evidently remained so.

"Ridiculous, Decker! The very reason we want to 'restructure' the Federation is because it limits itself exclusively to interplanetary affairs. A plot against Kamedon would be strictly out of character."

"But you have to admit that the Federation would hardly be dismayed if the people lost faith in the government and the planet ground to a halt."

"You've got a point there, but you must realize that the Restructurist movement will go on, with or without Kamedon. And you can't go around looking for a Federation plot every time something goes wrong."

"I suppose you're right," Eiselt reluctantly agreed.

"Of course I'm right! So let's not worry about the Federation or Restructurism. Let's worry about Morgan City. I don't want to have to call in the IMC."

Eiselt blanched. "The Interstellar Medical Corps is pro-Federation! Asking them for help is like going to the Federation itself!"

"Well, then," Caelen said pointedly, "I hope you've got some sort of a plan on how to tackle this."

"I've got the start of a plan. Those isolated cases might provide us with a clue. I'd like to have every one of them flown to the capital as soon as possible."

"Good idea," Caelen agreed, swallowing another stimulant.

After two weeks of testing and interviewing patients from the outlying districts, Eiselt was able to hand Dr. Caelen a piece of paper with a date scrawled on it.

"Remember that day?" he said.

Caelen hesitated. "No, can't say I do." Daily he and all the other victims had grown more haggard and exhausted. Remembering was an effort. "Almost a year ago… wait! Wasn't this the day of the accident in Dr. Sebitow's lab?"

"Correct. And how does this strike you: every case I've interviewed was in Morgan City when the accident occurred!"

Caelen slumped in his seat. "Sebitow's ray," he muttered.

"What's that supposed to mean?"

"I don't know. No one really knew except Sebitow—and he's dead."

Eiselt's tone showed his exasperation. "But the department gave him the money! You must know what he was working on!"

"What do you know about administration, Decker?" the older man flared. "How do you handle a man who is one of the greatest medical minds in the galaxy but who has no concept of politics, who has no loyalty to anything but his work? To Nathan Sebitow the Federation and the Restructurist movement were just words! The only way to keep a man like that working for you is to give him full rein. A number of other planets had offered him unlimited funds and unlimited freedom so we had to match them. He said he was onto something big and wanted the money immediately, so we gave it to him."

"But don't you have any idea what he was doing?"

Caelen paused. "All we know is that he was working on high-penetration radiation with neuronal effects. When he worked out a few bugs he was going to give us a full report. Decker, you don't think the Respiratory Center could have been affected, do you?"

"Not a chance," Eiselt replied with a slow shake of his head. Your Respiratory Center is intact and functional. Were any of Sebitow's records recovered?"

"None."

"But wasn't he still alive when they found him? I remember a report about Sebitow being taken to a hospital… did he say anything?"

"He said a few words," Caelen replied, "but they didn't make too much sense."

"Remember what they were? It might give us a lead."

"Not really. Something about an over-reaction, I think."

"Please try to remember!" Eiselt urged.

Caelen shrugged. "We had a recorder going when he came around. If you think it's important, go down to Hearn's office and he'll play it for you."

Dr. Hearn, too, was gaunt and haggard and really didn't want to be bothered with retrieving a recording of Dr. Sebitow's last words. His last stimulant was wearing off.

"I'll tell you what he said, Dr. Eiselt: 'Over-reaction… danger… tell… ens… ' That was all."

"Yes, but I'd like to hear it myself. I know what you're going through but I'm trying to find a key to this mess. Please get it."

Wearily, Hearn went to a file, pulled out a cartridge and fitted it into a viewer. For seemingly interminable minutes Eiselt watched the injured Dr. Sebitow toss his bandaged head and mumble incoherently. Suddenly, the man opened his eyes and shouted, "Over-reaction!… Danger! Tell… ens…" and then relapsed into mumbles. Hearn switched it off.

"What did he mean by 'ens'?" Eiselt asked.

Hearn shrugged. "That puzzled us for a while until we remembered that his chief assistant's name was Endicott. He must have wanted someone to tell Endicott something but never finished the sentence."

"Endicott? Where is Endicott?"

"Dead too."

Eiselt rose wordlessly and started for the door.

"We've got to get to the bottom of this soon, Doctor," he heard Hearn say behind him. Stimulant supplies are diminishing. The Department of Production is so understaffed that it hasn't been able to issue the latest production quota and so factories and mills all over the continent have had to shut down. We've had food riots in some areas because the

Department of Distribution has fouled up its scheduling. There's even talk of a march on Morgan City to demand more competence and efficiency in the handling of public affairs!"

"I'm doing the best I can!" Eiselt gritted.

"I know you are, and you're doing it almost single-handedly. It's just that I dread the thought of having to call in the IMC. But I fear it must come to that if we don't get a breakthrough soon."

"Never! If we can't lick this thing, they certainly can't do any better," he declared, approaching Hearn's desk.

"Come now, Doctor," Hearn replied. "I know you're a dedicated Restructurist, as are we all, but let's be realistic. The IMC has the brains, talents and resources of a thousand worlds at its disposal. You can't hope to compare our facilities with theirs."

Eiselt slammed his fist on the desk top. "We'll solve this and we'll do it without the help of the IMC!"

"I hope you're right," Hearn said softly as he watched Eiselt storm from the office. "And I hope it's soon."

———

Eiselt managed to cool his temper by the time he made his daily call to Sally. As her face came into focus on the viewscreen, he noticed that she looked distraught.

"Something wrong, honey?" he asked.

"Oh, Decker!" she cried. "They've gone!"

"Who?"

"Almost everyone! Students, faculty, administrators, fishermen, shopkeepers, everyone! They chartered groundcars and flitters and started out for Morgan City this morning!"

Eiselt remembered the march Hearn had mentioned. "What about Doctor Bain?"

"Oh, he's still here. His wife wants me to stay with them until you get back. Maybe I'd better take her up on it."

The exodus from town had made her somewhat anxious and Eiselt wished he could be with her.

"Good idea," he said. Bain would look after her. After all, she was his patient and in her eighth month and if her husband couldn't be there, someone should keep an eye on her. "Get over there as soon as possible and tell them I'll be eternally grateful!"

She ran a hand nervously through her brown hair. "Okay. Any luck so far?"

"No. Every time I think I'm onto something, I wind up in a dead end."

The frustration was evident in her husband's voice and Sally figured that the best thing she could do for him was allow him to get back to his work.

"I'd better get packed now," she told him. "Call me tomorrow."

"I will," he promised and broke the connection.

Depression was unusual for Decker Eiselt. In the past his nervous energy had always carried him through the troughs as well as over the peaks. But he felt drained now. He took the elevator down to street level and dropped into a chair by the window. That was when he spotted the dog.

The dog's gait grabbed his attention; the uneven, limping stride reminded him of another dog... years ago... at the university.

Suddenly he was on his feet and racing for the elevator. He shot to the upper levels and burst into Caelen's office just as the man was about to take another stimulant capsule.

"Don't take that! I've got one more test to make and I want you to try and sleep while I'm doing it."

Caelen hesitated. "I'm afraid, Decker. I'm afraid I may not wake up one of these times."

"I'll be right there," he assured him. "I want to monitor your cortex while you sleep."

"Are you on to something, Decker?"

Eiselt pulled him to his feet. "I'll explain as I wire you up. Let's just say that I hope I'm wrong."

Supine on a table, a very groggy Dr. Caelen tried valiantly to focus his eyes on the oscilloscope screen and concentrate on what his younger colleague was saying.

"See that?" Eiselt remarked, pointing to a series of spikes. "There's an unusually high amount of cortical activity synchronized with respiration. Put that together with the symptoms of this epidemic, the nature of Sebitow's research and his last words and the result is pretty frightening. You see, I fear Sebitow's last words were a warning."

"A warning against what?"

"Telencephalization!"

He saw no sign of recognition in Caelen's eyes.

"It's a neurophysiologist's term," Eiselt explained. "If a lame dog out on the street hadn't reminded me of it, the concept never would have occurred to me."

"Forgive me, Decker, but I'm not following you."

Eiselt paused. "Maybe this will help you remember: the most common and effective means of illustrating telencephalization is to take an experimental animal and sever the spinal cord at midthorax, or at the neck. If that happened to a man, he'd lose the use of his legs in the first instance and also the use of his arms in the latter. But an animal with a severed spinal cord—a dog or possum, for instance—can still walk! His gait is often irregular but the point is he can still get around while a man is rendered helpless. Why? Because man has telencephalized his walking ability! As part of his evolution, the higher centers of man's nervous system have taken over many motor functions formerly performed by the lower, local centers.

"I have a theory that Sebitow might have developed a way to cause telencephalization, possibly for use as a rehabilitation technique… to let higher centers take over where damaged local centers are no longer effective. But I fear the city got a blast of the radiation he was using to induce this takeover and the symptoms we've seen led me to the conclusion that somehow the respiratory center has been telencephalized. The encephalogram seems to confirm this."

"But you said nothing was wrong with the respiratory center," Caelen rasped in a weak whisper.

"There's no pathology, but it seems that the voluntary areas of the forebrain are in command and are overriding the local peripheral sensors. Thus the diffuse respiratory malaise and broken breathing rhythm when you exercised. The voluntary areas of the cortex were starting to take over. They are nowhere near as efficient nor as sensitive as the local centers such as the pressoreceptors in the lungs and the chemoreceptors in the aorta and carotid arteries which work directly through the respiratory center without going near the cortex. But because of telencephalization, the respiratory center is no longer responsive to the local centers. And there lies the problem.

"It boils down to this: You and all the other victims are breathing on the border of consciousness! This means you stop breathing when unconscious! Without oxygen the acidity of your blood goes up and the local chemoreceptors start screaming. But the respiratory center no longer responds and so impulses are finally relayed to the cortex; the cortex is roused and you wake up gasping for air. That's the theory. I want to monitor the voluntary areas to confirm or deny it; if activity there falls off as respiration falls off, then we'll know I'm right."

"What'll we do if you're right?" Caelen asked.

Rather than tell him that he didn't have the faintest idea, Eiselt pulled a blanket over him. "Try to sleep." The exhausted administrator closed his eyes. Eiselt watched him a minute, then went over to the drug cabinet and filled a syringe with a stimulant. Just in case.

As he sat and watched the oscilloscope, a dull roar filtered up from the street. Going to the window, he saw a shouting, gesticulating crowd marching below. They were frightened, and they were angry, and they wanted to know what was wrong. Kamedon had been running so smoothly... now, chaos. Some areas were receiving no food while others received more than they could use; some factories were shut down while others received double quotas; and no one could be sure when he would next be paid. What was happening? The famous efficiency of Kamedon was breaking down and the people wanted to know why.

Someone broke a window. Somebody else followed suit. Fascinated, Eiselt watched the march turn into a mob scene in a matter of minutes.

He glanced over at Dr. Caelen and realized with a start that the man had stopped breathing. He cursed as he noted the reduced cortical activity on the 'scope. Telencephalization of the respiratory center—no doubt about it now.

He put a hand on Caelen's shoulder and shook him. No response. Looking closer, he noticed a blue tinge to the man's lips. With frantic haste he found a vein and injected the stimulant, then hooked up a respirator.

Slowly, as normal breathing returned, Dr. Caelen's eyelids opened to reveal two dull orbs. Cortical activity had increased on the oscilloscope.

Decker Eiselt's shoulders slumped with relief—and defeat. He was beaten. Telencephalization was an evolutionary process—although in this case the evolution was suicidal—and he had no way of combating it, no way of returning command to the local centers. The only hope for Dr. Caelen—and Kamedon—was the IMC. And Eiselt knew he would have to be the one to call them in.

They would be gracious rescuers, of course, and would do their work skillfully and competently. The IMC would find a solution, rectify the situation and then leave, no doubt refusing to accept payment, explaining that they were only too glad to have such an opportunity to expand the perimeters of neurophysiology.

But it would soon be known throughout the settled galaxy that Kamedon, the pride of the Restructurist movement, had found it necessary to call in the IMC. And pro-Federation propagandists were sure to waste no time in drawing an ironic comparison between Restructurist philosophy and the syndrome which had afflicted Morgan City.

He could see it now: "Centralists suffering from overcentralization!"

To put it mildly, the near future was going to be a most difficult period.

Outside, the roar of the mob redoubled.

"The Man with the Anteater" (*Analog*, July 1971) is even less subtle than "Higher Centers" and, in many ways... ridiculous. After the fictitious book excerpt, the narrative starts off with a few paragraphs directed straight at the reader—something I'd consider verboten only a few years later. In the finale I pull a Melville: I stop the narrative to give a short lecture on antbears. Oy. As with "Higher Centers," I think Campbell bought it because he was sympatico to its underlying individualism. But as mentioned before, I was learning in public.

The Man with the Anteater

No discussion of galactic business, of course, would be complete without mention of Interstellar Business Advisers. Armed with the tried-and-true maxims of a free-market economy and a number of new and daring precepts for the conduct of business on an interstellar scale, IBA played an important part in shaping the course of trade in the galaxy.

The company was founded by one Joseph Finch, a man whose figure has taken on an almost mythical air in the annals of galactic trade. The most far-fetched stories concern the period before the founding of IBA, when Finch was still a resident of Earth—

Excerpt from *Galactic Business: A History*
by Emmerz Fent

On a steamy summer morning, Joe and Andy the anteater stepped out into their backyard and surveyed their domain. Thirty-eight, slight of frame and a bit on the homely side, Joe Finch didn't exactly cut a heroic figure. But he was looked up to as a hero by many nonetheless. And there were, of course, many who thought of him as a stupid, eccentric, thick-headed, bull-headed reactionary. But they seemed to be in the minority.

You see, in a world that functions with the smoothness of a well-oiled machine, the man who insists on deciding when to shift his own gears becomes a hero of sorts. A man with few friends, who had yet to meet his wife, whose sister and brother-in-law, unable to cope with Earth any longer, were living as splinter colonists on a planet called Dasein II somewhere out in nowhere,

Finch was a loner. And in a highly collectivized, planned and patented society, loners, if they can avoid being swallowed whole and digested, become heroes.

Finch was mentally running through his plan to manipulate Arthur Gordon, Chief Administrator of Earth. Gordon was either a social idealist or a power-monger—the two not always distinguishable—and Finch knew from certain sources that Gordon was planning to manipulate him. The thing to do was to make Gordon show his hand before he was completely ready, and the strike going on at the Finch House plant right now could be the perfect lever.

"Stay here, Andy," he told his pet. "And if you get hungry, help yourself." Andy scanned the dry, virtually grassless yard and trotted off in the direction of a promising mound with his huge, furry tail held straight out behind him and his agile tongue seemingly licking his snout in anticipation.

"Don't overdo it or you'll have to go back on synthe-meat and formic acid," Finch warned. Andy glanced over his shoulder and stuck out his tongue.

Finch went out front, started up an old transporter with the words Finch House printed on the sides and back, and drove off toward Pete Farnham's machine shop.

As the last of the new equipment was being loaded, Farnham turned to Finch. "You sure you want to go through with this, Joe?"

"Look, Pete," Finch said, wiping his forehead on his sleeve, "you designed this stuff so I'd be able to increase my output by about another half without increasing my overhead or labor costs."

Farnham looked annoyed. "I'm not talking about that. I'm talking about the union... it's on strike, remember? They're very unhappy about losing their overtime."

"If the union had its way," Finch growled, "I'd still be using

Gutenberg presses."

"But it's against the law to cross a picket line! Why don't you just wait it out as usual or maybe bribe the union president? All hell's going to break loose if you go through with this."

Finch locked the back of the transporter with a solid click. "That might be just what I'm after. Besides, this is as good a time as any to challenge a rotten law. Gordon's been pushing things a bit too..." His voice trailed off as he saw Farnham climbing into the cab. "Where do you think you're going?"

"With you, of course," Farnham replied and hefted a length of pipe. "I spent a lot of time designing that equipment and the only way it'll ever get to prove itself is if you get to use it. Now let's get moving."

...*the pickets/a truck in their midst/hey! /stop 'em! /get them! /Hold 'em/ don't let 'em through! stop 'em!! Stomp 'em!!/but chain and bricks and barricades and bodies give way/a face looms/flail at it. /Someone fires a shot/miss! / The police arrive/made it!!/The pickets are being held outside and the police will deal with you later...*

Joe Finch watched the roiling crowds from atop the Earth Building. "You just can't figure people, Andy," he told the pet he had insisted on bringing with him. "They clamor for a law to be passed and then celebrate a man who breaks it."

"I believe you're oversimplifying the situation, Joe," said a voice behind him.

Finch turned to see Arthur Gordon: big, graying, about sixty, the man on whose "invitation" he had come to the Earth Building. It was their first meeting and the Chief Administrator of Earth got things off on the wrong foot by calling him "Joe;" Finch believed first names were for personal friends only.

"Oh, how's that, Arthur?" he replied, noting the CA's wince.

"Well, I mean...it seems you've become a symbol to them—"

(My, what a phony smile you have, Arthur Gordon.)

"...a symbol of Individuality—"

(I'll bet he uses a capital "I" when he spells that word.)

"And Individuality is something each of them feels he has lost."

(Whose fault is that?)

"I imagine that some of them, deep in their hearts, actually hate you for maintaining a quality they've lost."

(I can think of a few union roughnecks who won't have to go that deep.)

"As a matter of fact—"

"Get to the point!" Finch finally interrupted. "Why did you 'invite' me here rather than have me arrested for breaking the picket law?"

Gordon's fixed smile was replaced by one of a more genuine nature. "Okay, Mr. Finch, I will be more to the point, although what I've been saying isn't far from it. Let's go into my office."

It was not until Finch was seated across the desk from him in the Chief Administrator's spacious main office that Gordon began to speak.

"Mr. Finch, the reason I did not have you arrested is very simple: you are the only man on this planet who can be described as a hero."

"I think you've got the wrong definition of a hero, Mr. CA. I'm not a hero. I've never done a heroic thing in my life. I may stand out in a crowd, but otherwise I think you're overestimating me."

Gordon frowned. "I don't think I overestimate you at all. The public is hungry for an idol and you, unwilling as you may be, are the prime candidate. In fact your unwillingness to cooperate with the idol-seekers only increases your popularity. To them you're the last of a rare species. Just look at you! You wander around with an antbear at your heels, you're making a pile of money in an industry that should have been extinct shortly after the development of telestories, you had a shyster lawyer wheedle a private home for you so you could raise ants for that ridiculous pet of yours and now you've taken to busting picket lines!"

"Nobody keeps me out of my own business," Finch stated flatly and finally.

"I wonder about that," Gordon mused. "This is hardly the first strike at your plant... You've bargained with the union before, why did you choose to defy it this time? Planning to challenge the Picket Law?"

"Would it do me any good to try?" Finch replied in a noncommittal tone.

"Maybe. I never liked the law. Didn't like it when it was passed and I like it even less at the moment."

Finch cracked his knuckles. "The Picket Law is a natural consequence of legalizing the picket line. You see, a picket line makes it possible to kidney-punch anyone trying to enter the building currently under siege and sooner or later you don't cross a picket line if you know what's good for you. Then, with typical political logic, crossing a picket line was declared illegal 'in order to prevent violence during strikes.'"

Gordon snorted. "I've heard all this before, Mr. Finch. And I didn't ask you here to reprimand your extralegal activities nor to discuss the Picket Law with you. Instead of having you arrested, I'd rather make a deal."

"I had a feeling you'd find some use for me."

The CA ignored the remark. "Look, Finch, here's the situation: we've become an incredibly complex society here on Earth; the average man feels like a cog, feels a loss of worth. Oh, I know it sounds very trite but unfortunately it's very true. We've been warned about this for centuries but it's something that's almost impossible to prevent, even when you can see it coming.

"You, however, have somehow overcome it all. You've bucked convention, legal restrictions… even technology! You've become a symbol of the Individuality people instinctively feel they've lost and want desperately to regain. And I've found a way to give it to them!"

Finch smirked. "How? Pills?"

Gordon was not in a light mood. "No, the plan's a little more complicated than that. It's a daring plan and will frighten people at first; they'll want the end but they'll balk at the means. Unless—"

"Unless what?"

"Unless someone they admire not only endorses it but actively promotes it."

Finch shook his head as if to clear it. "Wait a minute. Let's just go back a bit. You're building up to the means and I don't even know what the end really is supposed to be."

Gordon strode to a bookshelf and pulled out a huge volume.

"Ever hear of Gregor Black?" he asked as he laid the book on the desk.

"Some sort of technosociologist, wasn't he?" Finch replied. "But I believe his disciples are calling him 'Noah' Black now."

"Right. His theory was that both the individual and society are best served when the individual is doing the job for which he is best suited: the old 'right man for the right job' maxim. He figured that not only would you achieve maximum productivity but you'd also allow the individual the personal satisfaction and sense of fulfillment that comes from doing what he can do best."

"Where is he now?" Finch asked.

Gordon had opened the volume and was flipping through the pages. "Oh, somewhere in the Ninth Quadrant, I believe."

Finch snapped his fingers. "That's right! His group was outlawed so they decided to apply for a splinter colony."

Ninety years ago they took up the government's offer to any large enough group that wanted to settle an Earthclass planet and got free, one-way transportation to the prospective utopia of their choice. Since they were registered as a splinter colony, the planet was then declared off limits to all government traffic and Black and company could do whatever they wanted with it.

"I'd love to know who dreamed up the splinter colony idea," Finch said with a smile and a shake of the head. "It's probably one of the few deals in history in which everybody gets what he wants: the government not only colonizes world after world, but it gets rid of all the local dissidents to boot. And the dissidents get their own world on which to live the way they wish."

Gordon was not listening, however. Pointing to the book on his desk, be said, "Here's the reason Black's group was outlawed: the Assessor."

"I remember the name," Finch remarked. "Gregor Black's miracle machine."

"Don't be too light with the Assessor... nor with old Gregor. He designed quite a machine. With the Assessor screening a population you wouldn't have, say, a potential physicist or chemist doing menial labor because his talents and abilities were never discovered and never developed. Nor would you have incompetents in important positions because of 'connections.' It's too bad the Assessor jumbled the minds of a few of his followers during testing—that's why its use was outlawed."

"Jumbled, hell!" Finch snorted. "It turned a few of his faithful followers into vegetables!"

"Well, you've got to remember that 'electrohypnosis'—which was the term for mind-probing in those days—was still in the experimental stages. Its use was integral to the Assessor but its control had not yet been perfected. Thus, the tragic accidents."

Finch yawned. "Just as well. Never would have worked anyway."

Gordon smiled and leaned over his desk. "Oh, but it has!"

"You mean you've heard from Black's splinter colony? I wouldn't put too much faith in..."

"No, no," the CA. interrupted, "it has worked right here on Earth!"

"Where?"

"The Rigrod Peninsula."

"So that's what all the secrecy's been about."

Gordon was enthused now: "We started a colony out there twenty-six years ago using a thousand deserted children, each about a year old. Each was 'assessed' once a year for the first twenty years and education was modified and directed for each in accordance with the Assessor's findings; we were thus able to give them twenty years of education in roughly fifteen. Six years ago they were all given the option of either going into their assigned fields or returning to the mainland."

He paused dramatically. "All stayed."

Finch affected a surprised expression. He had a few contacts in the government and knew all about the Rigrod experiment.

"And the advances in technology, the arts, the life sciences, business and hundreds of other fields in these past six years have been incredible!"

"I can see how it would work," Finch said, "but why tell me about it?"

"Because it's going to take a massive selling job to get the public to accept it and my advisers think that endorsements by popular personalities would be the best technique. You, Joe Finch, are going to help convince the public that the Assessor is the greatest thing ever to come along."

"Oh, really? Not without a little more than a spiel from you, I'm afraid."

Gordon sobered. "What do you mean?"

"I mean I want to see Rigrod and see exactly what it's like. If this Assessor can do all you say it can, then I'll back you on it. But I want to see for myself."

"I'm afraid not," the CA frowned. "We've allowed free access of outside information into Rigrod but all outsiders have been barred. We can make no exceptions."

"Better make one this time."

"Need I remind you, Mr. Finch, that your situation in regard to the law at the moment is quite precarious?"

"I endorse nothing sight unseen," Finch stated. He was gambling now, gambling that the Finch endorsement was important enough to the CA to make him back down. "And besides, you've said nothing about my legal situation after I endorse the Assessor... how will I stand then?"

If you're going to bluff, don't do it halfheartedly.

Gordon studied Finch with narrowed eyes and nodded slowly. "All right. All right, dammit! I'll publicly denounce the Picket Law and have the charges dropped after we go to Rigrod."

"Well, Andy," Finch said, scratching his pet's snout, "looks like we're going on a trip soon... and at government expense, no less."

The Rigrod Peninsula had been turned into a minor city, a tiny nation of a thousand. Order and symmetry ruled its design and new structures of unique conceptualization were on the rise. The inhabitants came out in force to meet Joe Finch. They were only physically isolated here and the figure of the crusty individualist with his ever-present antbear companion was immediately recognized.

He wandered through the crowd of residents commenting on this and that, answering questions and shaking proffered hands. He was impressed. These people were friendly, articulate and every one a specialist in his or her field. But there was a subtle undercurrent here, an undercurrent he had been sure he would find.

After the tour, Gordon and Finch retired to the CA's Rigrod offices. Finch was skimming through a manuscript he had found on the desk. It was called "Interstellar Business: A Theory," by Peter J. Paxton.

"This Paxton is good," he told the beaming Gordon. "His logistical concepts will revolutionize interstellar trade. Does he need a publisher?"

"Sorry, Joe," Gordon laughed," but Rigrod is setting up its own publishing house—and it will be a telestories format." He was needling Finch and enjoying it. Changing the subject, he asked, "Well, now that you've seen our little project, what do you think of it?"

Now the touchy part: to stall for time. "I don't know. There's something about this setup that bothers me."

"What could bother you? It's the perfect society! Utopia!"

"The whole idea of utopia makes me more than a little nervous," Finch replied. "Can you give me a week or two to think on it?"

"I'll give you a week, Finch. That should give you plenty of time to assimilate what you've seen here today. But remember, those charges still stand."

"Yes, I'm aware of that. But don't you think the endorsement would hold more weight if it wasn't so obvious that we had made a deal?"

"You have a point," the CA admitted and paused, thinking. "Why don't we try this: I'll get the charges dropped if you give me a tentative affirmation."

"Okay, Mr. Gordon. It's a deal."

And the Chief Administrator of Earth made good his promise the very next day.

When Gordon and two other men burst into the Finch backyard, they found that he was not alone. Andy was there and so was a young, fair-haired man in his mid-twenties. Gordon instantly recognized him.

"Paxton! It figures I'd find you here! Go inside. I've something to discuss with Mr. Finch!"

The young man was cowed by the wrathful CA. He looked to Finch and Finch nodded toward the door.

"Do as he says. He brought a couple of his bully-boys along so we'd better humor him."

When Paxton had disappeared into the house, Finch turned to Gordon. "Now what the hell is all this about?"

"You're under arrest, Finch!" Gordon roared.

"What for?" Andy raised his head and wondered who was making all this noise on such a pleasant afternoon.

"You know very well what for... for destroying a government project!"

"You mean the Rigrod experiment?"

"Yes! The Rigrod experiment! The whole structure of the Assessor-built society started to break down soon after your visit. You did something out there. I'm going to find out what it was. I don't care how popular you are, you're going to tell me."

"I'll tell you what I did," said Finch. "I visited the place. That's all. You were with me all the time."

"You pulled something—" Gordon began.

"Damn right I did," Finch interrupted with a snort. "I destroyed that project willfully and with malice aforethought. And I did you a favor by doing it. It was bound to happen sooner or later! You thought you were creating the perfect society by basing it on human individuality, by making the best use of individual abilities. You took care of individuality... fine! But you forgot all about individualism!

"It never occurred to you that many people wouldn't be happy doing 'what they can do best.' As a matter of fact, many people don't give a damn about what they can do best. They're more interested in doing what they like to do, what they want to do. There might be a musician playing at the music center tonight who could be a brilliant physicist if he wanted to be, but he likes music instead. In an Assessor-built society, however, he'd be working with mathematical formulae instead of chord progressions. He'd sit around envying musicians for just so long and then he'd either rebel or go mad. When are people like you going to learn that utopia is a fool's game?"

Gordon was in a cold rage. The project, which was to be a monument to his name, was being torn to shreds by this man in front of him. He spoke through clenched teeth: "But why didn't they rebel before you showed up? The project was working perfectly until then."

"You've had no trouble on the peninsula until now," Finch explained, "because you've been working with a biased sample. Those kids have been told all their lives that they are pioneers, that they'll be the ones to prove that man can have utopia. And so all the square pegs in the round holes—the equivalents of our hypothetical musician-physicist—keep mum on the hope that their discontent will pass... they don't want to destroy 'man's chance at utopia' by a hasty decision. And in keeping mum they never find out that there are others like themselves.

"Then Joe Finch comes along.

"And I'm not a hero, Gordon. I'm a crackpot, an eccentric, a nut. I've known about Rigrod for over a decade now and spent that time building up a reputation as a rugged individualist. Many times I felt foolish but the press and the vid played right into my hands. I've been a walking publicity stunt for the last ten years. That's why my pet is an antbear instead of a dog—although I wouldn't trade Andy for anything now. I've been hoping for a chance to get to Rigrod and you gave it to me. And that was all I needed.

"Allowing someone with a reputation as a crackpot individualist to wander through the Rigrod Peninsula is like introducing a seed crystal to a supersaturated solution: all the underlying threads of doubt and discontent start to crystallize. But don't blame me! Blame yourself and your inane theories and ambitions! You were a fool to be taken in by Black's theory, you were a fool to bring me to the project and you were a fool to think that I'd have anything at all to do with such a plan!"

Gordon finally exploded. "Arrest him!" he told the two guards who had been standing idly by.

The guards, of course, did not know anything about antbears. The antbear has been long used in the areas to which it is indigenous as a watchdog. Its forelimbs have monstrous claws which it uses for digging into termite hills but it can rear up on its hind legs and use these claws for defense. And the antbear has an uncanny ability to roar like a lion.

The two guards were quickly made aware of these facts. Andy startled them with a roar as they made their first move toward Finch. A few swipes with his claws and the guards were down and gashed and bleeding.

Andy stood beside Finch and huffed warily as his master scratched his snout. Finch turned to the livid Chief Administrator.

"Now get out of here and take your friends with you."

"All right, Finch. You've won for now. But let me warn you that your life here on Earth from now on will be hell! And don't get any ideas about getting off-planet... you're staying right here!"

———

But Joe Finch had been far ahead of the CA. He had already sold his house, a printing firm had bought his machinery and all the properties of Finch House had been picked up by a telestories outfit. A handsome bribe had reserved two seats and one animal passage out from Earth on a moment's notice, and Joe Finch, Peter J. Paxton and Andy were well into primary warp toward Ragna before Arthur Gordon had any idea they had left Earth.

With Finch's money and organizational experience and Paxton's business theories, Interstellar Business Advisers was born and grew with the expanding Federation. And Joe, at long last able to put aside his role of superindividualist, found a woman who loved him—and anteaters, too—and it wasn't too long before Joe junior came along. But that's another story.

I'd intended this SF beauty-and-the-beast tale for John W. Campbell Jr. and *Analog*. It pokes at the question: *What is human?*—a question I'd explore in greater depth decades later in *Sims*. Campbell died just as I was finishing it. His replacement, Ben Bova, passed on it, so I sold it the following year to Vincent McCaffrey at *Fiction*; it appeared in issue #4 in 1973. I knew a lot more story was hiding in those pages but medical school was demanding the bulk of my time, so I let it go despite all the possibilities perking under the surface.

This is the first time the original story has been reprinted since 1973. As I reread it for this collection, I itched to change the passive constructions and cut the exclamation points, but I let them stay. It was what it was and it is what it is. And yes, once again, I was learning to write in public.

He Shall Be John

As he lay bleeding at the side of the road where he had been left for dead, the tery heard the approach of stealthy footsteps. He had no fear then that the soldiers were returning because stealth was hardly their way. He opened his mouth to cry out but found that his parched throat would utter no sound. With the greatest effort he rolled onto his back and raised an arm in the hope that someone would see it above the tall grass that surrounded him.

The footsteps quickened in his direction and suddenly there were four faces staring down at him—*human* faces. His heart sank; he had expected another tery. Now, he would no doubt be slain immediately.

The humans glanced at each other and nodded silently.

Then one with blonde hair turned and disappeared into the bushes. The others—to the tery's surprise—bent over him and began to brush away the flies and gnats that had been plaguing his wounds. All this without a single word.

Their silence puzzled him for they were obviously on their guard; but what had they to fear in these forests except Kitru's troops? And what had humans to fear from Kitru? Kitru slew only teries.

The fair-headed one returned from the bushes with a horse and, with the utmost gentleness and coordination of effort, the four men lifted the tery and laid him across the animal's back. Again, no word had been spoken. Perhaps they were outlaws, but even so, the tery began to think them overly cautious in their silence... the soldiers were long gone.

But further speculation was postponed as the horse began to move for its uneven step jostled the tery and a few of his barely-clotted wounds reopened.

The path they traveled was unknown to the tery, passing through dank grottos of huge, foul-hued fungi, that grew to twice the height of a man and skirting masses of writhing green tendrils all too willing to pull any hapless creature within reach toward a gaping central maw. After what seemed to be an interminable length of time, the group passed through a particularly dense thicket and came upon a clearing and a camp.

The tents were crude, of odd shapes and sizes, and scattered here and there in no particular arrangement. The inhabitants, too, offered little uniformity of design, ranging from frail to overweight. This was hardly what the tery had expected. He had envisioned a group of lean and wolfish outlaws; they would have to be so to hold their own against Kitru's seasoned troops. But there were women and children here and a number of them took leave of their cooking and playing to stare at him as he passed. These people certainly didn't look like outlaws... and the silence was oppressive.

His four rescuers set the tery down before a hut near the center of the camp. One of them called out, "Adriel!" The first and only word spoken during the entire episode.

A girl emerged, young—seventeen summers, perhaps—slightly overweight but not unpretty. Seeing the tery, she dropped to his side and examined his wounds.

"He's cut up pretty bad," she said. "Why'd you bring him back?"

"Those are sword wounds," one of the men said with some impatience. "That can only mean Kitru's men." He shrugged. "He's running from the same thing we are—might as well help him if we can."

"That was nice of you," Adriel said with a smile.

The man shrugged again. "I suppose so. Where's your father?"

Adriel rose and pointed to a far corner of the camp. "Over there somewhere."

The man nodded and left and the girl ducked back inside the hut. She re-emerged with a wet rag and knelt beside the tery. He was riding the ragged edge of consciousness then and the last thing he remembered as everything faded into blackness was the cool wet cloth wiping the dirt and dried blood from his face and a soft voice cooing, "Poor thing, poor thing..."

A huge man with a bushy red beard came up and Adriel turned to him.

"Father! Are Kitru's men exterminating the teries, too?"

He nodded and squatted beside her. "Yes, I'm afraid they are. Overlord Mekk's decree applies not only to us but to the teries and even to some of the more bizarre plants—at least that's what the Leader told us. It's also rumored Mekk will soon visit Kitru's keep and Kitru wants very much to please the Overlord." He paused a moment, then: "This creature was found too near the camp for comfort. It means that Kitru's men are ranging far from the keep. We must move on!"

He rose to his feet and stood with hands on hips, letting his eyes rove the weirdly silent camp. All motion ceased abruptly as everyone turned to face the big man. After a short pause, he turned back to Adriel and the camp dissolved into a flurry of activity.

"As soon as you finish binding his wounds, gather your things. We move!"

Adriel nodded and hastened her ministrations.

They numbered near fifty, these strange, silent folk, and their wordless coordination was fascinating to watch: with incredible swiftness they broke camp, loaded their pack animals and started off through the sun-filtered forest toward a new and safer location. Still weak from his wounds, the tery was bound to a drag behind one of the horses. Adriel walked beside him, neither happy nor unhappy, neither contented nor frustrated... lonely, rather. The tery thought that for the daughter of a chief-at least her father *seemed* to be the chief—to be lonely was unusual, even if she was slightly plump.

As they moved through the trees, a young man came up and put a hand on her shoulder. He was well built with an easy smile and curly brown hair that dangled over his forehead.

"How's the Finder today?" he asked Adriel.

She sighed. "How do you think, Dennel?"

"Same old problem?"

Adriel nodded.

"Will you ever understand?" he asked with a grin. "Speech is a burden for us: thoughts flash as entities between us, whole concepts transfer from one to another in an instant! We don't leave you out on purpose. It's just that... well, why walk on your hands when you can use your feet?"

"I know what you're trying to say, Dennel, but it doesn't keep me from feeling left out. Back at the keep I could at least go and find somebody to talk to. But here... here I'm the only one who was born without the Talent."

"But the Talent came out in you in a different way! You're a Finder!"

"I can *find* possessors of the Talent, sure! But I can't communicate with them. I'm cut off!"

"But your ability to find makes you the most valuable member of the tribe; through you we can find potential members to add to our ranks!"

"That still doesn't keep me from feeling like a cripple," she replied sulkily.

In the silence that followed, the tery had time to ponder what he had just heard. He now understood why these humans were fleeing Kitru. They, like the teries, were products of the Great Sickness of long ago and were thus on Mekk's extermination list. His mother had mentioned them once; they were called *psi-people*. That explained the eerie silence of the camp: they spoke with their minds!

"How's the tery?" Dennel asked and Adriel brightened. "Coming along, poor thing. He heals fast."

"Well, at least he's not a talker and not too ugly." He laughed. "Looks like a cross between a big baboon and some wiry breed of bear!"

The tery disliked Dennel's tone but had to agree with the comparison. He was about the height of a man when he walked upright although he much preferred to go on all fours. His hands were large, twice the size of a man's, and he was covered from head to toe with coarse black fur.

"Some teries can be taught to speak, you know. I saw one with a traveling musical troupe that came through the keep a few years ago; that was before Mekk declared them—*and* us—'unholy.'"

"Really? Do you think I could teach this one to talk?"

Dennel shook his head. "I doubt it. First of all, you've got to start them young if you're going to have any success. And secondly, you have to be lucky and get one who can be taught. The degree of intelligence varies greatly from one to another. "

"Oh," she said with obvious disappointment. "I thought I might have someone to talk to."

"They can't *think*, Adriel. All they can do is mimic sounds. And I'm not so sure you'd want a talker around. It's quite chilling to hear an animal speak to you. Some of them are so good you'd actually think they had a mind."

"I guess it would be a little frightening at that," Adriel admitted.

The tery could have destroyed Dennel's misinformed theories in an instant for he was a 'talker' and had no doubts about his ability to think. But he kept to himself. If these humans found the thought of a talking tery repugnant, how would they feel if they knew that this animal was listening in on their conversation and understanding every word?

By the way," Adriel asked, "just what does the word 'tery' mean?"

Dennel shrugged. "I haven't the faintest idea. As far as I know they've always been called teries. The name probably originated during the Great Sickness."

Dennel excused himself and walked toward the front of the train and the tery scrutinized the psi folk around him. He began to understand Adriel's predicament. Glances would pass between individuals, someone would smile, another would laugh, but speech was used only on the pack animals to keep them moving. Adriel was a very lonely girl.

The train halted at dusk and the tery was finally freed from the drag and allowed to take a few painful steps. Adriel had done an excellent job of cleaning and binding his wounds; his animal vitality would take care of the rest.

She appeared carrying two bowls. "Hungry?" she asked with a smile.

He had been given some milk during the day and tonight some raw meat was added to his diet. As the tery ate, Adriel examined his bandages and murmured soothingly.

"Looks like you're coming along fine. You'll be back to your old self in no time." She sobered suddenly. "Then I suppose you'll take off into the bush again. You don't have to go, you know. We'll treat you well here, really we will."

Silently, the tery considered this.

Later, well fed and freshly bandaged, the tery loped beside Adriel toward the central fire where her father and a few others sat in silence. The bearded man smiled as she knelt beside him. The tery remained in the background, watching, listening.

"We were just discussing our future," her father told her, "and it looks as if we'll be spending years in these forests." He glanced sharply at Dennel whose face flickered on the far side of the flames. "Haven't I asked you to use your tongue when my daughter is present? If not out of kindness then at least out of courtesy!"

Grudgingly, Dennel spoke. "But you haven't given my ideas due consideration, Komak. We could make ourselves very useful to Kitru—and to Mekk himself. Think of the intelligence network we could form for him! Why, he'd know what was going on in every one of his provinces!"

"You're dreaming," Komak said. "Practicality can't touch Mekk nowadays. He's become a religious fanatic and the priests have poisoned his mind against anything that does not bear True Shape - and that seems to include our minds. No, Mekk is unreachable. And Kitru... Kitru fears Mekk and dares not disobey him."

"But we could be useful!" Dennel persisted.

"You mean 'used,' don't you?"

"No—"

"A man is only what he proves himself to be," Komak interrupted. "Right now we're fleeing for our lives but your alternative strikes me as worse. Should we prove ourselves to be slaves? Tools of a tyrant? I think not, even if he permitted us to live that long. We can only run for now, but the Leader promised that someday we'd return—and on our own terms!"

"Where is the Leader?" Adriel asked. "I thought he was supposed to join us."

"He was. I don't know what happened to him. It's very possible that he met with the very fate he warned us against. If we only knew who he was we could find out if anything has happened to him."

"I'm suspicious of this so-called 'Leader,'" Dennel said. "Where did he get all his advance information and why wouldn't he reveal his identity?"

Komak shrugged. "We know that his information was correct for soon after we fled, those who were publicly known to possess the Talent were declared outlaws. We escaped just in time."

Dennel snorted. "True, but how did he manage to find those who were *not* known to have the Talent? Adriel is the only Finder in the province. I fear a trap, Komak."

"Well, if there's to be a trap, the Leader will have caught himself—because he contacted each and every one of us via the Talent. So he's on Mekk's extermination list along with the rest of us."

On that note of finality Adriel retired to her hut and oral conversation ceased. The tery dozed off.

He was well enough to travel the next day and left the train of the psi-folk as it moved deeper into the forest. He was not deserting his rescuers; he intended to stay with them for he had nowhere else to go and they seemed well organized. The raw meat and milk of the night before had restored his strength and he made his way quickly through the lush foliage. He knew where he was going and knew what he would find.

The hunting had been particularly good two days before.

The tery hunted with a club and a club was all he needed. He was early in returning to the clearing around the cave that served as a home for him and his parents and intended to surprise his parents with the two large rabbits he had bagged. But it was he, however, who was destined to be surprised: steel-capped, leather-jerkined strangers had invaded the clearing.

Keeping low, he crept through the small plot where they tried to grow a few edibles. The tery noticed something huddled among the corn stalks to his left and crawled over to investigate. His father lay there. A big, coarse brute who was happiest when he could sit in the sun and watch with eternal wonder the growth of the things his mate had taught him to plant, he had been pierced by a dozen feathered shafts and the red of his life was pooled on the ground beside him. Rage and fear fought for dominance but the tery held himself to the ground and continued toward the cave, hoping...

His mother, her head nearly severed from her body, lay in the mouth of the cave. All control shattered then and, screaming hoarsely and swinging his club before him, the tery charged.

The utter ferocity of his attack astonished him and certainly did the same for the soldiers. The archers were caught off guard but the troopers' swords were already bared. The first of the group lifted his blade as the tery closed but the creature batted it aside and swung his club for the trooper's head. The man ducked but not quickly enough and the tery had one less opponent facing him. His club swung again and connected with the shoulder of another who went down screaming. There were too many of them, however, and all were seasoned warriors. Before he could inflict any more real damage, the club was sliced from his hands and a sword point bared three of his ribs.

The tery ran. And he would have escaped easily had not the captain thought to order his men to horse.

"Don't run him through!" he heard the captain yell. "Just keep slicing at him!"

It was great sport. The troopers were excellent horsemen and cut the tery off, then surrounded him and sliced away, then let him escape and run a short distance only to cut him off again. He was an exhausted, bloody ruin by the time he finally collapsed in a field of tall grass.

"If he's not dead now," the captain panted as he stared down at the tery from atop his mount, "he soon will be. Let the jackals finish him!"

And so they left him to the scavengers. Luckily, the psi-folk found him first.

The tery remembered that captain's face.

———————

The clearing was much as he had left it—except for the vultures. He chased them away and, at the risk of reopening some of his deeper wounds, went about the grisly task of placing the bodies of his parents inside the cave.

His father had been a wild, bearish creature, born of equally wild parents and raised in the forests. His mother was different—no two teries are alike unless genetically related. Graceful in a simian way, she had been captured as an infant and brought up in the keep when Kitru's father was lord there. That was in the time before Mekk issued his proclamation calling for the extermination of everything that did not bear True Shape and it was considered fashionable then to have a tery or two around the court who could speak and converse on educated subjects. His mother was such; she would delight visitors with her singing, her recounting of history and the many poems she had memorized. But she escaped to the forests long ago.

There she met her mate who could speak not at all and could not learn to speak; for although he had the intelligence, he had gone too long without ever speaking. He did manage to communicate in other ways, however, and soon a tery child was born to them.

The little tery's mother taught him to speak and taught him of his origin—how the Great Sickness caused changes in many of the world's living things and that his ability to think was one of those changes. These were things she had learned during her stay at the keep. The cub was bright, curious and eager and readily learned to speak, though his voice had a gruff, discordant sound.

He said nothing, however, as he climbed the hillside above the cave and pried loose stone after stone until a minor land- slide covered the mouth of his former home. He had cut all ties with the past now. He was a fugitive tery and would stay with the fugitive humans he had met.

And he remembered that captain's face.

Around midday the tery started back. The psi-folk would have been on
the move all day so he traveled on an angle to his earlier path in order
to intercept them. Entering a grassy copse, he heard voices ahead and
carefully went to investigate.

Six troopers, obviously a scouting party, were resting in the shade
as their horses grazed nearby. The tery felt a blinding rush of hatred
but caution prevailed and he remained in cover. He was still somewhat
weak from his wounds and the

long journey had tired him. And even under optimum conditions,
a headlong rush would have been suicidal. The tery circled them and
continued on his way. His hour would come, he knew. He had only to
wait.

He came upon the psi-folk shortly thereafter. They too had stopped
to rest and eat. Adriel, overjoyed at the sight of the tery, jumped up
from her midday meal and ran toward him.

"It's the tery!" she cried. "He's come back!" She fell to her knees
beside him and threw her arms around his neck. "You came back!" she
whispered as she hugged him. "They said you were gone for good but
I knew you'd come back!"

Pleasant as it was, the tery had no time for such a welcome. He had
just realized that the scouting party's line of march would lead it close
to this site, so close that discovery would be unavoidable. The party
numbered only six so there was no danger of attack, but should they
be allowed to return to the keep with even a general knowledge of the
whereabouts of the folk, extermination would soon follow.

He had to warn them.

But how? He dared not speak for fear of letting them know he was
a talker... *and* a thinker; for a warning would indicate reasoning ability. The tery could not be sure that their sympathy for his loneness in
the vast forests would overcome their repugnance at having a talking,
thinking, *comprehending* animal in their midst. He had to find another
way.

He broke from Adriel and ran to her father. Wrapping long fingers
about the leader's arm, he tried to pull him away from the fire.

"Adriel!" Komak shouted, angered at being disturbed. "Get your
pet away from me and let me eat in peace!"

"I'll bet he's hungry," she said and went to get some meat.

This obviously wasn't working. Only one recourse remained.

Bolting for the forest, he ignored Adriel's pleading calls and disappeared into the brush. It didn't take him long to find the scouts; they were dangerously close and headed on a collision course. Picking up a large stone, he climbed out on a limb that overhung their path and waited.

They were walking their mounts single file through the dense undergrowth and grumbling about the heat and difficult traveling. As the last man passed below, the tery hurled the rock at his head and leaped from the tree. The stone drove the trooper's steel cap into his skull with a dull clank and his horse reared as the tery had grabbed the bloodied helmet and disappeared.

Hopefully, the loss of a man—whether temporarily or permanently the tery couldn't be sure—would throw the scouts into enough confusion to allow the psi-folk time enough to prepare a move against them.

Carrying the helmet in his teeth and running as fast as his four limbs would carry him, the tery burst upon the campsite and went directly to Komak. The sight of a steel cap with fresh *blood* around the rim was all the bearded man needed to set him into action. He shot to his feet and glanced around. In an instant the camp was thrown into frenzied activity.

"What is it, father?" Adriel asked, aware that an order had been given.

"Troopers! Your pet has brought us a warning. I never expected them to come this far into the forest but the tery was gone only a few minutes. They must be nearly upon us!"

She blanched. "What'll we do?"

"There's only one thing we *can* do," he replied with a shrug. "We haven't got time to run—although Dennel seems to think that would be the best course." He glared across the clearing at the youth who stood uncertainly amid the fluster. "But finding a recently abandoned campsite is the next best thing to finding the group itself. It wouldn't be long before they tracked us down. All we can do is set a trap and hope there aren't too many of them."

Komak's plan turned out to be fiendishly simple. The fires were quickly doused and the women and children, along with everything in the camp, were sent on their way from the clearing. Twenty men with strung bows concealed themselves in the surrounding bushes. The tery went along with Adriel for a time, then doubled back to the campsite.

As he watched from a nearby tree, the scouting party - one member with a bare and bloodied head—cautiously entered the clearing. One by one they inspected the fire sites for warmth and conversed in low tones. Komak watched until he was certain the entire party had revealed itself. And when he had used the Talent to make sure that each invader would receive his share of the arrows about to be loosed, his mental command caused twenty bows to *thrum* simultaneously.

It dawned on the tery then that with greater numbers and a greater desire to fight, the psi-folk could rule the forests completely.

A hero of sorts, the tery had earned his place in the tribe and found himself fondly regarded by most of its members, especially Adriel. The girl was convinced that she could teach her new pet to speak and began giving him lessons at meal time. She would hold up a piece of meat and say, "Food ... food." At first the tery would ignore the promptings but soon came to realize how desperately she wanted him to speak. And so, three days after the skirmish—after the bodies had been carefully buried in the brush and the troopers' horses added to their own—the tribe made another camp and the tery pleased his mistress by following her persistent example.

Pretending great effort, he rasped, "Food."

Adriel stared in wide-eyed wonder.

"Food," he repeated.

Komak was sitting nearby and turned his head at the unfamiliar voice. "Was that...?"

"Yes!" Adriel said breathlessly. "It was him! He spoke! Did you hear him? He spoke!" She quickly gave the tery the piece of meat she had been holding and held up another, but further demonstration of his new found ability was halted by the arrival of one of the point men Komak had sent out.

After a few minutes of telepathic conversation, Komak turned to his daughter. "Looks like we'll be needing you. Adriel."

She shot him a questioning glance. "Why?"

"Seems there's an isolated village about a mile to the east. There are about forty inhabitants and one or two may have the Talent. It's up to you to find them."

Adriel and her father returned three hours later. With them were a youth and a middle-aged man and woman. As they gathered around the fire the woman spoke.

"Now tell us what this is all about," she said. Her features were sharp and her jet hair was drawn back severely. "And use your tongues so my husband will understand."

"Well," Komak began slowly, "a few months ago a man who called himself 'the Leader' contacted us one by one—using the Talent—and told us to flee to the forests. He said that there was to be an addition to Mekk's decree against the teries: all those who possessed the Talent were to be considered sacrilegious and exterminated just as if they were teries. All those publicly known to be psi-folk were to be executed immediately. As for the more discreet possessors of the Talent, Mekk would arrive in time with a Finder and weed them out."

The woman smirked. "Ridiculous!"

"That thought occurred to us, too, but most of those who were publicly known decided to take no chances and fled. Sure enough, the new decree arrived and the ones who remained behind were slaughtered."

This statement seemed to have the desired impact for the three newcomers glanced at each other fearfully.

Komak continued. "The Leader contacted all the unknown psis then and told everyone to gather at a certain spot in the forest. He would join us later." Komak spread his hands. "He never showed up, however. It's very possible that Mekk arrived with the Finder ahead of schedule and caught the Leader in the keep. Whoever he was, we owe him our lives."

After a pause, the man said, "What do you want with us?"

"Nothing," Komak replied. "We're only offering you the chance to join us."

The man shook his head. "We're pretty isolated out here. I used to travel to the keep once in a while and no one seemed to know that our village existed. And no one in the village knows that my wife and son possess the Talent except me. I think we can risk staying where we are."

"But don't forget that Mekk himself will be in the province—soon if not already—and Kitru will spare no effort to impress the Overlord."

"I still think we'd rather stay where we are than become forest nomads," the man replied. "But we thank you for warning us." He put one arm around his wife and the other around his son and the trio walked slowly back to their village. .

"Isn't it rare for a psi to marry a non-psi?" Adriel asked after they were gone.

Komak nodded. "Very. The rapport between two psis is far and away more intimate that anything a non-psi can experience. But the woman and her son were the only psis we found so it might be that she never even knew she had the Talent until her son was born."

"I wish them well," Adriel said. "It must take a lot of backbone to risk extermination as they are doing."

"Speaking of backbone," her father remarked, "have you noticed that Dennel has been gone for the last few days?"

She nodded. "I was going to ask you about that. Did you send him off for something?"

"Hardly. He's scared to death. Back at the old clearing when we laid that ambush for the scouting party, it was all I could do to keep him from throwing down his bow and bolting. He claims we'd be better off if we split up into smaller groups. That way, in the event of an all-out attempt to do away with us, we could be fairly sure that some would survive to carry on the Talent."

"That sounds reasonable."

"On the surface, it does. But I really don't think Dennel is all that interested in preserving the Talent; preserving Dennel is his main concern." Komak paused, then grinned pointedly. "Besides, there are definite advantages to moving with a large group of individuals who can communicate silently and instantaneously. I think the lad just wants to run and I wouldn't worry too much about him. He'll be back.

Komak was right. Dennel returned after a few days but kept to himself, no doubt ashamed of his behavior. And Adriel and the tery got to know each other, so to speak. She taught him more words and devoted most of her day to him. She would rest her hand on his back and talk to him as they wandered the leafy glades near the camp. She hadn't the slightest suspicion that he could understand her but that his ears were for her alone, that he was not secretly carrying on a mental conversation with someone else at the same time—something which, the tery gathered, had happened more than once in the past.

"You're lucky, you know," she told him as they sat on a grassy knoll and watched the brightly colored tree-things go about their daily routines. "Nothing holds you down. You can come and go as you please and you're at home with us or away from us. But me... I'm stuck here with a bunch of people who feel insulted if they have to use their tongues!"

She laughed. "I thought I was going to be a lady once—can you believe that? A nobleman's son took a fancy to me and I thought I'd someday be living in the upper quarters of the keep. Then Mekk went and issued his decree and I've

spent the past few months living like a savage."

The tery came to think of Adriel as a wonderful creature—fresh, young, ready to burst into womanhood at any moment and only a fanged, barrel-chested beast at her side to share the experience. She wanted to love and be loved, to stop running; she longed for the stability she would have had had she not been born a Finder.

And the tery became a substitute for everything she desired. A thousand tiny kindnesses were showered upon him. She would put much time and effort into preparing the meat for his dinner and carved and painted a bowl from which to eat it. She learned the use of the loom so that he wouldn't have to sleep on the bare ground.

The two were driven closer and closer together by the void of silence which separated them from the others. They became inseparable... almost. For now and again the tery would make a solo journey to the rock choked mouth of a certain cave.

On one such occasion he returned at dusk from a day- long journey to find the camp in silent chaos. The women were gathering up their utensils and the men were arming themselves. Adriel was nowhere to be seen. The tery loped into her hut and found it empty. Her father was waiting for him when he emerged.

"Looking for your mistress?" he asked grimly and laid a gentle hand on the creature's head.

The tery immediately sensed that something was wrong for Komak rarely paid any attention to him and never spoke to him at all.

"Well, she walked off with Dennel and horse tracks in the area indicate that they were both grabbed by Kitru's men. We're going after them now and you might as well come along."

The tery waited to hear no more. He knew the location of the keep and plowed a direct course for it. He had to reach it before the psi-folk. The odds were against them there in both numbers and position. They might excel as guerrillas, but in an attack on an armed fortress manned by seasoned troops they would be cut down like rabble.

He felt he could accomplish more alone. He had been raised in the forest with a club as his only weapon—he either learned stealth or he went hungry. He seldom went hungry.

And Adriel! A Finder would be valuable to Kitru but the tery knew the girl would never cooperate against her father—not until they had broken her. He banished visions of Adriel being tortured. He had to remain calm if he was going to help her at all. But if they had harmed her... if they had harmed her...

The keep was a darker blot against a darkened sky when the tery reached it. The high outer wall was crudely made of rough stone and his long fingers found easy holds as he scuttled his way upward. He reached the top and hung just below it until the sentry had passed, then scuttled over behind him. With neither arms nor clothing nor accouterments, he was a shadow on the battlements and made his way toward the main tower unseen. He had no idea of where to find Adriel but reasoned that the lord of the keep would pick the most imposing structure for his quarters. And Kitru would know the whereabouts of Adriel.

The tery scuttled across the short space between the outer wall and the main tower and stood at the massive base of the structure, pondering his next move. The wall of the tower was pierced here and there by narrow windows which the tery judged wide enough to allow him entrance, so he began to climb. He had traveled only three man-heights when a shout from below caused him to freeze and hug the wall.

"Ho! You there on the tower wall! What are you doing?"

The doors to the trooper barracks flew open and there was the sound of running feet in the darkness below.

The same voice spoke again. "Alright, you! I've got a crossbow now... start coming down. No tricks or I'll spit you with a bolt!"

The tery saw the lowest window not far above him and made a sudden frantic effort to reach it. True to his word, the trooper below loosed a bolt. The missile grazed his ear and smashed against the stone in front of his face. Fragments of the wall peppered his eyes and the tery lost his precarious grip as he recoiled. He landed below with a *thud* and found himself surrounded by a squad of menacing figures.

"Someone get a torch and let's see who we've got here."

The torch was quickly brought and the troopers recoiled in surprise of their captive.

"It's one of those damn beasts!" exclaimed a trooper with a pike. He drew back the weapon as the tery made ready to lunge to the side. "This'll finish..."

"Stop!" cried a voice and the troopers turned to see who had dared to tell them not to kill a tery.

A young man stepped forward into their midst: Dennel.

"Just who are you to be giving orders around here?" the man with the pike asked belligerently.

"Never mind that," Dennel said. "Just let me tell you that if that tery is killed, Kitru will have your head. This particular beast could be very valuable to him."

The trooper paused, uncertain. He resented being told what to do by some civilian upstart but, if the man was telling the truth, he had no desire to be on the receiving end of Kitru's wrath.

He turned to the man beside him. "Get the captain."

There followed a short period of tense waiting in which the tery put aside his surprise at finding Dennel free within the keep and tried to find an avenue of escape. There was none. His back was to the tower and fully a dozen armed troopers formed a tight semi-circle around him.

Half dressed, his eyes puffy from sleep, the captain arrived and the tery felt an involuntary growl escape his throat. This was the officer who had ordered the slaughter of his parents.

"What's going on here?" the captain demanded angrily.

"This man says Kitru will have my head if this tery is slain," said the trooper with the pike.

The captain turned to Dennel. "Oh, so it's you. How do you happen to come to speak for Kitru?"

"Because I know this beast," Dennel replied. "It's the girl's pet and she's very attached to it."

"What do I care about the Finder's pet?" the captain asked.

"A lot. Because the Finder is very important to Kitru. Mekk arrives in a few days and it will be quite a feather in Kitru's cap if he can present the Overlord with a Finder... even more so if he can also present him with a lever with which to make the girl cooperate. This beast might just be that lever."

The captain pondered this. Knowing Dennel for a coward and a traitor to his kind, he despised the young man. Yet he was right about the Finder's value. Kitru had promised Dennel amnesty in return for delivery of the Finder and had held off the launching of a full scale attack against the psi-folk for fear of injuring the girl. But now that the girl was safe in the keep, the psi-folk would soon be wiped out. The captain smiled inwardly... Kitru had told him Dennel would be the first to go when Mekk arrived.

"I think you have a point," the captain told Dennel, then turned to the troopers. "Take this creature below and throw him in with crazy Rab—they'll make good company for each other."

This brought a laugh from all the men and broke the tension.

As the tery was being taken toward a sunken stairway, he heard Dennel speaking to the captain.

"I think we ought to present Kitru with this news immediately. He'll be most pleased..."

"Below" consisted of a small underground chamber broken up into three small cells. There appeared little need for incarceration facilities at the keep. Executions were no doubt much cheaper. Sharp pike tips prodded the tery into a dark cell and the lone guard locked the door behind him.

Amid harsh barks of laughter someone yelled, "Company for you, Rab!"

The laughter faded as the tery watched the troopers file out. The guard reseated himself by the entrance and, in the wan torchlight that filtered through the grate in his cell door, the tery tried to figure the workings of the lock, something he had never seen before.

"You're a man, aren't you?" came a gentle voice from behind him. "I can tell by the way you look at that lock."

The tery turned to see a filthy, bearded, bedraggled man who looked old at first, but on closer inspection, proved to be somewhere between youth and middle age.

"Can you speak?" he asked.

"I can speak," the tery grated, "but I'm not a man."

It felt strange, speaking, He had never really spoken to anyone but his mother in his entire life. He had repeated words and sentences to make Adriel happy, but that really wasn't speech.

"Oh, you're a man alright, it's just that nobody ever told you so."

"They call you *crazy* Rab," the tery said pointedly.

"And I must look the part!" Rab laughed. "But anyone who's been locked up in a hole for months without a bath, clean clothes or good food will start to look a little crazy! But I assure you I'm not! And I assure you that you're quite as human as I am."

The tery snorted. "Don't play with me! I may not be human but neither am I a foo!!"

"But you *are* human!"

"I know what I am! I'm a tery, a product of the Great Sickness."

"And I'm a heretic for knowing that you're not!" Rab shouted, then eased his voice. "Sit down and let me tell you what I've learned. You'll find it hard to believe but I can prove it all."

Reluctantly, the tery complied. He felt instinctively that there was no escape from the cell and the conversation he had overheard between Dennel and the captain had eased his fears about Adriel being in any immediate danger. And maybe this mad human would help him if humored.

"First off," Rab began, "I've suspected since my youth that the tery was not the mutated beast everyone suspects him to be. In fact, I more than suspect it, I knew it."

"How did you 'know' it?" the tery asked.

"Never mind *how*, let it suffice for the moment that I did. I began to search out old manuscripts from as far back as the time of the Great Sickness. Our language has changed much since then but I did manage to decipher them and found many obtuse references to a group of people called 'The Shapers.' Just who they were and what they did was never explained. It seemed to be taken for granted. All this whetted my appetite for more so I searched deep into some

of the old ruins that dot the forest here and there and came upon some old, very old volumes. They were in perfect condition, printed on incredibly thin sheets of metal. I finished deciphering them a few months ago and brought them to

Kitru."

He paused and smiled grimly. "That was a stupid thing to do. I deserve to be called 'Crazy Rab' for that one act alone! You see, I had learned some incredible things in those volumes. I learned that our would is just a colony of a larger race, that our ancestors came here from the sky—it's crazy, I know, but those volumes are real and obviously not a product of our culture!

"It seems that our ancestors were banned from the mother world and settled here to build their own culture. They were known as 'teratologists' and toyed with the stuff which gives a thing its shape, which makes a child resemble its parents. They believed in making each being perfect but somehow a perverted element came to power and shape became a plaything for the rulers. They created monstrous plants and made beasts look like men and men look like beasts. That's why you're called a 'tery'—you're a product of the teratologists."

The tery was frankly skeptical. "Where are these Shapers now?"

"They died in the Great Sickness," Rab replied. "The final volume I discovered says that the Shapers caused a change in something called a 'virus' and the Great Sickness swept through the world, reducing our ancestors' civilization to rubble. We are the survivors."

The tery regarded his fellow captive thoughtfully. The man seemed quite sane and spoke with utter conviction. And if those metallic volumes actually existed...

"Where are the volumes now?" the tery asked.

"Kitru has them. When I went to him with my information and told him that he must stop killing the teries because they were human, he laughed aloud. He said that it made no difference whether they were human or not because a new decree was coming from Mekk calling for the extermination of the psi-folk. He threw me out with my books. When I went back again the following week, he confiscated my books and imprisoned me as a heretic. My fate is to be decided when Mekk arrives."

"What of these psi-folk?" the tery asked. "Are they—?"

Rab nodded. "They're teries, too... the highpoint of the Shapers' talents. They had hoped to start a race of mental communicators but there are few of us left and our numbers dwindle daily."

"'Us?'" the tery asked.

"You might as well know," Rab said with a shrug. "Everyone will know when Mekk arrives with his Finder. Yes, I have the Talent. I'm also a Finder. When Kitru mentioned the new decree on its say from Mekk, I warned every psi I could find. Luckily most of them believed me and fled. I should have followed my own advice."

"Then you're the Leader!"

Rab glanced sharply at the tery. "How did you know I used that title?"

The tery quickly explained how he had spent the past few weeks and the circumstances which had brought him to the keep.

Rab jumped to his feet and began pacing the cell. "Komak is doing exactly what Kitru wants him to do. They'll be slaughtered! We've got to stop them!"

"The only way to do that is to return Adriel," the tery said. "But we've got to get out of here first."

"Right! And here's how we'll do it..."

The dozing guard was startled to wakefulness by shrill cries of fear and pain from the cell where Rab and the tery were confined. Grabbing a torch from its wall-brace, he rushed to the cell and peered through the grate. The flickering light showed the tery in ferocious assault upon the screaming Rab. The guard hesitated a moment, then decided that it would be best for him to intervene. Kitru only imprisoned those whom he wanted kept alive for a while; if one of the prisoners was killed, the guard knew it would be on his head.

Unlocking the cell door, he entered with the torch held before him. His plan was to back the tery away from Rab and then drag the man out and put him in a separate cell. As he neared the struggling pair, the tery looked up and shrank away from the flames...

As he expected, the beast was afraid of fire. What he hadn't expected, however, was an attack from Rab who leaped from the floor and grabbed his sword arm. The guard went to strike him with the torch but felt it wrenched from his grasp by the tery who had suddenly lost his fear of fire. In one motion the tery lifted him from the floor and hurled him against the stone wall. The guard rolled to the floor and lay still.

Rab regarded the tery with new respect. "You're quite as powerful as you look, my friend. But now to the tower. As one of the court scholars I had the run of the keep and I believe I know how we can gain the stairs of the main tower without being seen. After that we'll have to depend on luck."

Cautiously, they emerged into the courtyard and noted the positions of the sentries. Rab darted along a deeply shadowed wall with the tery close behind; he paused at a flimsy wooden door, peered within and found it dark and empty.

"This is the kitchen," he whispered, once inside. "They prepare the food for the keep's higher-ups." He pointed to a narrow door off to the left. "That leads to a passage which opens directly onto the stairs of the main tower. The scullions use it to deliver food at mealtime. I doubt very much if anyone will be watching it now."

They opened the door and felt their way along the inky passage. Torchlight filtered through cracks in another door far ahead and they soon found themselves on the massive circular stairway of the main tower.

Rab glanced around and sighed with relief. "No guards. No one's looking for danger from the inside. Come. We've got to get to the top if we're to find Kitru."

Wordlessly, the tery assumed the lead. Adriel was near now, he could feel it as he glided up the stairs. Suddenly he caught the sound of descending footsteps and voices in low conversation. He recognized Dennel's tones. Whirling, he motioned to Rab to stay where he was and went ahead alone. As he voices grew nearer, he recognized one other: the captain.

A window opening broke the wall above him. The tery reached it with a powerful leap and concealed himself within its shadow.

"...so you must agree that it was a good thing I happened along when I did," Dennel was saying.

"Yes," the captain said, nodding as they came into view. The two of them were alone. "Kitru was very pleased. He'll be even more pleased if we can take her father alive when the psi-folk attack the keep."

As they passed his window, the tery leaped and landed behind them with but a whisper of sound. The pair spun in surprise but Dennel put a hand on the captain's arm as the latter bared his sword.

"It's the girl's tery!" Dennel said.

"So I see. But he's supposed to be locked up below." The captain growled. "Someone will get the lash for this!"

"Put your sword away and I'll see if I can coax him over here. He knows me but he's not so sure of you... and he's of no use to anyone dead."

Hesitantly, the captain complied and Dennel, speaking in a soothing, gentle voice, edged closer to the tery. "Don't worry, boy. We're not going to hurt you. We'll take you to your mistress. She's right up those stairs. That's who you're looking for, aren't you? I'm sure she'll be glad to see you."

When he was close enough, Dennel put out his hand and began to stroke the fur on the back of the tery's neck. He glanced at the captain with a smile. "See, he's quite docile."

"Let's hope so," the captain replied as he moved closer. "Look at the size of those arms... and those hands!"

Those were the captain's last words. The tery's right hand shot out and went around his throat as he rose on his hind legs and lifted the officer clear of the steps.

"Parent slayer!" he rumbled with his grating voice.

The tery held him there and watched the terror in the captain's eyes as he fumbled for his sword. Then, with one quick, powerful movement, he smashed the man's head against the rough stone of the wall and cracked it like an egg. A grisly stain remained on the stones as he loosed his grip and let him drop.

Dennel shrank against the wall as the tery turned on him.

The captain had been armed so the tery had struck him first. Now he could concentrate fully on Dennel. The sound of speech from the lips of a stupid beast had shaken Dennel, the idea that such a creature could entertain ideas of vengeance horrified him.

The tery took him by the throat and shook him like a limp doll. "Traitor!" he hissed. "To save yourself you betrayed all of your kind!"

The tery left him on the stairs next to the captain and a second wet, red stain marred the stone wall.

"I'd know you were human now even if I hadn't found those ancient volumes," Rab whispered from the shadows. He had watched the entire scene in silence. "In the past few moments you've displayed craft, deceit, revenge and outrage at betrayal. For better or for worse, my friend, you're as human as I am... or as they were."

As the tery pondered this in silence, Rab moved past him and continued the ascent. Following almost absently, the tery's mind whirled in confusion. Was he truly human after all? The thought had never even occurred to him in the past

but as he began to look back on his life with the psi-folk, he was struck by the ease with which he had accepted them, having never been close to humans before. Not only had he accepted them, he had been drawn back to them after initial contact.

Further speculation was terminated by Rab's hand on his shoulder. They had reached the top of the stairway and a great oaken door barred their way. Hearing a voice within, Rab gently pushed it open.

A lean, greying man stood in the center of the room and the tery heard Rab mutter, "Kitru!"

The lord of the keep swayed as he poured red liquid from a silver flagon. On the floor beside him, bound and battered, lay Adriel, either asleep or unconscious.

"I know how to handle you now, stubborn little wench!" he said with a thick voice. "The howls of your beloved pet should make you more compliant."

The tery dropped all caution at the sight of Adriel and burst into the room. Kitru was obviously surprised by the intrusion but reacted instinctively and the tery found himself at the end of a sharpened length of gleaming steel. Rab entered then.

"So you've escaped, I see," Kitru said, showing not the slightest sign of fear. He knew he was a good swordsman and all that threatened him here were an unarmed scholar and an animal. The wine he had consumed merely bolstered his confidence. "You were a fool to come here, Rab."

"We came for the girl," Rab stated coolly.

"'We?'"

"Yes. This tery is a friend of the girl's. He's going to take her back to her people."

Kitru laughed aloud. *"Friend?* Oh, I'm afraid you really are crazy, Rab! This is her pet."

"I am a man," the tery said and Kitru took an, involuntary step backward.

The tery was not quite sure why he had said it—he could not quite believe it as yet. The declaration had escaped him involuntarily.

"You're not a man! Kitru sneered. "You're a filthy animal who can mimic a few words!"

"How strange," Rab goaded. "I was just thinking the same thing about you."

Enraged, Kitru roared and aimed a cut at the tery's throat, figuring to catch the beast off guard and then dispose of Rab at his leisure. He lunged wildly, however, and the tery leaped aside and aimed a balled fist at the back of the keep lord's neck. Kitru went down without a cry and lay still, his head at an unnatural angle.

Rab inspected the body. "You've had quite a night. First you kill one of Kitru's officers, then a traitor, then Kitru him- self. And all quite efficiently."

But the tery had already forgotten Kitru and was kneeling beside Adriel. The girl's face was bruised and swollen but she did not appear to be seriously hurt. As he lifted her in his arms, he heard an exclamation from Rab.

"The books! They're here!"

He rushed over to a stack of three metallic volumes in a far corner of the room. Reaching over to Kitru's great bed, he pulled the cover from it and wrapped the books within. Even at a distance, the tery could see that there was something strange, *alien* about those volumes.

"We've lost so much of the old knowledge already," Rab said, slinging the bundle over his shoulder, "I'm going to see to it that we don't lose anymore. And who knows ... someday the larger race of which we are a part may find us again. Until then, the psi-folk will guard the knowledge of our origin."

Escape was less difficult than the tery had expected. Rab found a rope in one of the store rooms at the base of the tower and they made their way unseen to the top of the outer wall.

"The sentry's at the other end," Rab said, securing the rope to a wooden support. "We've got to reach the ground before he gets back here. The only reason we haven't been spotted yet is that all eyes are directed outward. But once we're down, run as you've never run before because they'll surely see us!"

Rab threw the rope over the side and the tery motioned him to go first. With Adriel over his shoulder, the tery waited until Rab was down, then cautiously began his descent, hoping desperately that the rope would hold against the double burden.

As soon as the tery's feet touched the ground, Rab whispered, "Run!" and run they did. Their swiftly moving forms were immediately spotted and a call went out from one of the sentries. But before many arrows could be loosed, they were out of accurate range for even the keep's archers. The trees closed in on them and they were safe. After putting a little more distance between themselves and the keep, Rab called for a halt and dropped his bundle of books to the sward.

He noticed that the tery still held Adriel in his arms. "Why don't you put her down," he panted, "and we'll see if we can bring her around."

"That won't be necessary," the tery said tightly. He had never been so close to Adriel as he had been in the past few minutes. Her warmth, her softness were having an effect on him, awakening a timeless ache deep within.

"What do you mean?" Rab asked.

"We're not going to rejoin the psi-folk," the tery replied with sudden decision. "We'll find a life of our own in the forest and no one will ever hurt her again."

Rab studied his companion. "I don't think that would be wise," he said softly.

"I'm a human, am I not? You said so yourself. And right now I feel very human! She loves me-she's told me so many times."

"She loves you as a beast. But will she love you as a man? The choice must be hers. And if you don't let her make it then you're no better than Kitru or the captain who slew your parents!" Rab's voice softened. "And there are some hard facts you must accept: your offspring will carry your shape—or at least part of it. Your ancestors were deformed at the whim of some diseased mind and this act has been perpetuated for generations. It might be best for you to decide to bring their colossal joke to an end—let it go no further than you."

The tery's voice was thick as he spoke. "I would find that easy to say if the only mark the Shapers had left upon me was the ability to speak with my mind—a gift rather than a curse! It's easy to speak of letting the curse go no further if someone else must make the decision!"

A grim smile played about Rab's mouth. "Why do you think I've spent most of my life looking for a link between teries and humans? I told you I knew there was a link—how do you think I knew?"

"You...?"

Rab nodded. "I was born with a tail, as was my mother and her sister and their mother before them." He barked a harsh laugh. "What amusement my ancestors must have caused some depraved Shaper! Normal in every way except for a tail! Luckily my mother had a sister who could help her and I was no sooner out of the womb than the tail was cut off flush with my body. My father never had the slightest inkling that I was a tery for when the tail is cut off at birth, the scar is virtually invisible. But I've decided that the Shapers have laughed long enough: I shall father no children."

The tery eyed Rab intently. He had known the man for only a short time but had come to trust him. He knew Rab was not lying now. Very gently, he put Adriel down in the grass. She began to stir.

"She must never know, Rab."

Rab shook his head. "She must know sooner or later," he said, glancing at the cloth-wrapped volumes. "But we'll break the news of origins gently to the psi-folk. I'll have them thinking of you as a man before they know that you really are one! And the first step will be to give you a name."

Adriel could not travel quickly so it was not until the next day that they intercepted the psi-folk. The instant that Rab telepathically communicated with the folk, he was recognized as the Leader. Speaking for the benefit of Adriel and the tery, he outlined what had happened.

"So there's not much danger of pursuit at the moment with both Kitru and one of his top officers dead," he concluded. "By the time the keep is reorganized, we'll be so deep into the forest they'll never find us!"

He turned to Komak who stood with his arm around his daughter and beamed with joy and relief. "You really owe Adriel's return to the tery," he told him. "Does he have a name?"

Adriel shook her head. "We never thought to give him one. He's always been just 'the tery.'"

"Well then, I think we should call him *John*."

"But John is a man's name," Komak said.

"He shall be John nonetheless," the leader stated with a glance in the tery's direction.

Adriel is asleep now and it's nearly dawn as the tery lies across the entrance to her tent and watches the sky lighten. They'll all be moving deeper into the forest soon where they'll grow strong and possibly find some more of their kind. Overlord Mekk has no idea that his overthrow is brewing here. They will survive.

And John the tery will remain here with these people and with Adriel. For he is her pet, her companion, her guardian and lover removed. He is with her always. That is all he asks.

On June 18, 2018, the FDA's nationwide ban on trans fats went into effect. New York City, California, and Philadelphia had the dubious honor of leading the way onto that slippery slope, but now the federal government has dictated to all 330 million Americans what they cannot eat. "Nanny state" has become a cliché, but how else can you describe this sort of policy?

Yes, trans fats are bad for you. You should avoid them if you want to keep your heart healthy. I avoid them when I can, but that's my choice. You may have different priorities. I wouldn't think of stopping you from eating all the trans fats you wish (wouldn't stop you from mainlining heroin, either, but that's another issue) because it's your right to mess up your body. After all, you own it.

Or do you?

As we move toward a single-payer national health system, don't be so sure. You will have less and less say about how you wish to treat that body. Watch as the erosion of your already-diminished individual rights accelerates. If the hive is paying for your health care, then the hive is going to demand a say in behaviors that it considers hazardous to your (its) health.

It's only logical.

Lots of behaviors, lots of unhealthy ingestibles and inhalables are going to become illegal or, better yet (for the hive), be taxed to the point where you won't be able to afford them. And we all know what that situation creates: black markets.

It's only logical.

So logical that it inspired a 2009 episode of "American Dad." In "Live and Let Fry," the town has banned trans fats, and Dad goes to bootleggers for "food that tastes good." After it aired, some of my readers wrote asking if I thought my story "Lipidleggin'" had been had ripped off. Maybe yes, maybe no. I'd simply asked the next question 30 years sooner.

Back in the '70s, when a national health care system was a major political topic, I weighed in with a guest editorial in *Analog* magazine ("And now, from the people who brought you Vietnam and Watergate…") and with my fiction.

With tongue planted firmly in cheek, I wrote this cautionary tale about a day when saturated fats would be banned. I saw how it *could* happen, but never for a moment did I believe it *would* happen. Not in a free country like our U.S. of A. But trans fats and 32-ounce soft drinks *have* been banned. What next? Butter?

I tried a first draft of "Lipidleggin'" in the third person but wasn't happy with it. For the hell of it, I switched to first person present tense, a voice I usually dislike. But it worked here. George Scithers made a few well-considered suggestions and bought it for *Asimov's*. It has been reprinted many times since.

David Moore wrote and directed an excellent adaptation that's collected with two other short films on the DVD *Others: The Tales of F. Paul Wilson*.

Connections: Gurney is Repairman Jack's Uncle; he's the ancestor Peter LaNague is trying to trace in Chapter Eight of *An Enemy of the State*. (Rebelliousness can be genetic, I guess.)

Lipidleggin'

Butter.

I can name a man's poison at fifty paces. I take one look at this guy as he walks in and say to myself, "Butter." He steps carefully, like there's something sticky on the soles of his shoes. Maybe there is, but I figure he moves like that because he's on unfamiliar ground. Never seen his face before and I know just about everybody around.

It's early yet. I just opened the store and Gabe's the only other guy on the buying side of the counter, only he ain't buying. He's waiting in the corner by the checkerboard and I'm just about to go join him when the new guy comes in. It's wet out—not raining, really, just wet like it only gets up here near the Water Gap—and he's wearing a slicker. Underneath that he seems to have a stocky build and is average height. He's got no beard and his eyes are blue with a watery look. Could be from anywhere until he takes off the hat and I see his hair. It's dark brown and he's got it cut in one of those soup-bowl styles that're big in the city.

Gabe gives me an annoyed look as I step back behind the counter, but I ignore him. His last name is Varadi—sounds Italian but it's

Hungarian—and he's got plenty of time on his hands. Used to be a Ph.D. in a philosophy department at some university in Upstate New York till they cut the department in half and gave him his walking papers, tenure and all. Now he does part-time labor at one of the mills when they need a little extra help, which ain't near as often as he'd like.

About as poor as you can get, that Gabe. The government giraffes take a big chunk of what little he earns and leave him near nothing to live on. So he goes down to the welfare office where the local giraffes give him food stamps and rent vouchers so he can get by on what the first group of giraffes left him. If you can figure that one out...

Anyway, Gabe's got a lot of time on his hands, like I said, and he hangs out here and plays checkers with me when things are slow. He'd rather play chess, I know, but I can't stand the game. Nothing happens for too long and I get impatient and try to break the game open with some wild gamble. And I always lose. So we play checkers or we don't play.

The new guy puts his hat on the counter and glances around. He looks uneasy. I know what's coming but I'm not going to help him out. There's a little dance we've got to do first.

"I need to buy a few things," he says. His voice has a little tremor in it and close up like this I figure he's in his mid-twenties.

"Well, this is a general store," I reply, getting real busy wiping down the counter, "and we've got all sorts of things. What're you interested in? Antiques? Hardware? Food?"

"I'm not looking for the usual stock." (*The music begins to play*)

I look at him with my best puzzled expression. "Just what is it you're after, friend?"

"Butter and eggs."

"Nothing unusual about that. Got a whole cabinet full of both behind you there." (*We're on our way to the dance floor*)

"I'm not looking for that. I didn't come all the way out here to buy the same shit I can get in the city. I want the real thing."

"You want the real thing, eh?" I say, meeting his eyes square for the first time. "You know damn well real butter and real eggs are illegal. I could go to jail for carrying that kind of stuff." (*We dance*)

Next to taking his money, this is the part I like best about dealing with a new customer. Usually I can dance the two of us around the subject of what he really wants for upwards of twenty or thirty minutes if I've a mind to. But this guy was a lot more direct than most and didn't waste any time getting down to the nitty-gritty. Still, he wasn't going to rob me of a little dance. I've got a dozen years of dealing under my belt and no green kid's gonna rob me of that.

A dozen years... doesn't seem that long. It was back then that the giraffes who were running the National Health Insurance program found out that they were spending way too much money taking care of people with diseases nobody was likely to cure for some time. The stroke and heart patients were the worst. With the presses at the Treasury working overtime and inflation getting wild, it got to the point where they either had to admit they'd made a mistake or do something drastic. Naturally, they got drastic.

The president declared a health emergency and Congress passed something called the National Health Maintenance Act which said that since certain citizens were behaving irresponsibly by abusing their bodies and thereby giving rise to chronic diseases which resulted in consumption of more than their fair share of medical care at public expense, it was resolved that, in the public interest and for the public good, certain commodities would henceforth and hereafter be either prescribed or strictly rationed. Or something like that.

Foods high in cholesterol and saturated fats headed the list. Next came tobacco and any alcoholic beverage over 30 proof.

Ah, the howls that went up from the public. But those were nothing compared to the screams of fear and anguish that arose from the dairy and egg industry which was facing immediate economic ruin. The Washington giraffes stood firm, however—it wasn't an election year—and used phrases like "bite the bullet" and "national interest" and "public good" until we were all ready to barf.

Nothing moved them.

Things quieted down after a while, as they always do. It helped, of course, that somebody in one of the drug companies had been working on an additive to chicken feed that would take just about all the cholesterol out of the yolk. It worked, and the poultry industry was saved.

The new eggs cost more—of course—and the removal of most of the cholesterol from the yolk also removed most of the taste, but at least the egg farmers had something to sell.

Butter was out. Definitely. No compromise. Too much of an "adverse effect on serum lipid levels," whatever that means. You use polyunsaturated margarine or you use nothing. Case closed.

Well, almost closed. Most good citizen-type Americans hunkered down and learned to live with the Lipid Laws, as they came to be known. Why, I bet there's scads of fifteen-year-olds about who've never tasted real butter or a true, cholesterol-packed egg yolk. But we're not all good citizens. Especially me. Far as I'm concerned, there's nothing like two fried eggs—fried in *butter*—over easy, with bacon on the side, to start the day off. Every day. And I wasn't about to give that up.

I was strictly in the antiques trade then, and I knew just about every farmer in Jersey and Eastern Pennsylvania. So I found one who was making butter for himself and had him make a little extra for me. Then I found another who was keeping some hens aside and not giving them any of the special feed and had him hold a few eggs out for me.

One day I had a couple of friends over for breakfast and served them real eggs and toast with real butter. They almost strangled me trying to find out where I got the stuff. That's when I decided to add a sideline to my antique business.

I figured New York City to be the best place to start so I let word get around the antique dealers there that I could supply their customers with more than furniture. The response was wild and soon I was making more money running butter and eggs than I was running Victorian golden oak. I was a lipidlegger.

Didn't last, though. I was informed by two very pushy fellows of Mediterranean stock that if I wanted to do any lipid business in Manhattan, I'd either have to buy all my merchandise from their wholesale concern, or give them a very healthy chunk of my profits.

I decided it would be safer to stick close to home. Less volume, but less risky. I turned my antique shop up here by the Water Gap—that's the part of New Jersey you can get to without driving by all those refineries and reactors—into a general store.

A dozen years now.

"I heard you had the real thing for sale," the guy says.

I shake my head. "Now where would you hear a thing like that?"

"New York."

"New York? The only connection I have with New York is furnishing some antique dealers with a few pieces now and then. How'd you hear about me in New York?"

"Sam Gelbstein."

I nod. Sam's a good customer. Good friend, too. He helped spread the word for me when I was leggin' lipids into the city. "How you know Sam?"

"My uncle furnished most of his house with furniture he bought there."

I still act suspicious—it's part of the dance—but I know if Sam sent him, he's all right. One little thing bothers me, though.

"How come you don't look for your butter and eggs in the city? I hear they're real easy to get there."

"Yeah," he says and twists his mouth. "They're also spoiled now and again and there's no arguing with the types that supply it. No money-back guarantees with those guys."

I see his point. "And you figure this is closer to the source."

He nods.

"One more question," I say. "I don't deal in the stuff, of course"— still dancing—"but I'm curious how a young guy like you got a taste for contraband like eggs and butter."

"Europe," he says. "I went to school in Brussels and it's all still legal over there. Just can't get used to these damned substitutes."

It all fit, so I go into the back and lift up the floor door. I keep a cooler down there and from it pull a dozen eggs and a half-kilo slab of butter. His eyes widen as I put them on the counter in front of him.

"Is this the real thing?" he asks. "No games?"

I pull out an English muffin, split it with my thumbs, and drop the halves into a toaster I keep under the counter. I know that once he tastes this butter I'll have another steady customer. People will eat ersatz eggs and polyunsaturated margarine if they think it's good for them, but they want to know the real thing's available. Take that away from them and suddenly you've got them going to great lengths to get what they used to pass up without a second thought.

"The real thing," I tell him. "There's even a little salt added to the butter for flavor."

"Great!" He smiles, then puts both hands into his pockets and pulls out a gun with his right and a shield with his left. "James Callahan, Public Health Service, Enforcement Division," he says. "You're under arrest, Mr. Gurney."

He's not smiling anymore.

I don't change my expression or say anything. Just stand there and look bored. But inside I feel like someone's wrapped a length of heavy chain around my gut and hooked it up to a high speed winch.

Looking at the gun—a snub-nosed .32—I start to grin.

"What's so funny?" he asks, nervous and I'm not sure why. Maybe it's his first bust.

"A public health guy with a gun!" I'm laughing now. "Don't that seem funny to you?"

His face remains stern. "Not in the least. Now step around the counter. After you're cuffed we're going to take a ride to the Federal Building."

I don't budge. I glance over to the corner and see a deserted checkerboard. Gabe's gone—skittered out as soon as he saw the gun. Mr. Public Health follows my eyes.

"Where's the red-headed guy?"

"Gone for help," I tell him.

He glances quickly over his shoulder out the door, then back at me. "Let's not do anything foolish here. I wasn't crazy enough to come out here alone."

But I can tell by the way his eyes bounce all over the room and by the way he licks his lips that, yes, he was crazy enough to come out here alone.

I don't say anything, so he fills in the empty space. "You've got nothing to worry about, Mr. Gurney," he says. "You'll get off with a first offender's suspended sentence and a short probation."

I don't tell him that's exactly what worries me. I'm waiting for a sound: the click of the toaster as it spits out the English muffin. It comes and I grab the two halves and put them on the counter.

"What are you doing?" he asks, watching me like I'm going to pull a gun on him any minute.

"You gotta taste it," I tell him. "I mean, how're you gonna be sure it ain't oleo unless you taste it?"

"Never mind that." He wiggles the .32 at me. "You're just stalling. Get around here."

But I ignore him. I open a corner of the slab of butter and dig out a hunk with my knife. Then I smear it on one half of the muffin and press the two halves together. All the time I'm talking.

"How come you're out here messin' with me? I'm smalltime. The biggies are in the city."

"Yeah." He nods slowly. He can't believe I'm buttering a muffin while he holds a gun on me. "And they've also bought everyone who's for sale. Can't get a conviction there if you bring in the 'leggers smeared with butter and eggs in their mouths."

"So you pick on me."

He nods again. "Someone who buys from Gelbstein let slip that he used to connect with a guy from out here who used to do lipidlegging into the city. Wasn't hard to track you down." He shrugs, almost apologizing. "I need some arrests to my credit and I have to take 'em where I can find 'em."

I don't reply just yet. At least I know why he came alone: He didn't want anyone a little higher up to steal credit for the bust. And I also know that Sam Gelbstein didn't put the yell on me, which is a relief. But I've got more important concerns at the moment.

I press my palm down on top of the muffin until the melted butter oozes out the sides and onto the counter, then I peel the halves apart and push them toward him.

"Here. Eat."

He looks at the muffin all yellow and drippy, then at me, then back to the muffin. The aroma hangs over the counter in an invisible cloud and I'd be getting hungry myself if I didn't have so much riding on this little move.

I'm not worried about going to jail for this. Never was. I know all about suspended sentences and that. What I am worried about is being marked as a 'legger. Because that means the giraffes will be watching me and snooping into my affairs all the time. I'm not the kind who takes well to being watched. I've devoted a lot of effort to keeping a low profile and living between the lines—"living in the interstices," Gabe calls it. A bust could ruin my whole way of life.

So I've got to be right about this guy's poison.

He can't take his eyes off the muffins. I can tell by the way he stares that he's a good-citizen type whose mother obeyed all the Lipid Laws as soon as they were passed, and who never thought to break them once he became a big boy.

I nudge him. "Go ahead."

He puts the shield on the counter and his left hand reaches out real careful, like he's afraid the muffins will bite him. Finally, he grabs the nearest one, holds it under his nose, sniffs, then takes a bite. A little butter drips from the right corner of his mouth, but it's his eyes I'm watching. They're not seeing me or anything else in the store… they're sixteen years away and he's ten years old again and his mother just fixed him breakfast. His eyes are sort of shiny and wet around the rims as he swallows. Then he shakes himself and looks at me. But he doesn't say a word.

I put the butter and eggs in a bag and push it toward him.

"Here. On the house. Gabe will be back any minute with the troops so if you leave now we can avoid any problems."

He lowers the gun but still hesitates.

"Catch those bad guys in the city," I tell him. "But when you need the real thing for yourself, and you need it fresh, ride out here and I'll see you're taken care of."

He shoves the rest of the muffin half into his mouth and chews furiously as he pockets his shield and gun and slaps his hat back on his head.

"You gotta deal," he says around the mouthful, then lifts the bag with his left hand, grabs the other half muffin with his right, and hurries out into the wet.

I follow him to the door where I see Gabe and a couple of the boys from the mill coming up the road with shotguns cradled in their arms. I wave them off and tell them thanks anyway. Then I watch the guy drive off.

I guess I can't tell a Fed when I see one, but I can name anybody's poison. Anybody's.

I glance down at the pile of newspapers I leave on the outside bench. Around the rock that holds it down I can see where some committee of giraffes has announced that it will recommend the banning of Bugs Bunny cartoons from theaters and the airwaves. The creature, they say, shows a complete disregard for authority and is not fit viewing for children.

Well, I've been expecting that and dubbed up a few minidisks of some of Bugs' finest moments. Don't want the kids around here to grow up without the Wabbit.

I also hear talk about a coming federal campaign against being overweight. Bad health risk, they say. Rumor has it they're going to outlaw clothes over a certain size. That's just rumor, of course... still, I'll bet there's an angle in there for me.

Ah, the giraffes. For every one of me there's a hundred of them.

But I'm worth a thousand giraffes.

This was another sale to George Scithers when he was editing *Asimov's*. His acceptance note was, "I'll take the fish," and he gave it the cover with a Jack Gaughan painting.

"To Fill…" is part of my LaNague Federation future, but has its origins here on Earth in my childhood. When I was young, my father was an indefatigable fisherman. He would surf-cast at dawn or at sunset, sit on the bulkheads of the Manasquan Inlet as the tides changed, or go out on a party boat or a friend's private yacht whenever anyone needed an extra hand. Often he'd bring me along. I never saw the attraction of fishing—or any kind of killing sport, for that matter. But it certainly seems more sporting than hunting. I mean, you aren't putting a harmless, graceful, defenseless herbivore in the cross-hairs of a telescopic sight mounted on a superb killing weapon and snuffing out its life with a twitch of your index finger. A fish has to choose your bait and you have to reel him in before he's able to spit the hook. It's fairer, but the odds still don't seem even.

And sometimes as we trolled through the chum out there on the Atlantic, I'd watch the way the fish would hit or avoid the lines and wonder who was playing with whom. This story is the result of those childhood wonderings.

The title comes from "The Rime of the Ancient Mariner."

I don't go fishing anymore.

Connections: Dalt and Pard (*Healer*) wandered a lot. One of their stops (mentioned in the novel) was a planet named Gelk where he worked as a chispen fisherman. Here's the story about the man Dalt crewed with. It takes place after his visit, but will give you an idea of what he was doing when he was aboard.

To Fill the Sea and Air

*D*uring the period in question there were two items on the interstellar market for which supply could never equal demand. The intricate, gossamer carvings of the Vanek were one, valued because they were so subtly alien and yet so appreciable on human terms. The other was filet of chispen, a seafood delicacy with gourmet appeal all across Occupied Space. The flavor… how does one describe a unique gustatory experience, or the mild euphoria that attends consumption of sixty grams or more of the filet?

Enough to say that it was in high demand in those days. And the supply rested completely on the efforts of the individual chispen fishers on Gelk. Many a large interstellar corporation pressed to bring modern methods to the tiny planet for a more efficient harvesting of the fish, but the ruling council of Gelk forbade the intrusion of outside interests. There was a huge profit to be made and the council members intended to see that the bulk of it went into their own pockets.

from *Stars for Sale:*
An Economic History of Occupied Space
by Emmerz Fent

*I*magine the sea, smooth slate gray in predawn under a low drifting carapace of cloud. Imagine two high, impenetrable walls parallel on that sea, separated by ten times the height of a tall man, each stretching away to the horizon. Imagine a force-seven gale trapped between those walls and careening toward you, beating the sea below it to a furious lather as it comes.

Now… remove the walls and remove the wind. Leave the onrushing corridor of turbulent water. That was what Albie saw as he stood in the first boat.

The chispies were running. The game was on.

Albie gauged it to be a small school, probably a spur off a bigger run to the east. Good. He didn't want to hit a big run just yet. There were new men on the nets who needed blooding, and a small school like the one approaching was perfect.

He signaled to his men at their posts around the net, warning them to brace for the hit. Out toward the sun stood a long dark hull, bristling amidships with monitoring equipment. Albie knew he was being watched but couldn't guess why. He didn't recognize the design and closed his right eye to get a better look with his left. The doctors had told him not to do that. If he had to favor one of his eyes, let it be the artificial one. But he couldn't get used to it—everything always looked grainy, despite the fact that it was the best money could buy. At least he could see. And if he ever decided on a plastic repair of the ragged scar running across his right eyebrow and orbit, only old friends would know that a chispie wing had ruined that eye. And, of course, Albie would know.

He bore the chispies no animosity, though. No Ahab syndrome for Albie. He was glad to be alive, glad to lose an eye instead of his head. There were no prosthetic heads around.

Most of the experienced men on the nets wore scars or were missing bits of ears or fingers. It was part of the game. If they didn't want to play, they could stand on shore and let the chispies swim by unmolested. That way they'd never get hurt. Nor would they get those exorbitant prices people all over Occupied Space were willing to pay for filet of chispen.

Turning away from the dark skulking hull, Albie trained both eyes on the chispies. He leaned on the wheel and felt the old tingling in his nerve ends as the school approached. The middle of his sixth decade was passing, the last four of them spent on this sea as a chispen fisher... and still the same old thrill when he saw them coming.

He was shorter than most of the men he employed; stronger, too. His compact, muscular body was a bit flabbier now than usual, but he'd be back to fighting trim before the season was much older. Standing straight out from his cheeks, chin, and scalp was a knotty mane of white and silver shot through with streaks of black. He had a broad, flat nose, and the skin of his face, what little could be seen, showed the ravages of his profession. Years of long exposure to light from a star not meant to shine on human skin, light refracted down through the atmosphere and reflected up from the water, had left his dark brown skin with a texture similar to the soles of a barefoot reefclimber, and lined it to an extent that he appeared to have fallen asleep under the needle of a crazed tattooist with a penchant for black ink and a compulsion for cross-hatching. Eyes of a startling gray shone out from his face like beacons in the night.

The stripe of frothing, raging water was closer now. Albie judged it to be about twenty meters across, so he let his scow drift westward to open the mouth of the net a little wider. Thirty meters seaward to his right lay the anchor boat manned by Lars Zaro, the only man in the crew older than Albie. The floats on the net trailed in a giant semicircle between and behind them, a cul-de-sac ringed with ten scows of Albie's own design—flat-bottomed with a centerboard for greater stability—each carrying one gaff man and one freezer man. The two new hands were on freezer duty, of course. They had a long way to go before they could be trusted with a gaff.

Albie checked the men's positions—all twenty-six, counting himself, were set. Then he glanced again at the big ship standing out toward the horizon. He could vaguely make out GelkCo I emblazoned across the stern. He wondered why it was there.

"Incredible! That school's heading right for him!"

"Told you."

Two men huddled before an illuminated screen in a dark room, one seated, the other leaning over his shoulder, both watching the progress of the season's first chispen run.

The main body of the run was a fat, jumbled streak of light to the right of center on the screen, marking its position to seaward in the deeper part of the trench. They ignored that. It was the slim arc that had broken from the run a few kilometers northward and was now heading directly for a dot representing Albie and his crew that gripped their attention.

"How does he do it?" the seated man asked. "How does he know where they're going to be?"

"You've just asked the question we'd all like answered. Albie uses outdated methods, decrepit equipment, and catches more than anyone else on the water. The average chispen fisher brings home enough to support himself and his family; Albie is rich and the two dozen or so who work for him are living high."

"Well, we'll be putting an end to that soon enough, I guess."

"I suppose we will."

"It's almost a shame." The seated man pointed to the screen. "Just look at that! The school's almost in his net! Damn! It's amazing! There's got to be a method to it!"

"There is. And after seeing this, I'm pretty sure I know what it is."

But the standing man would say no more.

Albie returned his attention to the onrushing school, mentally submerging and imagining himself at one with the chispies. He saw glistening blue-white fusiform shapes darting through the water around him in tightly packed formation just below the surface. Their appearance at this point differed markedly from the slow, graceful, ray-like creatures that glide so peacefully along the seabottoms of their winter spawning grounds to the south or the summer feeding grounds to the north. With their triangular wings spread wide and gently undulating, the chispies are the picture of tranquility at the extremes of their habitat.

But between those extremes...

When fall comes after a summer of gorging at the northern shoals, the chispen wraps its barbed wings around its fattened body and becomes a living, twisting missile hurtling down the twelve-hundred-kilometer trench that runs along the coast of Gelk's major landmass.

The wings stay folded around the body during the entire trip. But should something bar the chispies' path—a net, for instance—the wings unfurl as they swerve and turn and loop in sudden trapped confusion. The ones who can build sufficient momentum break the surface and take to the air in a short glide to the open sea. The chispen fisher earns his hazard pay then—the sharp barbed edges of those unfurled wings cut through flesh almost as easily as air.

With the school almost upon him, Albie turned his attention to the net floats and waited. Soon it came: a sudden erratic bobbing along the far edge of the semi-circle. There were always a few chispies traveling well ahead of their fellows and these were now in the net.

Time to move.

"Everybody hold!" he yelled and started moving his throttle forward. He had to establish some momentum before the main body of the school hit, or else he'd never get the net closed in time.

As the white water speared into the pocket of net and boats, Albie threw the impeller control onto full forward and gripped the wheel with an intensity that bulged the muscles of his forearms.

The hit came, tugging his head back and causing the impeller to howl in protest against the sudden reverse pull. As Albie turned his boat hard to starboard and headed for Zaro's anchorboat to complete the circle, the water within began to foam like green tea in a blender. He was tying up to Zaro's craft when the first chispies began breaking water and zooming overhead. But the circumscribed area was too small to allow many of them to get away like that. Only those who managed to dart unimpeded from the deep to the surface could take to the air. The rest thrashed and flailed their wings with furious intensity, caroming off the fibrous mesh of the net and colliding with each other as the gaffers bent to their work.

The game was on.

The boats rocked in the growing turbulence and this was when the men appreciated the added stability of centerboards on the flat-bottomed scows. Their helmets would protect their heads, the safety wires gave them reasonable protection against being pulled into the water, but if a boat capsized... any man going into that bath of sharp swirling seawings would be ribbon-meat before he could draw a second breath.

Albie finished securing his boat to Zaro's, then grabbed his gaff and stood erect. He didn't bother with a helmet, depending rather on forty years of experience to keep his head out of the way of airborne chispies, but made sure his safety wire was tightly clipped to the back of his belt before leaning over the water to put his gaff to work.

There was an art to the gaffing, a dynamic synthesis of speed, skill, strength, courage, agility, and hand-eye coordination that took years to master. The hook at the end of the long pole had to be driven under the scales with a cephalad thrust at a point forward of the chispen's center of gravity. Then the creature's momentum had to be adjusted—never countered—into a rising arc that would allow the gaff-handler to lever it out of the water and onto the deck of his scow. The freezer man—Zaro in Albie's case—would take it from there, using hand hooks to slide the flopping fish onto the belt that would run it through the liquid nitrogen bath and into the insulated hold below.

Albie worked steadily, rhythmically, his eyes methodically picking out the shooting shapes, gauging speed and size. The latter was especially important: Too large a fish and the pole would either break or be torn from his hands; too small and it wasn't worth the time and effort. The best size was in the neighborhood of fifty kilos—about the weight of a pubescent human. The meat then had body and tenderness and brought the highest price.

Wings slashed, water splashed, droplets flashed through the air and caught in Albie's beard. Time was short. They had to pull in as many as they could before the inevitable happened. Insert the hook, feel the pull, lever the pole, taste the spray as the winged beastie angrily flapped the air on its way to the deck, free the hook and go back for the next. It was the first time all year Albie had truly felt alive.

Then it happened as it always happened: The furious battering opened a weak spot in the net and the school leaked free into the sea. That, too, was part of the game. After a moment of breath-catching, the men hauled in the remains of the net to pick up the leftovers, the chispies too battered and bloodied by their confused and frantic companions to swim after them.

"Look at that, will you?" the seated man said. "They broke out and now they're heading back to the main body of the run! How do you explain that?" The standing man said nothing and the seated one looked up at him. "You used to work for Albie, didn't you?"

A nod in the dimness. "Once. Years ago. That was before I connected with GelkCo."

"Why don't you pay him a visit? Never know... he might come in handy."

"I might do that—if he'll speak to me."

"Oh? He get mad when you quit?"

"Didn't quit. The old boy fired me."

"Hello, Albie."

Albie looked up from where he sat on the sand in a circle of his men, each with a pile of tattered net on his lap. The sun was lowering toward the land and the newcomer was silhouetted against it, his features in shadow. But Albie recognized him.

"Vic? That you, Vic?"

"Yeah, Albie, it's me. Mind if I sit down?"

"Go ahead. Sand's free." Albie gave the younger man a careful inspection as he made himself comfortable. Vic had been raised a beach rat but that was hard to tell now. A tall man in his mid-thirties, he was sleek, slim, and dark with blue eyes and even features. The one-piece suit he wore didn't belong on the beach. His black hair was slicked back, exposing a right ear bereft of its upper third, a physical trait acquired during his last year on the chispen nets. Restoration would have been no problem had he desired it, but apparently he preferred to flaunt the disfigurement as a badge of sorts. It seemed to Albie that he had broken Vic in on the nets only a few days ago, and had sacked him only yesterday. But it had been years... eleven of them.

He tossed Vic a length of twine. "Here. Make yourself useful. Can I trust you to do it right?"

"You never let a man forget, do you?" Vic said through an uncertain smile.

"That's because I don't forget!" Albie knew there was a sharp edge on his voice; he refused to blunt it with a smile of his own.

The other men glanced at each other, frowning. Albie's mellow temperament was legend among the fishermen up and down the coast, yet here he was, glowering and suffusing the air with palpable tension. Only Zaro knew what lay behind the animosity.

"Time for a break, boys," Zaro said. "We'll down a couple of ales and finish up later."

Albie never allowed dull-witted men out on the nets with him: They took the hint and walked off.

"What brings you back?" he asked when they were alone.

"That." Vic pointed toward the ship on the horizon.

Albie kept his eyes down, concentrating on repairing the net. "Saw it this morning. What's GelkCo I mean?"

"She's owned by the GelkCo Corporation."

"So they call it GelkCo I? How imaginative."

Vic shrugged and began patching a small hole in the net before him, his expression registering surprise and pleasure with the realization that his hands still knew what to do.

"The Council of Advisors put GelkCo together so the planet could deal on the interstellar market as a corporation."

"Since when do you work for the C. of A.?"

"Since my fishing career came to an abrupt halt eleven years ago." His eyes sought Albie's but couldn't find them. "I went into civil service then. Been on a research and development panel for the Council."

"Civil service, eh?" Albie squinted against the reddening light. "So now you get taxes put into your pay instead of taken out."

Vic was visibly stung by the remark. "Not fair, Albie. I earn my pay."

"And what's this corporation supposed to sell?" Albie said, ignoring the protest.

"Filet of chispen."

Albie smiled for the first time. "Oh, really? You mean they've still got chispies on their minds?"

"That's all they've got on their minds! And since I spent a good number of years with the best chispen fisher there is, it seemed natural that I be put in charge of developing the chispen as a major export."

"And that ship's going to do it?"

"It has to!" Vic said emphatically. "It must. Everything else was tried before they came to me—"

"Came to me first."

"I know." Vic could not suppress a smile. "And your suggestions were recorded as not only obscene, but physically impossible as well."

"That's because they really aren't interested in anything about those fish beyond the price per kilo."

"Perhaps you're right, Albie. But that boat out there is unique and it's going to make you obsolete. You won't get hurt financially, I know. You could've retired years ago... and should have. Your methods have seen their day. That ship's going to bring this industry up to date."

"Obsolete!" The word escaped behind a grunt of disgust.

Albie seriously doubted the C of A's ability to render anything obsolete... except maybe efficiency and clear thinking. For the past few years he had been keeping a careful eye on the Council's abortive probes into the chispen industry, had watched with amusement as it tried every means imaginable to obtain a large supply of chispen filet short of actually going out and catching the fish.

The chispies, of course, refused to cooperate, persisting in migratory habits that strictly limited their availability. They spawned in the southern gulf during the winter and fattened themselves on the northern feeding shoals during the summer, and were too widely dispersed at those two locales to be caught in any significant numbers. Every spring they grouped and ran north but were too lean and fibrous from a winter of mating, fertilizing and hatching their eggs.

Only in the fall, after a full summer of feasting on the abundant bait fish and bottom weed indigenous to their feeding grounds, were they right for eating, and grouped enough to make it commercially feasible to go after them. But Gelk's Council of Advisors was convinced there existed an easier way to obtain the filet than casting nets on the water. It decided to raise chispen just like any other feed animal. But chispies are stubborn. They won't breed in captivity, nor will they feed in captivity. This held true not only for adult fish captured in the wild, but for eggs hatched and raised in captivity, and even for chispen clones as well.

The Council moved on to tissue cultures of the filet but the resultant meat was said to be nauseating.

It eventually became evident to even the most dunderheaded member of the Council that there weren't going to be any shortcuts here. The appeal of chispen filet was the culmination of myriad environmental factors: The semi-annual runs along the coast gave the meat body and texture; the temperature, water quality, and bottom weed found only on their traditional feeding shoals gave it the unique euphorogenic flavor that made it such a delicacy.

No, there was only one way to supply the discriminating palates of Occupied Space with filet of chispen and that was to go out on the sea and catch them during the fall runs. They had to be pulled out of the sea and flash-frozen alive before an intestinal enzyme washed a foul odor into the bloodstream and ruined the meat. No shortcuts. No easy way out.

"I didn't come to gloat, Albie. And I mean you no ill will. In fact, I may be able to offer you a job."

"And how could a lowly old gaffer possibly help out on a monstrosity like that?" He turned back to his net repair.

"By bringing fish into it."

Albie glanced up briefly, then down again. He said nothing.

"You can't fool me, Albie. Maybe all the rest, but not me. I used to watch you... used to see you talking to those fish, bringing them right into the net."

"You think I'm a psi or something?" The voice had laughter all around the edges.

"I know it! And what I saw on the tracking screen this morning proves it!"

"Crazy."

"No. You're a psi! Maybe you don't even know it, but you've got some sort of influence over those fish. You call them somehow and they come running. That's why you're the best."

"You'll never understand, will you? It's—"

"But I do understand! You're a psi who talks to fish!"

Albie's dark lids eclipsed his eyes until only slim crescents of light gray remained.

"Then why," he said in a low voice, "did I have such a rotten season eleven years ago? Why did I have to fire the best first mate I ever had? If I'm a psi, why couldn't I call the chispies into the net that season? Why?"

Vic was silent, keeping his eyes focused on the dark ship off shore. As he waited for an answer, Albie was pulled pastward to the last time the two of them had spoken.

It had been Albie's worst season since he began playing the game. After an excellent start, the numbers of chispen flowing into the freezers had declined steadily through the fall until that one day at season's end when they sat in their boats and watched the final schools race by, free and out of reach.

That was the day Albie hauled in the net out there on the water and personally gave it a close inspection, actually cutting off samples of net twine and unraveling them. What he found within sent him into a rage.

The first mate, a young man named Vic who was wearing a bandage on his right ear, admitted to replacing the usual twine with fiber-wrapped wire. As Albie approached him in a menacing half-crouch, he explained quickly that he thought too many fish had been getting away. He figured the daily yield could be doubled if they reinforced the net with something stronger than plain twine. He knew Albie had only one hard-and-fast rule among his crew and that was to repair the net exclusively with the materials Albie provided—no exceptions. So Vic opted for stealth, intending to reveal his ploy at season's end when they were all richer from the extra fish they had caught.

Albie threw Vic into the sea that day and made him swim home. Then he cut the floats off the net and let it sink to the bottom. Since that day he had made a practice of being present whenever the net was repaired.

A long time passed before Albie started feeling like himself again. Vic had been in his crew for six years. Albie had taken him on as a nineteen-year-old boy and had watched him mature to a man on the nets. He was a natural. Raised along the coast and as much at home on the sea as he was on land, he was soon a consummate gaffer and quickly rose to be the youngest first mate Albie had ever had. He watched over Vic, worried about him, bled with him when a chispie wing took a piece of his ear, and seriously considered taking him in as a partner after a few more years. Childless after a lifelong marriage to the sea, Albie felt he had found a son in Vic.

And so it was with the anger of a parent betrayed by one of his own that Albie banished Vic from his boats. He had lived with the anguish of that day ever since.

"There's lots of things I can't explain about that season," Vic said. "But I still think you're a psi, and maybe you could help turn a big catch into an even bigger one. If you want to play coy, that's your business. But at least come out and see the boat. I had a lot to do with the design."

"What's in this for you, Vic? Money?"

He nodded. "Lots of it. And a place on the Council of Advisors."

"That's if everything goes according to plan. What if it fails?"

"Then I'm through. But that's not a realistic concern. It's not going to be a question of failure or success, just a question of how successful." He turned to Albie. "Coming out tomorrow?"

Albie's curiosity was piqued. He was debating whether or not to let Zaro take charge of the catch tomorrow... he'd do an adequate job... and it was early in the season...

"When?"

"Midmorning will be all right. The scanners have picked up a good-sized run up at the shoals. It's on its way down and should be here by midday."

"Expect me."

A hundred meters wide and at least three times as long: Those were Albie's estimates. The ship was like nothing he had ever seen or imagined... a single huge empty container, forty-five or fifty meters deep, tapered at the forward end, and covered over with a heavy wire mesh. Albie and Vic stood in a tiny pod on the port rim that housed the control room and crew quarters.

"And this is supposed to make me obsolete?"

"Afraid so." Vic's nod was slow and deliberate. "She's been ready since spring. We've tested and retested—but without chispies. This'll be her christening, her first blooding." He pointed to the yellow streak creeping down the center of the scanning screen. "And that's going to do it."

Albie noticed a spur off the central streak that appeared to be moving toward a dot at the left edge of the screen.

"My, my!" he said with a dry smile. "Look at those chispies heading for my boats—even without me there to invite them in."

A puzzled expression flitted briefly across Vic's features, then he turned and opened the hatch to the outside.

"Let's go up front. They should be in sight now."

Under a high white sun in a cloudless sky, the two men trod the narrow catwalk forward along the port rim. They stopped at a small observation deck where the hull began to taper to a point. Ahead on the cobalt sea, a swath of angry white water, eighty meters wide, charged unswervingly toward the hollow ship. A good-sized run—Albie had seen bigger, but this was certainly a huge load of fish.

"How many of those you figure on catching?"

"Most of them."

Albie's tone was dubious. "I'll believe that when I see it. But let's suppose you do catch most of them—you realize what'll happen to the price of filet when you dump that much on the market at once?"

"It will drop, of course," Vic replied. "But only temporarily, and never below a profitable level. Don't worry: The Council has it all programmed. The lower price will act to expand the market by inducing more people to take advantage of the bargain and try it. And once you've tried filet of chispen..." He didn't bother to complete the thought.

"Got it all figured out, eh?"

"Down to the last minute detail. When this ship proves itself, we'll start construction on more. By next season there'll be a whole fleet lying in wait for the chispies."

"And what will that kind of harvesting do to them? You'll be thinning them out... maybe too much. That's not how the game's played, Vic. We could end up with no chispies at all someday."

"We'll only be taking the bigger ones."

"The little guys need those bigger ones for protection."

Vic held up a hand. "Wait and see. It's almost time." He signaled to the control pod. "Watch."

Water began to rush into the hold as the prow split along its seam and fanned open into a giant scoop-like funnel; the aft panel split vertically down the middle and each half swung out to the rear. The ship, reduced now to a huge open tube with neither prow nor stern, began to sink.

Albie experienced an instant of alarm but refused to show it. All this was obviously part of the process. When the hull was immersed to two-thirds of its depth in the water, the descent stopped.

Vic pointed aft. "There's a heavy metal grid back there to let the immature chispies through. But there'll be no escape for the big ones. In effect, what we're doing here is putting a huge, tear-proof net across the path of a major run, something no one's dared to do before. With the old methods, a run like this would make chowder out of anything that tried to stop it."

"How do you know they won't just go around you?"

"You know as well as I do, Albie, these big runs don't change course for anything. We'll sit here, half-sunk in the water, and they'll run right into the hold there; they'll get caught up against the aft grid, and before they can turn around, the prow will close up tight and they're ours. The mesh on top keeps them from flying out."

Albie noticed Vic visibly puffing with pride as he spoke, and couldn't resist one small puncture: "Looks to me like all you've got here is an oversized, motorized seining scoop."

Vic blinked, swallowed, then went on talking after a brief hesitation.

"When they're locked in, we start to circulate water through the hold to keep them alive while we head for a plant up the coast where they'll be flash-frozen and processed."

"All you need is some cooperation from the fish."

Vic pointed ahead. "I don't think that'll be a problem. The run's coming right for us."

Albie looked from the bright anticipation in Vic's face to the ship sitting silent and open-mawed, to the onrushing horde of finned fury. He knew what was going to happen next but didn't have the heart to say it. Vic would have to learn for himself.

The stars were beginning to poke through the sky's growing blackness. Only a faint, fading glow on the western horizon remained to mark the sun's passing. None of the moons was rising yet.

With the waves washing over his feet, Albie stood and watched the autumn aurora begin to shimmer over the sea. The cool prevailing breeze carried smoke from his after-dinner pipe away toward the land. Darkness expanded slowly and was almost complete when he heard the voice.

"Why'd you do it, Albie?"

It wasn't necessary to turn around. He knew the voice, but had not anticipated the fury he sensed caged behind it.

"Didn't do a thing, Vic." He kept his eyes on the faint, wavering flashes of the aurora, his own voice calm.

"You diverted those fish!"

"That's what you'd like to believe, I'm sure, but that's not the way it is." The run had been almost on top of them. The few strays that always travel in the lead had entered the hold and slammed into the grate at the other end.

Then the run disappeared. The white water evaporated and the sea became quiet. In a panic, Vic had run back to the control pod where he learned from the scanner that the run had sounded to the bottom of the trench and was only now rising toward the surface... half a kilometer aft of the ship. Vic had said nothing, glaring only momentarily at Albie and then secluding himself in his quarters below for the rest of the day.

"It's true!" Vic's voice was edging toward a scream. "I watched your lips! You were talking to those fish... telling them to dive!"

Albie swung around, alarmed by the slurred tones and growing hysteria in the younger man's voice. He could not make out Vic's features in the darkness, but could see the swaying outline of his body. He could also see what appeared to be a length of driftwood dangling from his right hand.

"How much've you had to drink, Vic?"

"Enough." The word was deformed by its extrusion through Vic's clenched teeth. "Enough to know I'm ruined and you're to blame."

"And what's the club for? Gonna break my head?"

"Maybe. If you don't agree to straighten out all the trouble you caused me today, I just might."

"And how do you expect me to do that?"

"By guiding the fish into the boat instead of under it."

"Can't do that, Vic." Albie readied himself for a dodge to one side or the other. The Vic he had known on the nets would never swing that club. But eleven years had passed... and this Vic was drunk. "Can't do it as I am now, and I sure as hell won't be able to do it any better with a broken head. Sorry."

There followed a long, tense, silent moment. Then two sounds came out of the darkness: one, a human cry—half sob, half scream of rage; followed by the grating thud of wood hurled against wet sand. Albie saw Vic's vague outline slump into a sitting position.

"Dammit, Albie! I trusted you! I brought you out there in good faith and you scuttled me!"

Albie stepped closer to Vic and squatted down beside him. He put the bit of his pipe between his teeth. The bowl was cold but he didn't bother relighting it.

"It wasn't me, Vic. It was the game. That ship of yours breaks all the rules of the game."

"'The game'!" Vic said, head down, bitterness compressing his voice. "You've been talking about games since the day I met you. This is no game, Albie! This is my life... my future!"

"But it's a game to the chispies. That's what most people don't understand about them. That's why only a few of us are any good at catching them: Those fish are playing a game with us."

Vic lifted his head. "What do you take me for—?"

"It's true. Only a few of us have figured it out, and we don't talk it around. Had you stayed with me a few years longer, I might have told you if you hadn't figured it out for yourself by then. Truth is, I'm no psi and I don't direct those fish into my net; they find their way in on their own. If they get caught in my net, it's because they want to."

"You've been out on the nets too long, Albie. Chispies can't think."

"I'm not saying they can think like you and me, but they're not just dumb hunks of filet traveling on blind instinct, either. Maybe it only happens when they're packed tight and running, maybe they form some sort of hive-mind then that they don't have when they're spread out. I don't know. I don't have the words or knowledge to get across what I mean. It's a gut feeling... I think they look on the net as a game, a challenge they'll accept only if we play by the rules and give them a decent chance of winning."

He paused, waiting for another wisecrack from Vic, but none came. He continued. "They can gauge a net's strength. Don't know how, but they do it. Maybe it's those few fish always traveling in the lead... if they find the net too strong, if there's no chance of them breaking out, they must send out some kind of warning and the rest of the run avoids it. Sounds crazy, I know, but there's one inescapable fact I've learned to accept and apply, and it's made me the best: The weaker the net, the bigger the catch."

"So that's why you fired me when you found out I was repairing the nets with wire!"

"Exactly. You were hunting for a shortcut with the chispies and there aren't any. You made the net too strong, so they decided to play the game somewhere else. I wound up with the worst season I ever had."

"And I wound up in the water and out of a job!" Vic began to laugh, a humorless sound, unpleasant to hear. "But why didn't you explain this then?"

"Why didn't you come to me when you wanted to experiment with my nets? Why didn't you go buy your own tear-proof net and try it out on your own time? I may have overreacted, but you went behind my back and betrayed my trust. The entire crew went through pretty lean times until the next season because you broke the rules of the game!"

Vic laughed again. "A game! I must be drunker than I thought—it almost makes sense!"

"After forty years of hauling those winged devils out of the water, it's the only way I can make sense out of it."

"But they get caught and die, Albie! How can that be a game for them?"

"Only a tiny portion of the run challenges me at a time, and only a small percentage of those go into the freezer. The rest break free. What seems like a suicide risk to us may be only a diversion to them. Who knows what motivates them? This is their planet, their sea, and the rules of the game are entirely up to them. I'm just a player—one who figured out the game and became a winner."

"Then I'm a loser, I guess—the biggest damn loser to play." He rose to his feet and faced out toward the running lights of the GelkCo I as it lay at anchor a league off shore.

"That you are," Albie said, rising beside him and trying to keep his tone as light as possible. "You built the biggest, toughest damn net they've ever seen, one they'd never break out of... so they decided not to play."

Vic continued to stare out to sea, saying nothing.

"That's where you belong," Albie told him. "You were born for the sea, like me. You tried your hand with those stiff-legged land-roamers on the Council of Advisors and came up empty. But you and me, we're not equipped to deal with their kind, Vic. They change the rules as they go along, trying to get what they want by whatever means necessary. They sucked you in, used you up, and now they're gonna toss you out. So now's the time to get back on the water. Get out there and play the game with the chispies. They play hard and fast, but always by the same rules. You can die out there, but not because they cheated."

Vic made no move, no sound.

"Vic?"

No reply.

Albie turned and walked up the dune alone.

"ALBIEEEEEE!"

One of the dock hands came running along the jetty. Albie had just pushed off and was following his crew into the early morning haze. He idled his scow and waited for the man to get closer.

"Guy back at the boathouse wants to know if you need an extra hand today."

Albie held his breath. "What's he look like?"

"I dunno," the dock hand said with a shrug. "Tall, dark hair, a piece missing from his right—"

Albie smiled through his beard as he reversed the scow. "Tell him to hurry... I haven't got all day!"

And out along the trench, the chispies moved in packs, running south and looking for sport along the way.

Here you have one of the cornerstones of the Secret History.

By the mid-1970s I'd read most of the original Conan stories by Robert E. Howard and decided to try my hand at a little sword and sorcery myself. But I didn't want simply to rehash Howard. I decided to put my own stamp on it by writing a sword and sorcery tale in which the barbarian warrior never draws his sword. Gary Hoppenstand took it for his semi-prozine, *Midnight Sun*, but returned it with a kill fee when he had to discontinue the magazine. (Now *that's* class.)

Soon afterward I placed it with Gerald Page's *Heroic Fantasy* from DAW Books. The barbarian was named Glaeken and the evil wizard he faced called himself Rasalom. I forgot about those two until a few years later when I needed to cast two ancient foes for a novel I planned to call *The Keep*.

Demonsong

"Ho, outlander!" cried the burlier of the two men-at-arms stationed before the city's newsboard. His breath steamed in the chill post-dawn haze. "You look stout of arm, poor of cloak, and lame of brain—this notice from the prince should interest you!"

"He'd have to be an outlander to be interested," his companion muttered through a gap-toothed leer. "No one from around here's going to take the prince up on it."

The first scowled. "The prince ought to go himself! Then maybe we'd get a real man on the throne. Musicians and pretty-boys!" He spat. 'The palace is no longer a fit place for a warrior. Wasn't like that like that during his father's reign."

The other nodded and the pair walked off without a backward glance.

The outlander hesitated, then approached the elaborately handwritten notice. He ran long fingers through his dusty red hair as he stared at it. The language was fairly new to him and, although he spoke it passably, reading was a different matter. The gist of the notice was an offer of 10,000 gold grignas to the man who would undertake a certain mission for Prince Iolon. Inquiries should be made at the palace.

The outlander fingered his coin pouch; a few measly coppers rattled within. He didn't know the weight of a grigna, but if it was gold and there were 10,000 of them...money would not be a problem for quite some time. He shrugged and turned toward the palace.

The streets of Kashela, the commercial center of Prince Iolon's realm, were alive at first light. Not so the palace. It was well-nigh mid-morning before Glaeken was allowed entrance. The huge antechamber was empty save for an elderly blue-robed official sitting behind a tiny desk, quill in hand, a scroll and inkwell before him.

"State your business," he said in a bored tone, keeping his eyes on the parchment.

"I've come to find out how to earn those 10,000 grignas the prince is offering."

The old man's head snapped up at Glaeken's unfamiliar accent. He saw a tall, wiry, red-headed man—that hair alone instantly labeled him a foreigner—with high coloring and startlingly blue eyes. He wore leather breeches, a shirt of indeterminate color girded by a broad belt that held a dirk and longsword; he carried a dusty red cloak over his left shoulder.

"Oh. A northerner, eh? Or is it a westerner?"

"Does it matter?"

"No...no, I suppose not. Name?"

"Glaeken,"

The quill dipped into the well, then scratched out strange black letters on the scroll. "Glaeken of what?"

"How many Glaekens do you have in this city?"

"None. It's not even in our tongue."

"Then Glaeken alone will do."

The air of finality to the statement caused the official to regard the outlander with more careful scrutiny. He saw a young man not yet out of his third decade who behaved with an assurance beyond his years.

A youth with oiled locks and dressed in a clinging white robe entered the antechamber then. He gave Glaeken a frankly appraising stare as he sauntered past on his way to the inner chambers.

"Captain of the palace guard, I presume," Glaeken said blandly after the epicene figure had passed from sight.

"Your humor, outlander, could cost you your head should any of the guard hear such a remark."

"What does the prince want done?" he said, ignoring the caveat.

"He wants someone to journey into the eastern farmlands and kill a wizard."

"He has an army, does he not?"

The official suddenly became very interested in the scroll. "The captains have refused to send their men."

Glaeken mulled this. He sensed an air of brooding discontent in palace, an undercurrent of frustration and hostility perilously close to the surface.

"No one has tried to bring in this wizard then? Come, old man! The bounty surely didn't begin at 10,000 gold pieces."

"A few squads were sent when the problem first became apparent, but they accomplished nothing."

"Tell me where these men are quartered. I'd like to speak to them."

"You can't." The official's eyes remained averted. "They never came back."

Glaeken made no immediate reply. He fingered his coin pouch, then tapped the heel of his right hand against the butt of his longsword.

Finally: "Get a map and show me where I can find this wizard."

Glaeken dallied in one of those nameless little inns that dot the back streets on any commercially active town. He sat by the window. The shutters were open to let out the sour stench of last night's spilled ale, and the late morning sunlight glinted off the hammered tin goblet of cheap wine that rested on the table before him. The harlot in the corner eyed him languidly...this foreigner might prove interesting. A little early in the day for her talents, but perhaps if he stayed around a little longer...

A commotion arose on the street and Glaeken peered out the window to find its source. A squat, burly, misshapen hillock of a man with a square protruding jaw was trudging by, a large, oddly shaped leather case clutched with both arms against his chest. Behind him and around him ran the local gang of street youths, pushing, shoving and calling.

The wooden heels of their crude boots clacked as they scampered about; all wore a makeshift uniform of dark green shirts and rough brown pants.

"Ho, Ugly One!" cried a youth who seemed to be the leader, a lean, black-haired adolescent with a fuzzy attempt at a beard shading his cheeks. "What've y'got in that case? Give us a look! It truly must be something to behold if you're clutching it so tightly. Give us a look!"

The man ignored the group, but this only incited them to greater audacity. They began pummeling him and trying to trip him, yet the man made no attempt to protect himself. He merely clutched the case closer and tighter. Glaeken wondered at this as he watched the scene. This "Ugly One's" heavy frame and thickly muscled arms certainly appeared strong enough to handle the situation. Yet the well-being of the leather case seemed his only concern.

The leader gave a signal and he and his followers leaped upon the man. The fellow kept his footing for a while and even managed to shake a few of the attackers off his back, but their numbers soon drove him to the ground. Glaeken noted with a smile of admiration that the man twisted as he fell so that he landed on his back with the case unharmed. Only a matter of a few heartbeats, however, before the case was torn from his grasp.

With the loss of his precious possession, the little man became a veritable demon, cursing, gnashing his teeth, and struggling with such ferocity that it took the full strength of eight of the rowdies to hold him down.

"Be still, Ugly One!" the leader commanded as he stood near Glaeken's window and fumbled with the clasps on the case. "We only want to see what you've got here."

As the last clasp gave way, the case fell open and from it the leader pulled a double-barreled harmohorn. The shouts and scuffling ceased abruptly as all in sight, rowdy and bystander alike, were captured by the magnificence of the instrument. The intricate hand-carved wood of the harmohorn glistened in the sun under countless coats of flawlessly applied lacquer. A reed instrument, rare and priceless; in the proper hands it was capable of producing the most subtle and devious harmonies known to man. The art of its making had long been lost, and the musician fortunate enough to possess a harmohorn was welcomed— nay, sought—by all the royal courts of the world.

The squat little man redoubled his efforts against those restraining him.

"Damage that horn and I'll have your eyes!" he screamed.

"Don't threaten me, Ugly One!" the leader warned.

He raised the instrument aloft at if to smash it on the stones at his feet. In doing so he brought the horn within Glaeken's reach. To this point the outlander had been neutral, refusing to help a man who would not help himself. But now he knew the reason for the man's reluctance to fight, and the sight of the harmohorn in the hands of street swine disturbed him.

The horn abruptly switched hands.

The leader spun in surprise and glared at Glaeken.

"You!" he yelled, leaning in the window. "Return that before I come in and get it!"

"You want to come in?" Glaeken said with a tight smile. "Then by all means waste no time!"

He grabbed the youth by his shirt and pulled him half way through the window.

"Let go of me, red-haired dog!" he screeched.

"Certainly." And Glaeken readily replied, but not without enough of a shove to ensure that the youth would land sprawled in the dust.

Scrambling to his feet, the leader turned to his pack. "After him!"

They forgot the man they were holding and charged the inn door. But Glaeken was already there, waiting and ready.

He smiled as he met their attack and laughed as it moved out to the street where he darted among them, striking and kicking and wreaking general havoc upon their ranks. But these youths were hardly novices at street brawls, and when they realized that their opponent, too, was well experienced in the dubious art, they regrouped and began to stalk him.

"Circle him!" said the leader and his followers responded with dispatch. Before the menacing ring could close, however, the pack found itself harassed from an unexpected quarter.

"Ugly One" was upon them. Having regained his feet and sized up the situation, the little man charged into the pack with the roar of an angry bull. He was enraged to the point of madness and a smiling Glaeken stepped back to watch as the street youths were hurled and scattered about like jackstraws. A complete rout seemed inevitable. It was then that Glaeken glanced at the leader and saw him pull a dirk from within his shirt and lunge.

The blade never found its target. Glaeken moved and yanked the pack leader off his feet by his long hair; he pulled the knife from his grasp and extended his grimy neck over his knee. All fighting stopped as everyone watched the tableau of Glaeken and the pack leader.

"You should be slain outright," Glaeken said, toying with the dirk over the terrified youth's vulnerable throat. "And no one would miss you or mourn you."

"No!" he cried as he saw the cold light in Glaeken's eyes. "I meant no harm!"

Glaeken used the point to scratch an angry, ragged red line ear to ear across the leader's throat.

"A good street brawl is one thing, my young friend, but if I see you show your steel to the back of an unarmed man again, I'll finish the job this scratch has begun."

So saying, he lifted the youth by his hair and shoved him toward his companions. The green-shirted pack and its frightened leader wasted no time then in fleeing the scene.

"Ugly One" turned to Glaeken and extended his hand. "I thank you, outlander. I am called Cragjaw, although I assure you I was not given that name by my parents."

"No thanks called for," Glaeken said, clasping the hand. "A street brawl at midday is a good spirit-lifter." He did not offer his own name in return.

"I prefer quieter ways to amuse myself," Cragjaw muttered as he stooped to pick up the empty leather case.

The barmaster was sheathing a dirk of his own as they reentered. The contested musical instrument lay on the bar before him.

"I guarded the harmohorn well while you were out on the street!" he shouted to Cragjaw.

"And what would you have done with it if he hadn't been able return to claim it?" Glaeken asked with a knowing grin.

The barmaster shrugged and eyed the horn as Cragjaw returned it to its case.

"I suppose I would have had to sell it to someone... I have no talent for such an instrument."

Glaeken threw a coin on the bar. "That's for the wine," he said turned toward the door.

Cragjaw laid a hand on his arm. "At least let me buy you a cup before you go."

"Thanks, no. I'm riding the East Road and already I've tarried too long."

"The East Road? Why, I must travel that way, too. Would you mind a companion for a ways?"

"The roads are free," said Glaeken.

Glaeken's mount, a stallion called Stoffral, took him eastward from Kashela at an easy walk. Cragjaw ambled beside him on a chestnut mare.

"You're a Northerner, aren't you?" the shorter man observed.

"In a way, yes."

"You never told me your name."

"It is Glaeken."

"Glaeken..." Cragjaw paused before continuing. "Stories circulate among the wine cups in the back rooms of the court of Prince Iolon—in whose service I am presently employed as a musician—and in the taverns about a man named Glaeken. He's said to live in the Western Isles and is supposedly young and flame-haired like yourself."

"Interesting," Glaeken remarked. "And what are these tales?"

"Well, he is called Glaeken-the-Laugher by some and it is said that he once led the dreaded Nightriders who pillage vast areas of the Western Isles."

Glaeken nodded for his companion to continue.

"I know only what I've heard, but 'tis said that each of these raiders rides a monstrous bat with a body the size of a horse and wings like ketch sails that sweep the night. The tales tell of an evil king named Marag who was the favorite target of the Nightriders and who sent many champions against them with the quest to bring back the head of the Nightrider lord. But shortly after each set out, a monster bat would fly over Marag's hold and drop the latest champion's body into the courtyard.

"Finally, a man named Glaeken, who had refused to be the king's champion for many years, was called into Marag's court. And there in a steel cage suspended from the ceiling sat the damsel in whose company this Glaeken had been often seen. Now, they say that Glaeken had no serious future plans for the young lady but felt somewhat responsible for her present predicament. So he traveled to the pinnacle fortress of the Nightriders where he challenged and beat their lord in a contest of swords."

"And did he bring the head to Marag?" Glaeken asked.

"That and more, for it seems that by tradition the Nightriders must claim as leader the man who fairly defeats the reigning lord. This Glaeken returned with his new followers and taught Marag a grisly lesson." Cragjaw glanced at his companion. "Could you be that Glaeken?"

"A good tale, my friend, but how could I and this bat-rider be one and the same? How could I be pillaging the Western Isles at night and ride the East Road in Prince Iolon's domain with you today? Quite impossible."

"Not so," said Cragjaw with a sly grin. "For it is also said that after a year or two with the Nightriders, the man named Glaeken grew restless and dissatisfied. He left them to their own devices and no one knows where he travels now." The squat little man made a point of clearing his throat. "Where travel you now, Glaeken?"

"To Elder Cavern in the eastern farmlands."

"Elder Cavern! Why, that's in the very center of the plague area. Nothing out there but dying farms and..." Cragjaw's voice faded as he seemed to remember something. "Oh, I see. You must have answered the Prince's notice."

Glaeken nodded. "It seems that the mystery of the region's woes has been cleared up. They've discovered that a sorcerer named Rasalom—a giant of a man, I'm told—entered the cavern nearly two years ago. Not too long thereafter the crops, the cattle, and the farmers in the area began to sicken. Rasalom has been neither seen nor heard from since, and the Prince's advisors seem certain that he's still in the cavern."

"So the infamous Rasalom is behind it all," Cragjaw muttered. "We've long thought it to be a plague of some sort, released from the cavern after eons of sleep."

"The prince's advisors were rather vague about the plague," Glaeken said. "Do you know what it's like?"

"Stories vary, but most agree that the victims complain of a throbbing in the head and ears and slowly begin to lose their strength, becoming very lethargic. Soon they cannot get out of bed and eventually they waste away and die. But what puzzled the court physicians was the curious fact that all victims seem to improve and recover when moved out of the area. No one could give a reason for this...but sorcery explains it well: Rasalom has laid a curse of some sort on the region."

"So it would seem," Glaeken agreed.

"But what purpose could he have? Why would he want to lay waste the eastern farmlands—for not only do people sicken and die out there, but cattle and crops as well."

Glaeken shrugged. "Why is not my concern. I admit that I'm somewhat curious, but my task is merely to bring back Rasalom himself, or some proof of his demise, such as his Ring of Chaos, whatever that may be."

"'Tis rumored to be the most potent focus of power for black sorcery this side of the Netherworld. You will have to slay Rasalom to gain it, and that will not be easy." He shuddered. "Not only does that wizard have the black arts at his command, but he is said to stand half again as tall as a tall man, and be three times as broad in the shoulders. No wonder Iolon has to send an outlander! No local man would set foot in Elder Cavern! I hope the prince is paying you well."

"I seldom take on a gainless task." Glaeken replied.

"If that's true, then why did you aid me against those street thugs?"

Glaeken smiled. "I was quite willing to let them have their fun with you until I saw the harmohorn. I have a weakness for music and consequently a respect for musicians."

They came to a crossroads when and Cragjaw turned his horse to the north.

"We part here, Glaeken," he said. "I go to the prince's summer quarters to prepare entertainment for the arrival of his entourage tomorrow. I would bid you ride south and have no further thought of Elder Cavern, but I know you'll not heed me. So instead I bid you luck and hope to see you at the summer palace soon with either Rasalom or his ring. One word of warning though: travel quickly. Few who venture into that land nowadays are ever seen again."

Glaeken waved and headed east. He did not quicken his pace.

The land was arid and vegetation generally scarce in Iolon's domain, but as Glaeken penetrated into the eastern farmlands he became aware of an almost total lack of greenery. Bark-shedding trees lifted their dry, stunted, leafless branches skyward in silent supplication for surcease of—what? And the further east he moved, the darker became the sky; gray clouds slid by, twisting, churning, writhing, and rolling as if suffering from an agony of their own as they passed over the region.

Long-rotted cattle carcasses dotted the fields on both sides of the road, the hides dried and matted and close-fitting in death, perfectly outlining the skeleton within. Glaeken saw no evidence that scavengers had been at the carrion, and then realized that he had not seen a single trace of beast or fowl since he'd entered the region. Even vultures shunned this place.

The motionless air became thick and heavy as he pushed on, his lungs labored at their task. As evening consolidated the gray of the sky to black, Glaeken was glad to dismount. He built a fire not too far off the road between a dead tree and a large stone. He gave Stoffral free rein to find what nourishment he could in the lifeless, desiccated grasses nearby, but the horse seemed to have lost all appetite. Glaeken, too, felt no hunger, unusual after half a day's ride, but managed to force down some dried beef and stale wine.

He was strangely tired and this gave him some concern. He had never been one to believe in sorcerers and evil magic, considering them little more than tales designed to frighten children. The only magic he'd ever seen had been the work of charlatans. Yet for a man of his age and fitness to feel so lethargic after a mere six hours on horseback was decidedly unnatural. Maybe there was something to this curse after all.

He moved away from the heat of the fire and sat with his back against the rock. The oppressive silence made him uneasy. Even the nightbugs were quiet. He glanced about…no pairs of feral eyes reflected the firelight from the darkness around his little camp. That, too, was unusual. Slowly, his eyes grew heavy. Against his better judgment he allowed himself to doze.

…*the sound grows in his brain by imperceptible degrees, a ghastly, keening, wailing cacophony of madness that assaults his sanity with murderous intensity…and as the volume increases there appear wild, distorted visages of evil, countless blank-eyed demons howling with mindless joy, screaming louder and louder until he is sure he must go mad…*

Glaeken found himself awake and on his feet, sweat coursing along his skin in runnels. The fire had burned down to a fitful glow and all was quiet. He shook his head to clear it of the dream and glanced around for Stoffral. Gone!

Fully alert to danger now, Glaeken began shouting the horse's name. Stoffral was too loyal a beast to desert him. His third shout was answered by a faint whinny from behind the rock. Glaeken cautiously peered into the darkness and saw the dim form of his mount on the ground. He ran to its side and made a careful check. The horse had suffered no harm and Glaeken concluded that Stoffral must be a victim of the same lethargy afflicting his master.

He slapped the horse's flanks in an effort to rouse the beast back to its feet but to no avail. Stoffral's strength seemed completely drained. Glaeken remembered the cattle carcasses along the road and swore that his steed would not suffer a similar fate. He stalked to the fire and lifted a branch that had been only partially consumed. Fanning it in the air until the tip glowed cherry with heat, he applied the brand to Stoffral's right hindquarter. Amid the whiff of singed hair and the hiss of searing flesh, the horse screamed in pain and rose on wobbly legs.

Glaeken could not help but cast a fearful glance over his shoulder as he steadied his mount; horses were rare and highly valued creatures in the land where he had been raised, and any man caught doing harm to one was likely to be attacked by an angry mob. But pain or not, scar or not, Stoffral was on his feet now and somewhat revived. That was all that mattered at the moment. And the horse seemed to know instinctively that the act had been done without malice.

Replacing the saddle on Stoffral's back, he packed it with everything but the jerked beef, the waterskin, and the half-dozen torches he had fashioned before leaving Kashela. Then he shouted and slapped the horse's flanks and chased him back down the road. Hopefully, Stoffral would await his master beyond the zone of danger.

Glaeken waited a moment, then shouldered his pack and began walking in the opposite direction. He'd have preferred to wait until morning...travel would be easier in the light. But Glaeken's doubts about the supposed curse on the eastern farmlands had been thoroughly shaken. Perhaps something truly evil was afoot in the region. For all he knew, morning might prove too late if he waited for it. So he traveled in darkness.

Dawn lightened the perpetual overcast as Glaeken stood before the high arched entrance to Elder Cavern. He felt as if his eyes had been torn out and replaced with heated coals. His head buzzed and hummed; his sword had become a drag anchor. The very air weighed upon him like a stone. He stood swaying, questioning the wisdom of entering the opening before him. His strength had steadily declined during the night and he was now so weakened that he seriously entertained thoughts of abandoning his mission.

Everything seemed so hopeless. With barely strength enough to stand, he'd be insane to challenge a giant in stature and sorcery such as Rasalom. Yet he forced himself to stagger toward the cavern maw.

Part of his fogged brain screamed to turn back, but he kept pushing forward. He could not turn back, for he would never make it to the crossroads; he'd end up like the rotting cattle he'd had passed yesterday.

Why not simply lay down and die then?

Because he could not pass up the slim chance that he might find a way to outwit Rasalom. And of course the golden reward was a lure, as was his need to learn what lay behind the curse that weighed upon this region like a plague. And beneath it all, driving him like a whip, was that peculiar aspect of his nature that insisted he see a task through to its finish.

As he was engulfed by the darkness within, Glaeken paused, removed the tinderbox from his sack and ignited one of the torches. The flame flickered light off the walls and made marching armies of the stalactite and stalagmite shadows as he moved. His shuffling feet kicked up smelly clouds of dust that irritated his nose. He knew the odor well—bat dung, and none of it fresh. Even the bats were gone.

The tunnel sloped at a steep angle and the roof bore down on him until he had to walk in a slight crouch. The walls glistened with moisture as he plunged deeper and deeper into the earth, and his torch would hiss as it brushed against them. The odd, persistent humming in his brain grew louder and more distracting as he moved. He could only hope that the tunnel would lead him directly to Rasalom.

The passage broadened into a wider, higher chamber and Glaeken cursed as the torchlight revealed the problem he had hoped not to meet: three other tunnels opened into this same chamber. As he slumped against the wall in near complete exhaustion, his torch sagged and dipped into a brackish puddle. In sudden total darkness he fumbled for the tinderbox to light a fresh torch, then froze. Down the tunnel to the right trickled the faintest hint of illumination.

Glaeken forgot about torch and tinderbox and stumbled along the passage toward the beckoning tendrils of light. Rounding a corner he found himself in a dim, long-shadowed room. The walls were smooth and bare except for a few oil lamps flickering in sconces. A huge, throne-like chair rested in a dark corner, otherwise the room was empty.

Wary, Glaeken started to draw his broadsword as he moved further into the room, but the weight of it seemed so enormous to his weakened muscles that he let it slide back into its scabbard. He rested his hand instead on the handle of his dirk.

A massive door appeared to be cut into the wall to his right. Eyes darting constantly about the room, Glaeken approached it. He saw no latch, no ring, no handle, but the arcuate scratches on the floor before it were proof that the door did in some way swing open. Yet try as he might, he could not see how.

A voice rasped behind him: "There's a hidden latch."

The nape of his neck tingling with fear and surprise, Glaeken wheeled and peered closely at the massive chair in the corner. The seat lay immersed in Stygian shadow. He moved closer and faintly made out a human outline. Grabbing an oil lamp from the wall, he held it high.

As the shadows receded Glaeken saw that he faced a lank-haired skeleton of a man dressed in a robe once richly embroidered but now tattered and torn, foul and filthy.

"You must be strong-willed to have come this far," said the seated figure in a voice like rats' feet scurrying over dried corn husks.

"Who are you?" Glaeken demanded.

"I am called Rasalom."

"I was told Rasalom is a giant of a man, not a mere bag of bones."

"I am he, nevertheless," Rasalom replied with a grin that was horrible to behold. "You no doubt started on your journey with visions of a terrible struggle against a huge, sword-wielding wizard. You foresaw a mighty battle with flashes of steel and shouts of fury. Yet look at us now: you can barely stand and I have not the strength to cast the most elementary of weirds." He barked a harsh laugh. "What a comedy we play!"

But Glaeken could see no humor in the situation. He spoke with desperate determination.

"I've come in the name of Prince Iolon to put an end to this curse you've laid on the land."

"I know all about Iolon and his reward," Rasalom snarled. "He wants you to bring back Rasalom or his ring." He fumbled within his robe and withdrew a large ring of intricately worked gold. It was set with a small, spherical black stone, so black that it seemed to absorb all light, appeared to be a rent in the very fabric of existence, a tiny portal to the nothingness beyond. The ring dangled from a golden chain.

"You wish the Ring of Chaos?" he said. "Here...take it. It no longer fits me and I have no further need of it."

Glaeken stiffened visibly at the offer.

Rasalom smiled again. "No trick, I assure you. For why should I want to keep a mere Ring of Chaos when soon I shall be an integral part of Chaos itself?" The warlock's eyes began to glow as he spoke. "I, Rasalom, have called forth the twelve hundred idiot demons of the Amphitheater! It took two years to complete the task. Each of the twelve hundred had to be summoned by a separate spell, and each spell took its toll. I was once as you were told—a huge, robust man. Look at me now! But I care not. Eternity is mine!"

Glaeken's expression mirrored his doubts about Rasalom's sanity.

"I don't blame you for thinking me mad. But beyond that stone door you tried so futilely to move lies the Amphitheater of Chaos, and therein are assembled the twelve hundred idiot demons... the Choir of Chaos. They exist only to sing. There is no curse on the land... only their singing. For they sing to Chaos itself and the vibration of their song strikes discord in the life processes of all living things."

"But you—"

"I am protected, for I am performing The Task. And what a task it is! The Lords of Chaos are wise. They know that to extend their domain they must occasionally accept new blood into their ranks. But the newcomer must prove beyond all doubt that he is worthy. So The Task was set, an ordeal that only a practitioner of the greatest skill and stamina could hope to accomplish. For each of the twelve hundred demons of the choir sucks a little bit of life from the one who calls it forth. I have raised them all and yet I still live! I am wasted but I have succeeded!"

"If this is success," Glaeken said, "what would be failure?"

"Ah, but you see, within the Amphitheater the embryo of my new form gestates, slowly incorporating my being into its own as it matures. The time for parturition draws nigh. Soon I shall be eternal and all this world my domain!"

Glaeken remained unconvinced. "Your sorcery has wasted your mind as well as your body, Rasalom. Lift your curse and give me the ring and I shall leave you to your delusions. Refuse and my blade will end everything for you."

"You doubt my word?" the wizard rasped. "I tell you there is no curse! The Choir of Chaos sings and its song is slow death to all within reach of it! You are dying as we speak, my foolish interloper. And you cannot threaten me with death, for that would only accelerate the embryo's progress. I welcome death at this moment—it will bring my rebirth that much closer!"

Glaeken shook his head in dismay. How do you deal with a madman?

"Go!" Rasalom cried. "See for yourself! Pull the handle on the lamp by the door. The passage leads to the Amphitheater. View the Choir of Chaos. See my masterwork, and die!"

Wordlessly, wearily, Glaeken shuffled to the door. If Rasalom were mad, this would prove it. If sane, then Glaeken's life—nay, his whole world—was in grave danger.

He pulled down on the lamp handle. It moved easily. Behind the wall he heard the clank of weights as they were released. Slowly, the door swung open to reveal a narrow passage lit with oil lamps similar to those in the room. The throbbing hum was louder here. Glaeken moved into the passage and saw another stone door at its end. This one was equipped with a ring latch. He grasped the ring and pulled on it, doubting very much that he had strength left to budge it. But the hinges were perfectly balanced and the stone slab swung toward him.

He repeated this procedure with the three identical subsequent doors and each time the hum increased in volume until at the final door it had risen to a muted scream. This door was doubly thick and vibrated with the intensity of the sound behind it. But it swung as easily as the others when Glaeken pulled on the ring.

The sound was a physical thing, washing over him with a volume and intensity that drove him to his knees. He crouched on the edge of a precipice and before him lay the Amphitheater of Chaos, an inverted cone, mistily illuminated by light that filtered up from the unguessed depths below. Carved into the rounded walls that sloped upward to the pointed roof were twelve hundred niches, and in each of those niches huddled one of the twelve hundred idiot demons.

Blank-eyed and mindless they were, shaped in every deformity imaginable and unimaginable. Faces suffused with an insane, malignant glee, they howled and caterwauled in tones that ranged from far below to far above those audible to the human ear. No two tones harmonized, all was discord and conflict. Glaeken now knew the origin of his dream the night before...the Choir of Chaos was assembled and at work.

His gaze shifted from the howling demons to the ebon sphere that floated in the center of the Amphitheater. It appeared to be a thin-membraned ball of inky fluid, suspended above and before him by no visible means. The eyes of each of the twelve hundred were fixed steadily upon it.

Glaeken noticed a slight swirling movement within the sphere and recoiled at a fleeting glimpse of a dark, nameless shape and two glowing malevolent eyes.

The embryo of Rasalom's new form floated there in its inky amnion, suspended on a placenta of sound from the Choir of Chaos. Rasalom was not mad—he had been telling the truth.

Suddenly Glaeken gave in to a sudden urge to sing. He had no idea where it came from. Perhaps it was a feeble effort to counteract the effect of the sound that pressed down on him with such ferocity...perhaps the glimpse of those eyes in the sac had pushed him to the brink of madness and the song offered a tenuous link to sanity. He didn't know, he simply began singing.

He lifted his voice in the hymn of praise to the goddess Eblee, a sweet simple song known the world over. And his effort did not go unnoticed. The demons of the Choir pulled their gaze away from the amniotic sac and glared at him with unrestrained fury. Perhaps the merest trace of coherent melody within the Amphitheater interfered with the gestative process, for Glaeken noticed a slight ripple coursing over the membranous surface of the sac.

In response, the twelve hundred increased their volume and Glaeken was knocked flat. Vision and awareness blurred as every fiber of his being screamed in anguish. Still he sang, clinging to the melody as a last thread to sanity; but he was fading, losing his grip on consciousness. His hoarse tones grew fainter as the Choir of Chaos attacked him with unwavering vocal fury.

And then Glaeken heard another sound, as out of place as the sun in a starry sky: the dulcet tones of a harmohorn had joined him in song. Blinking his eyes into focus, he turned his head and there behind him stood Cragjaw. Eyes closed, bathed in sweat, the squat little man was leaning against the wall and blowing a perfect modal harmony to Glaeken's song. Glaeken found new strength then and redoubled his vocal efforts.

Something began to happen in the Amphitheater. The flawless acoustics permeated the new sound throughout the huge chamber. If a touch of coherence had proved slightly disruptive before, the harmony of man-made instrument and human voice began to have a shattering effect. The twelve hundred demons became agitated, thrashing in their niches, their voices faltering. And this in turn had its effect on the embryo. The tortured membrane stretched and bulged from the rolling convulsions of the thing within. The glowing eyes pressed against the sac wall, glaring in unearthly rage.

Then came a weakening, a thinning, a tiny puncture, a rent—the membrane ruptured in an explosion of inky fluid as its contents burst free into the air. The sac and its partially formed occupant fell swiftly and silently into the mists below.

A howling scream of agony rose from the Choir of Chaos. The idiot demons ceased their song and flew into fits of rage, slamming themselves against the walls of their niches and finally hurtling over the edges and down. One by one, then in groups, and finally in a hellish rain, they followed the embryo back to the hell of their origin. And then...

Silence.

Glaeken had almost given up hope of ever experiencing it again. He remained prone and reveled in the lack of sound as strength and sanity surged back into his body.

"Ho, Cragjaw," he said finally, rising to his feet. "What brought you to this concert?"

Cragjaw sighed exhaustedly as he slipped the harmohorn back into its case. "I owed you a service so I came after you. Seems a good thing I did."

Together they stumbled back down the passage toward the antechamber.

"We are more than even, my friend," Glaeken said. "I did but aid you in a street brawl—and enjoyed it, too. You risked your life just by entering this region."

They arrived then in the antechamber and found Rasalom stretched out on the floor halfway between the throne chair and the doorway. Dead.

Glaeken reached into the withered sorcerer's robe, pulled out the Ring of Chaos, and snapped the chain.

"That cannot be Rasalom!" Cragjaw exclaimed. "And where did he come from? I didn't see him when I passed through!"

"It's Rasalom, all right. The curse is broken but I suppose Iolon will want to have the ring before he gives me the reward."

Cragjaw started to speak as they headed for the surface, hesitated, then started again.

"Ah, Glaeken, I fear I bring bad news. When I reached the summer palace I learned that Iolon had been overthrown by his army. There will be no reward, I'm afraid."

Glaeken took this news in silence and continued walking. Receiving no reply, Cragjaw continued.

"I too am out of work. The generals have no liking for the harmohorn. Their tastes in music are a bit coarse for my skills, running more to naked girls with tambourines and bells. Knowing they would not honor Iolon's promise of a reward, I traveled to warn you that you would be imperiling yourself for naught. I found your horse on the way—he is well—and thought you might be in some I danger, so I rode my own horse nearly into the ground and ran the rest of the way on foot in an effort to catch you before you entered the cavern. I was too late. But I heard this awful caterwauling within and followed the sound. You know the rest."

Glaeken nodded appreciatively. "But what made you bring the harmohorn?"

"You don't think I'd leave it unguarded, do you?" Cragjaw replied indignantly. "It never leaves my side!"

"I suppose you sleep with it, too?"

"Of course!"

Glaeken smiled and tucked the Ring of Chaos into his belt. "Ah, well, the quest has been rewarding in one way if not another. I may not come away a rich man but at least I've found a friend among you strange easterners."

"Strange easterners, are we?" Cragjaw said with a gleam in his eye as they reached the mouth of the cavern. "Then you must be from the Western Isles after all!"

With the late morning sun warm on his face, Glaeken offered only a good-natured laugh in reply.

THE EIGHTIES

Ah, the '80s. "That libertarian sci-fi guy" decided to change course and pursue his first love—horror fiction—where he made a big splash with *The Keep*. He joined King and Straub on the bestseller lists and, with novels like *The Tomb*, *The Touch*, and *Black Wind*, took part in defining modern American horror fiction.

Movies and TV came knocking with mixed results.

I turned 40 during the decade—in 1986, to be exact. Something happened to me at forty. Something turned up the rheostat on the creative juices. Throughout my thirties I'd always been one novel ahead of myself—Dutch-ovening the characters and ideas of the next book or story while I wrote the current one. After forty, the ideas exploded.

Short-fictionwise during the six years pre-40 (1980-through '85) I wrote:

"Green Winter" (short)
"Be Fruitful and Multiply" (short)
"Soft" (short)
"The Last ONE MO' ONCE GOLDEN OLDIES REVIVAL" (short)
"Dydeetown Girl" (novella)
From 1986 through 1989, however...
"DatTayVao" (short)
"Traps" (short)
"The Years the Music Died" (short)
"Ménage a Trois" (novelette
"Doc Johnson" (short)
"Cuts" (short)
"Wires" (novella)
"Muscles" (short)
"Faces" (novelette)

"Tenants" (short)
"Feelings" (novelette)
"Kids" (novella)
"Buckets" (short)
"The Tenth Toe" (short)
"A Day in the Life" (novelette)
"Glim-Glim" (teleplay)
"Rumors" (drabble)
"Christmas Thingy" (short)
"Biosphere" (comic script)
"Slasher" (short)
"The Barrens" (novella)
"Definitive Therapy" (short)
"Topsy" (short)
"Rockabilly" (short)
"Bob Dylan, Troy Jonson, and the Speed Queen" (short)
"Pelts" (short)

Yikes! I cranked out all that in the '80s while writing *The Keep*, *The Tomb*, *The Touch*, *Black Wind*, *Reborn*, starting *Reprisal*, expanding *The Tery*, cobbling together *Dydeetown World*, and assembling and writing all the introductions to *Soft & Others*. AND—cannot forget: practicing family medicine full time.

I know...I can't believe it either. Of course, some weren't pubbed till years later, but they were all *written* in that period. I know because during the '80s I started keeping a chronology of my output and that's what it says.

I do know how I got it done, though, which leads me to...

A Method for Part-Time Writers
By the time the '80s rolled around I realized that to have a writing career I'd need a steady output to feed my readers. But I was a part-timer. I had a day job that didn't allow me to bang out 10 pages a day like my full-time fellows.

But I could write 3 pages a day.

And the next day I could write 3 more.

In operant terms, writing a book is a long task with the reward not only distant, but not even assured. So we must find incremental rewards along the way. Writing a few good pages a day can be their own reward. And if they're not so good, well, tomorrow's will be better.

Here's what worked for me as a part-timer:

I found that a minimum of 3 first-draft double-spaced pages per day did the trick. That's 21 per week. At that rate you've got over 540 pages in 6 months, which is a decent-sized novel.

In writing those 3 pages per day, I avoided tinkering with them, because that stalls you by fooling you into thinking you're still writing. You're not. And you're losing momentum. Get them down and then leave them alone and go on to the next 3. The time to fix and hone them is after you've finished that all-important first draft (what I call the vomit draft). You'll know your characters better then and can go back and make meaningful edits and additions.

Worry about quality later. Get that vomit draft done.

As someone said, *You can fix bad pages; you can't fix no pages.*

Print out that sentence and tape it to your monitor: It's key.

When I was practicing full time I'd use my commutes to the office and the hospital to compose my next three pages in my head so I'd be primed when I sat down to write. That's a key point: *Turn off the damn radio or the podcast and remove the damn earbuds.* Stop wasting valuable time listening to other people's words. You're a writer. When you're driving or walking around you should be working on *your* words—the words you want to tell other people. Compose your pages ahead of time so you can spew them when you sit before the keyboard.

Another key is writing every day—*every* day—to maintain the narrative flow. Often if you leave days between, you lose momentum and it's hard to bring your writing up to speed again.

I work from an outline—mostly to make sure I can end the novel satisfactorily with the catharsis I've been promising my reader—but I almost always deviate from it. I will end up where I originally intended, but along the way I find better paths to take me there.

I start at Chapter One and proceed from there. That works best for me. I have key scenes visualized ahead of time but I like to see events unfold in sequence because I can monitor motivation and causality as I go along, making sure each scene builds from the last and reaches for the next. That's when it becomes apparent that what worked well in outline doesn't always hold up in fully fleshed text.

If I wrote scenes out of sequence and connected them later (as do some writers I know) I'd miss this, or find I can't use a scene I'd spent a lot of time on.

Increments. Keep moving those grains of sand.

(end of lecture)

Later in the '80s I started my career as annual bridesmaid to the various literary awards in our field. My novella "Dydeetown Girl" made the final ballot for the 1987 Nebula Award from the Science Fiction Writers of America. Then '88 became another bridesmaid year—twice that time when both "Traps" and "DatTayVao" made the final ballot for the Bram Stoker short story award from the Horror Writers of America. The kiss of death. They split the vote and I lost. In '89 I was a bridesmaid again when *Black Wind* was a finalist for the Bram Stoker Award for novel. It lost but who can grouse about finishing close behind *The Silence of the Lambs*? I almost voted for it over my own novel. (Yeah, right.)

The '80s also saw the publication of my first short story collection, *Soft & Others*—"16 Stories of Wonder and Dread" from my first two decades as a professional writer. (Maybe I should have subtitled the collection, "Watch Wilson Learn to Write.") A lot of readers told me how much they liked the introductions to the stories; a few said they liked the intros better than some of the stories. (Wise-asses.)

Novels and Novellas

The Keep

THE KEEP was my first horror novel and I threw myself and everything else into it. I began it in 1979 when the horror fiction out there consisted mostly rewrites of *Carrie* and *'Salem's Lot*—small-town, narrow-focus horror. I decided to go widescreen. I'd been reading a lot of Robert Ludlum and you can see the influence of his paranoia/trust-no-one motifs weaving through the story. You might say the international thriller had a one-night stand with cosmic horror and conceived *The Keep*.

Because it occupies its own little historical neverneverland in the Transylvania Alps on the eve of WWII, *The Keep* doesn't date. It's held up very nicely through the decades. First published in 1981, it's never been out of print and is generally considered a classic of the genre. Who can ask for more?

The novel was instigated by Quinn Yarbro's *Hotel Transylvania*, a marvelous book dealing with a sympathetic vampire. My contention to Quinn, however, was that there's no such thing as a sympathetic vampire. They're obligate parasites. But I was intrigued with the story possibilities of a vampire *pretending* to be on your side. From there I notched it up and said, What if he's not only pretending to be your ally, but pretending to be a vampire as well—to hide the fact that he's something much worse? A stepwise progression of What-ifs led me to stir supernatural good and evil into a cauldron with human good and evil, add a soupçon of the temptation to try to fight evil with evil, a dash of a crisis of faith, and see what sort of stew resulted.

For characters, I went back to a story I'd written just the year before. Glaeken and Rasalom first met in a story called "Demonsong" in *Heroic Fantasy*.

My agent sold the novel to Hollywood before we had a publisher. The Hollywood agent pitched it as "Nazi vs vampires" and you couldn't get a better log line than that—at least not in 1980.

The vampire idea is the book's big red herring. I purposely set the story in the Transylvanian Alps to predispose the reader—and the characters—to a vampire. Then I took all those typical trappings and turned them on their heads. Great fun.

The crosses were a stumbling block. I wanted them there. I loved the visual of cross-studded stone walls to reinforce the vampire red herring. But I was using a non-Christian mythology as the bedrock of the story, so how did I explain the décor? Then I came up with the hilt of a sword and everything fell into place.

The Tomb

It began with a dream . . .

A nightmare, actually. Sometime in 1981, after publication of *The Keep*. I was working on another novel that would eventually become *Reborn* and running into walls—things simply were not gelling. What I remembered of the nightmare was being chased by a monster or demon of some sort—I couldn't remember a thing about how it looked, just that it was after me—and no matter what I shot at it, threw at it, cut it with, the damn thing kept coming.

I remember waking and feeling out of breath, as if I'd been running. I realized much later that it was a frustration dream—I was frustrated as all hell with the new novel, and I wound up physically battling its avatar in my dream.

Or maybe not. Who knows?

Doesn't matter. What does matter was my urge to capture that terror and frustration in a story. But I didn't want the protagonist to die on that roof (in my mind I was still the guy in jeopardy), so I had to come up with a character who could survive the encounter—someone a lot tougher and with a lot more survival skills than I. So I started inventing this tough guy and, because of my worldview, decided to make him a sort of gut anarchist—a guy whose nonconformity arises from his nature rather than from books he's read. A guy attached to our society by the slimmest and most fragile of threads. Jason Bourne was hot then, so I did my turn-it-on-its-head thing and made him an anti-Jason Bourne—with no black-ops, SEAL, or Special Forces training, no CIA or police background, no connection to officialdom. In other words, no safety net. No one in the government he could call on. He has to rely on his own wits and his own network.

The result was Repairman Jack. And by the time I'd fleshed him out in my head, I knew I had to write about him—now. I filed the proto-*Reborn* away and, working fore and aft from that battle on the Manhattan rooftop, started on what became *The Tomb*.

My biggest challenge was to come up with a suitable *thing* for the battle. But I didn't need that to start the book. I could write on without a name or even a description of the beastie. Once I came up with one I could backfill the details.

I could have patched together some Lovecraftian or demonic creation, but that wasn't good enough. I wanted to avoid Christian mythology as well. I was looking for something with a fabled history from a fabled land. For some reason—maybe I was thinking of the *Necronomicon*—I gravitated toward ancient Arabia. Once there I naturally latched onto the djinni (twisted into "genie" by the French). The archetypal, lamp-dwelling, three-wish djinn was *not* what I needed, but I figured it must have a dark side I could exploit.

Thus, my initial working title was *Djinni*. In fact the original hanging file remains in one of my cabinets, and that title still remains on the label.

As I wrote, I researched djinn folklore and didn't find anything I could use. How about India instead? Its swarming, overpopulated pantheon had to yield *something*. And yet I spent a lot of time coming up empty.

Don't forget, this was 1982. ARPANET was known to only a few DoD and academic geeks; the Internet hadn't been linked up and the primitive early version of the World Wide Web was a decade away.

I had to go to *libraries*, folks. I had to spend hours pawing through file cards and hunting through the stacks for often mis-shelved books. I flipped through every volume under the "India" subject heading and every "demon" under the title heading. *Months* of searching.

To make a point, I just googled "india +demon" and got 307,000 hits in 0.36 seconds.

I hope you appreciate how lucky we are these days.

By chance I happened upon a juvenile called *The Demons of Rajpur* by Molly and Betsy Bang. They retold tales from Bengali folklore about a demon known as a "rakosh," a fierce creature who devoured human flesh.

Cool.

Also a shape shifter.

Not cool. I didn't want to open that narrative can of worms. So I did what every self-respecting storyteller does in a situation like this: I tossed out the shape shifting.

The Bang sisters used "rakoshes" as their plural. This sounded clunky to me. I still saw my "Djinni" label every day, so I made the plural "rakoshi." I learned after *The Tomb* was published that the Bangs had used an obscure spelling (Bengali, perhaps?) of the demons known throughout India as *rakshasa*.

No matter. I now had my title (and it wasn't *The Tomb*).

Rakoshi (very early on it was *Rakoshi!* but I later dropped the exclamation point) was my first novel to employ this wondrous thing I'd heard about from Joe Haldeman: a word processor. Following his lead, I bought an Apple II+. The dot-matrix manuscript of the finished novel went straight to Pat Golbitz who'd edited *The Keep* at Wm. Morrow. She promptly rejected it, calling it "bloated and overwritten," but remaining vague as to any other reasons.

Let me tell you, that stung. I vehemently disagreed with her at the time; but after editing the scan files for a reprint edition in the '90s, I realized she had a point. I don't think it was bloated, but it was certainly overwritten. I found loads of passive voice and embarrassing redundancies: People crouching down, smoke rising up, the dying mother rakosh falling to her death "trailing smoke and flame behind her." (Like where else would she trail them? Ahead of her? Nice trick.) I trimmed it down with textual liposuction.

The good news was that I didn't have to change the characters. At all. They held up just fine. The problem was all the excess verbiage I forced them (and the reader) to wade though.

But as for rejecting an overwritten book…overwriting can be edited. I had the feeling something else was going on. Was it Jack's anarchic, seditious, subversive, under-the-radar lifestyle? I'll never know.

I'm long past any hard feelings but I would have loved to have been a fly on the inner wall of Pat's skull when she opened her *New York Times Book Review* and saw the novel on the Bestsellers list.

So the book went from Wm. Morrow to Whispers Press for a

limited hardcover edition, and to Berkley, the folks who'd made *The Keep* a paperback bestseller. They planned to do the same for *Rakoshi*. But Berkley had a problem with the title. After going through the editing, the copyediting, the page proofs, I got a call from the publisher herself, Rena Wolner. Permit me to approximate the conversation:

RW: *Paul, we need to change the title.*

Me: *What's wrong with* Rakoshi?

RW: *It's too foreign a word. It will put people off.*

Me: *As I recall, Trevanian's* Shibumi *didn't put people off.*

RW: *That's different.* Rakoshi *won't work.*

(To her credit, Rena could have said, "I know Trevanian and you're no Trevanian," but spared me.)

Me: *I assume you have something in mind.*

RW: *We need a cover and a title that will echo* The Keep: "*The Something.*" *I'm thinking* The Tomb.

Me: (stunned silence)

RW: *We can use an Indian temple on the cover with the same perspective as on* The Keep.

Me: *But-but there's no tomb in the novel.*

RW: *No one will care.*

Me: *Man, I don't know . . .*

RW: *The sales department thinks this is important. They figure we can ship an extra quarter-million copies with a name change.*

(Confession: Right here I'm doing some quick math...my percentage of the cover price times 250,000...yow. Nice bonus.)

Still . . .

Me: *But how do we get around having no tomb in the novel?*

RW: *No one will notice, and if they do, they won't care. Trust me on this.*

Bottom line: I agreed. Part of it was selling out, I suppose. But intimidation had a lot to do with it. I was vulnerable after being rejected by Wm. Morrow, and here I was getting the hard sell from my new publisher herself. I caved.

Looking back, Rena was right. The name change helped propel the novel onto bestseller lists all over the country. And yes, even though I've had many readers question me as to the lack of a tomb, they're a drop in the bucket, a minuscule percentage of the million-plus people who've read the novel during the three-plus decades since its publication.

Yes, Rena was right. People don't care.

But I do. And I've never completely let it go. In the context of a mass market edition, Rena was right. But later, in the noughts, when Borderlands Press wanted to do a limited edition, an epicurean entree designed for biblioconnoisseurs, I requested they publish it under the original title. And they did.

The Touch

Remember, I mentioned the Miracle Cure in regard to *Healer*. I return to it with a vengeance here—a whole novel full of them.

Not much to say about *The Touch*, other than it arose from my experiences as a medical practitioner. You see patients you've come to know develop diseases for which there's no cure. You wish for a miracle. Well, *The Touch* provides that miracle via the mysterious Dat-Tay-Vao. Dr. Alan Bulmer is passed the power to heal with a simple touch. It lasts one hour a day, but it comes with a price. For every Yang there must be a Yin, right? Working title was *The Power*.

Almost everyone in the novel returns for *Nightworld*.

I ran into a problem with Putnam which wanted to issue it as a paperback original. I insisted on a hardcover. They finally gave in and did a small print run. I felt vindicated when they had to go back for a second run. Even more so when they had to do a third. (Heh-heh-heh.)

For the Borderlands Press deluxe edition in 2003—seventeen years after its first publication—I edited out anything that rooted the novel in the '80s. That meant Alan's recounting of his rock 'n' roll epiphany in 1955, which would have had him pushing 60 years of age. The tale was a direct swipe from my own life—something I try to avoid in my fiction. So, in case you have a later edition, here's what I cut:

(Alan is speaking to Sylvia as Chuck Berry's *Maybellene* plays, sparking a memory.)

"Let's see… it was back in the summer of fifty-five and I had two passions in the world: rocket ships and the Brooklyn Dodgers. On summer nights I liked to listen to the Bums in bed, but the noise of the radio would keep my younger brother awake. So my father bought me a little Japanese radio—shaped like a rocket, of course—that had a tiny earplug instead of a speaker; you tuned by pulling up or down on the nose cone.

"And so it was on a hot, muggy August night as I was trying to tune in the Brooklyn Bums that I came upon this strange music with a twanging bass and some guy singing about chasing a Cadillac and a girl named Maybellene. I'd heard of Elvis but had never actually heard his music. In those days a kid listened to what his parents listened to. And my folks listened to stations that played stuff like 'Mister

Sandman,' 'How Much Is That Doggie in the Window?', 'The Tennessee Waltz,' 'Shrimp Boats Is a-Comin',' and so forth. Get the picture? Those songs did nothing for me. But *this!* This went directly from the radio to my central nervous system. And then that manic guitar solo in the middle came on-here it is. Listen!"

Sylvia listened. Yes, it was certainly manic. So was Alan. She could almost see the tension pouring out of him.

"Anyway, I sat up in the dark, electrified by what was shooting out of that little earplug. It was my rock 'n' roll epiphany. And to top it off, the DJ—I later learned his name was Alan Freed—said something like, 'So nice, we'll play it twice,' and he *did!* He played the same damn song twice in a row! That was it—I was converted. Still liked the Dodgers, but I kept the radio tuned to WINS all night except during the commercials, when I checked out the score of the game. While my folks blithely assumed I was up in bed listening to the national sport, I was really listening to what some folks were calling 'nigger music.'"

And I was worried about his memory! Sylvia thought with a mental shake of her head.

Black Wind

Black Wind (working title: *Ronin*) was sparked by reading *At Dawn We Slept* which recounted how nicely the Pearl Harbor attack played into Roosevelt's desire to go to war against the Axis, hinting that Pearl might have been set up for attack. The more research I did, the more I believed it a possibility. That started *Black Wind* cooking. It simmered while I was writing *The Touch* and demanded to be written after I'd finished.

From a career perspective, not a great move; but my problem is I tend not to think of writing in career terms. *BW* was the next book ready to go, so I went with it, and it ended up taking me two years to research and write. I became fascinated with the history. A feudal social structure was trying to break into the 20th century industrial age. Kimonos and top hats. Katanas and machine guns. Social, political, industrial chaos pure and simple. To understand the Japanese back then, you have to study *on*. If you don't know about their hierarchy of personal and cultural obligations, nothing makes sense.

The Japanese movers and shakers knew they'd eventually be going to war with the US and had begun preparing for it back in the 1920s. So that's when I started my story. They needed to understand Americans and so they sent a boy to be raised among them. Matsuo was that boy. He develops a hatred of the casual, ambient racism of the times and his contempt for what he perceives as Americans' lack of honor. I never had a doubt that the story would end at ground zero in Hiroshima.

Matsuo's actions, and anything done by the Kakureta Kao sect, are pure fiction. The rest was painstakingly researched, going so far as to comb old newspapers to find out what people were thinking, wearing, driving, doing at the time of the novel.

I started *BW* as a horror novel but as I did more and more research, it gained sweep and scope. As it grew, the horror got pushed into a secondary role. I think it's my best novel—not my favorite, but my best. I'm perhaps inordinately proud of the fact that it was reprinted in Japan, and was most pleased when I found out the translator had just three or four minor things he had to change. My research paid off.

Putnam, publisher of *The Keep, The Tomb,* and *The Touch,* turned it down. "We love the story but have no idea how to market it." And I could see the problem. It's a World War II revisionist historical family saga horror novel (try saying that fast 3 times), a mix of cultural fanaticism and wrenchingly dark supernatural horror. How do you market that? Fortunately, Tom Doherty, head of Tor, loved it and went to bat for it.

BW received not a single bad review, but no one seemed to know where to position this mongrel. Neither the marketing department nor the booksellers knew what to do with it. Tom Doherty spent a lot of time and effort getting it out to the stores, but where do you shelve a World War II revisionist historical family saga horror novel? Consequently, despite the excellent reviews, it got lost.

Dydeetown World

"I gathered from the medium-size tyrannosaurus rex running loose in the yard that Jennings discouraged drop-in company."

I loved that line from the moment I thought of it, but I always had something else to write, something more pressing, so it sat unused in my notebook for ten years, an opening hook in search of a story. Finally, in 1984, I decided to put it to use. I'd recently finished *The Tomb* and my mind was still in the private-eye groove. The line gave me no choice—the story had to be science fiction. The line told me things. For instance, it implies a future where genetic engineering and/or cloning are so far advanced that a formerly extinct dinosaur (now available in small, medium, and large) patrolling a yard as a watch animal is a ho-hum situation. And if this future can supply clones of famous extinct reptiles, why not clones of famous dead people, too?

And then the wheels began turning.

My aim was a short story. Five, maybe six thousand words, tops. A quiet little SF tribute to Raymond Chandler whose work has given me such pleasure over the years. I was going to use all the clichés—the down-and-out P.I., his seedy friends, the tired, seamy city, the bar hang-out, the ruthless mobster, the whore with the heart of gold. But I was going to set it in the far future, in the LaNague future I had developed for the SF I'd written during the '70s. This story, however, was going to be set on the underbelly of that future, going to be grimy and disillu-sioned rather than bright and full of hope like its predecessors.

But despite the downbeat milieu, the story would be about freedom, friendship, and selfesteem. Beneath its hardboiled voice, its seamy set-tings and violent events (Cyber/p-i/scifi, as Forry Ackerman might have called it) were characters trying to maintain—or reestablish—a human connection.

The working title was "Lies" because that's mostly what it's about. We all say we revere the truth, but sometimes a lie can be stronger than the truth, *better* than the truth. There are vital lies—the ones that can give you hope, can give you the strength to keep going when the truth would break you. And sometimes, under the right circumstances, a lie can *become* the truth

I disappeared into the story, so much so that its word count came in at three times the projected length, with a new title: "Dydeetown Girl."

A novella. One that none of the sf magazines wanted because it was too much like detective fiction; and which the detective mags rejected because it was "sci-fi." I began to fear my ugly-duckling hybrid would be doomed to perpetual orphanhood. But thanks to Jim Baen and Betsy Mitchell it found a home in one of the *Far Frontiers* anthologies. From there it went on to reach the Nebula Awards final ballot for best novella of the year. My ugly duckling had become a swan.

And that would have been that if not for Betsy Mitchell who wanted more from its characters and milieu. She said if I did two more related novellas we could put them all together and publish them in book form. I told her that sounded nice, but I hadn't planned a series and I didn't have any more ideas along that line. She said, "Why don't you do some-thing with those urchins." (The urchins are illegal children living in the abandoned subways under the city—they have no rights, no official existence. They were glimpsed only in passing in the story, but Betsy's instincts had sensed something there.) I said I'd give it some thought, but since I was deep into *Black Wind* at the time, it fell off my radar.

Not Betsy's. This is a very persistent editor. She reminded me at every opportunity that she was still waiting for the next novella. Finally I started thinking about those urchins...

The results were "Wires" and "Kids," both published in Baen's *New Destinies* series of paperback anthologies.

So, *Dydeetown World* is a fusion of "Dydeetown Girl," "Wires," and "Kids." But it's not a collection. The two follow-up novellas were written with the idea of continuing the storylines developed in the first, of bringing Sig closer to the land of the emotionally able-bodied, and tying everything together at the end. Baen published it with a marvelous cover by Gary Ruddell in the summer of '89.

So that's the *Dydeetown World* story. Goes to show that you never know when a 5,000-word tip-of-the-hat to one of the Old Masters will turn into a novel. Although written for adults, *Dydeetown World* wound up on the American Library Association's list of "Best Books for Young Adults" and on the New York Public Library's recommended list of "Books for the Teen Age." Go figure.

Oh. And that neat narrative hook that got the whole process started? The Tyrannosaurus line that was going to open the story? I couldn't use it until page 15. Go figure. But think about that hook. In a story written in the mid-'80s I used a dinosaur cloned from reconstituted fossil DNA, but I tossed it off as background color.

If only I'd thought to stick a bunch of them in a park...

OTHER MEDIA

The Keep

I have bitched about this film at such length for so long that I don't want to waste too much space on it here.

Michael Mann, who seems to have a great visual sense, had no sense at all of this type of story and how to tell it. He either didn't understand how the story is constructed, or simply didn't care. He just wanted to do what he wanted to do: "A World War II fairy tale." I chose the Transylvanian Alps to set you up for a vampire. But even though a vampire is just a red herring in the book, Mann wanted no mention of it in his film. So if you do that, you take away the very reason the book is set in the Transylvania Alps. Might as well set it in the Swiss Alps.

Look, I know a novel needs to be changed when it goes to the screen—it's a completely different medium. No inner monologues—what you get is what you see. Subplots have to go, characters must be combined. But when your source novel is an international bestseller, you should be smart enough to realize that it must have something going for it. You don't rip out its heart and display a hollow carcass.

And the heart of any story is its characters. The major fault of Mann's film is that he did not build characters. The first half hour or so is slow but has wonderful possibilities. Then he starts leaving the novel and going off on his own. That's when things fall apart. You realize that all the frames wasted on those self-indulgent super close-ups of eyeballs and flaring matches could have been used to develop the characters a little more. Glaeken and Magda meet—cut to the two of them in bed. And he has everybody speaking with these pregnant pauses: "Nobody sleeps… (beat)… here." All that slo-mo and smoke (Joe Lansdale says it looks like a string of shampoo commercials.) And making poor Scott Glenn talk like a robot. Sheesh.

The result was a critical and financial disaster: halfstar and onestar ratings with headers like, "You can keep *The Keep*."

I remember the last line of Jeffrey Lyons review on TV: "It could have been wonderful." And that's the real heartbreak of the film: all the ingredients were there for a classic. He had a major studio and decent budget behind him, Oscar Winner John Box doing the sets, Scott Glenn, Jürgen Prochnow, Ian McKellen, Gabriel Byrne, and Alberta Watson in front of the camera. And it sucked. *All that—you had all that to work with and this is what you came up with?*

Truly, it could have, should have been wonderful.

I realize that Michael Mann did not do the final cut, but he had changed so much of the story and botched so much during production that I doubt the film was salvageable.

The Tomb

New World Pictures optioned the novel immediately upon publication. (Published November 1984, agreement signed before Christmas.) Tamara Asseyev (who had produced *Norma Rae*) was set to produce, but a combination of low-rent antics by Fred Olen Ray (he hijacked the title) and a lackluster script by Sargon Tamimi (they moved the action to Pasadena!) had the project dead in the water 18 months later. I dashed off a spec script in an eleventh-hour attempt to save it, but too late.

Maybe just as well. The rakoshi—the Bengali temple demons who provide the horror—would have presented an almost insurmountable challenge in those pre-CGI days. How do you make them look real? The line between horror and hilarity is a couple of nanometers thick. A rakosh is scary; a guy in a rubber suit is dumb.

I'd created a number of original action sequences for the screenplay and I wanted to protect them. I was unaware of the Writers Guild's manuscript registration service at the time, so I figured my best option was to copyright them in a story. They're all in "A Day in the Life."

This was not the end of Repairman Jack's involvement with Hollywood, however. Not by a long shot.

Glim-Glim

In the late '80s I got to know Tom Allen, story editor for *Tales from The Darkside*. In the spring of 1988 he asked me to drop by the Laurel offices on Broadway for a meeting, where I learned that Tom and the others at Laurel wanted me to do something for *Monsters*, the new half-hour syndicated show Laurel was preparing for the coming fall season as a companion to their *Tales from the Darkside*. The guidelines were simple but strict: one or two lead characters, one to three supporting characters, one monster; one or two interior locations, no exteriors; three segments with a 5/8/8-minute breakdown.

For years I'd been kicking around an idea for a sci-fi/monster story but never had the impetus to put it down on paper. Now I did. I sat myself down on a Thursday night, wrote out just enough to fill one singlespaced sheet, and sent the precis of "Glim-Glim" to Laurel on Friday morning.

Tom called a week later: they loved it. But on March 7, before we could make the deal official, the Writers Guild of America went on strike. I wasn't a member of WGA then (I am now—I had to join if I wanted to see "Glim-Glim" produced) but somehow I was on strike too. For five months.

But all in all my experience with Laurel was a good one. I might even say excellent. The producers there actually read books and have great respect for writers and the written word. The director checked with me every time he wanted to change a word or two of dialogue or to shift the focus of a scene—light years away from my experience with the filming of *The Keep*.

Due to the strike, "Glim-Glim" didn't run in December as originally planned. It first aired the week of January 30, 1989.

My only regret is that Tom Allen never saw "Glim-Glim." He died suddenly on September 30, 1988. I miss his warmth and wisdom and quiet intelligence.

The '80s non-novel fiction not included here:

"Dydeetown Girl" (novella—included in *Dydeetown World*)

"Wires" (novella—included in *Dydeetown World*)

"Kids" (novella—included in *Dydeetown World*)

"The Death of Balajuro" (an excerpt from *Black Wind*)

"Glim-Glim" (teleplay)

"Christmas Thingy" (written to read to my daughters—pubbed decades later as an illustrated children's book)

"Biosphere" (comic script)

"Definitive Therapy" (included in *Other Sandboxes*)

"Rockabilly" (included in *Other Sandboxes*)

STORIES FROM THE '80s

We forget (or has it been suppressed?) that for most of the 1970s a new ice age was a major worry. I'm talking about a parade of articles and warnings in *Time*, *Newsweek*, the Washington *Post*, the NY *Times*, etc., etc.

Coincidentally, in the late 1970s, I came across an article in *Medical Tribune* about the successful transplantation of a mammalian nucleus into a plant cell. Naturally, having a SF turn of mind, and with the new-ice-age drumbeat hammering at me from the mass media, I foresaw all sorts of possibilities. I put the idea to use immediately, creating photosynthetic cattle for my third novel, *An Enemy of the State*, and making it the central idea for this piece. Stan Schmidt bought it for *Analog* and I promised him a series of stories in this future scenario, but never got around to writing them.

I probably never will. So "Green Winter" (*Analog*, January, 1981) is the first and last installment. This version, by the way, differs from the one Stan published. I had two endings. The *Analog* version left a ray of hope for humanity so I could continue the series.

Here it is:

GREEN WINTER

Everything was in its place. Why then were his feelings in such a chaotic state?

(...those eyes...he kept seeing *those eyes...he'd never looked a hairy in the eyes before...not while it was alive and near and afraid...*)

He shook himself irritably and sliced a few small pieces off the shank. Dropping them into a wooden bowl, he then reached over to place them in his daughter's lap.

Rana fended him off. "Get that away from me!"

She was physically and emotionally spent and Veneem did his best to be solicitous.

"Better eat it. You'll need all the nourishment you can get when regeneration starts, especially since there's no sunlight worth mentioning this time of year."

"I'm no cannibal." Her words were clipped and sharp.

"Don't be foolish—you must be starved. I know I am."

Rana eyed the fire in sulky concentration. "You didn't have to kill it."

"Yes, I did. And for more than one reason." He squatted before her with the bowl in his lap. "First of all, it hurt you. Nothing can hurt you and be allowed to live. Second, if we had brought it back alive as you wished—and I'm not really sure we could have—you'd have begun publicly spouting the madness Baken's put into your head. And that would mean the end of you. The Elders would have no choice then but to order your death. Third, because this catch makes me First Hunter beyond any doubt. And *last...*" He paused. (...*those eyes...that gibberish...almost like words...*)

"And last"—he was forcing himself to speak steadily—"I killed the hairy because it's the Law that all hairies are to be killed. They're very scarce now and we may never see one again. But if I should come upon another, I'll... I'll kill it. And that settles the matter."

Rana had slowly turned her gaze from the fire to her father as he spoke. She sensed something, something no one else could have detected. A slow smile spread across her face.

"You're bluffing! I thought I heard it in your voice and now I see it in your face: You're not so absolutely sure of yourself anymore, are you?"

"Of course I am!"

"Then go ahead!" She pointed to the bowl on his lap. "Roast hairy was always your favorite—eat your fill!"

Veneem picked up a slice of meat, hot and firm with a thin coating of grease that oozed onto his fingers.

(...*those eyes*...)

He dropped it back into the bowl. "I'm not hungry."

And now the darker ending...

Green Winter

The knife made a crisp, rasping sound as it sliced through Veneem's skin. The area over the left deltoid had been numbed with ice before the procedure and he felt only a sensation of pressure, a mild discomfort

The dark green of the epidermis parted cleanly to reveal the lighter dermis below. This in turn gave way and exposed the pink of the subcutaneous fat. Blood appeared in a slow, red ooze as the doctor completed the elliptical incision around the growth—a tiny hand and forearm this time, mottled green, with minute, articulated fingers.

Veneem had put off the excision for as long as he could because the growths so often withered and fell off on their own. But this one had kept on growing, so now he was back at Dr. Baken's adding another scar to his collection.

As the segment of skin supporting the growth was removed, blood filled the cavity and overflowed onto the arm. The doctor quickly wiped it away and began suturing. Three deft ties closed the wound. After a compress was applied and a clean cloth wrapped around the area to hold it in place, Veneem rose to his feet.

"See you in five or six days," Dr. Baken said, dropping the excised growth and the excess thread on the garbage pile in the corner. "Those sutures ought to be ready to be pulled by then."

Veneem nodded. He knew the routine.

"Tell me something," he said after a pause. "Don't I get an awful lot of these things?"

"No, not particularly. They're fairly common in regenerated limbs but the incidence varies between individuals. I've got a number of patients who need excisions far more often than you."

Veneem nodded with an overt lack of concern. He didn't want the doctor to think him overly concerned about his health—that would be unseemly for a hunter.

"How's Rana?" Baken asked.

The question surprised Veneem. The doctor had met his daughter, of course—he had been to the house often enough during the early stages of the arm's regeneration, and during Nola's final illness—but he didn't think Rana had made enough of an impression on the man that he'd be asking about her.

"She's well. If I can keep her out of trouble she'll make someone a fine wife someday."

Baken smiled. "If she stayed out of trouble, she wouldn't be Rana."

Veneem had to agree, yet he wondered how the doctor could make such a precise observation. He brushed the matter aside—everyone knew Rana. Now to the matter of settling the fee.

"Get you a rabbit for this—that do?"

"Nicely. Before the half-moon, if you can. My meat supply is getting low."

"You'll have it tomorrow or the next day."

He took his fur jacket from a hook on the wall and gingerly slipped his left arm in first. Veneem was of average height and heavily muscled, more so than most hunters, but moved with a feline grace that was the *sine qua non* of his profession. With the jacket cinched securely around him, he covered his shiny green scalp with a cloth cap, nodded brusquely to Baken, and stepped out into the cold.

His eyes immediately scanned the ground for game tracks. Sheer reflex—he knew he'd find nothing. The ground around Baken's hut was an indecipherable clutter of comings and goings and waitings-around. Pulling his horse out from the shelter, he slid up onto its bare back and trotted eastward along the road. Denuded trees stood stiff and still on either side as an icy gray sky threatened more snow.

Veneem liked snow. He detested the cold that came with it, but winter was inevitable, and so if it must be cold, let it snow. Let it be a wet snow that stuck to the trees and etched them in white against a darkening sky. Let it snow briefly, frequently, no more than a finger's breadth at a time—just enough to erase the stale tracks and highlight the fresh. At such times small-game hunting was as easy as picking wild berries.

He was perhaps halfway home when a movement, a darting shape in the thicket to his right, caused him to pull up his mount up sharply and peer into the gloom. His searching eyes found nothing. He could have sworn he'd seen a shadow moving in the tangle. A big shadow. Almost big enough to be a hairy. He cursed the overcast sky. If the sun was out he'd have a better chance for a second look ... if there was really anything there to see.

His eyes weren't what they used to be; hadn't been for a few years now. This was no casual admission—it was his most carefully guarded secret. He was a hunter and his eyes were his life, his reputation, his means of support, his protection—

Protection.

He snorted a disgusted puff of fog into the air. If his vision had been better, perhaps the bolt he'd loosed at that charging boar would have found its eye instead of glancing off its skull. Perhaps then the enraged beast wouldn't have butted Nola, half-crushing her chest, nor gored his left arm so badly that Dr. Baken had been forced to remove it at the shoulder. The arm took a full five seasons to regenerate. Nola died of the fever shortly after the accident.

And life had not been quite the same since.

No sound, no further movement came from the thicket. He strained to see but the outlines of objects began to blur beyond two man-lengths. He saw nothing out of the ordinary. Couldn't have been a hairy any-way—they simply weren't seen around here anymore. Just as well ... his crossbow was at home.

Giving the horse's flanks a jab with his leather-shod heels, he con-tinued on his journey. As he turned off the main road onto the path that led to his home, his gaze roamed the ground in search of wheel tracks. Finding none, he began to curse softly and steadily as he rode and was in a foul mood by the time he reached the house.

"Rana!" he called after tethering his horse to the nearest low-hanging branch.

The main structure of the house was a low dome of hardened clay with four small windows—boarded now against the cold—and a single entrance. Pushing aside the double hanging of cured hides that covered the doorway, he entered and called again.

"Rana!"

The girl came out of the smaller of the two sleeping rooms at the rear of the house. She had her father's long face and high cheekbones, but her dark eyes were her mother's. The fire in the hearth flickered off her face and bare scalp, darker green than usual now due to the increased time she was spending indoors. It was warm inside and she wore only a simple tunic that hid her thin, wiry frame and reduced her small breasts to an almost imperceptible swell.

"Something wrong?" She was nineteen summers and spoke with a clear, high voice.

"Yes! The delivery was to have been made at sunrise today. Absolutely no later—the Elders promised!"

"We still have some cheese left and there's plenty of meat."

"That's not the point. The supplies were supposed to be here by now and they are not."

"I'm sure you have a pretty good idea of why they're late," Rana said after a short pause.

"I don't have any such thing," he lied and pulled his jacket off with angry, jerking motions, oblivious to the discomfort he caused in his left arm.

Of course he knew why the supplies were late: The Elders disapproved of Rana and her overt disrespect for their authority, and this was how they chose to show it. They'd never have dared such a tactic while he was First Hunter, but many things had changed since the accident.

His home, for instance. Rana had moved easily and naturally into the void left in the household by her mother's death—preparing his meals, ministering to his arm while it regenerated, doing her best to keep his spirits up. But nothing she could do would fill the void in his spirit or allay his sense of loss or make him feel *complete* again. Only time would do that.

Time was a friend in that respect, and an enemy in others. Time, along with lots of sun-soaking, food, and rest, had replaced his left arm. But the time needed for convalescence had also preyed on his mind. The other hunters had seen to it that he was kept well stocked with provisions during the regenerative period; this was a tradition, but he'd chafed at being an invalid, dependent on the beneficence of others. He had always been a producer and the role of passive consumer did not sit well. He had been First Hunter before the accident. During his period of forced inactivity other hunters had vied for the vacant position. This was natural and he felt no resentment. However, by the time he was ready to go into the field again, his reputation had faded and he'd not found an opportunity to reassert his prominence. To date, no one in the enclave was generally recognized as First Hunter.

In ways he could see and in ways he could not, Rana had changed, too. She was now prone to long absences from home and to loud, pointed questions whenever she attended a plenum. For every point of the Law she had a *Why?* For every Revealed Truth she had a host of doubts. Rana had become a nettle in the collective breeches of the Elders.

And that could prove dangerous.

"They're goading you," she said. "They want you to bring me into line and this is their way of telling you."

"They'd be falling all over each other trying to supply me with farm goods if I were First Hunter again."

She came over and hugged him. "You *are* First Hunter as far as I'm concerned, and you should be treated as such. You bring more meat into the enclave than any two other hunters combined. It's only because of me that they've held back on restoring your title—they don't want a First Hunter who can't control his daughter."

Veneem ran the fingertips of his left hand lightly over the glossy green smoothness of Rana's scalp. He wanted to tell her that she was the center of his life right now, that although her flagrant disrespect for the Elders distressed him, he admired her fire. But he said nothing of his feelings. It never had been his way to show affection, and he couldn't change now.

"I guess I'm lucky you're not a farmer," she said, "or I'd have been taken off a long time ago."

His voice was a low growl. "Then there'd have been some dead Elders a long time ago. The Elders are the voice of God in the world—I believe that and I revere them as such. But they'll never hurt you, Rana. At least not while I breathe." He pushed her gently to arm's length and, resting both hands on her shoulders, gazed at her face. "But why do you do it? Why do you provoke them so?"

"Because everything they tell us is a lie! Everything!" The utter contempt in her voice made him cringe.

"How can you say that with such certainty? The Elders are older and wiser than either of us. And when they make a pronouncement, it is the Revealed Truth of God."

Rana's white teeth chewed briefly on her lower lip. "Some other time, Father."

"Don't toy with them," he said with an expression that matched the grimness of his tone. "You can push them only so far. If you should ever be deemed a threat to the order, even I won't be able to protect you."

The squeak of wheels and the clop of hooves from down the path halted further discussion as they both went to the door. The supply wagon had arrived.

"See?" Rana said, holding the hangings aside. "They've sent it late enough to irk you, but not late enough to bring you after them."

Orth, who had been driving the wagon since Veneem was a child, pulled the pair of horses to a stop in front of the house, set the brake, and slid from the seat—not as smoothly nor as quickly as he had of old, but still with an unmistakable sureness to his movements. He was swathed in furs and blankets to such an extent that he no longer looked quite human. Only his eyes showed through the wraps—quick, dark, darting pupils under heavy green lids ringed with the white lines of age.

"You're late, Orth," Veneem said in a low voice.

He knew he couldn't blame the old driver, but neither could he hide the menace in his mood as he went out to meet him.

"I know." Orth's voice was muffled by the layers of cloth covering the lower half of his face. "The Elders wouldn't let me load up until a short while ago. You're the first stop."

Veneem glanced back at Rana and shrugged. Still clad only in the thin tunic, she came out to help unload the milk, eggs, cheese, and flour.

"Did they give you any reason?" she asked, shivering in the breeze.

"Something about missing supplies. Somebody said it looked like a hairy got into the supply shed last night."

Veneem was reaching for a large wheel of cheese when he heard the word "hairy." His head snapped toward Orth while the rest of his body froze in position.

"A hairy? Last night?"

"Just talk. I wouldn't give it a second—"

Veneem whipped around in one abrupt motion and strode toward the house. Rana trotted after him carrying a basket of eggs.

"Where are you going?"

"After that hairy."

"But you heard Orth: just talk. Probably an excuse to make the wagon late."

"Any other time I'd agree with you. But I saw this one just a short while ago."

Passing through the doorway, he headed directly for the northwest corner of the room where he kept his crossbow.

Rana's eyes were wide as she followed him. "And you didn't go after it?"

"I didn't know it was a hairy then. I wasn't even sure I'd really seen anything. Now I know."

"But you can't leave now. It's past midday already."

He made no reply as he pulled his doubly thick hunting cloak from a peg and threw it over his shoulders. His respirations were rapid and his skin tingled with exhilaration. A hairy! There hadn't been a confirmed sighting in years and the last kill had been longer ago than he cared to remember.

He had to bag this one. It meant reaffirmation of his status as First Hunter. No matter how displeased the Elders were with his daughter, they'd have to publicly recognize his primacy if he brought in a hairy. He knew where to start the hunt—that gave him an edge—but he'd have to leave now if he was to have a chance. By morning the beast would be far from the region.

Rana waited for a reply. Receiving none, she hurried to her room and emerged with another crossbow.

"No, Rana," Veneem said in a matter-of-fact tone. "Not this time."

"*Especially* this time, Father. I've never seen a live hairy and may never get another chance—there just aren't any left around here."

"No." His voice was louder and firmer.

"Yes!" she hissed with sudden, unexplained intensity. "I've handled a bow and followed the trails with you and Mother since I was a child ... I will *not* be left out of this!"

Veneem knew from her tone and defiant posture that there was no point in arguing. She was showing her mother's side: When she made up her mind, that was that.

He girded his cloak around him with the broad belt that held his supply of hunting bolts, hefted his bow, and brushed past her on his way to the door.

"Get your horse then."

Outside, he helped Orth finish unloading the supplies as Rana hurried around to the lean-to behind the house. The supply wagon had been turned and was on its way down the path toward the road by the time she led her bridled horse around to the front.

Veneem was momentarily awed by her appearance. Only two years since her mother's death, yet in that short period she had grown from an awkward adolescent girl into a woman. She stood there, her eyes shining in anticipation, wearing her mother's hunting cloak with her mother's crossbow slung across her shoulder. His eyes suddenly blurred with excess moisture and his breath did not flow as easily as it should. Shuddering, he pulled himself up on the horse's back. Maybe he didn't deserve to be First Hunter again...he seemed to be losing his iron. If he kept on this way, he'd soon be a weepy, wilted old man before his time.

Expression set and teeth clenched, he gathered up the reins, gave the horse a harder than necessary kick, and raced off down the path. Rana hopped lightly onto her own mount and took chase.

They rode west at full gallop along the road toward the enclave center until Veneem pulled sharply to a halt and dismounted near a high thicket. Rana overrode the spot and walked her horse back. Veneem pushed his way into the chaotic tangle of leafless branches, thrashing about and cursing as the smaller twigs, stiff with winter, poked at him from all sides. Finally—

Tracks of cloth-wrapped feet. Tracks everywhere. Cheese rinds, too. It had been here. No doubt about it. Veneem followed the tracks a few paces into the trees, then called back over his shoulder.

"I knew it! Rana, bring the horses around!"

She led the animals back down the road until she found a break in the brush, then guided them through. Veneem awaited her in a clearing behind the thicket, a short distance from the road.

"Tether the horses there. It's headed toward the big rocks."

Rana did as she was bid and hurried after him. The trail was easy to follow.

"Did it ever occur to you," she said, coming abreast and matching his stride with her long thin legs, "that a hairy may be more than just a dumb animal?" She watched him carefully as he replied.

"Never said the hairies were dumb. In fact, they're the craftiest of all animals, as well as the tastiest. That's why they're such a prize."

"But the way they wrap their feet and bodies against the cold... doesn't that indicate a high level of intelligence to you?"

"Just imitation. They watch us, they steal our food and materials and copy what we do. They're just game animals. It's Revealed Truth."

"Revealed by whom?"

"Are we going to have to go through that again? You're courting sacrilege—just like at the last plenum when you made everyone so uncomfortable with your impertinence."

"Who revealed the 'truth' that the hairies are animals?" she repeated in a dogged tone.

"Don't ask foolish questions." His voice took on the singsong tone of a recitation: "God made us in his image and speaks through the Elders to guide us back to our place as the lords of creation. Revealed Truths are the word of God."

"God made us, did he?" A taunting smile seeped onto her face. "If that's so, then we're following the tracks of God."

This statement brought Veneem to an abrupt halt. Rana, too, stopped. They faced each other in silence, their breath steaming, streaming from nostrils and parted lips.

"What madness is this?" he said in a hoarse voice. "Why do you torment me with this blasphemy?"

"I don't mean to torment you, believe me. I just want you to know what I know. And now, while you're hunting a hairy...it seems to be the best time to tell you."

"Tell me what? That our most highly prized game animal is actually our Creator?" He started walking toward the rocks again. "I'm going to have Doctor Baken take a look at you tomorrow. Maybe he can come up with an elixir or something to—"

"Baken is my source of information!"

Once more Veneem stopped short. The answers to a number of niggling questions were suddenly clear. The doctor's inquiries about Rana this morning were also explained.

"Baken, eh? That's where you've been going when you disappear for a whole day." He snorted. "Who'd have thought? So he's the one who's been filling your head with this garbage. I'll have to have a little talk with Doctor Baken."

"He's a good man. We became friends while he was treating you and Mother after the accident."

"He's a fool and worse if he's taught you to blaspheme!"

Veneem resumed his pursuit of the hairy but found it almost impossible to focus his attention on the trail. Dr. Baken had somehow corrupted Rana's thinking. That in itself was bad. But more than a few ideas were at stake here: The heretical views Rana now held could endanger her life. That concerned him most. If she should ever start spouting such madness at a plenum—and she was impulsive enough to do just that given the proper provocation—the Elders would be duty bound to silence her. Forever.

And that would mean his end, as well. For he'd never allow anything to happen to her while he could raise a hand in her defense. She was all he had left. He had no one he could truly call a close friend— Nola had been that and a wife, too. They had formed a self-sufficient unit, the two of them—a threesome after Rana arrived. There had never been any need for outsiders.

Now they were two; no matter how wrong she was, they would not be divided.

They arrived at the big rocks, a pile of huge stone shards that rose above the forest and stretched away into the haze of the south. Veneem searched along the base of the formation until he found the place where the tracks disappeared.

"He started to climb here."

As he began to hoist himself up on the first rock in pursuit, Rana laid a gentle hand on his shoulder.

"Baken has books."

Veneem dropped back to the ground again but remained facing away from his daughter. Utter hopelessness began to settle upon him. Rana was getting in deeper and deeper. Hiding books from the Elders was punishable by death. He ground his teeth in frustration. He couldn't understand her—her constant questioning, her poking into things she should leave alone. Life was good under the Elders if you just tended to your business.

His voice was barely audible as he spoke the law: "Books are forbidden. They're to be turned over to the Elders as soon as they're found."

"That's so we won't find out what's inside them. Their authority would be destroyed if it became generally known that we're the descendants—worse, yet, the *creations*—of the hairies!"

"*Madness!*" He still refused to look at her.

"No! Baken's learned to read some of the books and he's teaching me. He's learned things. Incredible things. Things that go against everything we've ever been taught."

"I have no wish to hear them," he said as he found a foothold and began climbing the rocks.

Rana scrambled after him. "You're going to have to listen to me, Father. Baken told me of the time some hunters brought in the carcass of a pregnant bitch hairy. She'd been nearing her time when they got her and he was able to examine the unborn baby. He says it looked just like we do at birth!"

"Be quiet!" Veneem said angrily. He was climbing as quickly as he could, whether in pursuit of the hairy or to escape his daughter's blasphemies, he wasn't quite sure. "The beast will hear us coming!"

But Rana refused to be put off and kept pace. "Did you know that we're all born with pink skin and hair—hair on our heads and above our eyes? Sometimes fine hair on our arms and legs? And that our skin doesn't turn green until we've been exposed to light? Nobody talks about that...the same way nobody admits that if you took a hairy, sheared his fuzz, and stained him green, he'd look as human as we do! It's obvious to anyone with eyes that we come from the same stock."

Veneem halted his climb and turned to face Rana. Leaning his back against a rock, he studied her a moment before speaking. He hid his anger and adopted the tone of a patient parent speaking to a rather dull-witted child. He raised his forearms diagonally before him, right angles at the elbows, his palms on edge toward Rana. The tips of the right and left middle fingers touched lightly at eye level to form a point.

"This," he said, moving the right arm, "is the animal kingdom. This"—the left arm moved—"is the plant kingdom. At the apex are you and I and our kin: humanity, the highest form of life, the fusion of plant and animal. We have the best attributes of both kingdoms. In lean times we can take a certain amount of nourishment from the sun, and should we lose a limb we can grow a new one. No animal can do that. Yet we can move around and go where we wish, use our hands to build, and eat and drink in the winter months when the sun is weak. No plant can do that."

He sighed. "Don't you see? Not only does what you say go against Revealed Truth, it goes against common sense as well. The hairies belong solely to the animal kingdom. We are superior to them in every way. How could *they* have created us?"

"Baken says—"

"'Baken says'!" he mimicked. "'Baken says'! I'm sick of hearing about what Doctor Baken says! I'm after a game animal now—it's my job. If you cannot be silent, go wait by the horses!"

Rana persisted. "Baken says that long ago the hairies took a cell from a—"

"Cell? What's a cell?"

"As Baken explains it, it's one of the uncountable little capsules, invisibly small, that make up the bodies of every living thing."

It was Veneem's turn to taunt. "Look at me! How many 'cells' do you see?"

She said, "When you stand on a hill and look at the beach, how many grains of sand do you see?" She did not wait for an answer. "As I was saying, the hairies took a cell from a plant and removed its nucleus—that's the thing in the center of the cell that controls it—and replaced it with the nucleus from a cell of a hairy. For a while it was just a curiosity, but then they learned how to grow an entire organism from one of these cells. And then we were born. The hairies are the real humans...we're their creations."

Veneem made a contemptuous, snorting noise. "And you mock me for blindly accepting the teaching of the Elders! Look what you've just said: You've told me of something called a 'cell' which you admit you've never seen—*can't* see—and then about something else inside this 'cell.' Then you tell me that the beasts who have to steal food from us to survive the winter actually grew us from one of these mythical little capsules. Really, Rana! Who's the fool?"

"We're all fools for believing the Elders for so long! We—"

Veneem's right hand shot out and covered her mouth. A light shower of tiny sand particles had begun to fall, sliding and bouncing down from the rocks above, sprinkling their heads and shoulders.

"He's up there!" he whispered. "And if he has ears he's heard us."

Unslinging his bow, Veneem drew the gut string back to the last notch, set the trigger, and put one of his heaviest bolts in the groove. To his left was a break in the rocks, about a man-length or so wide. He sidled over and peered into it. Empty. A high-walled gully sloped upward for a short distance, then banked off to the right. With weapon at ready, he began his ascent.

The floor of the gully was smooth—it probably served as a water run-off during the spring—with patches of ice in scattered recesses. He heard a sudden loud crunch from up around the bend, then nothing. The sound was repeated, followed by a series of lesser noises, and then a large boulder bounded around the curve in the gorge and came rolling at him. Veneem gauged its path and ran upward toward the bend, allowing the stone to bounce off the far wall and pass him on his left.

Reaching the curve, he saw it—a buck hairy. Tall, thin, full mane on head and face; his torso and lower legs were wrapped in tattered cloth and he had just kicked loose a second boulder. With no time to aim properly, Veneem chanced a quick shot from waist level. The hairy howled in pain and clutched its left thigh as Veneem leaped to avoid the oncoming stone juggernaut.

Too late. He misjudged its ungainly wobbling roll and it struck him a glancing blow on the rib cage as it passed. Pain lanced up to his left shoulder and down along his flank as he fell on his back and began to slide down the gully headfirst. For a few heartbeats he could not draw a breath. Then, as his oxygen-starved mind was about to panic, air began to gush in and out of his lungs in ragged gusts. He hauled himself into a sitting position and waited for the pain to subside.

Rana had heard the wail of the wounded hairy and she now peered around the corner of the gully. Seeing her father leaning against the rocks with his hand pressed against his ribs, she dropped her bow and scurried up to his side.

"Are you all right?" Her expression was frantic.

Still gasping, Veneem nodded and pointed back the way they had come. "Help me up. I wounded him but he still might be dangerous."

Rana took his bow and his arm and led him back to safety. When they reached their previous position, Veneem sank to his knees.

"We'll let him bleed."

"Where'd you get him?"

"Leg."

Her eyes darted back and forth as her mind seemed to race. "Then we can take him alive!"

"*Never!*" Veneem was getting his wind back.

"We must! We may never get another chance like this to learn the truth about the hairies."

"I already *know* the truth!" He spat the words. "And it's part of the law that all hairies must be hunted down and killed like the wild game they are!"

Rana seemed ready to leap at him.

"How many 'game animals' have set a trap for you, Father? That's not just a wild beast up there!"

Veneem rose slowly, painfully to his feet. "No more of your fever dreams, please. I've more pressing matters to attend to. Silence, now!"

"No! I want you to think about what I've said before you kill it."

"I *am* thinking and I've *been* thinking. *You* must think! If the hairies had the power and the intelligence to create us, what happened to them? Where is their mighty civilization? Answer me that!"

"Baken says"—Veneem growled at the name—"that in their toying with the stuff of life they somehow altered one of the things that make us sick and a great plague swept the world. A famine followed. After that, those who didn't get sick or starve to death went mad, killing each other and destroying their cities. We survived. The plague had no effect on us and we could augment our nourishment by sun-soaking. We multiplied while they died.

"Only a few hairies are left. They hide in the ruined cities. That's why we're forbidden to go there—because we'd find out that the 'Truths' of the Elders are lies and their hold would be broken!"

"Very clever," Veneem said with a slow, sad shake of his head. "Doctor Baken has managed to twist everything. Everyone knows, and Revealed Truth confirms, that *we* built the cities ages ago. They are now forbidden because they were the cause of our fall from grace. When we built them we separated ourselves from the land and the sun. For that we were punished—the cities were destroyed by God and we were banished from them forever."

He rubbed his injured ribs gingerly, then snatched his bow from Rana.

"No more talk! I'm going to find another way up there, and when I get to him I'll finish him."

Rana watched him briefly as he began to reload the weapon, then wheeled and ran to the edge of the gully where she had dropped her own bow. After checking to see that the bolt was still in place, she called over her shoulder in a low voice:

"I'm going up this way. If I have to hit him in the other leg to bring him down, I will. But I'm going to take him alive."

Veneem's voice was strained as he jolted forward. "Stay out of there—he's still dangerous!"

Rana ignored him and entered the gully. He finished loading as quickly as he could and went after her. He watched as she moved swiftly, cautiously up the center of the gorge. She was almost to the bend when Veneem saw the stone. It was smaller than its predecessors—about the size of a human head—and had been thrown rather than rolled. It bounced once on the granite floor, then flew straight for Rana. She made to dive out of its way but slipped on an icy patch and fell against the far wall.

The bones of her right foot made a sickening noise as they were crushed.

Rana writhed on her side, her face contorted in agony. Low guttural sounds, half moan, half grunt, escaped between her clenched teeth as she tried to move the stone off her foot.

After a shocked, frozen instant, Veneem broke into a run and passed Rana without a second look. He had to reach the hairy before the next rock came. Rounding the bend, he saw the beast desperately trying to dislodge a larger stone, one that would surely finish Rana if it started to roll. But it was wounded—fresh blood covered its left leg—and its strength wasn't up to the task. When it saw the green fury that was Veneem charging up the gully, it began to retreat.

The hairy clawed and scrambled along the ledge, its wounded leg dragging like an anchor. Veneem thought he saw something almost like human fear in its eyes as it glanced over its shoulder at him, heard something almost human about the gibberish that burst from its mouth, sensed something almost human in the way it rolled on its back and frantically waved its hands as he stood within arm's length and aimed his crossbow at its head.

But it died like any other animal when the bolt split its skull.

"I think you're going to lose it," Veneem said as he gave Rana's foot a final inspection. It was swollen, misshapen, the skin had split in three places and showed numerous areas of brownish discoloration.

A fire was blazing in the hearth, dancing light off the smooth green of Rana's skin as she sat before it. Her wounded foot rested on a folded blanket which in turn rested on a short stool. The bleeding had stopped. The pain had not.

"You'll have to get Baken in the morning," she said.

"I'll not have that man near you."

"He's the only doctor in the enclave! If the foot must come off, he'll know where to cut. I won't let anyone else touch me."

Knowing she was right but refusing to admit it, Veneem said nothing. He turned to the hearth and rotated the spit. He was tired. It had been no easy task to carry Rana to the horses, then fetch the dead hairy, then guide all home. He was feeling his age, especially in his ribs and his left shoulder—there was blood on the dressing over this morning's incision but he hadn't got around to changing it yet.

But at least everything was in its place now. Rana was warming herself by the fire, the carcass of the hairy was dressed and hanging in the cold shed while Veneem roasted a piece of it on the spit. He had cut off the right shank as a celebratory feast of sorts; the rest would go to the central supply shed in the morning. A glance at Rana's wound and he realized there was probably something symbolic in the cut of meat he chose.

He sliced off a small piece and dropped it into a wooden bowl which he then placed in his daughter's lap.

"Come. Eat. You'll need all the nourishment you can get when regeneration starts, especially since there's no sunlight worth mentioning this time of year."

"Not hungry," she said. She was physically and emotionally spent and Veneem did his best to be solicitous.

"Of course you are. You haven't had this much activity in a long, long time. You must be ravenous. And this has always been your favorite."

"No." She swallowed hard—her salivary glands had been activated by the sight and smell of the meat. "You didn't have to kill it."

"Yes, I did. And for more than one reason." He squatted before her and took her hand. "First of all, it hurt you. Nothing can hurt you and be allowed to live. Second, if we had brought it back alive as you wished—and I'm not really sure we could have—you'd have begun publicly spouting the madness that Baken's put into your head. And that would mean the end of you. The Elders would have no choice then but to order your death. Third, because this catch makes me First Hunter beyond any doubt. And last..." He paused, catching and holding her gaze. "And last, I killed the hairy because it's the law that all hairies are to be killed. They're very scarce now and we might never see one again. But if I should come upon another, I'll kill it. And that settles the matter. I want no more discussion on it. Eat your dinner."

Rana sighed and picked up the piece of meat. It was hot and firm with a thin coating of grease that oozed onto her fingers. She nibbled at it. No sense in letting such a delicacy go to waste.

Back in 1981, Alan Ryan was editing *Perpetual Light*, an anthology for Warner Books comprised of stories about the religious experience. Over the years, Alan and I had compared our Jesuit educations—I'm a graduate of Xavier in Manhattan (yes... I was a Subway Commando) and Georgetown—and he thought I'd be an apt contributor.

The Jesuits taught us to think, to question, never to take anything purely at face value. They taught me to ask the next question long before Ted Sturgeon introduced me to the phrase. One result of all that thinking and questioning, at least for me, was an awareness of the negative effects of most religious movements, and I wound up questioning myself right out of the Church.

I used a variation of the BioCog unit as far back as *Healer* in the mid-seventies. The concept became a staple of cyberfiction.

"Be Fruitful" was the first story completed on my then brand-new Apple II+ using Applewriter I, a word processor that seems Paleolithic now, but was downright miraculous then.

The story was inspired by the rise of the religious right and the Moral Majority in the late 1970s. They've lost much of their clout nowadays, but never count them out. And Procreationism would be right up their alley.

Be Fruitful and Multiply

Saw God last week. Or maybe it was just St. Bartholomew. Looked more like Bartholomew, but could have been God.

He came to me in the night, a vision dangling from my ceiling, twisting slowly in the air like a corpse hanging from a gibbet. Said the birth rate was down. *Down.* Told me to warn everyone, especially the Church Elders. Told me to warn them right away.

But I've been so busy lately.

Actually, I'm afraid.

(11:40...about twenty minutes to spare)

They'll think I'm crazy. Paranoid, they'll say. But not if I can get everything organized. Not if I can show them in black and white that there's a plot afoot, a plot against the Church, a monstrous conspiracy that threatens everything generations of us have worked for. Been meaning to get organized for so long now, but can't seem to get going.

Maybe that's part of the conspiracy, too. Maybe—

For Birth's sake, don't start blaming your own foot-dragging on someone else. Next thing you know, your stubbed toe is someone else's fault...then the pimple on your chin...then your backache. Soon you're crazy.

I'm not crazy. My church, the only church, the Church of the Divine Imperative, is in danger. God told me so Himself. I may be the only one who knows. But I can prove it. At least I think I can. With God's help and without too much hindrance from Satan and His minions, the Elders will hear and believe. And act.

But got to get organized. Got to sound sane. I have my folks' files and scrapbooks from the old days. That'll help. If I can put the plot in historical perspective, the Elders will be more receptive.

To work. Start with a quote from St. Bartholomew. That'll grab them. They can't turn away from the words of the man who was the inspiration for the Church. And his words are as timely now as they were forty-odd years ago:

...So I say again to you, the Divine Imperative was God's first command to the first man and woman: "Be fruitful and multiply." This was not a casual remark. God created the earth as no more than a staging area. This planet, this life—they are no more than a first evolutionary step toward the ultimate destiny God has planned for His faithful. Nothing more than a staging area. In all the troubles through which you will pass, never forget that.

Words to remember, to be sure. Especially now.

After Bartholomew, how about these old pictures...everybody's so plump-ugly. Population was so sparse back then I guess they had to eat more than they needed. Almost obscene to look that well fed. No worry about looking like that nowadays...

Here's a magazine article from back then. The non-believers did a lot of empty speculation as the movement started to take hold. This looks like a good one:

...and sociologists are at a loss to explain it. Most of the Church's members were raised in the one- and two-child family units that have been the norm. Yet the whole thrust of the Church of the Divine Imperative runs contrary to the trends of the past few decades. Instead of limiting family size out of concern for the environment and a desire to pursue more personal goals of self-fulfillment,

*the Procreationists, as they call themselves, have laid aside their cultural, reli-
gious, and social backgrounds to band together in a compulsive drive to bring
as many new lives as possible into the world.*

It all started with a pamphlet called The Next Plateau *by an enigmatic
man known only as Bartholomew who is believed to have sprung from the
ranks of the now-defunct Christian Right. He is the source of Procreationist
theology—a dizzying mixture of right-to-life slogans, Far Eastern mysticism,
and rigid fundamentalism. Bartholomew's writings and passionate speeches
fired up a significant segment of a generation. Procreationism has caught on.
The Church of the Divine Imperative is spreading. Hopefully, for all our sakes,
it will be short-lived.*

Time Magazine

But we showed them—or at least my parents did. Being second-
generation Procreationist, I spent most of my life listening to my folks
and their friends swap tales about the early days of the Church. Must
have been exciting to be in the vanguard, to be shaping history. Wish I
could have been there.

The glory of it! They were outsiders in their day, struggling against
the Satan-inspired population-control forces that ran the governments
of the world. Hard to imagine today, with everybody Procreationist,
but back in the old days they were a tiny, persecuted minority. The
bureaucratic machinery and its allies in the media did their damned-
est—an appropriate word, that—to curb the growth of the Church. Said
we threatened to unbalance the environment, accelerate pollution, and
trigger famines. Ha!

Goes to show they never understood us. Tried psychoanalytical
parlor tricks to explain our growth. They were desperate for any explanation other than the truth: It was God's will.

Listen to this fool:

*These people are scared. They want a way out—that is all there is to it.
They look around and see shortages, unrest, economic and political uncertainty
on all sides, and it scares them. But do they pitch in and help? No! They make
things worse! They turn to mysticism and embrace practices that exacerbate
the very conditions which frighten them. It's mass insanity, that's what it is.*

And it's got to be stopped!

Senator Henry Mifflin (D-Neb)

Congressional Record

See? Never understood. The air is thick now, true, because the productive capacity of the entire race must be strained to the utmost to feed, clothe, and house us all. Food is scarce, yes, but there's enough to keep us going until the life force reaches the critical point, the signal to God that we are ready to be transported *en masse* to a higher plane of existence. Even non-believers will be translated to the next plateau. *Then* they'll believe.

Coming soon. I can feel it. We all can.

(11:48…better keep moving)

Getting sidetracked here. Let's see…the senator's remarks make a good lead-in to government attempts to control the Church. Knowing that the Church was doing God's work, the followers of Satan used the governments of the world to suppress it. Islamic and communist countries were the most successful—they simply outlawed us and that was that. But wherever there was a spark of democracy, we flourished. And once we were able to organize the faithful into voting blocks, no elected official could stand against us for long. Even after we had gained majority power, anti-Procreationist legislation was still introduced, but was consistently defeated when the final vote came around.

These headlines from some old newsstats ought to be dramatic enough:

BIRTH CONTROL
BILL ABORTED
New York *Daily News*

DEFEAT OF POPULATION CONTROL BILL A CERTAINTY
President Decries Dementia Sweeping Western World
New York Times

I was born three days after that last headline. Government opposition to the Church folded completely during the first five years of my life. By that time, every head of state and virtually every elected official was a Procreationist. Governments of the free world no longer hindered us because we *became* those governments. Soon, even the inner circles of the communist politburos came under our sway. The Islamic world took longer, but eventually saw the error of its ways, trading Mohammed for Bartholomew. The world was fast becoming Procreationist.

The media remained a problem for a while longer, probably because they were so full of queers. Queers feared us the most, and with good reason. They knew they were living in defiance of the Divine Imperative: They could not be fruitful and multiply, therefore they were an abomination. They offend God and all those who believe in God. But we soon put them in their proper place.

A golden age ensued. The Church continued to expand. It was not enough to have most of humanity as members of the Church— we wanted *everyone*. We inducted new members constantly. Some were reluctant at first, but eventually they saw the Light. Had to. If you weren't with us, you were most certainly against us. The Divine Imperative was frustrated and the goal delayed by anyone who refused to reproduce.

A holy time was upon us. There were pockets of resistance—heretics, die-hard reactionaries who refused to change their ways, queers, feminists—but they didn't last long. All the world was soon one with the Church. Or so I thought.

Something sinister occurred around my ninth birthday. No one recognized it as a threat then, but looking back now I can see the hand of the Devil.

This is the earliest report I could find in the library files:

LEARNING DEVICE TO SEEK MASS MARKET

London (AP)—Cognition Industries, Ltd., has announced development of a new microcircuit which will make mass distribution of its BioCognitive Learning Unit economically feasible. "It's a major breakthrough," said a spokesman for the Sheffield-based corporation. "Ten years from now there won't be a home without one."
New York Times

The company spokesman was wrong: Nearly every home contained a BioCog unit within *five* years, attached to the family vid set with up to a dozen headsets plugged in at once at the educational hours.

After a decade of widespread use, the results were astounding: ten-year-olds doing university-level work, autistic minds reached, brain-damaged kids formerly considered uneducable learning simple math and reading skills. Efforts were made to get BioCog units into as many homes as possible in every corner of the world. A triumphal time for the Church. Not only was the life force growing at an unprecedented rate, but our intellectual powers were increasing beyond our wildest dreams. All for the greater glory of God when He translated us to the next plateau.

Everyone was on guard, of course, for possible misuse of the BioCog device. Mind control was the big bugaboo at first, but that was proved impossible. On a subtler level, however, there was concern over the device's potential for influencing attitudes. Stringent laws were passed to assure the faithful that anti-Procreation ideas would never be put into their heads, nor into the heads of their children while they learned.

All went well until last year...

...last year...

Gayle and I produced our fourth life last year, a boy. Still remember how I felt as I cradled him in my arms, knowing I'd helped add another tiny increment to the life force, bringing us all that much closer to our goal...

—sidetracked again. Have to concentrate.

Last year, by the time of our fourth, the BioCog unit had become a part of our daily lives. Like all devout Procreationists, we were learning all we could before Translation, to be better prepared for whatever the next plateau might bring. The educational programs were all uniformly effective. And uniformly dull.

Then *The Bobby & Laura Show* made its debut on the late-night vid.

(11:55...*still some time left*)

Warm in here...palms sweaty...

The show was controversial from the start. A young couple—Laura, a sweet-looking blonde, Bobby darkly virile, both looking mid-twentyish and dressed in light blue kimonos—had been given an hour to explore methods of enhancing the emotional and physical responses of the procreational act. Discussion would take up the first half of the show; the final half would involve a demonstration via the BioCog unit.

Don't quite recall the details of the discussion that premier night, but the demonstration was unforgettable. I remember the screen dimming as we were instructed to don our headsets. Could see vague shapes of Bobby and Laura disrobing. Then the shapes came together and my body was electrified. Could almost feel Laura's hands on me. Sensations built slowly to a crescendo that was almost unbearable, leaving me weak and limp afterward. I remember turning to Gayle to find her staring at me with an odd expression on her face—she hadn't put her headset on.

Tried to explain it to her. Tried to convey the sensual and emotional warmth that flooded through me, but she just made a face and said it didn't seem right. Took her in my arms right then and showed her how right it was.

Gayle was hardly unique in her doubts about the propriety of the show. Many members of the Church felt there was something scandalous about it. The ensuing investigation revealed that Bobby and Laura were orthodox Procreationists with three lives—a little girl and a set of twin boys—to their credit. Their stated purpose was advancement of Church teachings into new areas. They wanted to explore all the roads of the procreational process in order to follow better the Divine Imperative. They had experimented and had discovered that the BioCog units could influence more than the cognitive areas of the brain, so they were employing the unit's abilities in the emotional and sensual areas as an educational adjunct to their discussions.

Their program was quickly cleared of any wrongdoing. It was, after all, discreetly staged and played only at a late hour. And besides, the reasoning went, weren't they merely doing God's work?

Aided by the notoriety of the investigation, the second *Bobby & Laura* drew the largest audience in the history of this country. Even Gayle put on a headset. She later agreed that it was a remarkably moving experience. Such a feeling of warmth, of being loved, of being needed, of belonging.

With the blessing of the Church, the show quickly moved into all the foreign mass media, vidcast at midnight in every time zone around the world. Dubbing or subtitles were used in the first half; no translation was necessary for the second. Billions began to look forward to the show each night. Crave it, in fact. Night shifts in factories were interrupted for *Bobby & Laura*. Even stories of hospital patients left unattended during the show.

I remember wondering about Bobby and Laura. Don't care how God-loving and righteous a couple is, they can't generate that level of emotional and physical intensity on a nightly basis. They either had a method of enhancing the signals they transmitted, or had recorded a library of their best procreational sessions and vidcast these to the eager billions wearing their headsets and waiting for the screen to dim.

So what? I'd ask myself. Only showed they were as human as the rest of us. The purpose of their show was not to set some sort of endurance record.

Still went through spasms of uneasiness, though. These would usually hit me after the nightly show was over and Gayle and I were falling asleep in each other's arms, spent without having moved a muscle.

Bobby & Laura had been on for well over a year when it came to me that we hadn't conceived our fifth life as planned. We both knew the reason: Our procreational activity had ebbed to the point where the only thing we did in bed was sleep. That was wrong. Evil. Contrary to everything we believed in. We felt guilty and ashamed.

And confused. Couldn't understand what was happening to me. Loved God and the Church as much as ever. My faith was still strong. Hard for me to admit this, but I'd lost all desire for Gayle as my procreational partner.

I wanted Laura.

Noticed Gayle's righteousness slipping, too. Did Bobby fill her thoughts as Laura did mine?

(11:58 ... better hurry)

Guilt made me keep all this to myself. Even noticed some hesitation to attend weekly services. Didn't feel as if I was doing my part to follow God's will. But forced myself to go.

Now I know I'm not alone. The vision told me the birth rate is down. Others have been afflicted as I have.

And I know why.

The Devil is sly and ever active. We thought the enemies of the Church had been eliminated. Thought them dispersed and discredited as heretics and blasphemers. Wrong. All wrong! They merely went underground and have been insidiously undermining God's will all along.

And their master plot is *Bobby & Laura!*

Had my suspicions for a long time now, but last week's vision convinced me: We have all become sensually jaded and emotionally dependent on that show. We are exposed to such peaks of pleasure and intimacy via the BioCog unit that the human contact demanded by God seems flat and ordinary.

THE BIOCOG IS AN INSTRUMENT OF THE DEVIL! THROUGH IT WE HAVE BECOME ADDICTED! EMOTIONALLY, PSYCHOLOGICALLY, PHYSIOLOGICALLY, AND NEUROLOGICALLY DEPENDENT ON BOBBY AND LAURA!

But not for long. I'm going to expose this hellish scheme tomorrow. I'll put an end to *The Bobby & Laura Show* for good. I'll reveal them for what they are. *(Only a minute to go)*

Exposure of the plot will mean no more Laura for me, but that doesn't matter. God's will is what matters. I can break this addiction and return to the True Path. We all can. I don't need the show. I can wash it away like sweat and dirt, leaving myself pure and clean for the coming Translation. (*Midnight*)

    Bobby & Laura is starting…Gayle's by the set … I'm going to join her … just for a few minutes…then I'll get back to this…

    …promise…

    …just as soon as the show's over… (*I'm coming, Laura!*)

I think of "Soft" as an AIDS story, possibly one of the very first pieces of fiction influenced by the syndrome.

I was a fairly regular reader of the CDC's *Morbidity and Mortality Report Weekly* back then and I remember seeing the 6/5/81 issue in which patients with the syndrome later to be known as AIDS were first described. The term wasn't coined until more than a year later ("HIV" came later still). Back when I began writing "Soft," AIDS was thought to be a result of the constellation of infections that were part and parcel of the urban male homosexual's life-style. There was talk also of a possible single etiologic agent, but that was only theory then.

Although directly triggered by a bodybuilder's remark that the whole country was going soft (I can be very literal at times), the story grew out of these reports. The real-life confusion seen in AIDS's early years is reflected in the confusion and vacillation displayed by the story's authorities regarding the etiology of the softness.

Even though not a pleasant piece, it's one of my most reprinted, even illustrated for a graphic anthology. *Publishers Weekly* called it "vivid and viscerally wrenching."

That's what I was shooting for.

Soft

I was lying on the floor watching TV and exercising what was left of my legs when the newscaster's jaw collapsed. He was right in the middle of the usual plea for anybody who thought they were immune to come to Rockefeller Center when—*pflumpf!*—the bottom of his face went soft. I burst out laughing.

"Daddy!" Judy said, shooting me a razorblade look from her wheelchair.

I shut up.

She was right. Nothing funny about a man's tongue wiggling

around in the air snake-like while his lower jaw flopped down in front of his throat like a sack of Jell-O and his bottom teeth jutted at the screen crowns-on, rippling like a line of buoys on a bay. A year ago I would have gagged. But I've changed in ways other than physical since this mess began, and couldn't help feeling good about one of those pretty-boy newsreaders going soft right in front of the camera. I almost wished I had a bigger screen so I could watch 21 color inches of the scene. He was barely visible on our 5-inch black-and-white.

The room filled with white noise as the screen went blank. Someone must have taken a look at what was going out on the airwaves and pulled the plug. Not that many people were watching anyway.

I flipped the set off to save the batteries. Batteries were as good as gold now. *Better* than gold. Who wanted gold nowadays?

I looked over at Judy and she was crying softly. Tears slid down her cheeks.

"Hey, hon—"

"I can't help it, Daddy. I'm so *scared!*"

"Don't be, Jude. Don't worry. Everything will work out, you'll see. We've got this thing licked, you and me."

"How can you be so sure?"

"Because it hasn't progressed in weeks. It's over for us—we've got immunity."

She glanced down at her legs, then quickly away. "It's already too late for me."

I reached over and patted my dancer on the hand. "Never too late for you, shweetheart," I said in my best Bogart. That got a tiny smile out of her.

We sat there in the silence, each thinking our own thoughts. The newsreader had said the cause of the softness had been discovered: a virus, a freak mutation that disrupted the calcium matrix of bones.

Yeah. Sure. That's what they said last year when the first cases cropped up in Boston. A virus. But they never isolated the virus, and the softness spread all over the world. So they began searching for "a subtle and elusive environmental toxin." They never pinned that one down either.

Now we were back to a virus. Who cared? It didn't matter. Judy and I had beat it. Whether we had formed the right antibodies or the right antitoxin was just a stupid academic question. The process had been arrested in us. Sure, it had done some damage, but it wasn't doing any more, and that was the important thing. We'd never be the same, but we were going to live.

"But that man," Judy said, nodding toward the TV. "He said they were looking for people in whom the disease had started and then stopped. That's us, Dad. They said they need to examine people like us so they can find out how to fight it, maybe develop a serum against it. We should—"

"Judy-Judy-Judy!" I said in Cary Grantese to hide my annoyance. How many times did I have to go over this? "We've been through all this before. I told you: It's too late for them. Too late for everybody but us immunes."

I didn't want to discuss it—Judy didn't understand about those kind of people, how you can't deal with them.

"I want you to take me down there," she said in the tone she used when she wanted to be stubborn. "If you don't want to help, okay. But I do."

"No!" I said that louder than I wanted to and she flinched. More softly: "I know those people. I worked all those years in the Health Department. They'd turn us into lab specimens. They'll suck us dry and use our immunity to try and save themselves."

"But I want to help somebody! I don't want us to be the last two people on earth!"

She began to cry again.

Judy was frustrated. I could understand that. She was unable to leave the apartment by herself and probably saw me at times as a dictator who had her at his mercy. And she was frightened, probably more frightened than I could imagine. She was only eighteen and everyone else she had ever known in her life—including her mother—was dead.

I hoisted myself into the chair next to her and put my arm around her shoulders. She was the only person in the world who mattered to me. That had been true even before the softness began.

"We're not alone. Take George, for example. And I'm sure there are plenty of other immunes around who are hiding like us. When the weather warms up, we'll find each other and start everything over new. But until then, we can't allow the bloodsuckers to drain off whatever it is we've got that protects us.

She nodded without saying anything. I wondered if she was agreeing with me or just trying to shut me up.

"Let's eat," I said with a gusto I didn't really feel.

"Not hungry."

"Got to keep up your strength. We'll have soup. How's that sound?"

She smiled weakly. "Okay...soup."

I forgot and almost tried to stand up. Old habits die hard. My lower legs were hanging over the edge of the chair like a pair of sand-filled dancer's tights. I could twitch the muscles and see them ripple under the skin, but a muscle is pretty useless unless it's attached to a bone, and the bones down there were gone.

I slipped off my chair to what was left of my knees and shuffled over to the stove. The feel of those limp and useless leg muscles squishing under me was repulsive but I was getting used to it.

It hit the kids and old people first, supposedly because their bones were a little soft to begin with, then moved on to the rest of us, starting at the bottom and working its way up—sort of like a Horatio Alger success story.

At least that was the way it worked in most people. There were exceptions, of course, like that newscaster. I had followed true to form: My left lower leg collapsed at the end of last month; my right went a few days later. It wasn't a terrible shock. My feet had already gone soft so I knew the legs were next.

Besides, I'd heard the sound.

The sound comes in the night when all is quiet. It starts a day or two before a bone goes. A soft sound, like someone gently crinkling cellophane inside your head. No one else can hear it. Only you. I think it comes from the bone itself—from millions of tiny fractures slowly interconnecting into a mosaic that eventually causes the bone to dissolve into mush. Like an on-rushing train far, far away can be heard if you press your ear to the track, so the sound of each microfracture transmits from bone to bone until it reaches your middle ear.

I haven't heard the sound in almost four weeks. I thought I did a couple of times and broke out in a cold, shaking sweat, but no more of my bones have gone. Neither have Judy's. The average case goes from normal person to lump of jelly in three to four weeks. Sometimes it takes longer, but there's always a steady progression. Nothing more has happened to me or Judy since last month.

Somehow, some way, we're immune.

With my lower legs dragging behind me, I got to the counter of the kitchenette and kneed my way up the stepstool to where I could reach things. I filled a pot with water—at least the pressure was still up—and set it on the Sterno stove. With gas and electricity long gone, Sterno was a lifesaver.

While waiting for the water to boil I went to the window and looked out. The late afternoon March sky was full of dark gray clouds streaking to the east. Nothing moving on West 16th Street one floor below but a few windblown leaves from God-knows-where. I glanced across at the windows of George's apartment, looking for movement but found none, then back down to the street below.

I hadn't seen anybody but George on the street for ages, hadn't seen or smelled smoke in well over two months. The last fires must have finally burned themselves out. The riots were one result of the viral theory. Half the city went up in the big riot last fall—half the city and an awful lot of people. Seems someone got the bright idea that if all the people going soft were put out of their misery and their bodies burned, the plague could be stopped, at least here in Manhattan. The few cops left couldn't stop the mobs. In fact a lot of the city's ex-cops had been *in* the mobs. Judy and I lost our apartment when our building went up. Luckily we hadn't any signs of softness then. We got away with our lives and little else.

"Water's boiling, Dad," she said from across the room.

I turned and went back to the stove, not saying anything, still thinking about how fast our nice rent-stabilized apartment house had burned, taking everything we had with it.

Everything gone...furniture and futures...gone. All my plans. Gone. Here I stood—if you could call it that—a man with a college education, a B.S. in biology, a secure city job, and what was left? No job. Hell—no *city*.

I'd had it all planned for my dancer. She was going to make it so big. I'd hang on to my city job with all those civil service idiots in the Department of Health, putting up with their sniping and their backstabbing and their lousy office politics so I could keep all the benefits and foot the bill while Judy pursued the dance. She was going to have it *all*. Now what? All her talent, all her potential...where was it going?

Going soft...

I poured the dry contents of the Lipton envelope into the boiling water and soon the odor of chicken noodle soup filled the room.

Which meant we'd have company soon.

I dragged the stepstool over to the door. Already I could hear their claws begin to scrape against the outer surface of the door, their tiny teeth begin to gnaw at its edges. I climbed up and peered through the hole I'd made last month at what had then been eye-level.

There they were. The landing was full of them. Gray and brown and dirty, with glinty little eyes and naked tails. Revulsion rippled down my skin. I watched their growing numbers every day now, every time I cooked something, but still hadn't got used to them.

So I did Cagney for them: "Yooou diiirty raaats!" and turned to wink at Judy on the far side of the fold-out bed. Her expression remained grim.

Rats. They were taking over the city. They seemed to be immune to the softness and were traveling in packs that got bigger and bolder with each passing day. Which was why I'd chosen this building for us: Each apartment was boxed in with pre-stressed concrete block. No rats in the walls here.

I waited for the inevitable. Soon it happened: A number of them squealed, screeched, and thrashed as the crowding pushed them at each other's throats, and then there was bedlam out there. I didn't bother to watch any more. I saw it every day. The pack jumped on the wounded ones. Never failed. They were so hungry they'd eat anything, even each other. And while they were fighting among themselves they'd leave us in peace with our soup.

Soon I had the card table between us and we were sipping the yellow broth and those tiny noodles. I did a lot of *mmm-gooding* but got no response from Judy. Her eyes were fixed on the walkie-talkie on the end table.

"How come we haven't heard from him?"

Good question—one that had been bothering me for a couple of days now. Where *was* George? Usually he stopped by every other day or so to see if we needed anything. And if he didn't stop by, he'd call us on the walkie-talkie. We had an arrangement that we'd both turn on our headsets every day at six P.M. just in case we needed to be in touch. I'd been calling over to George's place across the street at six o'clock sharp for three days running now with no result.

"He's probably wandering around the city seeing what he can pick up. He's a resourceful guy. Probably come back with something we can really use but haven't thought of."

Judy didn't flash me the anticipated smile. Instead, she frowned.

"What if he went down to the research center?"

"I'm sure he didn't. He's a trusting soul, but he's not a fool."

I kept my eyes down as I spoke. I'm not a good liar. And that very question had been nagging at my gut. What if George had been stupid enough to present himself to the researchers? If he had, he was through. They'd never let him go and we'd never see him again.

For George wasn't an immune like us. He was different. Judy and I had caught the virus—or toxin—and defeated it. We were left with terrible scars from the battle but we had survived. We *acquired* our immunity through battle with the softness agent. George was special—he had remained untouched. He'd exposed himself to infected people for months as he helped everyone he could, and was still hard all over. Not so much as a little toe had gone soft on him. Which meant—to me at least—that George had been *born* with some sort of immunity to the softness.

Wouldn't those researchers love to get their needles and scalpels into *him.*

I wondered if they had. George might have been picked up and brought down to the research center against his will. He told me once that he'd seen official-looking vans and cars prowling the streets, driven by guys wearing gas masks or the like. But that had been months ago and he hadn't reported anything like it since. Certainly no cars had been on this street in recent memory. I warned him time and again about roaming around in the daylight but he always laughed good-naturedly and said nobody'd ever catch him—he was too fast.

What if he'd run into someone faster?

Only one thing to do.

"I'm going to take a stroll over to George's just to see if he's okay."

Judy gasped. "No, Dad! You can't! It's too far!"

"Only across the street."

"But your legs—"

"—are only half gone."

I'd met George shortly after the last riot. I had two hard legs then. I'd come looking for a sturdier building than the one we'd been burned out of. He helped us move in here.

I was suspicious at first, I admit that. I mean, I kept asking myself, *What does this guy want?* Turned out he only wanted to be friends. And so friends we became. He was soon the only other man I trusted in this whole world. And that being the case, I wanted a gun—for protection against all those other men I didn't trust. George told me he had stolen a bunch during the early lootings. I traded him some Sterno and batteries for a .38 and a pump-action 12-gauge shotgun with ammo for both. I promptly sawed off the barrel of the shotgun. If the need arose, I could clear a room real fast with that baby.

So it was the shotgun I reached for now. No need to fool with it—I kept its chamber empty and its magazine loaded with #5 shells. I laid it on the floor and reached into the rag bag by the door and began tying old undershirts around my knees. Maybe I shouldn't call them knees; with the lower legs and caps gone, "knee" hardly seemed appropriate.

From there it was a look through the peep hole to make sure the hall was clear, a blown kiss to Judy, then a shuffle into the hall. I was extra wary at first, ranging the landing up and down, looking for rats. But there weren't any in sight. I slung the shotgun around my neck, letting it hang in front as I started down the stairs one by one on hands and butt, knees first, each flabby lower leg dragging alongside its respective thigh.

Two flights down to the lobby, then up on my padded knees to the swinging door, a hard push through and I was out on the street.

Silence.

We kept our windows tightly closed against the cold and so I hadn't noticed the change. Now it hit me like a slap in the face. As a lifelong New Yorker I'd never heard the city like this. Make that *not* heard. Even when there'd been nothing doing on your street, you could always hear that dull roar pulsing from the sky and the pavement and the walls of the buildings. The life sound of the city, the beating of its heart, the whisper of its breath, the susurrant rush of blood through its capillaries.

It had stopped.

The shiver that ran over me was not just the March wind's sharp edge. The street was deserted. A plague had been through here, but no contorted bodies were strewn about. You didn't fall down and die on the spot with the softness. No, that would be too kind. You died by inches, by bone lengths, in back rooms, trapped, unable to make it to the street. No public displays of morbidity. Just solitary deaths of quiet desperation.

In a secret way I was glad everyone was gone—nobody around to see me tooling across the sidewalk on my rag-wrapped knees like some skid row geek.

The city looked different from down here. When you have legs to stand on you never realize how cracked the sidewalks are, how *dirty*. The buildings, their windows glaring red with the setting sun that had poked through the clouds over New Jersey, looked half again as high as they had when I was a taller man.

I shuffled to the street and caught myself looking both ways before sliding off the curb. I smiled at the thought of getting run down by a truck on my first trip in over a month across a street that probably hadn't seen the underside of a car since December.

Despite the absurdity of it, I hurried across, and felt relief when I finally reached the far curb. Pulling open the damn doors to George's apartment building was a chore, but I slipped through both of them and into the lobby. George's bike—a light-frame Italian model ten-speeder—was there. I didn't like that. George took that bike everywhere. Of course he could have found a car and some gas and gone sightseeing and not told me, but still the sight of that bike standing there made me uneasy.

I shuffled by the silent bank of elevators, watching my longing expression reflected in their silent, immobile chrome doors. The fire door to the stairwell was a heavy one, but I squeezed through and started up the steps—backward. Maybe there was a better way, but I hadn't found it. It was all in the arms: Sit on the bottom step, get your arms back, palms down on the step above, lever yourself up. Repeat this ten times and you've done a flight of stairs. Two flights per floor. Thank the Lord or Whatever that George had decided he preferred a second-floor apartment to a penthouse after the final power failure.

It was a good thing I was going up backward. I might never have seen the rats if I'd been faced around the other way.

Just one appeared at first. Alone, it was almost cute with its twitching whiskers and its head bobbing up and down as it sniffed the air at the bottom of the flight. Then two more joined it, then another half dozen. Soon they were a brown wave, undulating up the steps toward me.

I hesitated for an instant, horrified and fascinated by their numbers and all their little black eyes sweeping toward me, then I jolted myself into action. I swung the scattergun around, pumped a shell into the chamber, and let them have a blast. Dimly through the reverberating roar of the shotgun I heard a chorus of squeals and saw flashes of flying crimson blossoms, then I was ducking my face into my arms to protect my eyes from the ricocheting shot. I should have realized the danger of shooting in a cinderblock stairwell like this. Not that it would have changed things—I still had to protect myself—but I should have anticipated the ricochets.

The rats did what I'd hoped they'd do—jumped on the dead and near-dead of their number and forgot about me. I let the gun hang in front of me again and continued up the stairs to George's floor.

He didn't answer his bell but the door was unlocked. I'd warned him about that in the past but he'd only laughed in that carefree way of his. "Who's gonna pop in?" he'd say. Probably no one. But that didn't keep me from locking mine, even though George was the only one who knew where I lived. I wondered if that meant I didn't really trust George.

I put the question aside and pushed the door open.

It stank inside. And it was empty as far as I could see. But there was this sound, this wheezing, coming from one of the bedrooms. Calling his name and announcing my own so I wouldn't get my head blown off, I closed the door behind me—locked it—and followed the sound. I found George.

And retched.

George was a blob of flesh in the middle of his bed. Everything but some ribs, some of his facial bones, and the back of his skull had gone soft on him.

I stood there on my knees in shock, wondering how this could have happened. George was *immune.* He'd laughed at the softness. He'd been walking around as good as new just last week. And now...

His lips were dry and cracked and blue—he couldn't speak, couldn't swallow, could barely breathe. And his eyes...they seemed to be just floating there in a quivering pool of flesh, begging me...darting to his left again and again...begging me...

For what?

I looked to his left and saw the guns. He had a suitcase full of them by the bedroom door. All kinds. I picked up a heavy-looking revolver—an S&W .357—and glanced at him. He closed his eyes and I thought he smiled.

I almost dropped the pistol when I realized what he wanted.

"No, George!"

He opened his eyes again. They began to fill with tears.

"George—I can't!"

Something like a sob bubbled past his lips. And his eyes ... his pleading eyes...

I stood there a long time in the stink of his bedroom, listening to him wheeze, feeling the sweat collect between my palm and the pistol grip. I knew I couldn't do it. Not George, the big, friendly, good-natured slob I'd been depending on.

Suddenly, I felt my pity begin to evaporate as a flare of irrational anger began to rise. I *had* been depending on George now that my legs were half gone, and here he'd gone soft on me. The bitter disappointment fueled the anger. I knew it wasn't right, but I couldn't help hating George just then for letting me down.

"Damn you, George!"

I raised the pistol and pointed it where I thought his brain should be. I turned my head away and pulled the trigger. Twice. The pistol jumped in my hand. The sound was deafening in the confines of the bedroom.

Then all was quiet except for the ringing in my ears. George wasn't wheezing anymore. I didn't look around. I didn't have to see. I have a good imagination.

I fled that apartment as fast as my ruined legs would carry me.

But I couldn't escape the vision of George and how he looked before I shot him. It haunted me every inch of the way home, down the now empty stairs where only a few tufts of dirty brown fur were left to indicate that rats had been swarming there, out into the dusk and across the street and up more stairs to home.

George...how could it be? He was immune.

Or was he? Maybe the softness had followed a different course in George, slowly building up in his system until every bone in his body was riddled with it and he went soft all at once. *God*, what a noise he must have heard when all those bones went in one shot. That was why he hadn't been able to call or answer the walkie-talkie.

But what if it had been something else? What if the virus theory was right and George was the victim of a more virulent mutation?

The thought made me sick with dread. Because if that were true, it meant Judy would eventually end up like George. And I was going to have to do for her what I'd done for George.

But what of me, then? Who was going to end it for *me*? I didn't know if I had the guts to shoot myself. And what if my hands went soft before I had the chance?

I didn't want to think about it, but it wouldn't go away. I couldn't remember ever being so frightened. I almost considered going down to Rockefeller Center and presenting Judy and myself to the leechers, but killed that idea real quick. Never. I'm no jerk. I'm college-educated. A degree in biology. I know what they'd do to us.

Inside, Judy had wheeled her chair over to the door and was waiting for me. I couldn't let her know.

"Not there," I told her before she could ask, and busied myself with putting the shotgun away so I wouldn't have to look her straight in the eyes.

"Where could he be?" Her voice was tight.

"I wish I knew. Maybe he went down to Rockefeller Center. If he did, it's the last we'll ever see of him."

"I can't believe that."

"Then tell me where else he can be."

She was silent.

I did Warner Oland's Chan: "Numbah One Dawtah is finally at loss for words. Peace reigns at last."

I could see that I failed to amuse, so I decided a change of subject was in order.

"I'm tired."

It was the truth. The trip across the street had been exhausting.

"Me, too." She yawned.

"Want to get some sleep?"

I knew she did. I was just staying a step or two ahead of her so she wouldn't have to ask to be put to bed. She was a dancer, a fine, proud artist. Judy would never have to ask anyone to put her to bed. Not while I was around. As long as I was able I would spare her the indignity of dragging herself along the floor.

I gathered Judy up in my arms. The whole lower half of her body was soft; her legs hung over my left arm like weighted drapes. It was all I could do to keep from crying when I felt them so limp and formless. My dancer...you should have seen her in *Swan Lake*. Her legs had been so strong, so sleekly muscular, like her mother's...

I took her to the bathroom and left her alone. Which left me alone with my daymares.

What if there really was a mutation of the softness and my dancer began leaving me again, slowly, inch by inch? What was I going to do when she was gone? My wife was gone. My folks were gone. What few friends I'd ever had were gone. Judy was the only attachment I had left. Without her I'd break loose from everything and just float off into space. I needed her...

When she was finished in the bathroom I carried her out and arranged her on the bed. I tucked her in and kissed her goodnight.

Out in the living room I slipped under the covers of the fold-out bed and tried to sleep. Useless. The fear wouldn't leave me alone. I fought it, telling myself that George was a freak case, that Judy and I had licked the softness. We were *immune* and we'd stay immune. Let everyone else turn into puddles of Jell-O, I wasn't going to let them suck us dry to save themselves. We were on our way to inheriting the earth, Judy and I, and we didn't even have to be meek about it.

But still sleep refused to come. So I lay there in the growing darkness in the center of the silent city and listened...listened as I did every night...as I knew I would listen for the rest of my life...listened for that sound...that cellophane crinkling sound...

This is a Just Deserts story.

Horror fiction is a great way of getting even. I've been a rock fan since a summer night in 1955 when I first heard Chuck Berry's "Maybellene" (see *The Touch* notes for details). Decades later I was reading a series of interviews with some of the originators of rock and how they were ripped off by DJs, record companies, and promoters—sometimes all wrapped up in a single slimy individual. I decided to get even for them.

Figuratively, of course. And with tongue set firmly in cheek.

Stu Schiff bought it for one of his *Whispers* anthologies.

The Last 'One Mo' Once Golden Oldies Revival

The announcer broke in with the news—right into the middle of a song by the latest New Wave sensation, Polio. Philip "Flip" Goodloe was gone. The father and seminal stylist of the rock 'n' roll guitar was dead.

Lenny Winter leaned back and took a long draw on the Royal Jamaican delicately balanced between his pudgy thumb and forefinger. He certainly didn't mind anybody cutting Polio's music short—this New Wave crap was worse than the stuff he jockeyed in his heyday. And he wasn't all that surprised about Flip.

Dead ... the Flipper was dead. Lenny had sensed that coming last week. The only disconcerting thing was it had happened so soon after seeing him. Fifteen or twenty years without laying eyes on Flip Goodloe, then Lenny visits him, then he's dead, all within a few days' time. Definitely disconcerting.

He listened for details about the death but none came. Only a hushed voice repeating that the major influence on every rocker who had ever

picked up an electric six-string was dead. Even guitarists who had
never actually heard a Flip Goodloe record owed him a debt because, as
the voice said, if you weren't directly influenced by Goodloe, you were
influenced by somebody who got his licks from somebody else who
got *his* licks from Flip Goodloe. "All riffs eventually lead to Goodloe,"
the voice said. It closed the break-in with: "...the exact cause of death is
unknown at this time."

"I can tell you the exact cause of death," Lenny muttered to the
empty room. "Smack. Flip Goodloe the hophead finally overjuiced
himself."

The disc jockey—whoops, sorry, they liked to be called "radio personalities" now—yanked the Polio record and put on "Mary-Liz," Flip's
first hit record. An instant Flip Goodloe retrospective was under way.

In spite of his personal knowledge of what a jerk Flip was, Lenny
Winter suffered a pang of nostalgia as the frenetic guitar notes and
wailing voice poured out of the twin Bose 901s in the corners of the
room. Nobody could play like the Flipper in his day. Flip didn't show-
boat and he didn't just doodle around the melody—he got behind his
bands and pushed, driving them 'til they were cooking at white heat.

Lenny Winter put his cigar down and pulled his considerable bulk
out of the recliner. He was pushing fifty-five and was at least that many
pounds overweight. He waddled over to the north wall of his trophy
room—one of the smaller of the eighteen rooms in his house. Where
was it, now? He scanned along rows of gold records. There—the 45
with the Backgammon label. "Mary-Liz" by Flip Goodloe. A million
sales, RIAA-certified. And beneath the title, the composer credit: (P.
Goodloe-L. Weinstein). Lenny smiled. Not too many people knew that
Lenny Winter's birth certificate read "Leonard Weinstein."

He wondered how many copies would sell in the inevitable surge of
interest after Flip's death. Look how many Lennon records moved after
he bought it. Lenny did not like to think of himself as one who made
money off the dead, but a buck was a buck, and half of all royalties from
sales and airplay of a good number of Flip's early songs belonged to
Lenny. So it was only fair that he got what was rightfully his. He made
a mental note to call BMI in the morning.

The radio segued into Goodloe's second big hit, "Little Rocker"—
another P. Goodloe-L. Weinstein composition. A gold copy of that, too,
was somewhere on the wall.

Those were the days when Lenny could do no wrong. Flip had it all
then, too. But he blew it. Lenny had managed to stay at or near the top.
Flip had been nowhere for years.

Which was why Lenny had visited him last week—to give the Flipper another chance.

He shook his head. What a mistake that had been.

It hadn't been easy to find Flip. He had moved back to Alexandria, Virginia, his old hometown. He still played an occasional solo gig in some of the M Street clubs in DC, but sporadically. He was unreliable. Club owners learned to expect him when they saw him. Everyone knew he was shooting shit again. No one had a phone number, but a bartender knew a girl who had gone home with him after a recent gig. Lenny found her. As expected, she was young and white. She remembered the address.

It was in a garden apartment complex that gave new meaning to the word "run-down." Waist-high weeds sprouted through cracks in the parking lot blacktop; a couple of stripped and rotting wrecks slumped amid the more functional cars; children's toys lay scattered over the dirt patch that had once been a lawn; on the buildings themselves the green of the previous coat of paint showed through cracks and chips in the current white coat, which was none too current.

This was where Flip Goodloe lived? Lenny shook his head. Flip could have had it all.

Building seven, apartment 4-D. Lenny pushed the bell button but heard no ring within. He did hear an acoustic guitar plunking away on the other side of the door, so he knocked. No answer. He knocked again, louder. The guitar kept playing, but not loud enough to drown out Lenny's pounding on the door. The player obviously heard Lenny; he was just ignoring him.

Typical.

He tried the doorknob. It turned. He went in.

A pigsty. That's what it was—a pigsty. Empty Kentucky Fried Chicken buckets caught the breeze from the door, rolling among the Big Mac boxes and countless candy bar wrappers littering the floor. Dust everywhere. The rug had once been red—possibly; hard to tell in the dim light. Cobwebs in all the ceiling corners. Clothes strewn everywhere. Acrid smoke layered out at three distinct levels in the air of the room, undulating sensuously in the draft.

And there in the middle of the room, sitting cross-legged like some black-skinned maharishi, his emaciated body naked but for a stained pair of jockey shorts, was Flip Goodloe, staring off into space while he picked and chorded an aimless melody from the Martin clutched before him. His hair was a rat's nest, looking like he had tried to weave a natural into dreadlocks but had given up halfway along.

"Flip," Lenny said, raising his voice to break through the noise. "*Flip!*"

Rheumy, red-rimmed eyes focused on Lenny through pinpoint pupils. A slow smile spread across Flip's features.

"Well, if it ain't my old friend, Lenny. Been seeing you on TV pushing those moldy oldies collections. You got fat, man. You look like Porky Pig on the tube. Yeah. L. Weinstein, a.k.a. Daddy Shoog, a.k.a. Lenny Winter, former dj, former owner of countless tiny record companies—bankrupt record companies—and now known as Mister Golden Oldies."

Lenny bowed—not an easy trick with his girth—more to escape the naked hostility in Flip's eyes and voice than to accept the sarcastic approbation.

"Oh, yeah. I almost forgot: former collaborator. I must be the only guy in rock who collaborated with someone who's never written a single lyric or note of music in his life."

Not the only, Lenny thought. Plenty of others.

Flip switched to a Kingfisher voice: "Ah guess dat makes yo' de collaborator, an' me de collaboratee."

"That's all water under the bridge, Flip," Lenny said, uncomfortable. This man had no class—no class at all. "Whatever disagreements we had in the past, we can bury now. I've got a deal for you. A great deal. It'll mean your comeback. Chuck Berry came back. You can, too—bigger than ever!"

Flip's smile finally faded. "What makes you think I wanna comeback?"

Lenny ignored the remark. Every has-been wants a comeback. He went on to explain the details of the ninth annual "One Mo' Once Golden Oldies Revival" tour, how it was going to be the biggest and best ever of its kind. And how he, Lenny Winter, out of the goodness of his heart, had decided to let Flip Goodloe headline the tour.

What he didn't say was that he needed Flip as headliner to put the icing on the cake, so to speak. The back-to-basics influence of the latest hits was having its effect, and Lenny was going to cash in on it. He'd always been able to pick up trends. It was his big talent, what had made him Daddy Shoog back in the old days. He sensed new interest growing in old-time rock 'n' roll, especially in the unpretentious, down-and-dirty, no-holds-barred guitar style of someone like the Flipper. Lenny could feel it in his gut—Flip Goodloe leading the bill would turn a successful, reasonably profitable tour into a gold rush.

He needed Flip. And he was going to get him. .

"Not interested," Flip said.

"You don't mean that. What else have you got going for you?"

"Religion, Lenny. I got religion."

Lenny kept his face straight but mentally rolled his eyes. Who's the guru this time?

"Born again?" he said.

"No way. I worship the great god Doolang."

"Doolang." Great.

"Yeah." Flip pointed toward the ceiling. "Behold His image."

Lenny squinted into the hazy air. Hanging from a thread thumbtacked to the ceiling was a wire coat hanger twisted into an "S"-like configuration...like a cross between a G-clef and a dollar sign.

"Doolang?"

"You got it. The God of Aging Rockers. I already burned my offering to Him and was just warming up to sing His favorite hymn."

"Is that what I smell? What did you burn?"

"Rod Stewart's latest." He giggled. "Know what hymn he likes best?"

Lenny sighed. "I'll bite—what?"

"'He's So Fine.' By the Chiffons. Remember?"

Lenny thought back. Oh, yeah: *Doolang-doolang-doolang.*

He laughed. "I get it."

Flip began to laugh, too. "I can also sing Him 'My Sweet Lord.' I'm not sure ol' Doolang knows the difference."

He laughed harder. He flopped back on the floor and spread his arms and laughed from deep in his gut.

Lenny saw the tracks on Flip's arms and his own laughter died, strangled in coils of pity and revulsion. Flip must have noticed the direction of his gaze, for he suddenly fell silent. He sat up and folded his arms across his chest, hiding the scars.

"Doolang don't mind if someone shoots up once in a while. Especially if they been blackballed out of the industry."

Fury blasted a wave of heat through him. A hopped-up Flip Goodloe would be a liability rather than an asset. There'd be a constant risk of his getting busted making a score in K.C. or Montgomery or some other burg and that would be it for the tour. Finis. Caput. Dead.

"Don't give me this Doolang crap!" Lenny shouted. "You're screwing up your—"

Flip was on his feet in a flash, his face barely an inch from Lenny's.

"Don't you *dare* take the name of the great god Doolang in vain! Your lips aren't even worthy to speak His name in praise! You'd better watch out, L. Weinstein. Doolang's pretty pissed at you. You've screwed more rockers than anybody else in history. One day He may decide to get even!"

That did it. The Flipper was completely *meshugge*. His brain was fried. He'd mainlined once too often.

Lenny pulled five C-notes from his wallet and threw them on the floor.

"Here! Buy yourself a nice load of smack, a bunch of schmaltzy records, and a truckload of coat hangers. Twist the hangers into cute little curlicues, burn the records, and shoot up to your heart's content. I don't want to hear about it!"

He spun and lurched out the door, away from the stink, away from the madness, away from the sight of the man he had ruined twenty years ago.

Twenty years…had it been that long?

A third Goodloe song, "Coin' Home," immediately followed the second. Flip's music was starting to get on his nerves. He went back to where he had left his cigar. Smoke ran straight up in a thin wavering line from the tip. Near the ceiling it curled into a twisted shape almost like a G-clef.

Lenny gave it passing notice as he knocked off the ash, then wandered around the trophy room in a pensive mood.

Flip had accused him of screwing more rockers than anyone else in history. A rotten thing to say. Sure, a lot of them *felt* screwed, but in truth they owed Lenny Winter a debt of thanks for giving them a chance in the first place. He'd pulled some fast ones—no use kidding himself—but he felt no guilt. In fact, he could not help but take a certain amount of pride in his fancy footwork.

He had realized early on the power wielded by a New York City DJ. He could make a new artist by raving about the record and playing it every half hour, or he could abort a career simply by losing the record. Those were heady days. Every agent, every manager, every PR man for every label was pushing gifts, trips, girls, and cash at him. He took everything they offered—except the cash.

Not to say he didn't want the dough. He wanted that most of all. But he saw the dangers from the start. For obvious reasons, you couldn't declare the money as income, and that left you open to a federal charge of income tax evasion if a scandal arose. You wouldn't just lose your job then—you could be headed for Leavenworth if the IRS boys built up a good case against you.

So cash was out for Lenny unless it could be laundered and declared. It nearly killed him to say no to all the easy dinero being pushed at him...until the spring of '55 when he came up with a revolutionary scam. It happened the day a portly Negro—that was what they were called then—from a small Washington, DC label brought in a regional hit called "Georgia-Mae" by someone named Flip Goodloe. Lenny knew instantly it was special. He'd never heard a guitar played that way. It seemed to feed directly into the central nervous system. His sixth sense told him this artist and this record had almost everything needed for a big hit. Almost.

"There's just one problem," Lenny had told the company rep. "That name won't play around here."

"Y'mean 'Flip'?" the black had said.

"No. I mean 'Georgia-Mae.' It's too hick, daddy. City kids won't dig it."

Hard to believe now that he actually talked like that in those days.

The black guy shrugged. "He wrote it, he can change it. What's in a name?"

"Everything, as far as this record's concerned. Tell him to change it to something more...American sounding, if you get my drift." The message was clear: Change it to a *white-sounding* name. "Then I can make it a biggy."

The black guy had been sharp. "*Can? Or will?*"

Lenny had been ready to do his silent routine and see what was offered when it struck him that he had just made a significant contribution to this Flip Goodloe's song. Fighting a burst of excitement that nearly lifted him from his chair, he spoke calmly, as if making a routine proposal.

"I want to go down as co-composer of this song and of the B-side as well. And if I make it a hit—which I will—I want half credit on his next ten releases."

The company rep had shaken his head. "Don't know about that. I don't think the Flipper will go for it."

Lenny wrote "L. Weinstein" on a slip of paper, then stood and opened the door to his office.

"He will if he wants to get out of DC." He handed the slip to the rep. "And that's the name of his new songwriting partner."

Lenny never did find out what transpired back in the offices of Backgammon Records, but four weeks later he received a promo 45 by Flip Goodloe called "Mary-Liz"—exactly the same song but for the name. And under the title was "(P. Goodloe-L. Weinstein)."

Lenny began to play it two or three times an hour that very night. The record went gold before the summer. Half of all composer royalties went to Lenny. All legal, all aboveboard and, he knew, utterly brilliant.

Not a stunt he could pull if a song came from the Brill Building or one of the other Tin Pan Alley tune mills, but it became a standard practice for Lenny with new artists who wrote their own material. Trouble was, there weren't enough of them.

Then it occurred to him: He had struck gold at the composer level. Why not get in on other levels?

So he did. He started a record company and a publishing company, found an *a-cappella* group with a few songs of their own, recorded them with an instrumental backup, and published their music. All without anyone having the slightest notion that the famous Lenny Winter was involved. Lenny then pushed the record on his show and more often than not it became a hit. Lenny knew nothing about music, could not sing a note. But he knew what would sell.

When sales for the record had dried up and all the royalties were in, Lenny closed up his operation and opened up down the street under a different name. The artists came looking for their money and found an empty office.

Lenny followed the formula for years, funneling all profits through Winter Promotions, the company he had set up to finance his plans for live rock 'n' roll shows, the kind Alan Freed was doing hand-over-fist business with in places like the Brooklyn Paramount.

"Down the Road and Around the Bend," another Flip Goodloe hit, started through the speakers.

Come on! Too bad about Flip being dead and all, but enough was enough.

Lenny went over to the tuner. He noticed some wires had fallen out from behind the system. They were twisted into a configuration that looked something like a dollar sign. He kicked them back out of sight and twisted the tuner dial a few degrees to the left until he caught the neighboring FM station.

The opening chords of "You're Mine Mine Mine" by the Camellows filled the room.

Lenny smiled and shook his head. This must be oldies night or something. He had recorded the Camellows on his Landlubber label back in '58. This was their only hit. Unfortunately, Landlubber records folded before any royalties could be paid. Such a shame.

He moved along the wall to a poster from the fall of '59 proclaiming his first rock 'n' roll show. His own face—younger, leaner in the cheeks—grinned from the top, and below ran a list of his stars, some of them the very same acts he had recorded and deserted during the preceding years. A great lineup, even if he did say so himself.

The shows—that was where the money was. Continuous shows ten A.M. 'til midnight for a week or two straight. One horde of pimple-pussed kids after another buying tickets, streaming in with their money clutched in their sweaty fists, streaming out with programs and pictures and records in place of that money. Lenny had wanted a piece of that action.

But he had to start small. He didn't have enough to bankroll a really big show the first time out, so he found the Bixby, a medium-sized theatre in Astoria whose owners, what with the movie business in a slump and all, were interested in a little extra revenue. The place was a leftover from those Depression-era movie palaces and not adequately wired for the lighting needed for a live show. No matter: A wad of bills stuffed into the pocket of the local building inspector took care of that permit. From then on it was full speed ahead. The acts were lined up, and he began the buildup on his radio show.

Opening night was a smash. Every show was packed for the first three days. He should have known then it couldn't last. Things were running too smoothly. A screwup was inevitable.

Lenny shifted his eyes to the right to where a framed newspaper photo showed his 1959 self dashing wide-eyed and fright-faced from a smoking doorway carrying an unconscious girl in his arms. That photo occupied a well-deserved place of honor in his trophy room. It had saved his ass.

She had wandered backstage after the fourth show to meet the great Lenny Winter, the Daddy Shoog of radio fame—a fifteen-year-old blonde who looked older and was absolutely thrilled when he let her sit in his dressing room. They had a few drinks—she found Seven and Seven "really neat-tasting"—and soon she was tipsy and hot and on his lap. As his hand was sliding under her skirt and slip and up along the silky length of her inner thigh, someone yelled "Fire!"

Lenny dumped her on the cot and ran to look. He saw the smoke, heard the screams from the audience, and knew with icy-veined certainty that even if he got out of here alive, his career as Daddy Shoog was dead.

He glanced back into his dressing room and saw that the kid had passed out. It wouldn't do to have a minor with a load of booze in her blood found dead of smoke inhalation in his dressing room. Wouldn't do at all. So he picked her up and ran for the stage door. By some incredible stroke of luck, a *Daily News* photog had been riding by, seen the smoke, and snapped Lenny coming out the door with his unconscious burden.

A hundred and forty-six kids died in the Astoria Bixby fire—most of them trampled by their fellow fans. Fingers of blame were pointed in every direction—at rock 'n' roll, at the building inspectors, at the fire department, at teenagers in general. Everywhere but at Lenny Winter. Lenny was safe, protected by that photo.

Because that picture made page one in the *News* and was picked up by the wire services. Lenny Winter, "known as 'Daddy Shoog' to his fans," was a hero. He had risked his life to save one of his young fans who had been overcome by smoke.

And when the payola scandal broke shortly thereafter in the winter of '60, that dear, dear photo carried him through. The Senate panels and the New York grand jury questioned everyone—even Dick Clark—but they left Daddy Shoog alone. He was a hero. You didn't bring a hero in and ask him about graft.

———

Looking back now, Lenny realized that it really hadn't mattered much what happened then. The whole scene was in flux. Alan Freed went down, the scapegoat for the whole payola scandal. Rock 'n' roll was changing. Even its name was being shortened to just plain "rock." Radio formats were changing, too. Lenny found himself out of the New York market in '62, and completely out of touch during the British invasion in the mid-sixties. Those were lean years, but he started coming back in the seventies with his series of "One Mo' Once Golden Oldies Revival" tours. He was no longer Daddy Shoog, but Mr. Golden Oldies. He sold mail-order collections of oldies on TV. He was a national figure again.

You can't keep a good man down.

A new song came on—"I'm on My Way" by the Lulus. A little bell chimed a sour note in the back of his brain. The Lulus had been one of his groups, too. Coincidence.

Lenny turned his attention back to the wall and spotted another framed newspaper clipping. He didn't know why he kept this one. Maybe it was just to remind himself that when Lenny Winter gets even, he gets *even*.

A 1962 UPI story. He could have cut it from the *Times* but he preferred the more lurid *News* version. The subject of the piece was Flip Goodloe and how he had been discovered *en flagrante* with a sixteen-year-old white girl. His career took the long slide after that. And even when it had all blown over, he had messed himself up too much with heroin to come back.

Strange how one thing leads to another, Lenny thought.

Shortly before the incident described in the article, Flip had refused to give Lenny any further composer credit on his songs. He had called Lenny all sorts of awful things like a no-talent leech, a bloodsucker, a slimeball, and other more colorful street-level epithets. Lenny didn't get mad. He got even. He knew Flip's fondness for young stuff—young *white* stuff. He found a little teenage slut, paid her to get it on with Flip, then sent in the troops. She disappeared afterward, so the case never came to trial. But the morals charges had been filed and the newspaper stories had run and Flip Goodloe was ruined.

To think: If it hadn't been for the teenybopper incident during the fire at the Bixby, Lenny might never have dreamed up the scam he pulled on Flip. Yes…strange how one thing leads to another.

But Flip's overdose. Maybe that was really Lenny's fault. Maybe the five hundred he had left the Flipper last week—guilt money?—had been too much cash at once. Maybe it had let him go out and get some really pure stuff. A lot of it. And maybe that was why he was dead—because of the money Lenny had left him.

The Lulus faded out, followed without commercial interruption or DJ comment by the Pendrakes' "I'm So Crazy for You."

Another of Lenny's groups from the fifties.

He felt a tingle crawl up from the base of his spine. What was going on here? Coincidence was one thing, but this made seven songs in a row he was connected with. Seven!

Lenny strode back to the tuner and spun the knob. Stations screeched by until the indicator came to rest in the nineties. Flip Goodloe once again shouted the chorus of "Little Rocker" from the speakers. Lenny gasped and gave the knob a vicious turn. Another screech and then the Boktones—another group on one of Lenny's short-lived labels—were singing "Hey-Hey Momma!"

Sweat broke out along Lenny's upper lip. This was crazy. It was Lenny Winter night all over the dial!

One more chance. Steadying his hand, he guided the indicator to the all-news station. The only tunes you ever heard there were commercial jingles. He found the number—

—and reeled away from the machine as the familiar opening riffs of "Mary-Liz" rammed against him.

With a quaking index finger stretched out before him, he forced himself forward and hit the power button. Silence. Blessed silence.

He realized he was trembling. Why? It was all just a coincidence, nothing more. The Flipper's death had put the stations into a retro-spective mood. They were playing old Goodloe tunes and other stuff from his era. And the all-news station...probably doing a feature on Goodloe, and Lenny had tuned in just as they were airing a sample of his work.

Sure. That was it.

So why not turn the radio back on? Why not indeed?

Because he had to go out now. Yes. Out. For some air. Lenny fled the trophy room and went to the front hall. It was spring but still cool out here along the Long Island Sound, and he'd need a coat. He pulled the closet door open and stopped. At first glance he thought the closet was empty. Then he saw the coats and jackets on the floor. They'd all fallen off their hangers.

And those hangers...they didn't look like hangers anymore.

They hung on the closet pole in a neat row, but they'd been twisted into an odd shape that was becoming too familiar...something like a cross between a G-clef and a dollar sign. They hung there, swaying gently, the light from the hall gleaming dully along the contorted lengths of wire.

Lenny stared at them dumbly, feeling terror expand with the mem-ory of where he had first seen that shape: Goodloe's apartment.

Flip had been squatting under a hanger shaped just like these when Lenny had last seen him. He'd called it the great god Doolang or some such nonsense. Just a junkie fever dream—but what had happened to these?

Someone was in the house! That was the only explanation.

Some buddy of Flip's had come here to twist these things into knots and scare him. Well, it was working. Lenny was terrified. Not of any supernatural mumbo-jumbo, but of the very idea of one of Flip's junkie friends in his house. Probably upstairs right now, waiting. He had to get out.

He snatched a coat from the floor and stumbled toward the front door. He'd be safer outside. He could run around to the garage and take the car. Then he'd phone the police and have them go through the house. That was the best way, the safest way.

As the door slammed behind him, he waited for a blast of cool air. It never came. Instead, it was warm out here. The air was stale, heavy with the smell and humidity of packed bodies. And it was dark...darker than it should be. Where were the lights of downtown Monroe?

Pain shot through Lenny's abdomen as his intestines twisted in fear. This wasn't his front yard. This was someplace else. He turned back to his front door. It was gone, replaced by a pair of wide, flat, swinging panels, each with a small glass rectangle at eye level. Through the glass he could see what appeared to be a lighted theatre lobby with Art Deco designs on the walls, popcorn machine and all. But deserted. He pounded on the doors, but it was like pounding against the base of a skyscraper; they didn't even rattle.

He turned. A light was growing out where the apron of his driveway should have been. Something was moved in the glow. As his eyes adjusted he could see rows of theatre seats stretching away on either side, and a filthy carpet leading down to a stage where the light continued to grow.

Noise filtered in like someone turning up the volume of an amplifier. Music: the driving rhythm of "Mary-Liz" and Flip Goodloe himself shouting the lyrics.

With his tongue cleaving to the roof of his mouth, Lenny took a faltering step or two toward the stage. It couldn't be.

But it was. No mistaking those gyrations, or the voice, or the riffs: the Flipper.

He heard crowd noises—cheers, hoots, shouts, hands clapping—and tore his gaze from the stage. The seats around him were filled with kids jumping up and down and gyrating wildly to the music. But there was no excitement in their slack faces, or in their cold eyes. Lenny knew this place. And he recognized those kids.

The Bixby in Astoria. But that was impossible—the Bixby was gone—burned out back in '59 during his first rock show and torn down a few months later.

Lenny ran back to the swinging doors and slammed against them. They still wouldn't budge. He pounded on the glass but there was no one in the outer lobby to hear. Had to find another way out, another exit. He was halfway down the aisle when he smelled it.

Smoke.

A cough. Another. Then someone shouted "Fire!" and the panic began. The crowd leaped out of its seats and surged into the aisle, enveloping Lenny like a hungry amoeba. As he went down under the press of panicked bodies, he caught a glimpse of the stage. Flip Goodloe was still up there, hurling his wild riffs into the smoky air, oblivious to the flames that ringed him. Flip smiled fiercely his way, and then Lenny was down, his back slamming against the filthy carpet.

Pain. Shoes kicked at him, heels high and low dug into his face and abdomen in frantic efforts to get by. Bodies fell on him. The weight atop him grew until he heard his ribs crack and shatter; but the lancinating pain from the bone splinters was overwhelmed by his hunger for air. He couldn't breathe! Stale air clogged in his lungs. The odor of old popcorn and dried chewing gum from the carpet was becalmed in his nasal passages.

Vision dimmed, tunneling down to a narrow circle of hazy light filtering through the chaos that swirled around him. And there on the ceiling of the theatre he saw a chandelier. But not the tasseled punchbowl affair that had hung in the old Bixby. This was a huge fluorescent tube, glowing redly, twisted into that same shape...the Doolang shape...

I'd originally intended to use a much shorter version of "Dat-tay-vao" as either a flashback or a prologue in *The Touch*, but no matter how I tried to work it in, it simply wouldn't fit. Used early on, it gave away too much of the mystery of what would be happening to Alan Bulmer in the body of the novel; inserted later, it seemed redundant. So I put it aside. (Never throw *any* writing away—unless it's a truly awful first novel.)

After the novel was finished I returned to it and fleshed it out to make it a stand-alone story—a prequel to *The Touch*. It appeared in the March 1987 issue of *Amazing Stories*. The story takes place exactly nineteen years before its publication…right about the time of *Reborn*, another novel in the Secret History of the World. The events in *Reborn* trigger the *Dat-tay-vao*'s migration to the US where it plays an important part in the teenage Jack books, and in the Secret History, as demonstrated in *Nightworld*.

Dat-Tay-Vao

1.

Patsy cupped his hands gently over his belly to keep his intestines where they belonged. Weak, wet, and helpless, he lay on his back in the alley and looked up at the stars in the crystal sky, unable to move, afraid to call out. The one time he'd yelled loud enough to be heard all the way to the street, loops of bowel had squirmed against his hands, feeling like a pile of Mom's slippery-slick homemade sausage all gray from boiling and coated with her tomato sauce. Visions of his insides surging from the slit in his abdomen like spring snakes from a novelty can of nuts had kept him from yelling again.

No one had come.

He knew he was dying. Good as dead, in fact. He could feel the blood oozing out of the vertical gash in his belly, seeping around his fingers and trailing down his forearms to the ground. Wet from neck to knees. Probably lying in a pool of blood...his very own homemade marinara sauce.

Help was maybe fifty feet away and he couldn't call for it. Even if he could stand the sight of his guts jumping out of him, he no longer had the strength to yell. Yet help was out there...the nightsounds of Quang Ngai streetlife...so near...

Nothing ever goes right for me. Nothing. Ever.

It had been such a sweet deal. Six keys of Cambodian brown. He could've got that home to Flatbush no sweat and then he'd have been set up real good. Uncle Tony would've known what to do with the stuff and Patsy would've been made. And he'd never be called Fatman again. Only the grunts over here called him Fatman. He'd be Pasquale to the old boys, and Pat to the younger guys.

And Uncle Tony would've called him Kid, like he always did.

Yeah. Would have. If Uncle Tony could see him now, he'd call him Shit-for-Brains. He could hear him now:

Six keys for ten G's? Whatsamatta witchoo? Din't I always tell you if it seems too good to be true, it usually is? Ay! Gabidose! Din't you smell no rat?

Nope. No rat smell. Because I didn't want to smell a rat. Too eager for the deal. Too anxious for the quick score. Too damn stupid as usual to see how that sleazeball Hung was playing me like a hooked fish.

No Cambodian brown.

No deal.

Just a long, sharp K-bar.

The stars above went fuzzy and swam around, then came into focus again.

The pain had been awful at first, but that was gone now. Except for the cold, it was almost like getting smashed and crashed on scotch and grass and just drifting off. Almost pleasant. Except for the cold. And the fear.

Footsteps...coming from the left. He managed to turn his head a few degrees. A lone figure approached, silhouetted against the light from the street. A slow, unsteady, almost staggering walk. Whoever it was didn't seem to be in any hurry. Hung? Come to finish him off?

But no. This guy was too skinny to be Hung.

The figure came up and squatted flatfooted on his haunches next to Patsy. In the dim glow of starlight and streetlight he saw a wrinkled face and a silvery goatee. The gook babbled something in Vietnamese.

God, it was Ho Chi Minh himself come to rob him.

Too late. The money's gone. All gone.

No. Wasn't Ho. Couldn't be. Just an old papa-san in the usual black pajamas. They all looked the same, especially the old ones. The only thing different about this one was the big scar across his right eye. Looked as if the lids had been fused closed over the socket.

The old man reached down to where Patsy guarded his intestines and pushed his hands away. Patsy tried to scream in protest but heard only a sigh, tried to put his hands back up on his belly but they'd weakened to limp rubber and wouldn't move.

The old man smiled as he sing-songed in gooktalk and pressed his hands against the open wound in Patsy's belly. Patsy screamed then, a hoarse, breathy sound torn from him by the searing pain that shot in all directions from where the old gook's hands lay. The stars really swam around this time, fading as they moved, but they didn't go out.

By the time his vision cleared, the old gook was up and turned around and weaving back toward the street. The pain, too, was sidling away.

Patsy tried again to lift his hands up to his belly, and this time they moved. They seemed stronger. He wiggled his fingers through the wetness of his blood, feeling for the edges of the wound, afraid of finding loops of bowel waiting for him.

He missed the slit on the first pass. And missed it on the second. How could that happen? It had been at least a foot long and had gaped open a good three or four inches, right there to the left of his belly button. He tried again, carefully this time...

...and found a thin little ridge of flesh.

But no opening.

He raised his head—he hadn't been able to do that before—and looked down at his belly. His shirt and pants were a bloody mess, but he couldn't see any guts sticking out. And he couldn't see any wound, either. Just a dark wet mound of flesh.

If he wasn't so goddamn fat he could see down there! He rolled onto his side—God, he was stronger!—and pushed himself up to his knees to where he could slump his butt onto his heels, all the time keeping at least one hand tight over his belly. But nothing came out, or even pushed against his hand. He pulled his shirt open.

The wound was closed, replaced by a thin, purplish vertical line.

Patsy felt woozy again. What's going on here?

He was in a coma—that had to be it. He was dreaming this.

But everything was so *real*—the rough ground beneath his knees, the congealing red wetness of the blood on his shirt, the sounds from the street, even the smell of the garbage around him. All so real...

Bracing himself against the wall, he inched his way up to his feet. His knees were wobbly and for a moment he thought they'd give out on him. But they held and now he was standing.

He was afraid to look down, afraid he'd see himself still on the ground. Finally, he took a quick glance. Nothing there but two clotted puddles of blood, one on each side of where he'd been lying.

He tore off the rest of the ruined shirt and began walking—very carefully at first—toward the street. Any moment now he would wake up or die, and this craziness would stop. No doubt 'bout that. But until then he was going to play out this little fantasy to the end.

2.

By the time he made it to his bunk—after giving the barracks guards and a few wandering night owls a story about an attempted robbery and a fight—Patsy had begun to believe that he was really awake and walking around.

It was so easy to say it had all been a dream, or maybe hallucinations brought on by acid slipped into his after-dinner coffee by some wise-ass. He managed to convince himself of that scenario a good half dozen times. And then he would look down at the scar on his belly, and at the blood on his pants...

Patsy sat on his rack in a daze.

It really happened! He just touched me and closed me up!

A hushed voice in the dark snapped him out of it.

"Hey! Fatman! Got any weed?"

It sounded like Donner from two bunks over, a steady customer.

"Not tonight, Hank,"

"What? Fatman's never out of stock!"

"He is tonight"

"You shittin' me?"

"Good night, Hank."

Actually, he had a bunch of bags stashed in his mattress, but Patsy didn't feel like dealing tonight. His mind was too numb to make change. He couldn't even mourn the loss of all his cash—every red cent he'd saved up from almost a year's worth of chickenshit deals with guys like Donner. All he could think about, all he could see, was that old one-eyed gook leaning over him, smiling, babbling, and touching him.

He'd talk to Tram tomorrow. Tram knew everything that went on in this goddamn country. Maybe he'd heard something about the old gook. Maybe he could be persuaded to look for him.

One way or another, Patsy was going to find that old gook. He had plans for him. Big plans.

3.

Somehow he managed to make it through breakfast without perking the powdered eggs and scrambling the coffee.

It hadn't been easy. He'd been late getting to the mess hall kitchen. He'd got up on time but had stood in the shower staring at that purple line up and down his belly for he didn't know how long, remembering the cut of Hung's knife, the feel of his intestines in his hands.

Did it really happen?

He knew it had. Accepting it and living with it was going to be the problem.

Finally he'd pulled on his fatigues and hustled over to the kitchen. Rising long before sunup was the only bad thing about being an army cook. The guys up front might call him a pogue but it sure beat hell out of being a stupid grunt in the field. *Anything* was better than getting shot at. Look what happened in Hue last month, and the whispers about My Lai. Only gavones got sent into the field. Smart guys got mess assignments in nice safe towns like Quang Ngai.

At least smart guys with an Uncle Tony did.

Patsy smiled as he scraped hardened scrambled egg off the griddle. He'd always liked to cook. Good thing too. Because in a way, the cooking he'd done for Christmas last year had kept him out of the fight this year.

As always, Uncle Tony had come for Christmas dinner. At the table Pop edged around to the big question: What to do about Patsy and the draft. To everyone's surprise, he'd passed his induction physical...

...another example of how nothing ever went right for him. Patsy had learned that a weight of 225 pounds would keep a guy his height out on medical deferment. Since he wasn't too many pounds short of that, he gorged on everything in sight for weeks. It would've been fun if he hadn't been so desperate. But he made the weight: On the morning of his induction physical the bathroom scale read 229.

But the scale they used downtown at the Federal Building read 224.

He was in and set to go to boot camp after the first of the year.

Pop finally came to the point: Could Uncle Tony maybe...?

Patsy could still hear the disdain in Uncle Tony's voice as he spoke around a mouthful of bread.

"You some kinda peacenik or somethin'?"

No, no, Pop had said, and went on to explain how he was afraid that Patsy, being so fat and so clumsy and all, would get killed in boot camp or step on a mine his first day in the field. You know how he is.

Uncle Tony knew. Everybody knew Patsy's fugazi reputation. Uncle Tony had said nothing as he poured the thick red gravy over his lasagna, gravy Patsy had spent all morning cooking. He took a bite and pointed his fork at Patsy.

"Y'gotta do your duty, kid. I fought in the big one. You gotta fight in this here little one." He swallowed. "Say, you made this gravy, dincha? It's good. It's real good. And it gives me an idea of how we can keep you alive so you can go on making this stuff every Christmas."

So Uncle Tony pulled some strings and Patsy wound up an army cook.

He finished with the cleanup and headed downtown to the central market area, looking for Tram. He smelled the market before he got to it—the odors of live hens, *thit heo*, and roasting dog meat mingled in the air.

He found Tram in his usual spot by his cousin's vegetable stand, wearing his old ARVN fatigue jacket. He'd removed his right foot at the ankle and was polishing its shoe.

"Nice shine, yes, Fatman?" he said as he looked up and saw Patsy.

"Beautiful." He knew Tram liked to shock passersby with his plastic lower leg and foot. Patsy should have been used to the gag by now, but every time he saw that foot he thought of having his leg blown off...

"I want to find someone."

"American or gook?" He crossed his right lower leg over his left and snapped his foot back into place at the ankle. Patsy couldn't help feeling uncomfortable about a guy who called his own kind gooks.

"Gook."

"What name?"

"Uh, that's the problem. I don't know."

Tram squinted up at him. "How I supposed to find somebody without a name?"

"Old papa-san. Looks like Uncle Ho."

Tram laughed. "All you guys think old gooks look like Ho!"

"And he has a scar across his eye"—Patsy put his index finger over his right eye—"that seals it closed like this."

4.

Tram froze for a heartbeat, then snapped his eyes back down to his prosthetic foot. He composed his expression while he calmed his whirling mind.

Trinh...Trinh was in town last night! And Fatman saw him!

He tried to change the subject. Keeping his eyes down, he said, "I am glad to see you still walking around this morning. Did Hung not show up last night? I warned you—he number ten bad gook."

After waiting and hearing no reply, Tram looked up and saw that Fatman's eyes had changed. They looked glazed.

"Yes," Fatman finally said, shaking himself. "You warned me." He cleared his throat. "But about the guy I asked you about—"

"Why you want find this old gook?"

"I want to help him."

"How?"

"I want to do something for him."

"You want do something for old gook?"

Fatman's gaze wandered away as he spoke. "You might say I owe him a favor."

Tram's first thought was that Fatman was lying. He doubted this young American knew the meaning of returning a favor.

"Can you find him for me?" Fatman said.

Tram thought about that. And as he did, he saw Hung saunter out of a side street into the central market. He watched Hung's jaw drop when he spotted Fatman, watched his amber skin pale to the color of boiled bean curd as he spun and hurriedly stumbled away.

Tram knew in that instant that Hung had betrayed Fatman last night in a most vicious manner, and that Trinh had happened by and saved Fatman with the *Dat-tay-vao*.

It was all clear now.

On impulse, Tram said, "He lives in my cousin's village. I can take you to him."

"Great" Fatman said, grinning and clapping him on the shoulder. "I'll get us a jeep!"

"No jeep," Tram said. "We walk."

"Walk?" Fatman's face lost much of its enthusiasm. "Is it far?"

"Not far. Just a few klicks on the way to Mo Due. A fishing village. We leave now."

"Now? But—"

"Could be he not there if we wait."

This wasn't exactly true, but he didn't want to give Fatman too much time to think. Tram watched reluctance and eagerness battle their way back and forth across the American's face. Finally...

"All right. Let's go. Long as it's not too far."

"If not too far for man with one foot, not too far for man with two."

5.

As Tram led Fatman south toward the tiny fishing village where Trinh had been living for the past year, he wondered why he'd agreed to bring the two of them together. His instincts were against it, yet he'd agreed to lead the American to Trinh.

Why?

Why was a word too often on his mind, it seemed. Especially where Americans were concerned. Why did they send so many of their young men over here? Most of them were either too frightened or too disinterested to make good soldiers. And the few who were eager for the fight hadn't the experience to make them truly valuable. They did not last long.

He wanted to shout across the sea: Send us seasoned soldiers, not your children!

But who would listen?

And did age really matter? After all, hadn't he been even younger than these American boys in the fight against the French at Dien Bien Phu fifteen years ago? But he and his fellow Vietminh had had a special advantage on their side. They had all burned with a fiery zeal to drive the French from their land.

Tram had been a communist then. He smiled at the thought as he limped along on the artificial foot, a replacement for the real one he'd lost to a Cong booby trap last year. Communist...he had been young at Dien Bien Phu and the constant talk from his fellow Vietminh about the glories of class war and revolution had drawn him into their ideological camp. But after the fighting was over, after the partition, what he saw of the birth pangs of the glorious new social order almost made him long for French rule again.

He'd come south then and had remained here ever since. He'd willingly fought for the South until the finger-charge booby trap had caught him at the knee; after that he found that his verve for any sort of fight had departed with his leg.

He glanced at Fatman, sweating so profusely as he walked beside him along the twisting jungle trail. He'd come to like the boy, but he could not say why. Fatman was greedy, cowardly, and selfish, and he cared for no one other than himself. Yet Tram had found himself responding to the boy's vulnerability. Something tragic behind the bluff and bravado. With Tram's aid, Fatman had gone from the butt of many of the jokes around the American barracks to their favored supplier of marijuana. Tram could not deny that he'd profited well by helping him gain that position. He'd needed the money to supplement his meager pension from the ARVN, but that had not been his only motivation. He'd felt a need to help the boy.

And he *was* a boy, no mistake about that. Young enough to be Tram's son. But Tram knew he could never raise such a son as this.

So many of the Americans he'd met here were like Fatman. No values, no traditions, no heritage. Empty. Hollow creatures who had grown up with nothing expected of them. And now, despite all the money and all the speeches, they knew in their hearts that they were not expected to win this war.

What sort of parents provided nothing for their children to believe in, and then sent them halfway around the world to fight for a country they had never heard of?

And that last was certainly a humbling experience—to learn that until a few years ago most of these boys had been blithely unaware of the existence of the land that had been the center of Tram's life since he'd been a teenager.

"How much farther now?" Fatman said.

Tram could tell from the American's expression that he was uneasy being so far from town. Perhaps now was the time to ask.

"Where did Hung stab you?" he said.

Fatman staggered as if Tram had struck him a blow. He stopped and gaped at Tram with a gray face.

"How...?"

"There is little that goes on in Quang Ngai that I do not know," he said, unable to resist an opportunity to enhance his stature. "Now, show me where."

Tram withheld a gasp as Fatman pulled up his sweat-soaked shirt to reveal the purple seam running up and down to the left of his navel. Hung had gut cut him, not only to cause an agonizing death, but to show his contempt.

"I warned you..."

Fatman pulled down his shirt. "I know, I know. But after Hung left me in the alley, this old guy came along and touched me and sealed it up like magic. Can he do that all the time?"

"Not all the time. He has lived in the village for one year. He can do it some of the time every day. He will do it many more years."

Fatman's voice was a breathy whisper. "Years! But how? Is it some drug he takes? He looked like he was drunk."

"Oh, no. *Dat-tay-vao* not work if you drunk."

"What won't work?"

"*Dat-tay-vao*...Trinh has the touch that heals."

"Heals what? Just knife wounds and stuff?"

"Anything."

Fatman's eyes bulged. "You've got to get me to him!" He glanced quickly at Tram. "So I can thank him...reward him."

"He requires no reward."

"I've got to find him. How far to go?"

"Not much." He could smell the sea now. "We turn here."

As he guided Fatman left into thicker brush that clawed at their faces and snagged their clothes, he wondered again if he'd done the right thing by bringing him here. But it was too late to turn back.

Besides, Fatman had been touched by the *Dat-tay-vao*. Surely that worked some healing changes on the spirit as well as the body. Perhaps the young American truly wanted to pay his respects to Trinh.

6.

He will do it many more years!

The words echoed in Patsy's ears and once again he began counting the millions he'd make off the old gook. God, it was going to be so great! And so easy! Uncle Tony's contacts would help get the guy into the states where Patsy would set him up in a "clinic." Then he would begin to cure the incurable.

And oh God the prices he'd charge.

How much to cure someone of cancer? Who could say what price was too high? He could ask anything—*anything*!

But Patsy wasn't going to be greedy. He'd be fair. He wouldn't strip the patients bare. He'd just ask for half—half of everything they owned.

He almost laughed out loud. This was going to be *so* sweet! All he had to do was—

Just ahead of him, Tram shouted something in Vietnamese. Patsy didn't recognize the word, but he knew a curse when he heard one.

Tram started running. They had broken free of the suffocating jungle atop a small sandy rise. Out ahead, the sun rippled off a calm sea. A breeze off the water brought blessed relief from the heat. Below lay a miserable ville—a jumble of huts made of odd bits of wood, sheet metal, palm fronds, and mud.,

One of the huts was burning. Frantic villagers were hurling sand and water at it.

Patsy followed Tram's headlong downhill run at a cautious walk. He didn't like this. He was far from town and doubted he could find his way back; he was surrounded by gooks and something bad was going down.

He didn't like this at all.

As he approached, the burning hut collapsed in a shower of sparks. To the side, a cluster of black pajama-clad women stood around a supine figure. Tram had pushed his way through to the center of the babbling group and now knelt beside the figure. Patsy followed him in.

"Aw, shit!"

He recognized the guy on the ground. Wasn't easy. He'd been burned bad and somebody had busted caps all over him, but his face was fairly undamaged and the scarred eye left no doubt that it was the same old gook who'd healed him up last night. His good eye was closed and he looked dead, but his chest still moved with shallow respirations. Patsy's stomach lurched at the sight of all the blood and charred flesh. What was keeping him alive?

Suddenly weak and dizzy, Patsy dropped to his knees beside Tram. His millions...all those sweet dreams of millions and millions of easy dollars were fading away.

Nothing ever goes right for me!

"I share your grief," Tram said, looking at him with sorrowful dark eyes.

"Yeah. What happened?"

Tram glanced around at the frightened, grieving villagers. "They say the Cong bring one of their sick officers here and demand that Trinh heal him. Trinh couldn't. He try to explain that the time not right yet but they grow angry and tie him up and shoot him and set his hut on fire."

"Can't he heal himself?"

Tram shook his head slowly, sadly. "No. *Dat-tay-vao* does not help the one who has it. Only others."

Patsy wanted to cry. All his plans...it wasn't *fair*!

"Those shitbums!"

"Worse than shitbums," Tram said. "These Charlie say they come back soon and destroy whole village."

Patsy's anger and self-pity vanished in a cold blast of fear. He peered at the trees and bushes, feeling naked with a thousand eyes watching him.

...*they come back soon*...

His knees suddenly felt stronger.

"Let's get back to town." He began to rise to his feet, but Tram held him back.

"Wait. He looking at you."

Sure enough, the old gook's good eye was open and staring directly into his. Slowly, with obvious effort, he raised his charred right hand toward Patsy. His voice rasped something.

Tram translated: "He say, 'You the one.'"

"What's that supposed to mean?"

Patsy didn't have time for this dramatic bullshit. He wanted out of here. But he also wanted to stay tight with Tram because Tram was the only one who could lead him back to Quang Ngai.

"I don't know. Maybe he mean that you the one he fix last night."

Patsy was aware of Tram and the villagers watching him, as if they expected something of him. Then he realized what it was: He was supposed to be grateful, show respect to the old gook. Fine. If it was what Tram wanted him to do, he'd do it. Anything to get them on their way out of here. He took a deep breath and gripped the hand, wincing at the feel of the fire-crisped skin—

Electricity shot up his arm.

His whole body spasmed with the searing bolt. He felt himself flopping around like a fish on a hook, and then he was falling. The air went out of him in a rush as his back slammed against the ground. It was a moment before he could open his eyes, and when he did he saw Tram and the villagers staring down at him with gaping mouths and wide, astonished eyes. He glanced at the old gook.

"What the hell did he do to me?"

The old gook was staring back, but it was a glassy, unfocused, sightless stare. He was dead.

The villagers must have noticed this too because some of the women began to weep.

Patsy staggered to his feet.

"What happened?"

"Don't know," Tram said with a puzzled shake of his head. "Why you fall? He not strong enough push you down."

Patsy opened his mouth to explain, then closed it. Nothing he could say would make sense.

He shrugged. "Let's go."

He felt like hell and just wanted to be gone. It wasn't only the threat of Charlie returning; he was tired and discouraged and so bitterly disappointed he could have sat down on the ground right then and there and cried like a wimp.

"Okay. But first I help bury Trinh. You help, too."

"What? You kidding me? Forget it!"

Tram said nothing, but the look he gave Patsy said it all: It called him fat, lazy, and ungrateful.

Screw you! Patsy thought.

Who cared what Tram or anybody else in this stinking sewer of a country thought? It held nothing for him anymore. All his money was gone, and his one chance for the brass ring lay dead and fried on the ground before him.

7.

As he helped dig a grave for Trinh, Tram glanced over at Fatman where he sat in the elephant grass staring morosely out to sea. Tram could sense that he was not grief-stricken over Trinh's fate. He was unhappy for himself.

So...he had been right about Fatman from the first: The American had come here with something in mind other than paying his respects to Trinh. Tram didn't know what it was, but he was sure Fatman had not had the best interests of Trinh or the village at heart.

He sighed. He was sick of foreigners. When would the wars end? Wars could be measured in languages here. He knew numerous Vietnamese dialects, Pidgin, French, and now English. If the North won, would he then have to learn Russian? Perhaps he would have been better off if the booby trap had taken his life instead of just his leg. Then, like Trinh, the endless wars would be over for him.

He looked down into the empty hole where Trinh's body soon would lie. Were they burying the *Dat-tay-vao* with him? Or would it rise and find its way to another? So strange and mysterious, the *Dat-tay-vao*...so many conflicting tales. Some said it came here with the Buddha himself, some said it had always been here. Some said it was as capricious as the wind in the choice of its instruments, while others said it followed a definite plan.

Who was to say truly? The *Dat-tay-vao* was a rule unto itself, full of mysteries not meant to be plumbed.

As he turned back to his digging, Tram's attention was caught by a dark blot in the water's glare. He squinted to make it out, then heard the chatter of one machine gun, then others, saw villagers begin to run and fall, felt sand kick up around him.

A Cong gunboat!

He ran for the tree where Fatman half sat, half crouched with a slack, terrified expression. He was almost there when something hit him in the chest and right shoulder with the force of a sledgehammer, and then he was flying through the air, spinning, screaming with pain.

He landed with his face in the sand and rolled. He couldn't breathe! Panic swept over him. Every time he tried to take a breath, he heard a sucking sound from the wound in his chest wall, but no air reached his lungs. His chest felt ready to explode. Black clouds encroached on his dimming vision.

Suddenly, Fatman was leaning over him, shouting through the typhoon roaring in his ears.

"Tram! Tram! Jesus God get up! You gotta get me outta here! Stop bleeding f'Christsake and get me out of here!"

Tram's vision clouded to total darkness and the roaring grew until it drowned out the voice.

8.

Patsy dug his fingers into his scalp.

How was he going to get back to town? Tram was dying, turning blue right here in front of him, and he didn't know enough Vietnamese to use with anyone else and didn't know the way back to Quang Ngai and the whole area was lousy with Charlie.

What am I gonna do?

As suddenly as they started, the AKs stopped. The cries of the wounded and the terrified filled the air in their place.

Now was the time to get out.

Patsy looked at Tram's mottled, dusky face. If he could stopper up that sucking chest wound, maybe Tram could hang on, and maybe tell him the way back to town. He slapped the heel of his hand over it and pressed.

Tram's body arched in seeming agony. Patsy felt something too— electric ecstasy shot up his arm and spread through his body like subliminal fire. He fell back, confused, weak, dizzy.

What the hell—?

He heard raspy breathing and looked up. Air was gushing in and out of Tram's wide-open mouth in hungry gasps; his eyes opened and his color began to lighten.

Tram's chest wasn't sucking anymore. As Patsy leaned forward to check the wound, he felt something in his hand and looked. A bloody lead slug sat in his palm. He looked at the chest where he'd laid that hand and what he saw made the walls of his stomach ripple and compress as if looking for something to throw up.

Tram's wound wasn't *there* anymore! Only a purplish blotch remained.

Tram raised his head and looked down at where the bullet had torn into him.

"The *Dat-tay-vao!* You have it now! Trinh passed it on to you! You have the *Dat-tay-vao!*"

I do? he thought, staring at the bullet rolling in his palm. Holy shit, I do!

He wouldn't have to get some gook back to the States to make his mint—all he had to do was get himself home in one piece.

Which made it all the more important to get the hell out of this village. Now.

"Let's go!"

"Fatman, you can't go. Not now. You must help. They—"

Patsy threw himself flat as something exploded in the jungle a hundred yards behind them, hurling a brown and green geyser of dirt and underbrush high into the air.

Mortar!

Another explosion followed close on the heels of the first, but this one was down by the waterline south of the village.

Tram was pointing out to sea.

"Look! They firing from boat." He laughed. "Can't aim mortar from boat!"

Patsy stayed hunkered down with his arms wrapped tight around his head, quaking with terror as the ground jittered with each of the next three explosions. Then they stopped.

"See?" Tram said, sitting boldly in the clearing and looking out to sea. "Even *they* know it foolish! They leaving. They only use for terror. Cong very good at terror."

No argument there, Patsy thought as he climbed once more to his feet.

"Get me out of here now, Tram. You owe me!"

Tram's eyes caught Patsy's and pinned him to the spot like an insect on a board. "Look at them, Fatman."

Patsy tore his gaze away and looked at the ville. He saw the villagers—the maimed and bleeding ones and their friends and families—looking back at him. Waiting. They said nothing, but their eyes...

He ripped his gaze loose. "Those Cong'll be back!"

"They need you, Fatman," Tram said. "You are only one who can help them now."

Patsy looked again, unwillingly. Their eyes...calling him. He could almost feel their hurt, their need.

"No way!"

He turned and began walking toward the brush. He'd find his own way back if Tram wouldn't lead him. Better than waiting around here to get caught and tortured by Charlie. It might take him all day, but—

"Fatman!" Tram shouted. "For once in your life!"

That stung. Patsy turned and looked at the villagers once more, feeling their need like a taut rope around his chest, pulling him toward them. He ground his teeth. It was idiotic to stay, but. . .

One more. Just one, to see if I still have it.

He could spare a couple of minutes for that, then be on his way. At least that way he'd be sure what had happened with Tram wasn't some sort of crazy freak accident.

Just one.

As he stepped toward the villagers, he heard their voices begin to murmur excitedly. He didn't know what they were saying but felt their grateful welcome like a warm current through the draw of their need.

He stopped at the nearest wounded villager, a woman holding a bloody, unconscious child in her arms. His stomach lurched as he saw the wound—a slug had nearly torn the kid's arm off at the shoulder. Blood oozed steadily between the fingers of the hand the woman kept clenched over the wound. Swallowing the revulsion that welled up in him, he slipped his hands under the mother's to touch the wound—

—and his knees almost buckled with the ecstasy that shot through him.

The child whimpered and opened his eyes. The mother removed her hand from the wound.

Make that *former* wound. It was gone, just like Tram's.

She cried out with joy and fell to her knees beside Patsy, clutching his leg as she wept.

Patsy swayed. He had it! No doubt about it—he had the goddamn

Dat-tay-vao! And it felt so good! Not just the pleasure it caused, but how that little gook kid was looking up at him now with his bottomless black eyes and flashing him a shy smile. He felt high, like he'd been smoking some of his best merchandise.

One more. Just one more.

He disengaged his leg from the mother and moved over to where an old woman writhed in agony on the ground, clutching her abdomen.

Belly wound...I know the feeling, mama-san.

He knelt and wormed his hand under hers. That burst of pleasure surged again as she stiffened and two slugs popped into his hand. Her breathing eased and she looked up at him with gratitude beaming from her eyes.

Another!

On it went. Patsy could have stopped at any time, but found he didn't want to. The villagers seemed to have no doubt that he would stay and heal them all. They knew he could do it and *expected* him to do it. It was so new, such a unique feeling, he didn't want it to end. Ever. He felt a sense of belonging he'd never known before. He felt protective of the villagers. But it went beyond them, beyond this little ville, seemed to take in the whole world.

Finally, it was over.

Patsy stood in the clearing before the huts, looking for another wounded body. He checked his watch—he'd been at it only thirty minutes and there were no more villagers left to heal. They all clustered around him at a respectful distance, watching silently. He gave himself up to the euphoria enveloping him, blending with the sound of the waves, the wind in the trees, the cries of the gulls. He hadn't realized what a beautiful place this was. If only—

A new sound intruded—the drone of a boat engine. Patsy looked out at the water and saw the Cong gunboat returning. Fear knifed through the pleasurable haze as the villagers scattered for the trees. Were the Cong going to land?

No. Patsy saw a couple of the crew crouched on the deck, heard the familiar *choonk!* of a mortar shell shooting out of its tube. An explosion quickly followed somewhere back in the jungle. Tram had been right. No way they could get any accuracy with a mortar on the rocking deck of a gunboat. Just terror tactics.

Damn those bastards! Why'd they have to come back and wreck his mood? Just when he'd been feeling good for the first time since leaving home. Matter of fact, he'd been feeling better than he could ever remember, home or anywhere else. For once, everything seemed *right*.

For once, something was going Patsy's way, and the Cong had to ruin it.

Two more wild mortar shots, then he heard gunfire start from the south and saw three new gunboats roaring up toward the first. But these were flying the old red, white, and blue. Patsy laughed and raised his fist.

"Get 'em!"

The Cong let one more shell go *choonk*! before pouring on the gas and slewing away.

Safe!

Then he heard a whine from above and the world exploded under him.

9.

...a voice from far away...Tram's. . .

"...chopper coming, Fatman...get you away soon... hear it?... almost here..."

Patsy opened his eyes and saw the sky, then saw Tram's face poke into view. He looked sick.

"Fatman!' You hear me?"

"How bad?" Patsy asked.

"You be okay."

Patsy turned his head and saw a ring of weeping villagers who were looking everywhere and anywhere but at him. He realized he couldn't feel anything below his neck. He tried to lift his head for a look at himself but didn't have the strength.

"I wanna see."

"You rest," Tram said.

"Get my head up, dammit!"

With obvious reluctance, Tram gently lifted his head. As Patsy looked down at what was left of him, he heard a high, keening wail. His vision swam, mercifully blotting out sight of the bloody ruin that had once been the lower half of his body. He realized that the wail was his own voice.

Tram lowered his head and the wail stopped.

I shouldn't even be alive!

Then he knew. He was waiting for someone. Not just anyone would do. A certain someone.

A hazy peace came. He drifted into it and stayed there until the chopping thrum of a slick brought him out; then he heard an American voice.

"I thought you said he was alive!"

Tram's voice: "He is."

Patsy opened his eyes and saw the shocked face of an American soldier.

"Who are you?" Patsy asked.

"Walt Erskine. Medic. I'm gonna—"

"You're the one," Patsy said. Somehow, he bent his arm at the elbow and lifted his hand. "Shake."

The medic looked confused. "Yeah. Okay. Sure."

He grabbed Patsy's hand and Patsy felt the searing electric charge.

Erskine jerked back and fell on his ass, clutching his hand. "What the *hell*?"

The peace closed in on Patsy again. He'd held on as long as he could. Now he could embrace it. One final thought arced through his mind like a lone meteorite in a starless sky. The *Dat-tay-vao* was going to America after all.

I usually *don't* write from experience and *do* write with a lot of dialogue. "Traps" is an exception to both of those usuals.

The story has no dialogue and is partially true. For a while I did have mice in my attic. And something else up there too. Because a couple of dead mice were devoured in the traps I'd set for them. I never did find out what else was up there, but when Alan Rogers asked me for a story for *Night Cry*, I began conjuring up possibilities as to what might have invaded my attic besides mice.

"Traps" is *very* close to home. It's set in the neighboring town south of where I was living at the time, the house is modeled on my own then, I have two daughters, and Hank has a lot of my attitudes.

I made up the final scene, though. Really.

Traps

S kippy Super Chunk peanut butter worked best.

Hank smeared it on the pedals of the four traps he'd bought. Victors. Something about the way the big red *V* in their logo formed itself around the shape of a mouse's head gave him a feeling that they knew what they were about.

Not that he took any pleasure in killing mice. He may not have had the bumper sticker, but he most certainly did brake for animals. He didn't like killing anything. Even ants. Live and let live was fine with him, but he drew the line at the threshold of his house. They could live long and prosper out *there*, he would live in *here*. When they came inside, it was war.

He'd had a few in the basement of their last house and caught them all with Skippy-baited Victors. But he always felt guilty when he found one of the little things dead in the trap, so frail and harmless-looking with its white underbelly and little pink feet and tail. The eyes were always the worst—shiny black and guileless, wide open and looking at him, almost saying, *Why? I don't eat much.*

Hank knew he could be a real sentimental jerk at times.

He consoled himself with the knowledge that the mouse didn't feel any pain in the trap. Better than those warfarin poisons where they crawl off to their nest and slowly bleed to death. With a trap, the instant the nibbling mouse disturbs the baited pedal, *wham!* it's on its way to mouse heaven before it knows what hit it.

Hank was doing this on the sly. Gloria wouldn't be able to sleep a wink if she thought there were mice overhead in the ceiling. And the twins, God, they'd want to catch them and make them pets and give them names. With the trip to Disney World just three days off, all they could talk about was Mickey and Minnie. They'd never forgive him for killing a mouse. Best to set the traps before they came home in the afternoon and dispose of the little carcasses in the morning after everyone was gone. Luckily, this was his slack season and he had some time at home to take care of it.

He wondered how the mice were getting in. He knew they were up there because he'd heard them last night. Something had awakened him at about 2:30 this morning—a noise, a bad dream, he didn't remember what—and as he was lying there spooned against Gloria he heard little claws scraping on the other side of the ceiling. It sounded like two or three of them under the insulation, clawing on the plasterboard, making themselves a winter home. He was ticked. This was a brand new two-story colonial, just built, barely lived in for six months, and already they had uninvited guests. And in the attic no less.

Well, they were in a woodsy area and it was fall, the time of year when woodsy things start looking for winter quarters. He wished them all a safe and warm winter. But not in this house.

Before setting the traps, he fitted a bolt on the attic door. The house had one of those swing-down contraptions in the hall ceiling right outside their bedroom. It had a pull-cord on this side and a folding ladder on the upper side. The twins had been fascinated with it since they moved in. The attic had always been off-limits to them, but you never knew. He had visions of one of them pulling the ladder down, climbing up there, and touching one of the traps. Instant broken finger. So he screwed a little sliding bolt in place to head off that trauma at the pass.

He took the four traps up to the attic and gingerly set the bows. As he stood on the ladder and spaced them out on the particle board flooring around the opening, he noticed an odd odor. The few times he had been up here before the attic had been filled with the clean smell of plywood and kiln-dried fir studs. Now there was a sour tint to the air. Vaguely unpleasant. Mouse b-o? He didn't know. He just knew that something about it didn't set well with him.

He returned to the second floor, bolted the ceiling door closed, and hit the switch that turned off the attic light. Everything was set, and well before Gloria and the girls got home.

Kate crawled into Hank's lap as he leaned back in the recliner and watched the six o'clock Eyewitness News. She was holding her well-thumbed "Mickey's book." As soon as Kim saw her, she ran in from the kitchen like a shot.

So with his two pale blonde seven-year-old darlings snuggled up against him, Hank opened up "Mickey's book" for the nightly ritual of the past two weeks. Not a book actually, just a brochure touting all the park's attractions. But it had become a Holy Book of sorts for the twins and they never tired of paging through it. This had to be their twentieth guided tour in as many days and their blue eyes were just as wide and full of wonder this time as the first.

Only three days to go before they headed for Newark Airport and the 747 that would take them south to Orlando.

Hank had come to see Disney World as a religious experience for seven-year-olds. Moslems had Mecca, Catholics had the Vatican, Japanese had Mount Fuji. Kids had Disney World on the East Coast and Disneyland on the West. Katie and Kim would start out on their first pilgrimage Thanksgiving morning.

He hugged them closer, absorbing their excitement. This was what life was all about. And he was determined to show them the best time of their lives. The sky was the limit. Any ride, any attraction, he didn't care how many times they wanted to go on it, he'd take them. Four days of fantasy at Mickey's Place with no real-world intrusions. No *Times*, no *Daily News*, no Eyewitness Special Reports, no background noise about wars or floods or muggings or bombings...or mousetraps.

Nothing about mousetraps.

The snap of the trap woke Hank with a start. It was faint, muffled by the intervening plasterboard and insulation. He must have been subconsciously attuned for it, because he heard it and Gloria didn't.

He checked the clock—12:42—and tried to go back to sleep. Hopefully, that was the end of that.

He was just dozing back off when a second trap sprang with a muffled snap. Two of them. Sounded like he had a popular attic.

He didn't know when he got to sleep again. It took a while.

When Hank had the house to himself again the next morning, he unbolted the ceiling door, pulled it down, and unfolded the ladder. Half way up, he hesitated. This wasn't going to be pleasant. He knew when he stuck his head up through that opening he'd be eye-level with the attic floor—and with the dead mice. Those shiny reproachful little black eyes...

He took a deep breath and stepped up a couple of rungs.

Yes, two of the traps had been sprung and two sets of little black eyes were staring at him. Eyes and little else. At first he thought it was a trick of the light, of the angle, but as he hurried the rest of the way up, he saw it was true.

The heads were still in the traps, but the bodies were gone. Little bits of gray fur were scattered here and there, but that was it. Sort of gave him the creeps. Something had eaten the dead mice. Something bigger than a mouse. A discomforting thought.

And that odor was worse. He still couldn't identify it, but it was taking on a stomach-turning quality.

He decided it was time for an inspection tour of the grounds. His home was being invaded. He wanted to know how.

He found the little buggers' route of invasion on the south side of the house. He had two heating-cooling zones inside, with one unit in the basement and one in the attic. The compressor-blowers for both were outside on the south side. The hoses to the upstairs unit ran up the side of the house to the attic through an aluminum leader.

That was how they were getting in.

There wasn't much space in the leader, but a mouse can squeeze through the tiniest opening. The rule of thumb—as all mouse experts knew—was that if it can get its head through, the rest of the body can follow. They were crawling into the leader, climbing up along the hoses inside, and following them into the attic. Simple.

But what had eaten them?

Up above the spot where the hoses ran through the siding, he noticed the triangular gable vent hanging free on its right side. Something had pulled it loose. As he watched, a squirrel poked its head out, looked at him, then scurried up onto the roof. It ran a few feet along the edge, jumped onto an overhanging oak branch, and disappeared into the reddening leaves.

Great! He was collecting a regular menagerie up there!

So much for the joys of a wooded lot. Gloria and he had chosen this semi-rural development because they liked the seclusion of an acre lot and the safety for the twins of living on a cul-de-sac. They both had grown up in New Jersey, and Toms River seemed like as good a place as any to raise kids. The house was expensive but they were a two-income family—she a teacher and he a CPA—so they went for it.

So far, theirs was the only house completed in this section, although two new foundations had just started. It would be nice to have neighbors. Until recently, the only other building in sight had been a deserted stone church of unknown age and long-forgotten denomination a few hundred yards south of here. The belfry of that old building had concerned him for a while—bats, you know. Very high rabies rate. But he spoke to the workmen when they bulldozed it down last week to start another cul-de-sac, and they told him they hadn't seen a single bat. Lots of animal droppings up there, but no bats.

He wondered: Would a squirrel eat a couple of dead mice? He thought they only ate nuts and berries. Maybe this one was a carnivore. Didn't matter. One way or another, something had to be done about that gable vent. He went to get the ladder.

———

He had everything taken care of by the time Gloria and the girls got home from their respective schools.

He'd tacked the gable vent back into place. He couldn't see how that squirrel had pulled it free, but it wouldn't get it out now. He also plugged up the upper and lower ends of the hose leader with an aerosol foam insulation he picked up at Home Depot. It occurred to him as he watched the mustard-colored gunk harden into a solid Styrofoam plug that he was cutting off the mouse exit as well as the mouse entryway. Hopefully they were all out for the day. When they came back they'd be locked out and would have to go somewhere else. And even more hopefully, the squirrel hadn't left a friend in the attic behind the resecured gable vent.

Hank hardly slept at all that night. He kept listening for the snap of a trap, hoping he wouldn't hear it, yet waiting for it. Hours passed. The last time he remembered seeing on the clock radio LED was 3:34. He must have fallen asleep after that.

Dawn was just starting to bleach out the night when the snap came. He came wide awake with the sound. The clock said 5:10. But the noise didn't end with that single snap. Whatever was up there began to thrash. He could hear the wooden base of the trap slapping against the attic flooring. Something bigger than a mouse, maybe a squirrel, was caught but still alive. He heard another snap and a squeal of pain. God, it was alive and hurt! His stomach turned.

Gloria rolled over and sat up, a silhouette in the growing light. She was still nine-tenths asleep.

Suddenly the attic went still.

He patted her arm and told her to lie down and go back to sleep.

She did. He couldn't.

He approached the attic door with dread. He did *not* want to go up there. What if it was still alive? What if it was weak and paralyzed but still breathing? He'd have to kill it. He didn't know if he could do that. But he'd have to. It would be the only humane thing to do. How? Drown it? Smother it in a plastic bag? He began to sweat.

This was crazy. He was wimping out over a rodent in his attic. Enough already! He flipped the attic light switch, slipped the bolt, and pulled on the cord. The door angled down on its hinges.

But it didn't come down alone. Something came with it, flying right at his face.

He yelled like a fool in a funhouse and batted it away. Then he saw what it was: one of the mousetraps. At first glance it looked empty, but when he went to pick it up, he saw what was in it and almost tossed his cookies.

A furry little forearm, no longer than the last two bones on his pinkie finger, was caught under the bow. It looked like it once might have been attached to a squirrel, but now it ended in a ragged bloody stump where it had been chewed off just below the shoulder.

Where the hell was the rest of it?

Visions of the squirrel chewing off its own arm swam around him until he remembered that auto-amputation only occurred with arresting traps, the kind that were chained down. Animals had been known to chew off a limb to escape those. The squirrel could have dragged the mousetrap with it.

But it hadn't.

Hank stood at the halfway point on those steps a long while. He finally decided he had wasted enough time. He clenched his teeth, told himself it was dead, and poked his head up. He started and almost fell off the stairs when he turned his head and found the squirrel's tail only two inches from his nose. It was caught in the bow of another trap—the second snap he had heard this morning. But there was no body attached.

This was getting a bit gory. He couldn't buy a squirrel chewing off its arm and then its tail. If anything, it would drag the tail trap after it until it got stuck someplace.

Nope. Something had eaten it. Something that didn't smell too good, because the attic was really beginning to stink.

He ducked down the ladder, grabbed the flashlight he always kept in the night table, then hurried back up to the attic. Light from the single bulb over the opening in the attic floor didn't reach very far. And even with daylight filtering in through the gable vents, there were lots of dark spots. He wanted the flashlight so he could get a good look along the inside of the eaves and into all the corners.

He searched carefully, and as he moved through the attic he had a vague sense of another presence, a faint awareness of something else here, a tantalizing hint of furtive movement just out of his range of vision.

He shook it off. The closeness up here, the poor lighting, the missing animal carcasses—it had all set his imagination in motion. He gave the attic a thorough going over and found nothing but a few droppings. Big droppings. Bigger than something a mouse or squirrel would leave. Maybe possum-sized. Or raccoon-sized.

Was that the answer? A possum or a coon? He didn't know much about them, but he'd seen them around in the woods, and he knew every time he put turkey or chicken scraps in the garbage, something would get the lid off the trash can and tear the Hefty bag apart until every last piece of meat was gone. Raccoons were notorious for that. If they'd eat leftover chicken, why not dead mice and squirrels?

Made sense to him. But how was it getting in? A check of the gable vent he'd resecured yesterday gave him the answer. It had been pulled free again. Well, he'd fix that right now.

He went down to his workshop and got a hammer and some heavy nails. He felt pretty good as he pounded them into the edges of the vent, securing it from the inside. He knew what he was up against now and knew something that big would be easy to keep out. No raccoon or possum was going to pull this vent free again. And just to be sure, he went over to the north side and reinforced the gable vent there.

That was it. His house was his own again.

Wednesday night was chaotic. Excitement ran at a fever pitch with the twins packing their own little suitcases full of stuffed animals and placing them by the front door so they'd be all set to go first thing in the morning.

Hank helped Gloria with the final packing of the big suitcases and they both fell into bed around midnight. He had little trouble getting off to sleep. There probably weren't any mice left, there weren't any squirrels, and he was sure no raccoon or possum was getting in tonight. So why stay awake listening?

The snap of a trap woke him around 3:30. No thrashing, no slapping, just the snap. Another mouse. A second trap went off ten minutes later. Then a third. Damn! He waited. The fourth and final trap sprang at 4:00 a.m.

Hank lay tense and rigid in bed and wondered what to do. Everybody would be up at first light, just an hour or so from now, getting ready for the drive to Newark Airport. He couldn't leave those mouse carcasses up there all the time they were away—they'd rot and the whole house would be stinking by the time they got back.

He slipped out of bed as carefully as he could, hoping the movement wouldn't awaken Gloria. She didn't budge. He grabbed the flashlight and closed the bedroom door behind him on his way out.

He didn't waste any time. He had to get up there and get rid of the dead mice before the girls woke up. These damn animals were really getting on his nerves. He slid the bolt, pulled down the door, and hurried up.

Hank stood on the ladder and gaped at the traps. All four had been sprung but lay empty on the flooring around him, the peanut butter untouched. No mice heads, no bits of fur. What could have tripped them without getting caught? It was almost like a game.

He looked around warily. He was standing in a narrow cone of light. The rest of the attic was dark. Very dark. The sense of something else up here with him was very strong now. So was the odor. It was worse than ever.

Imagination again.

He waved the flashlight around quickly but saw no scurrying or lurking shapes along the eaves or in the corners. He made a second sweep, more slowly this time, more careful. He crouched and moved all along the edges, bumping his head now and again on a rafter, his flashlight held ahead of him like a gun.

Finally, when he was satisfied nothing of any size was lurking about, he checked the gable vent.

It had been yanked loose again. Some of the nails had pulled free, and those that hadn't had ripped through the vent's plastic edge.

He was uneasy now. No raccoon was strong enough to do this. He didn't know many *men* who could do it without a crowbar. This was getting out of hand. He suddenly wanted to get downstairs and bolt the attic door behind him. He'd call a professional exterminator as soon as they got back from Orlando.

He spun about, sure that something had moved behind him, but all was still, all was dark but for the pool of light under the bulb. Yet...

Quickly now, he headed back toward the light, toward the ladder, toward the empty traps. As he sidled along, he checked in the corners and along the eaves one last time, and wondered how and why the traps had been sprung. He saw nothing. Whatever it was, if it had come in, it wasn't here anymore. Maybe the attic light had scared it off. If that was the case, he'd leave the light on all night. All *week*.

His big mistake was looking for it along the floor.

It got him as he came around the heating unit. He saw a flash movement as it swung down from the rafters—big as a Rottweiler, brown scruffy fur, a face that was all mouth with huge countless teeth, four clawed arms extended toward him as it held onto the beams above with still two more limbs—and that was all. It engulfed his head and lifted him off the floor in one sweeping motion. For a few spasming seconds his fingers tore futilely at its matted fur and his legs kicked and writhed silently in the air. As life and consciousness fled that foul smothering unbearable agony, he sensed the bottomless pit of its hunger and thought helplessly of the open attic door, of the ladder going down, and of Gloria and the twins sleeping below.

This is the companion piece to "The Last 'One Mo' Once Golden Oldies Revival'" and it appeared in another of Stu Schiff's *Whispers* collections for Doubleday.

It popped into my head as I was thumbing through the *Rolling Stone Rock Almanac* and noted all the deaths, injuries, drop-outs, and plain bad luck that had befallen every single major name in rock 'n' roll during a two-year period in the late fifties. They had dropped like the proverbial flies. Most people would say, "Isn't that something," and read on.

I, of course, saw a hideous conspiracy.

(I revisited this Nantucket house in *Harbingers*.)

The Years the Music Died

Nantucket in November. Leave it to Bill to make a mockery of security. And of me. The Atlantic looked mean today. I watched its gray, churning surface from behind the relative safety of the double-paned picture windows. I would have liked a few more panes between me and all that water. Would have liked a few *miles* between us, in fact.

Some people are afraid of snakes, some of spiders. With me, it's water. And the more water, the worse it is. I get this feeling it wants to suck me down. Been that way since I was a kid. Bill has known about the phobia for a good twenty years. So why did he do it? Bad enough to set up the meeting on this dinky little island, but to hold it on this narrow spit of land between the head of the harbor and an uneasy ocean with no more than a hundred yards between the two was outright cruel. And a nor'easter coming. If that awful ocean ever reared up...

I shuddered and turned away. But no turning away in this huge barn of a room with all these picture windows facing east, west, and north. Like a goddamn goldfish bowl. Not even curtains I could pull closed. I felt naked and exposed in this open pine-paneled space. Eight hours to go until dark blotted out the ocean. But then I'd still be able to *hear* it.

Why would my own son do something like this to me?

Security, Bill had said.

A last-minute off-season rental of an isolated house on a summer resort island in the chill of November. The Commission members could fly in, attend the meeting, then fly out again with no one ever knowing they were here. What could be more secure?

I'm a stickler for security, too, but this was ludicrous. This was—

Bill walked into the room, carefully not looking in my direction. I studied my son a moment: a good-looking man with dark hair and light blue eyes; just forty-four but looking ten years older. A real athlete until he started letting his weight go to hell. Now he had the beginnings of a hefty spare tire around his waist. I've got two dozen years on him and only half his belly.

Something was wrong with the way he was walking … a little unsteady. And then I realized.

Good Lord, he's drunk.

I started to say something but Bill beat me to it.

"Nelson's here. He just called from the airport. I sent the car out for him. Harold is in the air."

I managed to say, "Fine," without making it sound choked.

My son, half-lit at a Commission meeting, and me surrounded by water—this had a good chance of turning into a personal disaster. All my peers, the heads of all the major industries in the country, were downstairs at the buffet brunch. Rockefeller was on the island, and Vanderbilt was on his way; they would complete the Commission in its present composition. Soon they'd be up here to start the agenda. Only Joe Kennedy would be missing. Again. Too bad. I've always liked Joe. But with a son in the White House, we all had serious doubts about his objectivity. It had been a tough decision, but Joe had gracefully agreed to give up his seat on the Commission for the duration of Jack's presidency.

Good thing, too. I was glad he wouldn't be here to see how Bill had deteriorated.

His son's going down in history while mine is going down the drain.

What a contrast. And yet, on the surface, I couldn't see a single reason why Bill couldn't be where Jack Kennedy was. Both came from good stock, both had good war records and plenty of money behind them. But Jack had gone for the gold ring and Bill had gone for the bottle.

I wasn't going to begrudge Joe his pride in his son. All of us on the

Commission were proud of the job Jack was doing. I remember that inner glow I felt when I heard, "Ask not what your country can do for you; ask what you can do for your country." That's *just* the way I feel. The way everybody on the Commission feels.

I heard ice rattle and turned to see Bill pouring himself a drink at the bar.

"Bill! It's not noon yet, for God's sake!"

Bill raised his glass mockingly. "Happy anniversary, Dad."

I didn't know what to say to that. Today was nobody's anniversary.

"Have you completely pickled your brains?"

Bill's eyebrows rose. "How soon we forget. Six years ago today: November eighth, 1957. Doesn't that ring a bell?"

"No." I could feel my jaw clenching as I stepped toward him. "Give me that glass."

"That was the day the Commission decided to 'do something' about rock 'n' roll."

"So what?"

"Which led to February 3, 1959."

That date definitely had a familiar ring.

"You *do* remember February 3, don't you, Dad? An airplane crash. Three singers. All dead."

I took a deep breath. "That again."

"Not again. Still." He raised his glass. "*Salud.*" Taking a long pull on his drink, he dropped into a chair.

I stood over him. The island, the drinking...here was what it was all about. I've always known the crash bothered him, but never realized how much until now. What anger he must have been carrying around these past few years. Anger and guilt.

"You mean to tell me you're still blaming yourself for that?" The softness of my voice surprised me.

"Why not? My idea, wasn't it?"

"The plane crash was nobody's idea. How many times do we have to go over this?"

"There never seems to be a time when I *don't* go over it. And now it's November eighth, 1963. Exactly six years to the day after I opened my big mouth at the Commission meeting."

"Yes, you did." And how proud I was of him that day. "You came up with a brilliant solution that resolved the entire crisis."

"Hah! Some crisis!"

A sudden burst of rain splattered against the north and east windows. The storm was here.

I sat down with my back to most of the glass and tried to catch Bill's eye.

"And you talk about how soon *I* forget? You had a crisis in your own home—Peter. Remember?"

Bill nodded absently.

I pressed on. Maybe I could break through this funk he was wallowing in, straighten him out before the meeting.

"Peter is growing to be a fine man now and I'm proud to call him my grandson, but back in '57 he was only eleven and already thoroughly immersed in rock and roll—"

"Not 'rock *and* roll,' Dad. You've got to be the only one in the country who pronounces the 'and.' It's 'rock 'n' roll'—like one word."

"It's *three* words and I pronounce all three. But be that as it may, your house was a war zone, and you know it."

That had been a wrenching time for the whole McCready clan, but especially for me. Peter was my only grandson then and I adored him. But he had taken to listening to those atrocious Little Richard records and combing his hair like Elvis Presley. Bill banned the music from the house but Peter was defying everyone, sneaking records home, listening to it on the radio, plunking his dimes into jukeboxes on the way home from school.

But Bill's house was hardly unique. The same thing was happening in millions of homes all over the country. Everyone but the kids seemed to have declared war on the music. Old-line disc jockeys were calling it junk noise and were having rock and roll record-smashing parties on the air; television networks were refusing to broadcast Presley below the waist; church leaders were calling it the Devil's music, cultural leaders were calling it barbaric, and a lot of otherwise mild-mannered ordinary citizens were calling it nigger music.

They should have guessed what the result of such mass persecution would be: The popularity of rock and roll *soared*.

"But the strife in your home served a useful purpose. It opened my eyes. I say with no little pride that I was probably the only man in the country who saw the true significance of what rock and roll was doing to American society."

"You *thought* you saw significance, and you were very persuasive. But I don't buy it anymore. It was only music."

I leaned back and closed my eyes. *Only music...*

Bill was proving to be a bigger and bigger disappointment with each passing year. I'd had such high hopes for him. I'd even started bringing him to Commission meetings to prepare him to take my seat someday. But now I couldn't see him ever sitting on the Commission. He had no foresight, no vision for the future. He couldn't be trusted to participate in the decisions the Commission had to make. Nor could I see myself leaving my controlling interest in the family business to him.

I have a duty to the McCready newspaper chain: My dad started it with a measly little local weekly in Boston at the turn of the century and built it to a small string. I inherited that and sweated my butt to expand it into a publishing empire that spans the country today. There was no way in good conscience I could leave the McCready Syndicate to Bill. Maybe this was a signal to start paying more attention to Jimmy. He was a full decade younger but showing a *lot* more promise.

Bill had shown promise in '57, though. I'll never forget the fall meeting of the Commission that year when Bill sat in as a non-voting member. I was set to address the group on what I saw as an insidious threat to the country. I knew I was facing a tough audience, especially on the subject of music. I drew on every persuasive skill I had to pound home the fact that rock and roll was more than just music, more than just an untrained nasal voice singing banal lyrics to a clichéd melody backed by a bunch of guitar notes strung together over a drumbeat.

It had become a social force.

Music as a social force—I knew that concept was unheard-of, but the age of mass communication was here and life in America was a new game. I saw that. I had to make the Commission see it. The Commission had to learn the rules of the new game if it wanted to remain a guiding force. In 1957, rock and roll was a pivotal piece in the game.

Irritating as it was, I knew the music itself was unimportant. Its status as a threat had been created by the hysterically negative reaction from the adult sector of society. As a result, untold millions of kids under eighteen came to see it as *their* music. Everyone born before World War II seemed to be trying to take it away from them. So they were closing ranks against all the older generations. That frightened me.

It did not, however, impress the other members of the Commission.

So for weeks before our regular meeting, I hammered away, throwing facts and figures at them, sending newspaper accounts of rock and roll riots, softening them up for my pitch.

And I was good that day. God, was I good. I can still remember my closing words:

"And gentlemen, as you all know, the upcoming generation includes the post-war baby boom, making it the largest single generation in the nation's history. If that generation develops too much self-awareness, if it begins to think of itself as a group outside the mainstream, catastrophe could result.

"Consider, gentlemen: In ten years most of them will be able to vote. If the wrong people get their ear, the social and political continuity that this Commission has sworn to safeguard could be permanently disrupted.

"The popularity of the music continues to expand, gathering momentum all the time. If we don't act now, next year may be too late. We cannot silence this music, because that will only worsen the division. We must find a way to temper rock and roll...make it more palatable to the older generations, fuse it to the mainstream. Do that, and the baby boom generation will fall in line! Do nothing and I see only chaos ahead!"

But in the ensuing discussion it became quite clear that nobody, including myself, had the foggiest notion of how to change the music.

Then someone—I forget who—made a comment about how it was too bad all these rock and roll singers couldn't give up their guitars and go into the religion business like Little Richard had just done.

Bill had piped up then: "Or the Army. I'd love to see a military barber get a hold of Elvis Presley. Can't we get him drafted?"

The room suddenly fell silent as the Commission members—all of us— shared an epiphany:

Don't go after the music—go after the ones who make the music. Get rid of the raucous leaders and replace them with more placid, malleable types.

Brilliant! It might never have occurred to anyone without Bill's remark.

The tinkling of the ice in Bill's glass as he took another sip dragged me back to the present, to Nantucket and the storm. In what I hoped he would take as a friendly gesture, I slapped Bill on the knee.

"Don't you remember the excitement back then after the Commission meeting? You and I became *experts* on rock and roll. We listened to all those awful records, got to know all about the performers, and then we began to zero in on them."

Bill nodded. "But I had no idea where it was going to end."

"No one did. Remember making the list? We sat around for weeks, going through the entertainment papers and picking out the singers most closely associated with the music, the leaders, the trendsetters, the originals."

I still savor the memory of that time of closeness with Bill, working together with him, both of us tingling with the knowledge that we were doing something important.

Elvis was the prime target, of course. More than anyone else, he personified everything that was rock and roll. His sneers, his gyrations, everything he did on stage was a slap in the face to the older generations. And his too-faithful renditions of colored music getting airplay all over the country, the screaming, fainting girls at his concerts, the general hysteria. Elvis had to go first.

And he turned out to be the easiest to yank from sight. With the Commission's vast influence, all we had to do was pass the word. In a matter of weeks, a certain healthy twenty-two-year-old Memphis boy received his draft notice. And on March 24, 1958—a landmark date I'll never forget—Elvis Presley was inducted into the US Army. But *not* to hang around stateside and keep up his public profile. Oh, no. Off to West Germany. Bye-bye, Elvis Pelvis.

Bill seemed to be reading my thoughts. "Too bad we couldn't have taken care of everyone like that."

"I agree, son." Bill seemed to be perking up a little. I kept up the chatter, hoping to bring him out some more. "But someone would have smelled a rat. We had to move slowly, cautiously. That was why I rounded up some of our best reporters and had them start sniffing around. And as you know, it didn't take them long to come up with a few gems."

The singers weren't my only targets. I also wanted to strike at the ones who spread the music through the airwaves. That proved easy. We soon learned that a lot of the big-time rock and roll disc jockeys were getting regular payoffs from record companies to keep their new releases on the air. We made sure that choice bits of information got to congressmen looking to heighten their public profile, and we made sure they knew to go after Alan Freed.

Oh, how I wanted Freed off the air back then. The man had gone from small-time Cleveland dj to big-time New York music show impresario. By 1959 he had appeared in a line of low-budget rock and roll movies out of Hollywood and was hosting a nationwide music television show. He had become "Mr. Rock 'n' Roll." His entire career was built on the music and he was its most vocal defender.

Alan Freed had to go. And payola was the key. We set the gears in motion and turned to other targets. And it was in May, only two months after Presley's induction, that the reporters turned up another spicy morsel.

"Remember, Bill? Remember when they told us that Jerry Lee Lewis had secretly married his third cousin in November of '57? Hardly a scandal in and of itself. But the girl was only fourteen. *Fourteen!* Oh, we made sure the McCready papers gave plenty of press to that, didn't we. Within days he was being booed off the stage. Yessir, Mr. Whole Lotta Shakin' / Great Balls of Fire was an instant has-been."

I laughed, and even Bill smiled. But the smile didn't last.

"Don't stop now, Dad. Next comes 1959."

"Bill, I had nothing to do with that plane crash. I swear it."

"You told your operatives to 'get Valens and Holly off the tour.' I heard you myself."

"I don't deny that. But I meant 'off the tour'—not *dead!* We couldn't dig up anything worthwhile on them so I intended to create some sort of scandal. We discussed it, didn't we? We wanted to see them replaced by much safer types, by pseudo-crooners like Frankie Avalon and Fabian. I did *not* order any violence. The plane crash was pure coincidence."

Bill studied the ceiling. "Which just happened to lead to the replacement of Holly, Valens, and that other guy with the silly name—The Big Bopper—by Avalon, Fabian, and Paul Anka. Some coincidence!"

I said nothing. The crash *had* been an accident. The operatives had been instructed to do enough damage to the plane to keep it on the ground, forcing the three to miss their next show. Apparently they didn't do enough, and yet did too much. The plane got into the air, but never reached its destination. Tragic, unfortunate, but it all worked out for the best. I couldn't let Bill know that, though.

"I can understand why you lost your enthusiasm for the project then."

"But *you* didn't, did you, Dad? You kept right on going."

"I had a job to do. An important one. And when one of our reporters discovered that Chuck Berry had brought that Apache minor across state lines to work in his club, I couldn't let it pass."

Berry was one of the top names on my personal list. Strutting up there on stage, swinging his guitar around, duck-walking across back and forth, shouting out those staccato lyrics as he spread his legs and wiggled his hips, and all those white girls clapping and singing along as they gazed up at him. I tell you it made my hackles rise.

"The Mann Act conviction we got on him has crippled his career. And then later in '59 we finally spiked Alan Freed. When he refused to sign that affidavit saying he had never accepted payola, he was through.

Fired from WNEW-TV, WABC-TV, and WABC radio—one right after the other."

What a wonderful year.

"Did you stop there, Dad?"

"Yes." What was he getting at? "Yes, I believe so."

"You had nothing to do with that car crash in sixty—Eddie Cochran killed, Gene Vincent crippled?"

"Absolutely not!" *Damn!* The booze certainly wasn't dulling Bill's memory. That crash had been another unfortunate, unintended mishap caused by an overly enthusiastic operative. "Anyway, it remains a fact that by the middle of 1960, rock and roll was dead."

"Oh, I don't know about that—"

"Dead as a *threat*. What had been a potent, divisive social force is now a tiny historical footnote, a brief, minor cultural aberration. Only two years after we started, Elvis was out of the service but he was certainly not the same wild man who went in. Little Richard was in the ministry, Chuck Berry was up to his ears in legal troubles, Jerry Lee Lewis was in limbo as a performer, Alan Freed was out of a job and appearing before House subcommittees."

Bill tossed off the rest of his drink and glared at me. "You forgot to mention that Buddy Holly, Richie Valens, and Eddie Cochran were dead."

"Unfortunately and coincidentally, yes. But not by my doing. I say again: Rock and roll was dead then, and remains dead. Even Presley gave up on it after his discharge. He got sanitized and Hollywoodized and that's fine with me. More power to him. I bear him no ill will."

"There's still rock 'n' roll," Bill mumbled as he got up and stood by the bar, glass in hand.

"I disagree, son," I said quickly, hoping he wouldn't pour himself another. "I stay current on these things and I know. There's still popular music they *call* rock and roll, but it has none of the abrasive, irritating qualities of the original. Remember how some of those songs used to set your teeth on edge and make your skin crawl? That stuff is extinct."

"Some of it's still pretty bad."

"Not like it used to be. Its punch is gone. Dried up. Dead." I pointed to the radio at the end of the bar. "Turn that thing on and I'll show you."

Bill did. A newscast came on.

"Find some music."

He spun the dial until the sweet blend of a mixed duet singing "Hey, Paula" filled the room.

"Hear that? Big song. I can live with it. Find another so-called rock 'n' roll station." He did and the instrumental "Telstar" came on. "Monotonous, but I can live with that, too. Try one more." As a dj announced the number one song in the country, a twelve-string guitar opening led into "Walk Right In."

Bill nodded and turned the radio off. "I concede the point."

"Good. And you must also concede that the wartime and post-war generations are now firmly back in the fold. There are pockets of discontent, naturally, but they are small and isolated. There is no clear-cut dividing line—*that's* what's important. Jack's doing his part in the White House. He's got them all hot for his social programs like the Peace Corps and such where their social impulses can be channeled and directed by the proper agencies. They see themselves as part of the mainstream, *involved* in the social continuum rather than separate from it."

"And we saved them, Bill—you, me, and the Commission."

Bill only stared at me. Finally, he said, "Maybe we did. But I never really understood about Buddy Holly—"

I felt like shouting, but controlled my voice.

"Can't you drop that? I told you—"

"Oh, I don't mean the crash. I mean why he was so high on your list. He always struck me as an innocuous four-eyes who hiccupped his way through songs."

"Perhaps he was. But like Berry and Little Richard and Valens and Cochran, he had the potential to become a serious threat. He and the others originated the qualities that made the music so divisive. They wrote, played, and sang their own songs. That made me extremely uneasy."

Bill shook his head in bafflement. "I don't see..."

"All right: Let's suppose the Commission hadn't acted and had let things run their course. And now, here in sixty-three, the wartime and post-war baby boom generation is aware of itself and a group, psychologically separate and forming its own subculture within ours. A lot of them are voting age now, and next year is an election year. Let's say one of these self-styled rock and roll singers who writes his own material gets it into his head to use his songs to influence the generation that idolizes him. Think of it: a thinly disguised political message being played over and over again, on radios, TVs, in homes, in jukeboxes, hummed, sung in the shower by all those voters. With their numbers, God knows what could happen at the polls."

I paused for breath. It *was* a truly frightening thought.

"But that's all fantasy," I said. "The airwaves are once again full of safe, sane Tin Pan Alley tunes."

Bill smiled.

I asked, "What's so funny?"

"Just thinking. When I was in London last month I noticed that Britain seems to be going through the same kind of thing we did in '57. Lots of rock and roll bands and fans. There's one quartet of guys who wear their hair in bangs—can't remember the name now—that's selling records like crazy and packing the kids into the old music halls where they're screaming and fainting just like in Elvis Presley's heyday. And I understand they write and play and sing their own music, too."

I heard the windows at my back begin to rattle and jitter as hail mixed with the rain. I did not turn to look.

"Forget Britain. England is already a lost cause."

"But what if their popularity spreads over here and the whole process gets going again?"

I laughed. That was a good one.

"A bunch of Limeys singing rock and roll to American kids? That'll be the day."

But I knew that if such a thing ever came to pass, the Commission would be there to take the necessary measures.

Besides the Miracle Cure, one of my recurring themes is loss of control or loss of self: For one reason or another your values corrode, your moral underpinnings collapse, you become a lesser person than you wish to be, or do things that you never thought you'd sink to.

Take that, mix in memories of the old Lionel Atwill creeper *Night Monster* from the 1930s, and you get "Ménage à Trois."

After "Ménage" was published, I began thinking of other twists on Marta Gati's power. I remembered that I'd mentioned other members of her family in the course of the story, and so I put the other branch of the Gati family on a back burner and let them simmer. They stewed for years before I stumbled on the final twist that made me drop everything else and write *Sibs*.

Showtime made a lot of odd changes for the adaptation (with Karen Black, Daniel Craig, and Lena Headey) that launched its horror series, *The Hunger*, in 1997.

But here's the original. Here is where *Sibs* began. (Detective Burke, by the way, was borrowed from "The Cleaning Machine".)

Ménage à Trois

*B*urke noticed how Grimes, the youngest patrolman there, was turning a *sickly shade of yellow-green. He motioned him closer.*

"You all right?"

Grimes nodded. "Sure. Fine." His pitiful attempt at a smile was hardly reassuring. "Awful hot in here, but I'm fine."

Burke could see that he was anything but. The kid's lips were as pale as the rest of his face and he was dripping with sweat. He was either going to puke or pass out or both in the next two minutes.

"Yeah. Hot," Burke said. It was no more than seventy in the hospital room. "Get some fresh air out in the hall."

"Okay. Sure." Now the smile was real—and grateful. Grimes gestured

toward the three sheet-covered bodies. "I just never seen anything like this before, y'know?"

Burke nodded. He knew.

This was a nasty one. He swallowed the sour-milk taste that puckered his cheeks. In his twenty-three years with homicide he had seen his share of crime scenes like this, but he never got used to them. The splattered blood and flesh, the smell from the ruptured intestines, the glazed eyes in the slack-jawed faces—who could get used to that? And three lives, over and gone for good.

"While you're out there," he told Grimes, "check at the nurses' desk and find out where they lived. Get over there and dig up some background."

Grimes nodded enthusiastically. "Yes, sir."

Burke turned back to the room. Three lives had ended in there this morning. He was going to have to find out what those lives had been until now if he was ever going to understand this horror. And when he did get all the facts, could he ever really understand? Did he really want to?

———

Hot, sweaty, and gritty, Jerry Pritchard hauled himself up the cellar stairs and into the kitchen. Grabbing a beer from the fridge, he popped the top and drained half the can in one long, gullet-cooling swallow.

Lord, that was *good.*

He stepped over to the back door and pressed his face against the screen in search of a vagrant puff of air, anything to cool him off.

"Spring cleaning," he muttered, looking out at the greening rear acreage. "Right."

It felt like August. Who ever heard of eighty degrees in April?

He could almost see the grass growing. The weeds, too. That meant he'd probably be out riding the mower around next week. Old lady Gati had kept him busy all fall getting the grounds perfectly manicured; the winter had been spent painting and patching the first and second floors; April had been designated basement cleanup time; and now the grounds needed to be whipped into shape again.

An endless cycle.

Jerry smiled because that cycle meant job security. And job security meant he could work and eat here during the day and sleep in the gate-house at night, and never go home again.

He drained the can and gave it a behind-the-back flip into the brown paper bag sitting in the corner by the fridge.

Home...the thought pursued him. There had been times when he thought he'd never get out. Twenty-two years in that little house, the last six of them pure hell after Dad got killed in the cave-in of No.8 mine. Mom went off the deep end then. She'd always been super-religious, herding everyone along to fire-and-brimstone Sunday prayer meetings and making them listen to Bible readings every night. Dad had kept her in check somewhat, but once he was gone, all the stops were out. She began hounding Jerry about how her only son should join the ministry and spread the Word of God. She submerged him in a Bible-besotted life for those years, and he'd almost bought the package. She had him consulting the Book upon awakening, upon retiring, before eating, before going off to school, before buying a pair of socks, before taking a leak, until common sense got hold of him and he realized he was going mad. But he couldn't leave because he was the man of the house and there was his younger sister to think of.

But Suzie, bless her, ran off last summer at sixteen and got married. Jerry walked out a week later. Mom had the house, Dad's pension, her Bible, and an endless round of prayer meetings. Jerry stopped by once in a while and sent her a little money when he could. She seemed to be content.

Whatever makes you happy, he thought.

He'd taken his own personal Bible with him when he left. It was still in his suitcase in the gatehouse. Some things you just didn't throw away, even after you stopped using them.

The latest in a string of live-in maids swung through the kitchen door with old lady Gati's lunch dishes on a tray. None of the others had been bad looking, but this girl was a knockout.

"Hey, Steph," he said, deciding to put off his return to the cellar just a little bit longer. "How's the Dragon Lady treating you?"

She flashed him a bright smile. "I don't know why you call her that, Jerry. She's really very sweet."

That's what they all say, he thought, and then *wham!* They're out.

Stephanie Watson had been here almost six weeks—a record in Jerry's experience. Old lady Gati went through maids like a hay fever sufferer went through Kleenex. Maybe Steph had whatever it was old lady Gati was looking for.

Jerry hoped so. He liked her. Liked her a *lot*. Liked her short tawny hair and the slightly crooked teeth that made her easy smile seem so genuine; liked her long legs and the way she moved through this big old house with such natural grace, like she belonged here. He especially liked the way her blue-flowered print shift clung to her breasts and stretched across her buttocks as she loaded the dishes into the dishwasher.

She excited him, no doubt about that.

"You know," she said, turning toward him and leaning back against the kitchen counter, "I still can't get over the size of this place. Seems every other day I find a new room."

Jerry nodded, remembering his first few weeks here last September. The sheer height of this old three-storied Gothic mansion had awed him as he'd come through the gate to apply for the caretaker job. He had known it was big—everybody in the valley grew up within sight of the old Gati house on the hill—but had never been close enough to appreciate *how* big. The house didn't really fit with the rest of the valley. It wasn't all that difficult to imagine that a giant hand had plucked it from a faraway, more populated place and dropped it here by mistake. But the older folks in town still talked about all the trouble and expense mine owner Karl Gati had gone through to have it built.

"Yeah," he said, looking at his callused hands. "It's big, all right."

He watched her for a moment as she turned and rinsed out the sink, watched the way her blond hair moved back and forth across the nape of her neck. He fought the urge to slip his arms around her and kiss that neck. That might be a mistake. They had been dating since she arrived here—just movies and something to eat afterward—and she had been successful so far in holding him off. Not that that was so hard to do. Growing up under Mom's watchful Pentecostal eye had prevented him from developing a smooth approach to the opposite sex. So far, his limited repertoire of moves hadn't been successful with Steph.

He was sure she wasn't a dumb innocent—she was a farm girl and certainly knew what went where and why. No, he sensed that she was as attracted to him as he to her but didn't want to be a pushover. Well, okay. Jerry wasn't sure why that didn't bother him too much. Maybe it was because there was something open and vulnerable about Steph that appealed to a protective instinct in him. He'd give her time. Plenty of it. Something inside him told him she was worth the wait. And something else told him that she was weakening, that maybe it wouldn't be too long now before...

"Well, it's Friday," he said, moving closer. "Want to go down to town tonight and see what's playing at the Strand?"

He hated to sound like a broken record—movie-movie-movie—but what else was there to do in this county on weekends if you didn't get drunk, play pool, race cars, or watch TV?

Her face brightened with another smile. "Love it!"

Now why, he asked himself, should a little smile and a simple yes make me feel so damn good?

No doubt about it. She did something to him.

"Great! I'll—"

A deep, guttural woman's voice interrupted him. "Young Pritchard! I wish to see you a moment!"

Jerry shuddered. He hated what her accent did to the r's in his name. Setting his teeth, he followed the sound of her voice through the ornate, cluttered dining room with its huge needlepoint carpet and bronze chandeliers and heavy furniture. Whoever had decorated this house must have been awful depressed. Everything was dark and gloomy. All the furniture and decorations seemed to end in points.

He came to the semicircular solarium where she awaited him. Her wheelchair was in its usual position by the big bay windows where she could look out on the rolling expanse of the south lawn.

"Ah, there you are, young Pritchard," she said, looking up and smiling coyly.

She closed the book in her hands and laid it on the blanket that covered what might have passed for legs in a nightmare. The blanket had slipped once and he had seen what was under there. He didn't want another look. Ever. He remembered what his mother had always said about deformed people: that they were marked by God and should be avoided.

Old lady Gati was in her mid-sixties maybe, flabby without being fat, with pinched features and graying hair stretched back into a severe little bun at the back of her head. Her eyes were a watery blue as she looked at him over the tops of her reading glasses.

Jerry halted about a dozen feet away but she motioned him closer. He pretended not to notice. She was going to want to touch him again. God, he couldn't stand this!

"You called, ma'am?"

"Don't stand so far away, young Pritchard." He advanced two steps in her direction and stopped again. "Closer," she said. "You don't expect me to shout, do you?"

She didn't let up until he was standing right next to her. Except for these daily chats with Miss Gati, Jerry loved his job.

"There," she said. "That's better. Now we can talk more easily. "

She placed a gnarled, wrinkled hand on his arm and Jerry's flesh began to crawl. Why did she always have to touch him?

"The basement—it is coming along well?"

"Fine," he said, looking at the floor, out the window, anywhere but at her hungry, smiling face. "Just fine."

"Good." She began stroking his arm, gently, possessively. "I hope this heat wave isn't too much for you." As she spoke she used her free hand to adjust the blanket over what there was of her lower body. "I really should have Stephanie get me a lighter blanket."

Jerry fought the urge to jump away from her. He had become adept at masking the revulsion that rippled through his body every time she touched him. And it seemed she *had* to touch him whenever he was in reach. When he first got the caretaker job, he took a lot of ribbing from the guys in town down at the Dewkum Inn. (Lord, what Mom would say if she ever saw him standing at a bar!) Everybody knew that a lot of older, more experienced men had been passed over for him. His buddies had said that the old lady really wanted him for stud service. The thought nauseated him. Who knew if she even had—?

No, that would never happen. He needed this job, but there was nothing he needed that badly. And so far, all she had ever done was stroke his arm when she spoke to him. Even that was hard to take.

As casually as he could, he moved out of reach and gazed out the window as if something on the lawn had attracted his attention. "What did you want me to—?"

Stephanie walked into the room and interrupted him.

"Yes, Miss Gati?"

"Get me a summer blanket, will you, dear?"

"Yes, ma'am."

She flashed a little smile at Jerry as she turned, and he watched her until she was out of sight. Now if only it were Steph who couldn't keep her hands off him, he wouldn't—

"She appeals to you, young Pritchard?" Miss Gati said, her eyes dancing.

He didn't like her tone, so he kept his neutral. "She's a good kid."

"But does she *appeal* to you?"

He felt his anger rising, felt like telling her it was none of her damn business, but he hauled it back

"Why's that so important to you?"

"Now, now, young Pritchard, I'm only concerned that the two of you get along well. But not *too* well. I don't want you taking little Stephie away from me. I have special needs, and as you know, it took me a long time to find a live-in maid with Stephie's special qualities."

Jerry couldn't quite buy that explanation. He'd spotted something in her eyes when she spoke of Steph "appealing" to him, a hint that her interest went beyond mere household harmony.

"But the reason I called you here," she said, shifting the subject, "is to tell you that I want you to tend to the roof in the next few days."

"The new shingles came in?"

"Yes. Delivered this morning while you were in the basement. I want you to replace the worn ones over my room tomorrow. I fear this heat wave might bring us a storm out of season. I don't want my good furniture ruined by leaking water."

He guessed he could handle that.

"Okay. I'll finish up today and be up on the roof tomorrow. How's that?"

She wheeled over and cut him off as he tried to make his getaway.

"Whatever you think best, young Pritchard."

Jerry pulled free and hurried off, shuddering.

Marta Gati watched young Pritchard's swift exit.

I repulse him.

There was no sorrow, no self-pity attached to the thought. When you were born with twig-like vestigial appendages for legs and only half a pelvis, you quickly became used to rejection—you learned to read it in the posture, to sense it behind the eyes. Your feelings soon became as callused as a miner's hands.

He's sensitive about my little Stephie, she thought. Almost protective. He likes her. He's attracted to her. *Very* attracted.

That was good. She wanted young Pritchard to have genuine feelings for Stephie. That would make it so much better.

Yes, her little household was just the way she wanted it now. It had taken her almost a year to set it up this way. Month after month of trial and error until she found the right combination. And now she had it.

Such an arrangement would have been impossible while Karl was alive. Her brother would never have hired someone with as little experience as young Pritchard as caretaker, and he would have thought Stephie too young and too frail to be a good live-in maid. But Karl was dead now. The heart attack had taken him quickly and without warning last June. He had gone to bed early one night complaining of what he thought was indigestion, and never awoke. Marta Gati missed her brother and mourned his loss, yet she was reveling in the freedom his passing had left her.

Karl had been a good brother. Tyrannically good. He had looked after her as a devoted husband would an ailing wife. He had never married, for he knew that congenital defects ran high in their family. Out of their parents' four children, two—Marta and Gabor—had been horribly deformed. When they had come to America from Hungary, Karl invested the smuggled family fortune in the mines here and, against all odds, had done well. He saw to it that Lazlo, the younger brother, received the finest education. Lazlo now lived in New York where he tended to Gabor.

And Marta? Marta he had kept hidden away in this remote mansion in rural West Virginia where she had often thought she would go insane with boredom. At least she had been able to persuade him to decorate the place. If she had to stay here, she had a right to be caged in surroundings to her taste. And her taste was Gothic Revival.

Marta loved this house, loved the heavy wood of the tables, the carved deer legs of the chairs, the elaborate finials atop the cabinets, the ornate valances and radiator covers, the trefoil arches on her canopy bed.

But the decor could only carry one so far. And there were only so many books one could read, television shows and rented movies one could watch. Karl's conversational capacity had been limited in the extreme, and when he had spoken, it was on business and finance and little else. Marta had wanted to be out in the world, but Karl said the world would turn away from her, so he'd kept her here to protect her from hurt.

But Marta had found a way to sneak out from under his overprotective thumb. And now with Karl gone, she no longer had to sneak out to the world. She could bring some of the world into the house.

Yes, it was going to be so nice here.

"Tell me something," Steph said as she rested her head on Jerry's shoulder.

She was warm against him in the front seat of his old Fairlane 500 convertible and his desire for her was a throbbing ache. After the movie—a car-chase flick—he had driven them back here and parked outside the gatehouse. The top was down and they were snuggled together in the front seat watching the little stars that city people never see, even on the clearest of nights.

"Anything," he whispered into her hair.

"How did Miss Gati get along here before she had me?"

"A lady from town used to come in to clean and cook, but she never stayed over. You're the first live-in who's lasted more than a week since I've been working here. The old lady's been real choosy about finding someone after the last live-in...left."

Jerry decided that now was not the time to bring up the last maid's death. Steph was from the farmlands on the other side of the ridge and wouldn't know about her. Constance Granger had been her name, a quiet girl who went crazy wild. She had come from a decent, church-going family, but all of a sudden she became a regular at the roadside taverns, taking up with a different man every night. Then one night she became hysterical in a motel room—with two men, if the whispers could be believed—and began screaming at the top of her lungs. She ran out of the room jaybird naked and got hit by a truck.

Jerry didn't want to frighten Steph with that kind of story, not now while they were snug and close like this. He steered the talk elsewhere.

"Now you tell me something. What do you think of working for old lady Gati?"

"She's sweet. She's not a slave driver and the pay is good. This is my first job since leaving home and I guess I'm kinda lucky it's working out so well."

"You miss home?"

He felt her tense beside him. She never talked about her home.

"No. I...didn't get along with my father. But I get along just fine with Miss Gati. The only bad thing about the job is the house. It gives me the creeps. I get nightmares every night. "

"What about?"

She snuggled closer, as if chilled despite the warmth of the night.

"I don't remember much by morning, all I know is that they're no fun. I don't know how Miss Gati lived here alone after the last maid left. Especially her without any legs. I'd be frightened to death!"

"She's not. She tried out girl after girl. No one satisfied her till you came along. She's a tough one."

"But she's not. She's nice. A real lady. You know, I make her hot chocolate every night and she insists I sit down and have a cup with her while she tells me about her family and how they lived in 'the old country.' Isn't that nice?"

"Just super," Jerry said.

He lifted her chin and kissed her. He felt her respond, felt her catch some of the fervor running through him like fire. He let his hand slip off her shoulder and come to rest over her right breast. She made no move to push him away as his fingers began caressing her.

"Want to come inside?" he said, glancing toward the door of the gatehouse.

Steph sighed. "Yes." She kissed him again, then pulled away. "But no. I don't think that would be such a good idea, Jerry. Not just yet. I mean, I just met you six weeks ago."

"You know all there is to know. I'm not hiding anything. Come on."

"I want to...you know I do, but not tonight. It's time for Miss Gati's hot chocolate. And if I want to keep this job, I'd better get up to the house and fix it for her." Her eyes searched his face in the light of the rising moon. "You're not mad at me, are you?"

"Nah!" he said with what he hoped was a reassuring grin. How could he look into those eyes and be mad? But he sure as hell *ached*. "Crushed and heartbroken, maybe. But not mad."

She laughed. "Good!"

There's plenty of time, he told the ache deep down inside. And we'll be seeing a lot of each other.

"C'mon. I'll walk you up to the house."

On the front porch, he kissed her again and didn't want to let go. Finally, she pushed him away, gently.

"She's calling me. Gotta go. See you tomorrow."

Reluctantly, Jerry released her. He hadn't heard anything but knew she had to go. He wondered if her insides were as churned up as his own.

"Hurry and drink your chocolate before it gets cold," Marta Gati said as Stephie returned from down the hall.

Stephie smiled and picked up her cup from the bedside table. A lovely child, Marta thought. Simply lovely.

Her own cup was cradled in her hands. It was a little too sweet for her taste, but she made no comment. She was propped up on her bed pillows. Stephie sat in a chair pulled up to the side of the bed.

"And what did you and young Pritchard do tonight?" Marta said. "Anything special?"

She watched Stephie blush as she sipped her chocolate. Marta took a sip of her own to hide the excitement that swept through her. They're in love! This was perfect.

"How was the movie?" she managed to say in a calm voice.

Stephie shrugged. "It was okay, I guess. Jerry likes all those cars racing around and crashing."

"Don't you?"

She shrugged. "Not really."

"But you go because young Pritchard likes them. And you like him, don't you?"

She shrugged shyly. "Yes."

"Of course you do. And he likes you. I can tell. I just hope he hasn't taken any liberties with you."

Stephie's color deepened. Marta guessed she wanted to tell her it was none of her damn business but didn't have the nerve.

"No," Stephie said. "No liberties."

"Good!" Marta said. "I don't want you two running off and getting married. I need the both of you here. Now, finish your chocolate and get yourself to bed. Never let it be said I kept you up too late."

Stephie smiled and drained her cup.

Yes, Marta thought. A lovely girl.

———

The gatehouse was one room and a bathroom, furnished with a small desk, a chair, a bureau, and a hide-a-bed that folded up into a couch during the day. A sort of unattached motel room. But since he took his meals up at the house, it was all that Jerry needed.

The lights had been off for nearly an hour but he was still awake, rerunning his favorite fantasy, starring the voracious Steph and the inexhaustible Jerry. Then the door opened without warning and Steph stood there with the moonlight faintly outlining her body through the light cotton nightgown she wore. She said nothing as she came forward and crawled under the single sheet that covered him.

After that, no words were necessary.

Dawn light sneaking through the spaces between the venetian blinds on the gatehouse window woke Jerry. He was alone. After she had worn him out, Steph had left him. He sat on the edge of the hide-a-bed and cradled his head in his hands. In the thousand times he had mentally bedded Steph since her arrival, he had always been the initiator, the aggressor. Last night had been nothing at all like the fantasies. Steph had been in complete control—demanding, voracious, insatiable, a wild woman who had left him drained and exhausted. And hardly a word had passed between them. Throughout their lovemaking she had cooed, she had whimpered, she had moaned, but she had barely spoken to him. It left him feeling sort of...used.

Still trying to figure out this new, unexpected side to Steph, he walked up to the house for breakfast. The sun was barely up and already the air was starting to cook. It was going to be another hot one.

As he came in the back door he saw Steph heading out of the kitchen toward the dining room with old lady Gati's tray.

"Be with you in a minute," she called over her shoulder.

He waited by the swinging door and caught her as she came through. He slipped his arms around her waist and kissed her.

"Jerry, no!" she snapped. "Not here—not while I'm working!"

He released her. "Not your cheerful old self this morning, are you?"

"Just tired, I guess." She turned toward the stove.

"I guess you should be."

"And what's that supposed to mean?"

"Well, you had an unusually active night. At least I hope it was unusual."

Steph had been about to crack an egg on the edge of the frying pan. She stopped in mid-motion and turned to face him.

"Jerry...what on earth are you talking about?"

She looked genuinely puzzled, and that threw him.

"Last night...at the gatehouse...it was after three when you left."

Her cranky scowl dissolved into an easy smile.

"You must really be in a bad way!" She laughed. "Now you're believing your own dreams!"

Jerry was struck by the clear innocence of her laughter. For a moment, he actually doubted his memory—but only for a moment. Last night had been real. Hadn't it?

"Steph..." he began, but dropped it.

What could he say to those guileless blue eyes? She was either playing some sort of game, and playing it very well, or she really didn't
remember. Or it really never happened. None of those choices was the
least bit reassuring.

He wolfed his food as Steph moved in and out of the kitchen, attend-
ing to old lady Gati's breakfast wants. She kept glancing at him out of
the corner of her eye, as if checking up on him. Was this a game? Or had
he really dreamed it all last night?

Jerry skipped his usual second cup of coffee and was almost relieved
to find himself back in the confines of the cellar. He threw himself into
the job, partly because he wanted to finish it, and partly because he
didn't want too much time to think about last night. By lunchtime he
was sweeping up the last of the debris when he heard the sound.

It came from above. The floorboards were squeaking. And something else as well—the light sound of feet moving back and forth,
rhythmically. It continued as he filled a cardboard box with the last of
the dirt, dust, and scraps of rotten wood from the cellar. He decided to
walk around the south side of the house on his way to the trash bins.
The sound seemed to be coming from there.

As he passed the solarium, he glanced in and almost dropped the
box. Steph was waltzing around the room with an invisible partner in
her arms. Swirling and dipping and curtsying, she was not the most
graceful dancer he had ever seen, but the look of pure joy on her face
made up for whatever she lacked in skill.

Her expression changed abruptly to a mixture of surprise and
something like anger when she caught sight of him gaping through
the window. She ran toward the stairs, leaving Miss Gati alone. The
old lady neither turned to watch her go, nor looked out the window
to see what had spooked her. She sat slumped in her wheelchair, her
head hanging forward. For a second, Jerry was jolted by the sight: She
looked dead! He pressed his face against the solarium glass for a closer
look, and was relieved to see the gentle rise and fall of her chest. Only
asleep. But what had Steph been doing waltzing around like that while
the old lady napped?

Shaking his head at the weirdness of it all, he dumped the box in the
trash area and returned to the house through the back door. The kitchen
was empty, so he made his way as quietly as possible to the solarium
to see if Steph had returned. He found all quiet—the music off and old
lady Gati bright and alert, reading a book. He immediately turned back
toward the kitchen, hoping she wouldn't spot him. But it was too late.

"Yes, young Pritchard?" she said, rolling that r and looking up from her book. "You are looking for something?"

Jerry fumbled for words. "I was looking for Steph to see if she could fix me a sandwich. Thought I saw her in here when I passed by before."

"No, dear boy," she said with a smile. "I sent her up to her room for a nap almost an hour ago. Seems you tired her out last night. "

"Last night?" He tensed. What did she know about last night?

Her smile broadened. "Come now! You two didn't think you could fool me, did you? I know she sneaked out to see you." Something about the way she looked at him sent a sick chill through Jerry. "Surely you can fix something yourself and let the poor girl rest."

Then it hadn't been a dream! But then why had Steph pretended—? He couldn't figure it.

"Yeah. Sure," he said dully, his thoughts jumbled. "I can make a sandwich." He turned to go. "You should be about through with the basement by now," she said. "But even if you're not, get up to the roof this afternoon. The weatherman says there's a sixty percent chance of a thunderstorm tonight."

"Basement's done. Roof is next."

"Excellent! But don't work too hard, young Pritchard. Save something for Stephie."

She returned to her book.

Jerry felt numb as he walked back to the kitchen. The old lady hadn't touched him once! She seemed more relaxed and at ease with herself than he could ever remember—a cat-that-had-swallowed-the-canary sort of self-satisfaction. And she hadn't tried to lay a single finger on him!

The day was getting weirder and weirder.

———

Replacing the shingles on the sloping dormer surface outside old lady Gati's bedroom had looked like an easy job from the ground. But the shingles were odd, scalloped affairs that she had ordered special from San Francisco to match the originals on the house, and Jerry had trouble keeping them aligned on the curved surface. He could have used a third hand, too. What would have been an hour's work for two men had already taken Jerry three in the broiling sun, and he wasn't quite finished yet.

While he was working, he noted that the wood trim on the upper levels was going to need painting soon. That was going to be a hellish job, what with the oculus windows, the ornate friezes, cornices, brackets, and keystones. Some crazed woodcarver had had a field day with this stuff—probably thought it was "art." But Jerry was going to be the one to paint it. He'd put that off as long as he could, and definitely wouldn't do it in summer.

He pulled an insulated wire free of the outside wall to fit in the final shingles by the old lady's window. It ran from somewhere on the roof down to the ground—directly into the ground. Jerry pulled himself up onto the parapet above the dormer to see where the wire originated. He followed it up until it linked into the lightning rod on the peak of the attic garret. *Everything* connected with this house was ornate—even the lightning rods had designs on them!

He climbed back down, pulled the ground wire free of the dormer, and tacked the final shingles into place. When he reached the ground, he slumped on the bottom rung of the ladder and rested a moment. The heat from the roof was getting to him. His tee-shirt was drenched with perspiration and he was reeling with fatigue.

Enough for today. He'd done the bulk of the work. A hurricane could hit the area and that dormer would not leak. He could put the finishing touches on tomorrow. He lowered the ladder to the ground, then checked the kitchen for Steph. She wasn't there. Just as well. He didn't have the energy to pry an explanation out of her. Something was cooking in the oven, but he was too bushed to eat. He grabbed half a six-pack of beer from the fridge and stumbled down to the gatehouse. Hell with dinner. A shower, a few beers, a good night's sleep, and he'd be just fine in the morning.

It was a long ways into dark, but Jerry was still awake. Tired as he was, he couldn't get to sleep. As thunder rumbled in the distance, charging in from the west, and slivers of ever-brightening light flashed between the blinds, thoughts of last night tumbled through his mind, arousing him anew. Something strange going on up at that house. Old lady Gati was acting weird, and so was Steph.

Steph...he couldn't stop thinking about her. He didn't care what kind of game she was playing, she still meant something to him. He'd never felt this way before. He—

There was a noise at the door. It opened and Steph stepped inside. She said nothing as she came forward, but in the glow of the lightning flashes from outside, Jerry could see her removing her nightgown as she crossed the room. He saw it flutter to the floor and then she was beside him, bringing the dreamlike memories of last night into the sharp focus of the real and now. He tried to talk to her but she would only answer in a soft, breathless "uh-huh" or "uh-uh" and then her wandering lips and tongue wiped all questions from his mind.

When it was finally over and the two of them lay in a gasping tangle of limbs and sheets, Jerry decided that now was the time to find out what was going on between her and old lady Gati, and what kind of game she was playing with him. He would ask her in a few seconds... or maybe in a minute...soon...thunder was louder than ever outside but that wasn't going to bother him...all he wanted to do right now was close his eyes and enjoy the delicious exhaustion of this afterglow a little longer...only a little...close his eyes for just a few seconds...no more...

"Sleep well, my love."

Jerry forced his eyes open. Steph's face hovered over him in the flashing dimness as he teetered on the brink of unconsciousness. She kissed him lightly on the forehead and whispered, "Good night, young Pritchard. And thank you."

It was as if someone had tossed a bucket of icy water on him. Suddenly Jerry was wide awake. Young Pritchard? Why had she said that? Why had she imitated old lady Gati's voice that way? The accent, with its roll of the r, had been chillingly perfect.

Steph had slipped her nightgown over her head and was on her way out. Jerry jumped out of bed and caught her at the door.

"I don't think that was funny, Steph!" She ignored him and pushed the screen door open. He grabbed her arm. "Hey, look! What kind of game are you playing? What's it gonna be tomorrow morning? Same as today? Pretend that nothing happened tonight?" She tried to pull away but he held on. "Talk to me, Steph! What's going on?"

A picture suddenly formed in his mind of Steph going back to the house and having hot chocolate with old lady Gati and telling her every intimate detail of their lovemaking, and the old lady getting excited, *feeding* off it.

"What's going on?" Involuntarily, his grip tightened on her arm.

"You're hurting me!"

The words cut like an icy knife. The voice was Steph's, but the tone, the accent, the roll of the R, the inflection—all were perfect mimicry of old lady Gati, down to the last nuance. But she had been in pain. It couldn't have been rehearsed!

Jerry flipped the light switch and spun her around. It was Steph, all right, as achingly beautiful as ever, but something was wrong. The Steph he knew should have been frightened. The Steph before him was changed. She held herself differently. Her stance was haughty, almost imperious. And there was something in her eyes—a strange light. .

"Oh, sweet Jesus! What's happened to you?"

He could see indecision flickering through her eyes as she regarded him with a level stare. Outside, it began to rain. A few scattered fore-runner drops escalated to a full-scale torrent in a matter of seconds as their eyes remained locked, their bodies frozen amid day-bright flashes of lightning and the roar of thunder and wind-driven rain. Then she smiled. It was like Steph's smile, but it wasn't.

"Nothing," she said in that crazy mixed voice.

And then he thought he knew. For a blazing instant, it was clear to him:

"You're not Steph!"

In the very instant he said it he disbelieved it, but then her smile broadened and her words turned his blood to ice.

"Yes, I am...for the moment." The voice was thick with old lady Gati's accent, and it carried a triumphant note. "What Stephie sees, I see! What Stephie feels, I feel!" She lifted the hem of her nightgown. "Look at my legs! Beautiful, aren't they?"

Jerry released her arm as if he had been burned. She moved closer but Jerry found himself backing away. Steph was crazy! Her mind had snapped. She thought she was old lady Gati! He had never been faced with such blatant madness before, and it terrified him. He felt exposed, vulnerable before it. With a trembling hand, he grabbed his jeans from the back of the chair.

Marta Gati looked out of Stephie's eyes at young Pritchard as he struggled into his trousers, and she wondered what to do next. She had thought him asleep when she had kissed him good night and made the slip of calling him "young Pritchard." She had known she couldn't keep her nightly possession of Stephie from him for too long, but she had not been prepared for a confrontation tonight. She would try for sympathy first.

"Do you have any idea, young Pritchard," she said, trying to make Stephie's voice sound as American as she could, "what it is like to be trapped all your life in a body as deformed as mine? To be repulsive to other children as a child, to grow up watching other girls find young men and go dancing and get married and know that at night they are holding their man in their arms and feeling all the things a woman should feel? You have no idea what my life has been like, young Pritchard. But through the years I found a way to remedy the situation. Tonight I am a complete woman—*your* woman!"

"Stephanie!" young Pritchard shouted, fear and disbelief mingling in the strained pallor of his face. "Listen to yourself! You sound crazy! What you're saying is impossible!"

"No! Not impossible!" she said, although she could understand his reaction.

A few years ago, she too would have called it impossible. Her brother Karl had devoted himself to her and his business. He never married, but he would bring women back to the house now and then when he thought she was asleep. It would have been wonderful if he could have brought a man home for her, but that was impossible. Yet it hadn't stopped her yearnings. And it was on those nights when he and a woman were in the next bedroom that Marta realized she could sense things in Karl's women. At first she thought it was imagination, but this was more than mere fantasy. She could feel their passion, feel their skin tingling, feel them exploding within. And one night, after they both had spent themselves and fallen asleep, she found herself in the other woman's body—actually lying in Karl's bed and seeing the room through her eyes!

As time went on, she found she could enter their bodies while they slept and actually take them over. She could get up and walk! A sob built in her throat at the memory. To *walk*! That had been joy enough at first. Then she would dance by herself. She had wanted so much all her life to dance to waltz, and now she could! She never dared more than that until Karl died and left her free. She had perfected her ability since then.

"It will be a good life for you, young Pritchard," she said. "You won't even have to work. Stephie will be my maid and housekeeper during the day and your lover at night."

He shook his head, as if to stop her, but she pressed on.

"And when you get tired of Stephie, I'll bring in another. And another. You'll have an endless stream of young, willing bodies in your bed. You'll have such a good life, young Pritchard!"

A new look was growing in his eyes: belief.

"It's really you!" he said in a hoarse whisper. "Oh, my dear sweet Lord, it's really you in Steph's body! I...I'm getting out of here!"

She moved to block his way and he stayed back. He could have easily overpowered her, but he seemed afraid to let her get too near. She couldn't let him go, not after all her work to set up a perfect household.

"No! You mustn't do that! You must stay here!"

"This is sick!" he cried, his voice rising in pitch as a wild light sprang into his eyes. "This is the Devil's work!"

"No-no," she said soothingly. "Not the Devil. Just me. Just something—"

"Get away from me!" he said, backing toward his dresser. He spun and pulled open the top drawer, rummaged through it, and came up with a thick book with a cross on its cover. "Get away, Satan!" he cried, thrusting the book toward her face.

Marta almost laughed. "Don't be silly, young Pritchard! I'm not evil! I'm just doing what I have to do. I'm not hurting Stephie. I'm simply borrowing her body for a while!"

"Out, demon!" he said, shoving the Bible almost into her face. "*Out!*"

This was getting annoying now. She snatched the book from his grasp and hurled it across the room.

"Stop acting like a fool!"

He looked from her to the book and back to her with an awed expression. At that moment there was a particularly loud crash of thunder and the lights went out. Young Pritchard cried out in horror and brushed past her. He slammed out the door and ran into the storm.

Marta ran as far as the doorway and stopped. She peered through the deluge. Even with the rapid succession of lightning strokes and sheets, she could see barely a dozen feet. He was nowhere in sight. She could see no use in running out into the storm and following him. She glanced at his keys on the bureau and smiled. How far could a half-naked man go in a storm like this?

Marta crossed the room and sat on the bed. She ran Stephie's hand over the rumpled sheets where less than half an hour ago the two of them had been locked in passion. Warmth rose within her. *So good.* So good to have a man's arms around you, wanting you, needing you, *demanding* you. She couldn't give this up. Not now, not when it was finally at her disposal after all these years.

But young Pritchard wasn't working out. She had thought any virile young man would leap at what she offered, but apparently she had misjudged him. Or was a stable relationship within her household just a fool's dream? She had so much to learn about the outside world. Karl had kept her so sheltered from it.

Perhaps her best course was the one she had taken with the last housekeeper. Take over her body when she was asleep and drive to the bars and roadhouses outside of town. Find a man—two men, if she were in the mood—and spend most of the night in a motel room. Then come back to the house, clean her up, and leave her asleep in her bed. It was anonymous, it was exciting, but it was somehow...empty.

She would be more careful with Stephie than with the last housekeeper. Marta had been ill one night but had moved into the other body anyway. She had lost control when a stomach spasm had gripped her own body. The pain had drawn her back to the house, leaving the woman to awaken between two strangers. She had panicked and run out into the road.

Yes, she had to be very careful with this one. Stephie was so sensitive to her power, whatever it was. She only had to become drowsy and Marta could slip in and take complete control, keeping Stephie's mind unconscious while she controlled her body. A few milligrams of a sedative in her cocoa before bedtime and Stephie's body was Marta's for the night.

But young Pritchard wasn't working out. At least not so far. There was perhaps a slim chance she could reason with him when he came back. She had to try. She found him terribly attractive. But where could he be?

Sparks of alarm flashed through her as she realized that her own body was upstairs in the house, lying in bed, helpless, defenseless. What if that crazy boy—?

Quickly, she slid onto the bed and closed her eyes. She shut out her senses one by one, blocking off the sound of the rain and thunder, the taste of the saliva in her mouth, the feel of the bedclothes against her back. . .

...and opened her eyes in her own bedroom in the house. She looked around, alert for any sign that her room had been entered. Her bedroom door was still closed, and there was no moisture anywhere on the floor.

Good! He hasn't been in here!

Marta pushed herself up in bed and transferred to the wheelchair. She wheeled herself out to the hall and down to the elevator, cursing its slow descent as it took her to the first floor. When it finally stopped, she propelled herself at top speed to the foyer where she immediately turned the dead bolt on the front door. She noted with satisfaction that the slate floor under her chair was as dry as when she had walked out earlier as Stephie. She was satisfied that she was alone in the house.

Safe!

She rolled herself into the solarium at a more leisurely pace. She knew the rest of the doors and windows were secure. Stephie always locked up before she made the bedtime chocolate. She stopped before the big bay windows and watched the storm for a minute. It was a fierce one. She gazed out at the blue-white, water-blurred lightning flashes and wondered what she was going to do about young Pritchard. If she couldn't convince him to stay, then surely he would be in town tomorrow, telling a wild tale. No one would believe him, of course, but it would start talk, fuel rumors, and that would make it almost impossible to get help in the future. It might even make Stephie quit, and Marta didn't know how far her power could reach. She'd be left totally alone out here.

Her fingers tightened on the armrests of her wheelchair. She couldn't let that happen.

She closed her eyes and blocked out the storm, blocked out her senses. . .

. . .and awoke in Stephie's body again.

She leaped to the kitchenette and pulled out the drawers until she found the one she wanted. It held three forks, a couple of spoons, a spatula, and a knife—a six-inch carving knife.

It would have to do.

She hurried out into the rain and up the hill toward the house.

Jerry rammed his shoulder against the big oak front door again but only added to bruises the door had already put there. He screamed at it.

"In God's name—open!"

The door ignored him. What was he going to do? He had to get inside! Had to get to that old lady! Had to wring the Devil out of her! Had to find a way in! Make her give Steph back! His mother had warned him about this sort of thing. He could almost hear her voice between the claps of thunder: *Satan walks the earth, Jerome, searching for those who forsake the Word. Beware—he's waiting for you!*

Jerry knew the Devil had found him—in the guise of old lady Gati!

What was happening to Steph was all his fault! He ran back into the downpour and headed around toward the rear. Maybe the kitchen door was unlocked. He glanced through the solarium windows as he passed. His bare feet slid to a halt on the wet grass as he stopped and took a better look.

There she was: old lady Gati, the Devil herself, zonked out in her wheelchair.

The sight of her sitting there as if asleep while her spirit was down the hill controlling Steph's body was more than Jerry could stand. He looked around for something to hurl through the window, and in the next lightning flash he spotted the ladder next to the house on the lawn. He picked it up and charged the solarium like a jousting knight. Putting all his weight behind the ladder, he rammed it through the center bay window. The sound of shattering glass broke the last vestige of Jerry's control. Howling like a madman, he drove the ladder against the window glass again and again until every pane and every muntin was smashed and battered out of the way.

Then he climbed in.

The shards of glass cut his bare hands and feet but Jerry barely noticed. His eyes were on old lady Gati. Throughout all the racket, she hadn't budged.

Merciful Lord, it's true! Her spirit's left her body!

He stumbled over to her inert form and stood behind her, hesitating. He didn't want to touch her—his skin crawled at the thought—but he had to put an end to this. Now. Swallowing the bile that sloshed up from his stomach, Jerry wrapped his fingers around old lady Gati's throat. He flinched at the feel of her wrinkles against his palms, but he clenched his teeth and began to squeeze. He put all his strength into it—

—and then let go.

He couldn't do it.

"God, give me strength!" he cried, but he couldn't bring himself to do it. Not while she was like this. It was like strangling a corpse! She was barely breathing as it was!

Something tapped against the intact bay window to the right. Jerry spun to look—a flash from outside outlined the grounding wire from the lightning rods as it swayed in the wind and slapped against the window. It reminded him of a snake.

A *snake!* And suddenly he knew: It's a sign! A sign from God!

He ran to the window and threw it open. He reached out, wrapped the wire around his hands, and pulled. It wouldn't budge from the ground. He braced a foot against the windowsill, putting his back and all his weight into the effort. Suddenly, the metal grounding stake pulled free and he staggered back, the insulated wire thrashing about in his hands...just like a snake.

He remembered that snake-handlers' church back in the hills his mother had dragged him to one Sunday a few years ago. He had watched in awe as the men and women would grab water moccasins and cottonmouths and hold them up, trusting in the Lord to protect them. Some were bitten, some were not. Ma had told him it was all God's will.

God's will!

He pulled the old lady's wheelchair closer to the window and wrapped the wire tightly around her, tying it snugly behind the backrest of the chair, and jamming the grounding post into the metal spokes of one of the wheels.

"This is your snake, Miss Gati," he told her unconscious form. "It's God's will if it bites you!"

He backed away from her until he was at the entrance to the solarium. Lightning flashed as violently as ever, but none came down the wire. He couldn't wait any longer. He had to find Steph. As he turned to head for the front door, he saw someone standing on the south lawn, staring into the solarium. It was old lady Gati, wearing Steph's body. When she looked through the broken bay window and saw him there, she screamed and slumped to the ground.

"*Steph!*" What was happening to her?

Jerry sprinted across the room and dove through the shattered window onto the south lawn.

Marta awoke in her own body, panicked.

What has he done to me?

She felt all right. There was no pain, no—

My arms! Her hands were free but she couldn't move her upper arms! She looked down and saw the black insulated wire coiled tightly around her upper body, binding her to the chair. She tried to twist, to slide down on the chair and slip free, but the wire wouldn't give an inch. She tried to see where it was tied. If she could get her hands on the knot...

She saw the wire trailing away from her chair, across the floor and out the window and up into the darkness.

Up! To the roof! The lightning rods!

She screamed, "*Nooooo!*"

Jerry cradled Steph's head in his arm and slapped her wet face as hard as he dared. He'd hoped the cold pounding rain and the noise of the storm would have brought her around, but she was still out. He didn't want to hurt her, but she had to wake up.

"Steph! C'mon, Steph! You've got to wake up! Got to fight her!"

As she stirred, he heard old lady Gati howl from the solarium. Steph's eyes fluttered, then closed again. He shook her. "Steph! Please!"

She opened her eyes and stared at him. His spirits leaped.

"That's it, Steph! Wake up! It's me—Jerry! You've got to stay awake!"

She moaned and closed her eyes, so he shook her again.

"Steph! Don't let her take you over again!"

As she opened her eyes again, Jerry dragged her to her feet. "Come on! Walk it off! Let's go! You've got to stay awake!" Suddenly, her face contorted and she swung on him. Something gleamed in her right hand as she plunged it toward his throat. Jerry got his forearm up just in time to block it. Pain seared through his arm and he cried out.

"Oh, God! It's you!"

"*Yes!*" She slashed at him again and he backpedaled to avoid the knife. His bare feet slipped on the grass and he went down on his back. He rolled frantically, fearing she would be upon him, but when he looked up, she was running toward the house, toward the smashed bay window.

"No!"

He couldn't let her get inside and untie the old lady's body.

Steph's only hope was a lightning strike.

Please, God, he prayed. Now! Let it be now!

But though bolts crackled through the sky almost continuously, none of them hit the house. Groaning with fear and frustration, Jerry scrambled to his feet and sprinted after her. He had to stop her!

He caught her from behind and brought her down about two dozen feet from the house. She screamed and thrashed like an enraged animal, twisting and slashing at him again and again with the knife. She cut him along the ribs as he tried to pin her arms and was rearing back for a better angle on his chest when the night turned blue-white. He saw the rage on Steph's face turn to wide-eyed horror. Her body arched convulsively as she opened her mouth and let out a high-pitched shriek of agony that rose and cut off like a circuit being broken—

—only to be taken up by another voice from within the solarium. Jerry glanced up and saw old lady Gati's body jittering in her chair like a hooked fish while blue fire played all about her. Her hoarse cry was swallowed and drowned as her body exploded in a roiling ball of flame. Fire was everywhere in the solarium. The very air seemed to burn.

He removed the knife from Steph's now limp hand and dragged her to a safer distance from the house. He shook her.

"Steph?"

He could see her eyes rolling back and forth under the lids.

Finally, they opened and stared at him uncomprehendingly.

"Jerry?" She bolted up to a sitting position. "Jerry! What's going on?"

His grip on the knife tightened as he listened to her voice, searching carefully for the slightest hint of an accent, the slightest roll of an r. He detected nothing, but only one test would completely convince him.

"My name," he said. "What's my last name, Steph?"

"It's Pritchard, of course. But—" She must have seen the flames flickering in his eyes because she twisted around and cried out. "The house! It's on fire! Miss Gati—!"

She had said it perfectly! The real Steph was back! Jerry threw away the knife and lifted her to her feet.

"She's gone," he told her. "Burnt up. I saw her."

"But how?"

He had to think fast—couldn't tell her the truth. Not yet.

"Lightning. It's my fault. I must have messed up the rods when I was up on the roof today!"

"Oh God, Jerry!" She clung to him and suddenly the storm seemed far away. "What'll we do?"

Over her shoulder, he watched the flames spreading throughout the first floor and lapping up at the second through the broken bay window.

"Got to get out of here, Steph. They're gonna blame me for it and God knows what'll happen. "

"It was an accident! They can't blame you for that!"

"Oh, yes, they will!" Jerry was thinking about the ground wire wrapped around the old lady's corpse. No way would anyone think that was an accident. "I hear she's got family in New York. They'll see me hang if they can, I just know it! I've got to get out of here." He pushed her to arm's length and stared at her. "Come with me?"

She shook her head. "I can't! How—?"

"We'll make a new life far from here. We'll head west and won't stop till we reach the ocean." He could see her wavering. "Please, Steph! I don't think I can make it without you!"

Finally, she nodded.

He took her hand and pulled her along behind him as he raced down the slope for the gatehouse. He glanced back at the old house and saw flames dancing in the second-floor windows. Somebody down in town would see the light from the fire soon and then half the town would be up here to either fight it or watch it being fought. They had to be out of here before that.

It's gonna be okay, he told himself. They'd start a new life out in California. And someday, when he had the nerve and he thought she was ready for it, he'd tell her the truth. But for now, as long as Steph was at his side, he could handle anything. Everything was going to be all right.

———

Patrolman Grimes looked better now. He was back from the couple's apartment and stood in the hospital corridor with an open notebook, ready to recite.

All right," Burke said. "What've we got?"

"We've got a twenty-three-year-old named Jerome Pritchard. Came out here from West Virginia nine months ago."

"I mean drugs—crack, angel dust, needles, fixings."

"No, sir. The apartment was clean. The neighbors are in absolute shock. Everybody loved the Pritchards and they all seem to think he was a pretty straight guy. A real churchgoer—carried his own Bible and never missed a Sunday, they said. Had an assembly line job and talked about starting night courses at UCLA as soon as he made the residency requirement. He and his wife appeared to be real excited about the baby, going to Lamaze classes and all that sort of stuff."

"Crack, I tell you!" Burke said. "Got to be!"

"As far as we can trace his movements, sir, it seems that after the baby was delivered at 10:06 this morning, he ran out of here like a bat out of hell, came

back about an hour later carrying his Bible and a big oblong package, waited until the baby was brought to the mother for feeding, then...well, you know."

"Yeah. I know."

The new father had pulled a 10-gauge shotgun from that package and blown the mother and kid away. Then put the barrel against his own throat and completed the job.

"But why, dammit!"

"Well...the baby did have a birth defect."

"I know. I saw. But there are a helluva lot of birth defects a damn sight worse. Hell, I mean, her legs were only withered a little!"

Greystone Bay ("The City Horror Calls Its Own") was a shared-world anthology for horror fans. I read the first volume and was interested by the possibilities—a *Thieves' World* of contemporary horror. I wrote the editor, Charlie Grant, and told him the town definitely needed a doctor and that I'd be glad to supply him. He agreed, told me to give it a shot, and sent me the particulars on the town of Greystone Bay.

I wound up supplying the town with *two* doctors. One is pretty straight, but the other... the other is Doc Johnson. You don't mess with ol' Doc Johnson.

In 2008 I retconned the story from Grant's turf into my Secret History, calling the town Ludlum Bay and placing it near the Jersey Pine Barrens for the Garden State Horror Writers' anthology, *Dark Territories*. This is that version.

In 2014 I scripted it for Rachel Deering's *In the Dark* anthology for IDW. Matthew Dow Smith illustrated it.

Doc Johnson

"I think you'd better take the call on oh-one," Jessie said, poking her head into the consultation room.

I glanced up from the latest issue of *Cardiology* and looked at my wife. It was Monday morning and I had a grand total of three patients scheduled.

"Why?"

"Because I said so."

That's what I get for hiring my wife as my nurse-receptionist, but I had to keep overhead down until I built up a decent practice and could afford a stranger...someone I could reprimand without paying for it later at home. I had to admit, though, Jessie was doing a damn fine job so far. She wasn't letting the pregnancy slow her down a bit.

"Who is it?"

She shrugged. "Not sure. Says she's never been here before but says her husband needs a doctor real bad."

"Got it."

Never turn down a patient in need. Especially one who might be able to pay. I picked up the phone.

"Hello. Doctor Reid."

"Oh, Doctor," said a woman's voice. "My husband's awful sick. Can you come see him?"

"A *house call?*" After all, I was a board-eligible internist. House calls were for GPs and family practitioners, not specialists. "What's wrong with your husband, Mrs....?"

"Mosely—Martha Mosely. My husband, Joseph, he's...he's just not right. Sometimes he says he wants a doctor and sometimes he says he doesn't. He says he wants one now."

"Can you be a little more specific?"

If this Mosely fellow was going to end up in the hospital, I'd rather have him transported there first and then see him.

"I wish I could, Doctor, but I can't."

"Who's his regular doctor?"

"Doc Johnson."

Ah-ha!

"And why aren't you calling him?"

"Joe won't let me. He says he doesn't ever want to see Doc Johnson again. He only wants you."

I hesitated. I didn't want to get into the house-call habit, but as the new kid in town, I couldn't afford to pass up a chance to score some points.

"All right. Give me the address and I'll be out after dinner."

He doesn't ever want to see Doc Johnson again.

I thought about that as I drove out to the Mosely house. An odd thing to say. Most people in Ludlum Bay swore by Johnson. You'd think he walked on water the way some of them talked. Which wasn't making it any easier for me to get started in the Bay. I'd been living—quite literally—off the crumbs he left behind. Joseph Mosely appeared to be a crumb, so I was on my way to gather him up.

I turned south off Port Boulevard onto New Hope Road, watching the homes change from post-World War II tract homes to smaller, older houses on bigger lots. The January wind slapped at my car.

This was my first winter in Ludlum Bay and it was *cold*. I grew up in Florida, went to med school and did my internal medicine residency at Emory in Atlanta. My idea of cold and these New Jerseyans' idea of cold differed by a good twenty degrees.

The Bay natives like to say the nearness of the Atlantic tends to moderate the severity of the weather. Maybe that's true. According to the thermometer, it doesn't seem to get quite as cold here as it does inland, but I think the extra moisture sends the chill straight through to the bone.

But now the cold was locked outside the car and I was warm within. I had a bellyful of Jessie's tuna casserole, the Civic's heater-defrost system was blowing hard and warm. Snow blanketed the lawns and was banked on the curbs, but the asphalt was clean and dry. A beautiful, crystalline winter night for a drive. Too bad Jessie wasn't along. Too bad this wasn't a pleasure drive. People attach such rosy nostalgia to the house call, but here in the twenty-first century the house is a *lousy* place to practice medicine.

I slowed as the numbers on the mailboxes told me I was nearing the Mosely place. There: 620 New Hope Road. As I pulled into the driveway my headlamps lit up the house and grounds. I stopped the car halfway through the turn and groaned.

The Mosely house was a mess.

Every neighborhood has one. You know the type of house I mean. You drive along a street lined with immaculately kept homes, all with freshly painted siding and manicured lawns, all picture-perfect... except for one. There's always one house with a front yard where even the weeds won't grow; the Christmas lights are still attached to the eaves even though it might be June; if the neighborhood is lucky, only one rusting auto will grace the front yard, and the house's previous coat of paint will have merely peeled away, exposing much of the original color of the siding. If the neighborhood is especially cursed, the front yard will sport two or more automobile hulks in various stages of refurbishment, and the occupant will have started to paint the derelict home a hot pink or a particularly noxious shade of green and then quit halfway through.

The Mosely house was New Hope Road's derelict.

I turned off my engine and, black bag in hand, stepped out into the cold. No path had been dug through the snow anywhere I could see, but I found a narrow path where it had been packed down by other feet before me. It led across the front lawn. At least I think it was a lawn. The glow from a nearby streetlight limned odd bumps and rises all over the front yard. I could only guess at what lay beneath. A blanket of snow hides a multitude of sins.

I got a closer look at the house as I carefully picked my way toward it. The front porch was an open affair with its overhang tilted at a crazy angle. The paint was particularly worn and dirty up to a level of about two feet. Looked like a dog had spent a lot of time there but I saw no paw prints and heard no barking. The light from within barely filtered through the window shades.

The front door opened before I could knock. A thin, fiftyish woman wearing an old blue house dress and a stretched-out brown cardigan stood there with her hand on the knob.

"I'm terribly sorry, Doctor," she said in a mousy voice, "but Joe's decided he don't want to see a doctor tonight."

"What?" My voice went hoarse with shock. "You mean to tell me I came—"

"Oh, let him in, Martha!" said a rough voice from somewhere behind her. "Long as he's here, might as well get a look at him."

"Yes, Joe."

She stepped aside and I stepped in.

The air within was hot, dry, and sour. I wondered how many years since they'd had the windows open. A wood stove sat in a corner to my left. The only light in the room came from candles and kerosene lamps.

Joseph Mosely, the same age as his wife but thinner, sat in a rocker facing me. His skin was stretched tight across his high forehead and cheekbones. He had a full head lank hair and a three-day stubble.

Something familiar about him. As I watched, he sipped from a four-ounce tumbler clutched in his right hand; a half-empty bottle of no-name gin sat on a small table next to him. He stared at me. I've seen prosthetic eyes of porcelain and glass show more warmth and human feeling than Joe Mosely's.

"If that was your idea of a joke, Mr. Mosely—"

"Don't bother trying to intimidate me, Doctor Charles Reid. It's a waste of breath. Take the man's coat, Martha."

"Yes, Joe."

Sighing resignedly, I shrugged out of my jacket and turned to hand it to her. I stopped and stared at her face. A large black-and-purple hematoma, a good inch and a half across, bloomed on her right cheek. I hadn't noticed it when she opened the door. But now…I knew from the look of it that it couldn't be more than a couple of hours old.

"Better get the ice back on that bruise," he said to her from his rocker. "And careful you don't slip on the kitchen floor and hurt yourself again."

"Yes, Joe."

Clenching my teeth against the challenge that leaped into my throat, I handed her my coat and turned to her husband.

"What seems to be the problem, Mr. Mosely?"

He put the glass down and rolled up his right sleeve to show me a healing laceration on the underside of his forearm.

"This."

It ran up from the wrist for about five inches or so and looked to be about ten days to two weeks old. Three silk sutures were still in place.

My anger flared. "You brought me all the way out here for a suture removal?"

"*I* didn't bring you anywhere. You brought yourself. And besides—" He kicked up his left foot; it looked deformed within a dirty sock. "I'm disabled."

"All right," I said, cooling with effort. "How'd you cut yourself?"

"Whittling."

I felt like asking him if he'd been using a machete, but restrained myself.

"They sew it up at County General?"

"Nope."

"Then who?"

He paused and I saw that his eyes were even colder and flatter than before.

"Doc Johnson."

"Why'd he leave these three sutures in?"

'Didn't. Took them out myself. He won't ever get near me again—*ever!*" He half rose from the rocker. "I wouldn't take my *dog* to him if she was still alive!"

"Hey! Take it easy."

He calmed himself with another sip of gin.

"So why did *you* leave the last three in?"

He looked at the wound, then away.

"'Cause there's something wrong with it."

I inspected it more closely. It looked fine. The wound edges had knitted nicely. Doc Johnson had done a good closure. I found no redness or swelling to indicate infection.

"Looks okay to me."

I opened my bag, got out an alcohol swab, and dabbed the wound.

Then I took out scissors and forceps and removed those last three sutures.

"There. Good as new."

"There's *still* something wrong with it." He pulled his arm away to reach for the gin glass; he drained it, then slammed it down. "There's something in there."

I almost laughed. "Pardon me?"

"Something's *in* there! I can feel it move every now and then. The first time was when I started taking the sutures out. There! Look!" He stiffened and pointed to the scar. "It's moving now!"

I looked and saw nothing the least bit out of the ordinary. But I thought I knew what was bothering him.

"Here." I took his left hand and laid the fingers over the underside of his forearm. "Press them here. Now, open and close your hand, making a fist. There...feel the tendons moving under the skin? You've probably got a little scar tissue building up in the deeper layers next to a tendon sheath and it's—"

"Something's *in* there, damn it! Doc Johnson put it there when he sewed me up!"

I stood. "That's ridiculous."

"It's true! I wouldn't make up something like that!"

"Did you watch him sew you up?"

"Yeah."

"Did you see him put anything in the wound?"

"No. But he's sneaky. I know he put something in there!"

"You'd better lay off the gin." I closed my bag. "You're having delusions."

"Shoulda known," he said bitterly, reaching for his bottle. "You doctors think you've got all the answers."

I took my coat off a hook by the door and pulled it on.

"What's that supposed to mean? And haven't you had enough of that for one night?"

"*Damn* you!" Eyes ablaze with fury, he hurled the glass across the room and leaped out of the rocker. "Who the hell do you think you are to tell me when I've had enough!"

He limped toward me and then I remembered why he looked familiar. The limp triggered it: I had seen him dozens of times in the Port Boulevard shopping area, usually entering or leaving Elmo's liquors. He'd lied to me—he wasn't disabled enough to warrant a house call.

"You're drunk." I reached for the doorknob. "Sleep it off."

Suddenly he stopped his advance and grinned maliciously.

"Oh, I'll sleep, all right. But will *you?* Better pray nothing goes bad with this arm here, or you'll have another malpractice case on your hands. Like the one in Atlanta."

My stomach wrenched into a tight ball. "How do you know about that?"

I hoped I didn't look as sick as I felt.

"Checked into you. When I heard we had this brand-new doctor in town, fresh from a big medical center in Atlanta, I asked myself why a young, hot-shot specialist would want to practice in the Bay? So I did some digging. I'm real good at digging. 'Specially on doctors. They got these high an' mighty ways with how they dole out pills and advice like they're better'n the rest of us. Doctor Tanner was like that. That office you're in used to be his. I dug up some *good* dirt on Tanner but he disappeared before I could rub his face in it."

"Good night."

I stepped out on the porch and pulled the door closed behind me.

I had nothing else to say. I thought I'd left that malpractice nightmare behind me in Atlanta. The realization that it had followed me here threatened all the hopes I'd nursed of finding peace in Ludlum Bay. And to hear it from the grinning lips of someone like Joe Mosely made me almost physically ill.

I barely remembered the trip home. I seemed to be driving through the past, through interrogatories and depositions and sweating testimonies. I didn't really come back to the present until I parked the car and walked toward the duplex we were renting.

Jessie was standing on the front steps, wrapped in her parka, arms folded across her chest as she looked up at the stars under a full moon. Suddenly I felt calm. This was the way I had found her when we first met—standing on a rooftop gazing up at the night sky, looking for Jupiter. She owned two telescopes she used regularly, but she's told me countless times that a true amateur astronomer never tires of naked-eye stargazing.

She smiled as she saw me walk up. "How was the house call?"

I put on an annoyed expression. "Unnecessary." I wouldn't tell her about tonight. At least one of us should rest easy. I patted her growing belly. "How we doing in there?"

"You mean the Tap Dance Kid? Active as ever."

She turned back to the stars and frowned. I followed her upward gaze.

"What's the matter?"

"I don't know. Something weird about the stars out here."

They looked all right to me, except that I could see a hell of a lot more of them than I'd ever seen in Atlanta.

Jessie slipped an arm around my back and seemed to read my expression without looking at me.

"Yeah. I said *weird*. They don't look right. I could get out a star map and I know everything would look fine. But something's just not right up there. The perspective's different somehow. Only another stargazer would notice. Something's wrong."

I had heard that expression too many times tonight.

"The baby wants to go in," I said. "He's cold."

"*She's* cold."

"Anything you say."

I had trouble sleeping that night. I kept reliving the malpractice case and how I wound up scapegoat for a couple of department heads at the medical center. After all, I was only a resident and they had national reputations. I was sure they were sleeping well tonight while I lay here awake.

I kept seeing the plaintiff attorney's hungry face, hearing his voice as he tore me apart. I'm a good doctor, a caring one who knows internal medicine inside and out, but you wouldn't have thought so after that lawyer was through with me. He got a third of the settlement and I got the word that I shouldn't apply for a position on the staff when my residency was up. I supposed the big shots didn't want me around as a reminder.

Jessie wanted me to fight them for an appointment but I knew better. Every hospital staff application has a question that reads: "Have you ever been denied staff privileges at any other hospital?" If you answer *Yes*, they want to know all the particulars. If you say *No*, and later they find out otherwise, your ass is grass.

Discretion is the better part of valor, I always say. I knew they'd turn me down, and I didn't want to answer *yes* to that question for the rest of my life. So I packed up and left when my residency was over. The medical center reciprocated by giving me good recommendations.

Jessie says I'm too scared of making waves. She's probably right. She usually is. I do know I couldn't have made it through the trial without her. She stuck by me all the way.

She's right about the waves, though. All I want to do is live in peace and quiet and practice the medicine I've been trained for. That's all. I don't need a Porsche or a mansion. Just Jessie and our kids and enough to live comfortably. That's all I want. That's all I've ever wanted.

Wednesday afternoon, two days after the Mosely house call, I was standing on Doc Johnson's front porch, ringing his bell.

"Stop by the house this afternoon," he'd said on the phone a few hours ago. "Let's get acquainted."

I'd been in town seven months now and this was the first time he'd spoken to me beyond a nod and a good-morning while passing in the hall at County General. I couldn't use the excuse that my office was too busy for me to get away, so I accepted. Besides, I was curious as to why he wanted to see me.

I'd spotted Joe Mosely on my way over. He was coming out of the liquor store and saw me waiting at the light. He looked terrible. I wasn't sure if it was just the daylight or if he was actually thinner than the other night. His cheeks looked more sunken, his eyes more feverish. But his smile hadn't changed. The way he grinned at me had tied my stomach into a knot that was just now beginning to unravel.

I tried not to think of Mosely as I waited for someone to answer my ring. I inspected my surroundings. The Johnson house was as solid as they come, with walls built of the heavy gray native granite that rimmed the shore in these parts. Little mortar was visible. Someone had taken great pains to mate each stone nook and cranny against its neighbor. The resultant pattern was like the flip side of one of those thousand-piece Springbok jigsaw puzzles that Jessie liked to fiddle with.

His verandah here high on East Hill—the only real hill in town—offered a clear eastward view of the length and breadth of the bay all the way down to Blind Point; beyond the barrier island the Atlantic surged cold and gray. To the west lay the Parkway—the low drone of its traffic was audible most nights, but that was a minor concern when you considered how easy it made getting to places like picturesque Cape May to the south and glitzy Atlantic City to the north.

And beyond the Parkway, the deep and enigmatic Jersey Pine Barrens.

I could get used to this.

I thought about Doc Johnson. I'd heard he was a widower with no children, that his family had come over with Ludlum Bay's original settlers back in the seventeenth century. Doctors apparently came and went pretty regularly around the Bay, but "the Doc"—that's what the natives called him—was as constant as the moon, always available, always willing to come out to the house should you be too sick to go to him. If you were a regular patient of the Doc's he never let you down. People talked as if he'd always been here and always would. His practice seemed to encompass the whole town. That was impossible, of course. No one man could care for 20,000 people. But to hear folks talk—and to listen to the grumbling of the few other struggling doctors in town—that was the way it was.

The handle rattled and Doc Johnson opened the door himself. A portly man in his sixties with a full, friendly, florid face and lots of white hair combed straight back, he wore a white shirt, open at the collar, white duck pants, and a blue blazer with a gold emblem on the breast pocket. He looked more like a yacht club commodore than a doctor.

"Charles!" he said, shaking my hand. "So good of you to come! Come in out of the chill and I'll make you a drink!"

It wasn't as chilly as it had been the past few days but I was glad to step into the warmth. He was fixing himself a Sapphire gimlet with a dash of Cointreau and offered me one. I was through for the day, so I accepted. It was excellent.

He showed me around the house that one of his ancestors had built a couple of centuries ago. We made small talk during the tour until we ended up in his study before a fire. He was a gracious, amiable host and I took an immediate liking to him.

"Let's talk shop a minute," he said after I refused a refill on the gimlet and we'd settled into chairs. "I like to feel out a new doctor in town on his philosophy of medicine." His eyes penetrated mine. "Do you have one?"

I thought about that. Since starting med school I'd been so involved in learning whatever there was to know about medicine that I hadn't given much consideration to a philosophical approach. I was tempted to say *Keeping my head above water* but thought better of it. I decided to go Hippocratic.

"I guess I'd start with 'Above all else do no harm.'"

He smiled. "An excellent start. But how would triage fit into your philosophy, Horatio?"

"Horatio?"

"I'm an avid reader. You will forgive me a literary reference once in a while, won't you? That was to *Hamlet*. A strained reference, I'll grant you, but *Hamlet* nonetheless."

"Of course. But triage...?"

"Under certain circumstances we have to choose those who will get care and those who won't. In disasters, for instance: We must ignore those whom we judge to be beyond help in order to aid those who are salvageable."

"Of course. That's an accepted part of emergency care."

"But aren't you doing harm by withholding care?"

"Not if a patient is terminal. Not if the outcome will remain unchanged no matter what you do."

"Which means we must place great faith in our judgment, then, correct?"

I nodded. "Yes, I suppose so."

Where was this going?

"And what if one must amputate a gangrenous limb in order to preserve the health of the rest of the body? Isn't that doing harm of sorts to the diseased limb?"

I said, "I suppose you could look at it that way, but if the health of the good tissue is threatened by the infected limb, and you can't cure the infection, then the limb's got to go."

"Precisely. It's another form of triage: The diseased limb must be lopped off and discarded. Sometimes I find that triage must be of a more active sort where radical decisions must be made. Medicine is full of life-and-death decisions, don't you think?"

I nodded once more. What a baffling conversation.

"I understand you had the pleasure of meeting the estimable Joseph Mosely the other night."

The abrupt change of subject left me reeling for a second.

"I don't know if I'd call it a pleasure."

He barked a laugh. "There'd be something seriously wrong with you if you did. A despicable excuse for a human being. Truly a hollow man, if you'll excuse the Yeats reference—or is that Eliot? No matter. It fits Joe Mosely well enough: no heart, no soul. An alcoholic who abused his children mercilessly. I patched up enough cuts and contusions on his battered boys, and I fear he battered his only daughter in a far more loathsome way. They all ran away as soon as they were able. So now he abuses poor Martha when the mood suits him, and that is too often. Last summer I had to strap up three broken ribs on that poor woman. But she won't press charges. Love's funny, isn't it?"

"It is," I said. "But codependency isn't."

"You've got that right. Did you notice his mangled foot, by the way? That happened when he was working at the shoe factory. Talk is he stuck his foot in one of the machines on purpose, only he stuck it in farther than he intended and did too good a job of injuring himself. Anyway, he got a nice settlement out of it, which is what he wanted, but he drank it up in no time."

"I'm not surprised," I said, remembering his rapidly dwindling level in his gin bottle.

"And did you notice the lack of electricity? The power company caught him tampering with the meter and cut him off. I've heard he's blackmailing a few people in town. And he steals anything that's not nailed down. That cut on his arm I sewed up? That was the first time in all these years I'd ever had a chance to actually treat him. He tried to tell me he did it whittling. Ha! Never yet seen a right-handed man cut his right arm with a knife. No, he did that breaking into a house on Armondo Street. Did it on a storm window. Read in the *Gazette* how they found lots of blood at the scene and were checking ERs in the area to see if anybody had been sewn up. That was why he came to me. I tell you, he will make the world a brighter place by departing it."

"You didn't report him to the police?"

"No," he said levelly. "And I don't intend to. The courts won't give him his due. And calling the police is not my way of handling the likes of Joe Mosely."

I had to say it: "Mosely says you put something in the laceration when you sewed it up."

Doc Johnson's face darkened. "I hope you will consider the source and not repeat that."

"Of course not. I only mentioned it now because you were the accused."

"Good." He cleared his throat. "There's some things you should know about the Bay. We like it quiet here. We don't like idle chatter. You'll find that things have a way of working themselves out in their own way. You don't get outsiders involved if you can help it."

"Like me?"

"That's up to you, Charles. You can be an insider if you want to be. 'Newcomer' and 'insider' aren't mutually exclusive terms in Ludlum Bay. A town dies if it doesn't get *some* new blood. But discretion is all important. As a doctor in town you may occasionally see something out of the ordinary. You can take it as it comes, deal with it, and leave it at that—which will bring you closer to the inside. Or, you can talk about it a lot or maybe even submit a paper on it to something like the *New England Journal of Medicine*, and that will push you out. *Far* out. Soon you'd have to pack up and move away."

He stood and patted my shoulder.

"I like you, Charles. This town needs more doctors. I'd like to see you make it here."

"I'd like to stay here."

"Good! I do my own sort of triage on incoming doctors. If I think they'll work out, I send them my overflow." He sighed. "And believe me, I'm getting ready to increase my overflow. I'd like to slow down a bit. Not as young as I used to be."

"I'd appreciate that."

He gave me a calculating look. "Okay. We'll see. But first—"He glanced outside. "Well, here it comes!" He motioned me over to the big bay window. "Take a look!"

I stepped to his side and gazed out at the Atlantic—or rather, where the Atlantic had been. The horizon was gone, lost in a fog bank that was even now rolling into the bay itself.

Doc Johnson pointed south. "If you watch, you'll see Blind Pew disappear."

"Excuse me?"

He laughed. "Another reference, my boy. I've called Blind Point 'Blind Pew' ever since I read *Treasure Island* when I was ten. You remember Blind Pew, don't you?"

N. C. Wyeth's painting of the moonlit character suddenly flashed before my eyes. It had always given me the chills.

"Of course. But where's the fog coming from?"

"The Gulf Stream. For reasons known only to itself, it swings in here a couple of times a winter. The warm air from the stream hits the cold air on the land and then we have fog. And I do mean *fog*."

As I watched, lacy fingers of mist began to rise from the snow in the front yard.

"Yes, sir!" he said, rubbing his hands together and smiling. "This one's going to be a beauty!"

Mrs. Mosely called me Friday night.

"Doctor, you've got to come out and see Joe."

"No, thank you," I told her. "Once was quite enough."

"I think he's dying!"

"Then get him over to County General."

"He won't let me call an ambulance. He won't let me near him!"

"Then I'm sorry—"

"*Please*, Doctor Reid!" Her voice broke into a wail. "If not for him, then for me! I'm frightened!"

Something in her voice got to me. And I remembered that bruise on her cheek.

"Okay," I said reluctantly. "I'll be over in a half hour."

I knew I'd regret it.

The fog was still menacingly thick, and worse at night than during the day. At least you could pick out shadows in daylight. At night the headlights bounced off the fog instead of penetrating it. Like driving through cotton.

When I finally reached the Mosely place, the air seemed cooler and the fog appeared to be thinning. Somewhere above, moonlight struggled to get through. Maybe the predicted cold front from the west was finally moving in.

Martha Mosely opened the door.

"Thank you for coming, Doctor Reid. I don't know what to do! He won't let me touch him or go near him! I'm at my wit's end!"

"Where is he?"

"In bed."

She led me to a room in the back and stood at the door clutching her hands between her breasts as I entered.

By the light of the room's single flickering candle I could see Joe Mosely lying naked on the bed, stretched out like an emaciated corpse. In fact, for a moment I thought he was dead—his breathing was so shallow I couldn't see his chest move.

Then he turned his head a few degrees in my direction.

"So, it's you." His lips barely moved. The eyes were the only things alive in his face.

"Yeah. Me. What can I do for you?"

"First, you can close the door—with that woman on the other side."

Before I could answer, I heard the door close behind me. I was alone in the room with him.

"And second, you can keep your distance."

"What's the matter? Anything hurt?"

"No pain. But I'm a dead man. It's Doc Johnson's doing. I told you he put something in that cut."

His words were disturbing enough, but his completely emotionless tone made them even more chilling—as if whatever emotions he possessed had been drained away along with his vitality.

"You need to be hospitalized."

"No use. I'm already gone. But let me tell you about Doc Johnson. He did this to me. He's got his own ways and he follows his own rules. I've tailed him into the Pine Barrens a few times but I always lost him. Don't know what he goes there for, but it can't be for no good."

I took out my stethoscope as he raved. When he saw it, his voice rose in pitch.

"Don't come near me. Just keep away."

"Don't be ridiculous. I'm here. I might as well see if I can do anything for you."

I adjusted the earpieces and went down on one knee beside the bed.

"Don't! Keep back!"

I pressed the diaphragm over his heart to listen—

—and felt his chest wall give way like a stale soda cracker.

My left hand disappeared up to the wrist inside his chest cavity. And it was *cold* in there! I yanked it out and hurled myself away from the bed, not stopping until I came up against the bedroom wall.

"Now you've done it," he said in that passionless voice.

As I watched, a yellow mist began to ooze out of the opening. It slid over his ribs and along the sheet, and from there down to the floor, like the fog from dry ice.

I looked at Mosely's face and saw the light go out of his eyes.

He was gone.

A wind began blowing outside, whistling under the doors and banging the shutters. I glanced out the window on the far side of the room and saw the fog begin to swirl and tear apart. Suddenly something crashed in the front room. I pulled myself up and opened the bedroom door. A freezing wind hit me in the face with the force of a gale, tearing the door from my grip and swirling into the room. I saw Martha Mosely get up from the sofa and struggle to close the front door against the rage of the wind.

The bedroom window shattered under the sudden pressure and now the wind howled through the house.

The yellow mist from Mosely's chest cavity caught the gale and rode it out the window, slipping along the floor and up the wall and over the sill in streaks that gleamed in the growing moonlight.

Then the mist was gone and I was alone in the room with the wind and Joe Mosely's empty shell.

And then that shell began to crumble, caving in on itself piece by piece, almost in slow motion, fracturing into countless tiny pieces that in turn disintegrated into a gray, dust-like powder. This too was caught by the wind and carried out into the night.

Joe Mosely was gone, leaving behind not so much as a depression in the bedcovers.

The front door finally closed with Martha's efforts and I heard the bolt slide home. She walked up to the bedroom door but did not step inside.

"Joe's gone, isn't he?" she said in a low voice.

I couldn't speak. I opened my mouth but no words would come. I simply nodded as I stood there trembling.

She stepped into the room then and looked at the bed. She looked at the broken window, then at me. With a sigh she sat on the edge of the bed and ran her hand over the spot where her husband had lain.

My home phone rang at eight o'clock the next morning. It didn't disturb my sleep. I'd been awake all night. Part of the time I'd spent lying rigid in bed, the rest here in the kitchen with all the lights on, waiting for the sun.

An awful wait. When I wasn't reliving the scene in the Mosely bedroom I was hearing voices. If it wasn't Joe telling me that Doc Johnson had put something in his wound, it was the Doc himself talking about making life-and-death decisions, about triage, all laced with literary references.

I hadn't told Jessie a thing. She'd think I was ready for a straitjacket. And if by some chance she *did* believe, she'd want to pack up and get out of town. But where to? We had the baby to think of.

I'd spent the time since dawn going over my options. And when the phone rang, I had no doubt who was calling.

"I understand Joe Mosely is gone," Doc Johnson said without preamble.

"Yes."

...a hollow man...

"Any idea where?"

"Out the window." My voice sounded half dead to me. "Beyond that, I don't know."

...calling the police is not my way of handling the likes of Joe Mosely...

"Seen anything lately worth writing to any of the medical journals about?"

"Not a thing."

...the diseased limb has to be lopped off and discarded...

"Just another day in Ludlum Bay then?" Doc Johnson said.

"Oh, I hope not." I could not hide the tremor in my voice.

...sometimes triage has to be of a more active sort where radical decisions must be made...

He chuckled. "Charles, my boy, I think you'll do all right here. As a matter of fact, I'd like to refer a couple of patients to your office today. They've got complicated problems that require more attention than I can give them at this time. I'll assure them that they can trust you implicitly. Will you take them on?"

I paused. Even though my mind was made up, I took a deep breath and held it, waiting for some argument to come out of the blue and swing me the other way. Finally, I could hold it no longer.

"Yes," I said. "Thank you."

"Charles, I think you're going to do just fine in Ludlum Bay."

One of my all-time favorite stories is Ray Bradbury's "The October Game." I think it's a perfect horror sorry. But in his later years, Ray sort of backed away from it. I say "sort of" because I never heard him disown it, but I sensed that he thought he'd stepped over a line there, gone too dark. He wasn't that person anymore.

I'm starting to feel that way about "Cuts."

Wherever I go, people who've read *Silver Scream* never fail to mention "Cuts." I know it had great cathartic power for me. When David Schow approached me for a Hollywood-based story for *Silver Scream*, I knew immediately the kind of piece I'd do.

In the early '80s, Michael Mann adapted—screenplay and direction—my novel *The Keep* for Paramount. (Adapted? Well, he kept the title.)

I was still in a rage after seeing what he'd done to my baby. I blasted straight through "Cuts" and felt *wonderful* when I was finished. My mood was lighter, the world was brighter, even my digestion was better. I let it sit for a week or two before printing it out and reading it. When I finally did read it, I was shocked. I hadn't meant to allow so much pent-up rage to spill onto the page. I pride myself on my cool and this was a little too self-revelatory. I sent it to Dave as it was but mentioned that I might want to do a toned-down rewrite. Dave threatened me with bodily harm if I toned down a damn thing.

If you've read Schow's fiction you know he's quite inventive in the area of bodily harm. So I left it as it was. It's rivaled only by "Pelts" as my nastiest story.

But on rereading it now I think I know how Bradbury felt. I still think the film's a load of pretentious crap, but I'm no longer the person who wrote "Cuts."

Cuts

It started in Milo's right foot. He awoke in the dark of his bedroom with a pins-and-needles sensation from the lower part of his calf to the tips of his toes. He sat up, massaged it, walked around the bedroom. Nothing helped. Finally, he took a Darvocet and went back to bed. He managed to get to sleep but was awake again by dawn, this time with both feet tingling. In the wan light, he inspected his lower legs.

A thin, faintly red line around each leg about three inches up from the ankle. Milo snapped on the night table light for a closer look. He touched the line. It was more than a line—an indentation, actually, like something left after wearing a pair of socks too tight at the top. But it felt as if the constricting band were still there.

He got up and walked around. It felt a little funny to stand on partially numb feet but he couldn't worry about it now. In just a couple of hours he was doing a power breakfast at the Polo with Regenstein from TriStar and he had to be sharp. He padded into the kitchen to put on the coffee.

———

As he wove through LA's morning commuter traffic, Milo envied the drivers with their tops down. He would have loved to have his 380 SL opened up to the bright early morning sun. Truthfully, he would have been glad for an open window. But for the sake of his hair he stayed bottled up with the a-c on. He couldn't afford to let the breeze blow his toupee around. It had been especially stubborn about blending in with his natural hair this morning and he didn't have any more time to fuss with it. And this was his good piece. His back-up had been stolen during a robbery of his house last week, an occurrence that still baffled the hell out of him. He wished he didn't have to worry about wearing a rug. He had heard about a new experimental lotion that was supposed to start hair growing again. If that ever panned out, he'd be first on line to—

His right hand started tingling. He removed it from the wheel and fluttered it in the air. Still it tingled. The sleeve of his sports coat slipped back and he saw a faint indentation running around his forearm, just above the wrist. For a few heartbeats he studied it in horrid fascination.

What's happening to me?

Then he glanced up and saw the looming rear of a truck rushing toward his windshield. He slammed on the brakes and slewed to a screeching stop inches from the tailgate. Gasping and sweating, Milo slumped in the seat and tried to get a grip. Bad enough he was developing mysterious little constricting bands on his legs and now his arm, he had almost wrecked the new Mercedes. This sucker cost more than his first house back in the seventies.

When traffic started up again, he drove cautiously, keeping his eyes on the road and working the fingers of his right hand. He had some weird-shit disease, he just knew it, but he couldn't let anything get between him and this breakfast with Regenstein.

"Look, Milo," Howard Regenstein said through the smoke from his third cigarette in the last twenty minutes. "You know that if it was up to me the picture would be all yours. You know that, man."

Milo nodded, not knowing that at all. He had used that same line himself a million times—maybe *two* million times. If it was up to me...

Yeah, right. The great cop-out: I'm a nice guy and I have all the faith in the world in you but those money guys, those faithless, faceless Philistines who hold the purse-strings won't let guys with vision like you and me get together and make a great film.

"Well, what's the problem, Howie? I mean, give it to me straight."

"All right," Howie said, showing his chicklet caps between his thin lips. He was deeply tanned, wore thick horn-rimmed glasses; his close cropped curly hair was sandy-colored and lightly bleached. "Despite my strong—and, Milo, I do mean *strong*—recommendation, the money boys looked at the grosses for *The Hut* and got scared away."

Well. That explained a lot of things, especially this crummy table half hidden in an inside corner. The real power players, the ones who wanted everybody else in the place to see who they were doing breakfast with, were out in the middle or along the windows. Regenstein probably had three breakfasts scheduled for this morning. Milo was wondering what tables had been reserved for the others when a sharp pain stabbed his right leg. He winced and reached down.

"Something wrong?" Regenstein said.

"No. Just a muscle cramp."

He lifted his trouser leg and saw that the indentation above his ankle was deeper. It was actually a cut now. Blood oozed slowly, seeping into his sock. He straightened up and forced a smile at Regenstein.

"*The Hut*, Howie? Is *that* all?" Milo said with a laugh. "Don't they know that project was a loser from the start? The book was a bad property, a piece of clichéd garbage. Don't they know that?"

Howie smiled, too. "Afraid not, Milo. You know their kind. They look at the bottom line and see that Universal's going to be twenty mill in the hole on *The Hut*, and in their world that means something. And maybe they remember those PR pieces you did a month or so before it opened. You never even mentioned that the film was based on a book. Had me convinced the story was all yours, whole cloth."

Milo clenched his teeth. That had been when he had thought the movie was going to be a smash.

"I had a *concept*, Howie, one that cut through the bounds and limitations of the novel. I wanted to raise the level of the material but the producers stymied me at every turn."

Actually, he had been pretty much on his own down there in Haiti. He had changed the book a lot, made loads of cuts and condensations. He had made it "A Milo Gherl Film."

But somewhere along the way he had lost it. Unanimously hostile one-star reviews with leads like, "Shut *The Hut*" and "New Gherl Pix the Pits" hadn't helped. Twentieth had been pushing an offer in its television division and he had been holding them off—who wanted to do TV when you could do theatricals? But as the bad reviews piled up and the daily grosses plummeted, he grabbed the TV offer. It was good money, had plenty of prestige, but it was still television.

Milo wanted to do films, and very badly wanted in on the new package Regenstein was putting together for TriStar. Howie had Jack Nicholson, Bobby DeNiro, and Kathy Turner firm, and was looking for a director. More than anything else in his career, Milo wanted to be that director. But he wasn't going to be. He knew that now.

Well, at least he could use the job to pay the bills and keep his name before the public until *The Hut* was forgotten. That wouldn't be long. A year or two at most and he'd be back directing another theatrical. Not a package like Regenstein's, but something with a decent budget where he could do the screenplay and direct. That was the way he liked it— full control on paper and on film.

He shrugged at Regenstein and put on his best good-natured smile.

"What can I say, Howie? The world wasn't ready for *The Hut*. Someday, they'll appreciate it."

Yeah, right, he thought as Regenstein nodded noncommittally. At least Howie was letting him down easy, letting him keep his dignity here. That was important. All he had to do now was—

Milo screamed as pain tore into his left eye like a bolt of lightning. He lurched to his feet, upsetting the table as he clamped his hands over his eye in a vain attempt to stop the agony.

Pain! Oh Christ, pain as he had never known it was shooting from his eye straight into his brain. This had to be a stroke! What else could hurt like this?

Through his good eye he had a whirling glimpse of everybody in the dining room standing and staring at him as he staggered around. He pulled one hand away from his eye and reached out to steady himself. He saw a smear blood on his fingers. He took the other hand away. His left eye was blind, but with his right he saw the dripping red on his palm. A woman screamed.

"My God, Milo!" Regenstein said, his chalky face swimming into view. "Your eye! What did you do to your eye?" He turned to a gaping waiter. "Get a doctor! Get a fucking ambulance!"

Milo was groggy from the Demerol they had given him. In the blur of hours since breakfast he'd been wheeled in and out of the emergency room so many times, poked with so many needles, examined by so many doctors, x-rayed so many times, his head was spinning.

At least the pain had eased off.

"I'm admitting you onto the vascular surgery service, Mr. Gherl," said the bearded doctor as he pushed back one of the white curtains that shielded Milo's gurney from the rest of the emergency room. His badge said, *Edward Jansen, M.D.*, and he looked tired and irritable.

Milo struggled up the Demerol downgrade. "Vascular surgery? But my eye—!"

"As Dr. Burch told you, Mr. Gherl, your eye can't be saved. It's ruined beyond repair. But maybe we can save your feet and your hand if it's not too late already.

"*Save* them?"

"If we're lucky. I don't know what kind of games you've been into, but getting yourself tied up with piano wire is about the dumbest thing I've ever heard of."

Milo was growing more alert by the second now. Over Dr. Jansen's shoulder he saw the bustle of the emergency room personnel, saw an old black mopping the floor in slow, rhythmic strokes. But he was only seeing it with his right eye. He reached up to the bandage over his left. *Ruined?* He wanted to cry, but Dr. Jansen's piano wire remark suddenly filtered through to his consciousness.

"Piano wire? What are you talking about?"

"Don't play dumb. Look at your feet." Dr. Edwards pulled the sheet free from the far end of the gurney.

Milo looked. The nail beds were white and the skin below the indentations were a dusky blue. And the indentations had all become clean, straight, bloody cuts right through the skin and into the meat below. His right hand was the same.

"See that color?" Jansen was saying. "That means the tissues below the wire cuts aren't getting enough blood. You're going to have gangrene for sure if we don't restore circulation soon."

Gangrene! Milo levered up on the gurney and felt his toes with his good hand. *Cold!* "No! That's impossible!"

"I'd almost agree with you," Dr. Jansen said, his voice softening for a moment as he seemed to be talking to himself. Behind him, Milo noticed the old black moving closer with his mop. "When we did x-rays, I thought we'd see the wire embedded in the flesh there, but there was nothing. Tried Xero soft-tissue technique in case you had used fishing line or something, but that came up negative, too. Even probed the cuts myself but there's nothing in there. Yet the arteriograms clearly show that the arteries in your lower legs and right forearm are compressed to the point where very little blood is getting through. The tissues are starving. The vascular boys may have to do bypasses."

"I'm getting out of here!" Milo said. "I'll see my own doctor!"

"I'm afraid I can't allow that."

"You can't stop me! I can walk out of here anytime I want!"

"I can keep you seventy-two hours for purposes of emergency psychiatric intervention."

"Psychiatric!"

"Yeah. Self-mutilation. Your mind worries me almost as much as your arteries, Mr. Gherl. I'd like to make sure you don't poke out your other eye before you get treatment."

"But I didn't—!"

"Please, Mr. Gherl. There were witnesses. Your breakfast companion said he had just finished giving you some disappointing news when you screamed and rammed something into your eye."

Milo touched the bandage over his eye again. How could they think he had done this to himself?

"My God, I swear I didn't do this!"

"That kind of trauma doesn't happen spontaneously, Mr. Gherl, and according to your companion, no one was within reach of you. So one way or the other, you're staying. Make it easy on both of us and do it voluntarily."

Milo didn't see that he had a choice. "I'll stay," he said. "Just answer me one thing: You ever seen anything like this before?"

Jansen shook his head. "Never. Never heard of anything like it either." He took a sudden deep breath and smiled through his beard with what Milo guessed was supposed to be doctorly reassurance. "But, hey. I'm only an ER doc. The vascular boys will know what to do."

With that, he turned and left, leaving Milo staring into the wide-eyed black face of the janitor.

"What are you staring at?" Milo said.

"A man in *big* trouble," the janitor said in a deep, faintly accented voice. He was pudgy with a round face, watery eyes, and two days' worth of silvery growth on his jowls. With a front tooth missing on the top, he looked like Leon Spinks gone to seed for thirty years. "These doctors can't be helpin' what you got. You got a *Bocor* mad at you and only a *Houngon* can fix you."

"Get lost!" Milo said.

He lay back on the gurney and closed his good eye to shut out the old man and the emergency room. He hunted for sleep as an escape from the pain and the gut-roiling terror, praying he'd wake up and learn that this was all just a horrible dream. But those words wouldn't go away. *Bocor* and *Houngon*...he knew them somehow. Where?

And then it hit him like a blow—*The Hut*! They were voodoo terms from the novel, *The Hut*! He hadn't used them in the film—he'd scoured all mention of voodoo from his screenplay—but the author had used them in the book. If Milo remembered correctly, a *Bocor* was an evil voodoo priest and a *Houngon* was a good one. Or was it the other way around? Didn't matter. They were all part of Bill Franklin's bullshit novel.

Franklin! Wouldn't he like to see me now! Milo thought. Their last meeting had been anything but pleasant. Unforgettable, yes. His mind did a slow dissolve to his new office at Twentieth two weeks ago...

"Some conference!"

The angry voice startled Milo and he spilled hot coffee down the front of his shirt. He leaped up from behind his desk and bent forward, pulling the steaming fabric away from his chest. "Jesus H.—"

But then he looked up and saw Bill Franklin standing there and his anger cooled like fresh blood in an arctic breeze. Maggie's anxious face peered over Franklin's narrow shoulder.

"I tried to stop him, Mr. Gherl, honest I did, but he wouldn't listen!"

"You've been ducking me for a month, Gherl!" Franklin said in his nasal voice. "No more tricks!"

Maggie said, "Shall I call security?"

"I don't think that will be necessary, Maggs," he said quickly, grabbing a Kleenex from the oak tissue holder on his desk and blotting at his stained shirt front. Milo had moved into this office only a few weeks ago, and the last thing he needed today was an ugly scene with an irate writer. He could tell from Franklin's expression that he was ready to cause a doozy. Better to bite the bullet and get this over with. "I'll talk to Mr. Franklin. You can leave him here." She hesitated and he waved her toward the door. "Go ahead. It's all right."

When she had closed the door behind her, he picked up the insulated brass coffee urn and looked at Franklin. "Coffee, Billy-boy?"

"I don't want coffee, Gherl! I want to know why you've been ducking me!"

"But I haven't been ducking you, Billy!" he said, refreshing his own cup. He would have to change this shirt before he did lunch later. "I'm not with Universal anymore. I'm with Twentieth now, so naturally my offices are here." He swept an arm around him. "Not bad, ay?"

Milo sat down and tried his best to look confident, at ease. Inside, he was anything but. Right now he was a little afraid of the writer stalking back and forth before the desk like a caged tiger. Nothing about Franklin's physical appearance was the least bit intimidating. He was fair-haired and tall with big hands and feet attached to a slight, gangly frame. He had a big nose, a small chin, and a big Adam's apple—Milo had noticed on their first meeting two years ago that he could slant a perfectly straight line along the tips of those three protuberances. A moderate overbite did not help the picture. Milo's impression of Franklin had always been that of a patient, retiring, rational man who never raised his voice.

But today he was barging about with a wild look in his eyes, shouting, gesticulating, accusing. Milo remembered an old saying his father used to quote to him when he was a boy: *Beware the wrath of a patient man.*

Franklin had paused and was looking around the spacious room with its indirect lighting, its silver-gray floor-to-ceiling louvered blinds and matching carpet, the chrome and onyx wet bar, the free-form couches, the abstract sculptures on the Lucite coffee table and on Milo's oversized desk.

"How did you ever rate this after perpetrating a turkey like *The Hut*?"

"Twentieth recognizes talent when it sees it, Billy."

"My question stands," Franklin said.

Milo ignored the remark. "Sit down, Billy-boy. What's got you so upset?"

Franklin didn't sit. He resumed his stalking. "You know damn well what! My book!"

"You've got a new one?" Milo said, perfectly aware of which book he meant.

"No! I mean the only book I've ever written—*The Hut!*—and the mess you made out of it!"

Milo had heard quite enough nasty criticism of that particular film to last him a lifetime. He felt his anger flare but suppressed it. Why get into a shouting match?

"I'm sorry you feel that way, Billy, but let's face facts." He spread his hands in a consoling gesture. "It's a dead issue. There's nothing more to be done. The film has been shot, edited, released, and—"

"—and withdrawn!" Franklin shouted. "Two weeks in general release and the theater owners sent it back! It's not just a flop, it's a catastrophe!"

"The critics—killed it."

"Bullshit! The critics blasted it, just like they blasted other 'flops' like *Flashdance* and *Top Gun* and *Ernest Goes to Camp*. What killed it, Gherl, was word of mouth. Now I know why you wouldn't screen it until a week before it opened: You knew you'd botched it!"

"I had trouble with the final cut. I couldn't—"

"You couldn't get it to make sense! As I walked out of that screening I kept telling myself that my negative feelings were due to all the things you'd cut out of my book, that maybe I was too close to it all and that the public would somehow find my story in your mass of pretensions. Then I heard a guy in his early twenties say, 'What the hell was *that* all about?' and his girlfriend say, 'What a boring waste of time!' and I knew it wasn't just me." Franklin's long bony finger stabbed through the air. "It was you! You raped my book!"

Milo had had just about enough of this. "You novelists are all alike!" he said with genuine disdain. "You do fine on the printed page so you think you're experts at writing for the screen. But you're not. You don't know the first goddam thing about visual writing!"

"You cut the heart out of my story! *The Hut* was about the nature of evil and how it can seduce even the strongest among us. The plot was like a house of cards, Gherl, built with my sweat. Your windbag script blew it all down! And after I saw the first draft of the script, you were suddenly unavailable for conference!"

Milo recalled Franklin's endless stream of nit-picking letters, his deluge of time-wasting phone calls. "I was busy, dammit! I was writer-director! The whole thing was on my shoulders!"

"I warned you that the house of cards was falling due to the cuts you made. I mean, why did you remove all mention of voodoo and zombiism from the script? They were the two red herrings that held the plot together."

"Voodoo! Zombies! That's old hat! Nobody would pay to see a voo-doo movie!"

"Then why set the movie in Haiti, f'Christsake? Might as well have been in Pasadena! And that monster you threw in at the end? Where in hell did you come up with that? It looked like the Incredible Hulk in drag! I spent years in research. I slaved to fill that book with terror and dread—all you brought to the screen were cheap shocks!"

"If that's your true opinion—and I disagree with it absolutely—you should be glad the film was a flop. No one will see it!"

Franklin nodded slowly. "That gave me comfort for a while, until I realized that the movie isn't dead. When it reaches the video stores and the cable services, tens of millions of people will see it—not because it's good, but simply because it's there and it's something they've never heard of before and certainly have never seen. And they'll be direct-ing their rapt attention at your corruption of my story, and they'll see 'Based on the Novel by William Franklin' and think that the preten-tious, incomprehensible mishmash they're watching represents my work. And that makes me *mad*, Gherl! Fucking-ay crazy mad!"

The ferocity that flashed across Franklin's face was truly frighten-ing. Milo rushed to calm him. "Billy, look: Despite our artistic differ-ences and despite the fact that *The Hut* will never turn a profit, you were paid well into six figures for the screen rights. What's your beef?"

Franklin seemed to shrink a little. His shoulders slumped and his voice softened. "I didn't write it for money. I live off a trust fund that provides me with more than I can spend. *The Hut* was my first novel—maybe my only novel ever. I gave it everything. I don't think I have any more in me."

"Of course you do!" Milo said, rising and moving around the desk toward the subdued writer. Here was his chance to ease Franklin out of here. "It's just that you've never had to suffer for your art! You've had it too soft, too cushy for too long. Things came too easy on that first book. First time at bat you got a major studio film offer that actually made it to the screen. That hardly ever happens. Now you've got to prove it wasn't just a fluke. You've got to get out there and slog away on that new book! Deprive yourself a little! *Suffer!*"

"Suffer?" Franklin said, a weird light starting to glow in his eyes. "I should suffer?"

"Yes!" Milo said, guiding him toward the office door. "All great artists suffer."

"You ever suffer, Milo Gherl?"

"Of course." Especially this morning, listening to you!

"Look at this office. You don't look like you're suffering for what you did to *The Hut*."

"I did my suffering years ago. The anger you feel about *The Hut* is small change compared to the dues I've had to pay." He finally had Franklin across the threshold. "I'm through suffering," he said as he slammed the door and locked it.

From the other side of the thick oak door he thought he heard Franklin say, "No, you're not."

"Missing any personal items lately, mister?" said a voice.

Milo opened his good eye and saw the big black guy standing over him, leaning on his mop handle. What was *wrong* with this old fart? What was his angle?

"If you don't leave me alone I'm gonna call—" He paused. "What do you mean, 'personal items'?"

"You know—clothing, nail clippings, a brush or comb that might hold some of your hair. That kinda stuff."

A chill swept over Milo's skin like an icy breeze in July.

The robbery!

Such a bizarre thing—a pried-open window, a few cheap rings gone, his drawers and closets ransacked, an old pair of pajamas missing. And his toupee, the second-string hairpiece...gone. Who could figure it? But he had been shaken up enough to go out and buy a .38 for his night table.

Milo laughed. This was so ludicrous. "You're talking about a voodoo doll, aren't you?"

The old guy nodded. "It got other names, but that'll do."

"Who the hell *are* you?"

"Name's Andre but folks call me Andy. I got connections you gonna need."

"You need your head examined!"

"Maybe. But that doctor said he was lookin' for the wires that was cuttin' into your legs and your arm but he couldn't find them. That's because the wires are somewheres else. They around the legs and arm of a doll somebody made on you."

Milo tried to laugh again but found he couldn't. He managed a weak, "Bullshit."

"You believe me soon enough. And when you do, I take you to a *Houngon* who can help you out."

"Yeah," Milo said. "Like you really care about me."

The old black showed his gap-tooth smile. "Oh, I won't be doin' you a favor, and neither will the *Houngon*. He'll be wantin' money for pullin' you fat out the fire."

"And you'll get a finder's fee."

The smile broadened. "Thas right."

That made a little more sense to Milo, but still he wasn't buying. "Forget it!"

"I be around till three. I keep checkin' up on you case you change you mind. I can get you out here when you want to go."

"Don't hold your breath."

Milo rolled on his side and closed his eyes. The old fart had some nerve trying to run that corny scam on him, and in a hospital yet! He'd report him, have him fired. This was no joke. He'd lost his eye already. He could be losing his feet, his hand! He needed top medical-center level care, not some voodoo mumbo-jumbo...

...but no one seemed to know what was going on, and everyone seemed to think he'd put his own eye out. God, who could do something like that to himself? And his hand and his feet—the doc had said they were going to start rotting off if blood didn't get flowing back into them. What on earth was happening to him?

And what about that weird robbery last week? Only personal articles had been stolen. All the high-ticket stereo and video stuff had been left untouched.

God, it couldn't be voodoo, could it? Who'd even—?

Shit! Bill Franklin! He was an expert on it after all those years of research for *The Hut*. But he wouldn't...he couldn't...

Franklin's faintly heard words echoed in Milo's brain: No, you're not.

Agony suddenly lanced through Milo's groin, doubling him over on the gurney. Gasping with the pain, he tore at the clumsy stupid nightshirt they'd dressed him in and pulled it up to his waist. He held back the scream that rose in his throat when he saw the thin red line running around the base of his penis. Instead, he called out a name.

"Andy! Andy!"

Milo coughed and peered through the dim little room. It smelled of dust and sweat and charcoal smoke and something else—something rancid. He wondered what the hell he was doing here. He knew if he had any sense he'd get out now, but he didn't know where to go from here. He wasn't even sure he could find his way home from here.

The setting sun had been a bloody blob in Milo's rearview mirror as he'd hunched over the steering wheel of his Mercedes and followed Andy's rusty red pick-up into one of LA's seamier districts. Andy had been true to his word: He'd spirited Milo out of the hospital, back to the house for some cash and some real clothes, then down to the garage near the Polo where his car was parked. After that it was on to Andy's *Houngon* and maybe end this agony.

It *had* to end soon. Milo's feet were so swollen he was wearing old slippers. He had barely been able to turn the ignition key with his right hand. And his dick—God, his dick felt like it was going to explode!

After what seemed like a ten-mile succession of left and right turns during which he saw not a single white face, they had pulled to a stop before a dilapidated storefront office. On the cracked glass was painted:

M. Trieste
Houngon

Andy had stayed outside with the car while Milo went in.

"Mr. Gherl?"

Milo started at the sound and turned toward the voice. A balding, wizened old black, six-two at least, stood next to him. His face was a mass of wrinkles. He was dressed in a black suit, white shirt, and thin black tie.

Milo heard his own voice quaver: "Yes. That's me."

"You are the victim of the *Bocor*?" His voice was cultured, and accented in some strange way.

Milo pushed back the sleeve of his shirt to expose his right wrist. "I don't know what I'm the victim of, but Andy says you can help me. You've *got* to help me!"

He stared at the patch over Milo's eye. "May I see?"

Milo leaned away from him. "Don't touch that!" It had finally stopped hurting. He held his arm higher.

M. Trieste examined Milo's hand, tracing a cool dry finger around the clotted circumferential cut at the wrist. "This is all?"

Milo showed him his legs, then reluctantly, opened his fly.

"You have a powerful enemy in this *Bocor*," M. Trieste said, finally. "But I can reverse the effects of his doll. It will cost you five hundred dollars. Do you have it with you?"

Milo hesitated. "Let's not be too hasty here. I want to see some results before I fork over any money." He was hurting, but he wasn't going to be a sucker for this clown.

M. Trieste smiled. He had all his teeth. "I have no wish to steal from you, Mr. Gherl. I shall accept no money from you unless I can effect a cure. However, I do not wish to be cheated either. Do you have the money with you?"

Milo nodded. "Yes."

"Very well." M. Trieste struck a match and lit a candle on a table Milo hadn't realized was there. "Please be seated," he said and disappeared into the darkness.

Milo complied and looked around. The wan candlelight picked up an odd assortment of objects around the room: African ceremonial masks hung side by side with crucifixes on the wall; a long conga drum sat in a corner to the right while a statue of the Virgin Mary, her small plaster foot trodding a writhing snake, occupied the one on his left. He wondered when the drums would start and the dancers appear. When would they begin chanting and daubing him with paint and splattering him with chicken blood? God, he must have been crazy to come here. Maybe the pain was affecting his mind. If he had any smarts he'd—

"Hold out your wrist," M. Trieste said, suddenly appearing in the candlelight opposite him. He held what looked like a plaster coffee mug in his hand. He was stirring its contents with a wooden stick.

Milo held back. "What are you going to do?"

"Help you, Mr. Gherl. You are the victim of a very traditional and particularly nasty form of voodoo. You have greatly angered a *Bocor* and he is using a powerful *loa*, via a doll, to lop off your hands and your feet and your manhood."

"My left hand's okay," Milo said, gratefully working the fingers in the air.

"So I have noticed," M. Trieste said with a frown. "It is odd for one extremity to be spared, but perhaps there is a certain symbolism at work here that we do not understand. No matter. The remedy is the same. Hold your arm out on the table."

Milo did as he was told. His swollen hand looked black in the candlelight. "Is...is this going to hurt?"

"When the pressure is released, there will be considerable pain as the fresh blood rushes into the starved tissues."

That kind of pain Milo could handle. "Do it."

M. Trieste stirred the contents of the cup and lifted the wooden handle. Instead of the spoon he had expected, Milo saw that the man was holding a brush. It gleamed redly.

Here comes the blood, he thought. But he didn't care what was in the cup as long as it worked.

"Andre told me about your problem before he brought you here. I made this up in advance. I will paint it on the constrictions and it will nullify the influence of the *loa* of the doll. After that, it will be up to you to make peace with this *Bocor* before he visits other afflictions on you."

"Sure, sure," Milo said, thrusting his wrist toward M. Trieste. "Let's just get on with it!"

M. Trieste daubed the bloody solution onto the incision line. It beaded up like water on a freshly waxed car and slid off onto the table. Milo glanced up and saw a look of consternation flit across the wrinkled black face towering above him. He watched as the red stuff was applied again, only to run off as before.

"Most unusual," M. Trieste muttered as he tried a third time with no better luck. "I've never..." He put the cup down and began painting his own right hand with the solution. "This will do it. Hold up your hand."

As Milo raised his arm, M. Trieste encircled the wrist with his long dripping fingers and squeezed. There was an instant of heat, and then M. Trieste cried out. He released Milo's wrist and dropped to his knees cradling his right hand against his breast.

"The poisons!" he cried. "Oh, the poisons!"

Milo trembled as he looked at his dusky hand. The bloody solution had run off as before. "What poisons?"

"Between you and this *Bocor*! Get out of here!"

"But the doll! You said you could—!"

"There is no doll!" M. Trieste said. He turned away and retched. "There *is* no doll!"

With his heart clattering against his chest wall, Milo pushed himself away from the table and staggered to the door. Andy was leaning on his truck at the curb.

"Wassamatter?" he said straightening off the fender as he saw Milo. "Didn't he—?"

"He's a phony, just like you!" Milo screamed, letting his rage and fear focus on the old Black. "Just another goddam phony!"

As Andy hurried into the store, Milo started up his Mercedes and roared down the street. He'd drive until he found a sign for one of the freeways. From there he could get home.

And from home, he knew where he wanted to go...where he *had* to go.

"Franklin! Where are you, Franklin?"

Milo had finally found Bill Franklin's home in the Hollywood Hills. Even though he knew the neighborhood fairly well, Milo had never been on this particular street, and so it had taken him a while to track it down. The lights had been on inside and the door had been unlocked. No one had answered his knocking, so he'd let himself in.

"Franklin, goddamit!" he called, standing in the middle of the cathedral-ceilinged living room. His voice echoed off the stucco walls and hardwood floor. "Where are you?"

In the ensuing silence, he heard a faint voice say, "Milo? Is that you?"

Milo tensed. Where had that come from? "Yeah, it's me! Where are you?"

Again, ever so faintly: "Down here...in the basement!"

Milo searched for the cellar door, found it, saw the lights ablaze from below, and began his descent. His slippered feet were completely numb now and he had to watch where he put them. It was as if his feet had been removed and replaced with giant sponges.

"That you, Milo?" said a voice from somewhere around the corner from the stairwell. It was Franklin's voice, but it sounded slurred, strained.

"Yeah, it's me."

As he neared the last step, he pulled the .38 from his pocket. He had picked it up at the house along with a pair of wirecutters on his way here. He had never fired it, and he didn't expect to have to tonight. But it was good to know it was loaded and ready if he needed it. He tried to transfer it to his right hand but his numb, swollen fingers couldn't keep hold of the grip. He kept it in his left and stepped onto the cellar floor—

—and felt his foot start to roll away from him. Only by throwing himself against the wall and hugging it did he save himself from falling. He looked around the unfinished cellar. Bright, reflective objects were scattered all along the naked concrete floor. He sucked in a breath as he saw the hundreds of sharp curved angles of green glass poking up at the exposed ceiling beams. The looked like shattered wine bottles—big, green, four-liter wine bottles smashed all over the place. And in among the shards were scattered thousands of marbles.

"Be careful," said Franklin's voice. "The basement's mined." The voice was there, but Franklin was nowhere in sight.

"Where the hell are you, Franklin?"

"Back here in the bathroom. I thought you'd never get here."

Milo began to move toward the rear of the cellar where brighter light poured from an open door. He slid his slippered feet slowly along the floor, pushing the green glass spears ahead of him, rolling the marbles out of the way.

"I've come for the doll, Franklin."

Milo heard a hollow laugh. "Doll? What doll, Milo? There's just me and you, ol' buddy."

Milo shuffled around the corner into view of the bathroom. And froze. The gun dropped from his fingers and further shattered some of the glass at his feet. "Oh, my God, Franklin! Oh, my God!"

William Franklin sat on the toilet wearing Milo's rings, his old slippers, his stolen pajamas, and his other hairpiece. His left eye was patched and his feet and his right hand were as black and swollen as Milo's. There was a maniacal look in his remaining eye as he grinned drunkenly and sipped from a four-liter green-glass bottle of white wine. The cuts in his flesh were identical to Milo's except that a short length of twisted copper wire protruded from each. A screwdriver and a pair of pliers lay in his lap.

M. Trieste's parting words screamed through his brain: There is no doll!

"See?" Franklin said in a slurred voice. "You said I had to suffer."

Milo wanted to be sick. "Christ! What have you done?"

"I decided to suffer. But I didn't think I should suffer alone. So I brought you along for company. Sure took you long enough to figure it out."

Milo bent and picked up the pistol. His left hand wavered and trembled as he pointed it at Franklin. "You...you..." He couldn't think of anything to say.

Franklin casually tossed the wine bottle out onto the floor where it shattered and added to the spikes of glass. Then he pulled open the pajama top. "Right here, Milo, old buddy!" he said, pointing to his heart. "Do you really think you want to put a slug into me?"

Milo thought about that. It might be like putting a bullet into his own heart. He felt his arm drop. "Why...how...I don't deserve..."

Franklin closed his eye and grimaced. He looked as if he were about to cry. "I know," he said. "It's gone too far. Maybe you really don't deserve all this. I've always known I was a little bit crazy, but maybe I'm a lot crazier than I ever thought I was."

"Then for God's sake, man, loosen the wires!"

"No!" Franklin's eye snapped open. The madness was still there. "I entrusted my work to you. That's a sacred trust. You were responsible for *The Hut*'s integrity when you took on the job of adapting it to the screen."

"But I'm an artist, too!" Why was he arguing with this nut? He slipped the pistol into his front pocket and reached around back for the wire cutters.

"All the more reason to respect another man's work! You didn't own it—it was only on loan to you!"

"The contract—"

"*Means nothing!* You had a moral obligation to protect my work, one artist to another."

"You're over-reacting!"

"Am I? Imagine yourself a parent who has sent his only child to a reputable nursery school only to learn that the child has been raped by the faculty—then you will understand *some* of what I feel! I've come to see it as my sacred duty to see to it that you don't molest anyone else's work!"

Enough of this bullshit! If Franklin wouldn't loosen the wires, Milo would cut them off! He pulled the wire cutters from his rear pocket and began to shuffle toward Franklin, sweeping the marbles and daggers of glass ahead of him.

"Stay back!" Franklin cried. He grabbed the pliers and pushed them down toward his lap, grinning maliciously. "Didn't know I was left-handed, did you?" He twisted something.

Searing pain knifed into Milo's groin. He doubled over but kept moving toward Franklin. Less than a dozen feet to go. If he could just—

He saw Franklin drop the pliers and pick up the screwdriver, saw him raise it toward his right eye, the good eye. Milo screamed,

"NOOOOO!"

And then agony exploded in his eye, in his head, robbing him of the light, sending him reeling back in sudden impenetrable blackness. As he felt his feet roll across the marbles, he reached out wildly. His legs slid from under him and despite the most desperate flailings and contortions, he found nothing to grasp on the way down but empty air.

This is my homage to the Times Square of my teens. I came of age in Manhattan—knew how to get mugs of porter at McSorley's at age 16, where in Chinatown to buy fireworks (illegal in New York), and which of the grindhouse theaters along the Deuce had the least-sticky seats. It became a grim place in the late sixties and seventies after the assassinations and the riots, but now Disneyfication and pedestrian malls have swung it to the opposite, family-friendly pole. But preserved in "Muscles" is the Times Square I knew, a Times Square we'll never see again. A Times Square I miss.

Ed Ferman bought it for *The Magazine of Fantasy & Science Fiction*, I think maybe more for the setting than the story. He missed that Times Square too.

Muscles

Jay was dry, his mind a vast open plain, barren of the slightest sprig of an idea. It worried him no little bit.

He finished his coffee and sandwich at his desk, then sat there tapping a pencil on his blotter. He looked around the empty office. This was getting serious. He needed a lead story for next week's edition and he was completely blank.

He picked up the current issue of *The Light* lying open on his desk, exposing the weekly eye injury on page three. That was one of his rules: Every issue had to have an eye injury on page three, preferably with a photo. Page five was reserved for the weekly UFO story. The dependable appearance of features like those kept the regulars coming back week after week. But it was page one that caught the impulse buyers, and they were the gravy. He closed it over and scanned the front page.

FOUND IN SIBERIA!
TWO-HEADED BABY SPEAKS
ENGLISH AND RUSSIAN!

There followed an eyewitness account of the left head speaking Russian and the right answering in English—talk about internationalism!—along with a photo of a two-headed baby from the freak file.

Jay frowned. Another of his rules was that freaks were a last resort for the front page. The presence of one in this week's lead was testimony to the aridity of his current dry spell. But you had to go for the gross when you were competing against something as juicy as the Profumo scandal in the dailies.

He got up and walked around the tiny office, stopping before the front page of the March 15, 1959 issue framed on the wall. He'd only just started at *The Light* then, but he'd made his mark with that one. Even today they still considered it a masterpiece.

SECRET VATICAN PAPERS REVEAL:
RICHIE VALENS WOULD
HAVE BEEN NEXT POPE!

He shook his head at the memory. Boy, had that ever sold papers. The text had been the usual bullshit about secret information leaked by a deep contact who would talk only to *The Light*. A source in a place like the Vatican was a safe bet because the Vatican was so secretive anyway and naturally would be expected to deny the story. Of course, the tried-and-true standby was placing the source behind the Iron Curtain. No way anyone could prove you right or wrong when the story came from Siberia.

Look at me, he thought. Standing here reminiscing about 1959 like it was the good old days. Hell, it was only four years ago.

He shook his head. Acting like a has-been at thirty.

He needed some air, a walk, a change of scenery. Anything but these same old lousy walls.

He pulled on his coat and headed for the elevator. He knew where he wanted to go.

Ah, sleaze. Something in the air here in Times Square did something for Jay. Not any one particular thing. The amalgam stimulated him—a benny for his soul. And the Square looked especially sleazy today, buffeted by a chill wind under a low gray sky that promised rain or snow or a mix.

He wandered past the Tango Palace.

Continuous Dancing from 2 P.M. to 4 A.M.
to the Type of Music You Love
Presenting Beautiful Girls to Dance With

Then came the Square Theater showing a double bill of *The Immoral Mr. Teas* and *Wild Women of Wongo*, past the Garden Theatre with a double of *B-O-I-N-N-N-G!* and *Goldilocks and the Three Bares*, past Hubert's Museum and Flea Circus.

He'd been to the Tango Palace a number of times through the plain door and up the stairs to where the music was not the type he loved and the women not the kind he cared to dance with—and had seen the movies twice each. He knew the attractions of Hubert's by heart.

But he never got tired of the aura of the Square. The regulars here were living by their wits on the edge of the law, on the far side of truth, justice, and the American way. The skells, the sky-grifters, the street-hawkers, the streetwalkers all worked as hard at their trades as any straight, but they didn't want it straight. They wanted it their way. Jay could not deny a feeling of kinship.

Lighted headlines crawled around the Times Building—something about Kennedy and Khrushchev—while a guy in cowboy boots and a Stetson gave Jay the eye. He ignored both. A lot of women had told him he looked like Anthony Perkins and maybe it was true. Tall, very slim, dark brown hair and an angular face—a look useful in attracting women, but had its drawbacks in that it attracted certain men too. Not so popular, though, a couple of years ago when *Psycho* was such a hit.

Jay crossed the street and slowed when he came to Harold's Mondo Emporium where a line of about half a dozen guys was filing past the ticket window.

Harold's Mondo was a relative newcomer on the Square, a smaller, poor man's version of Hubert's Museum and Flea Circus. Hubert's had been on the Square since 1929. Ernie Rawson had opened up Harold's just last year. He'd sounded like he was going under when Jay had spoken to him a couple of weeks ago. Now he was doing gangbusters with the lunchtime crowd.

Jay showed his press card to the ticket girl and wandered inside to look around. Same old junk as Hubert's: a taxidermied two-headed cow, a snake charmer, a belly dancer, pickled punks, the trade's charming name for bottled embryos—25 bucks apiece from Del Rio, Texas. He came to a closed-off section with a separate admission. If Jay remembered correctly, the last time he was in it had housed "Sexology" lectures with visual aids by a professor from the Sorbonne. Uh-huh. Now it said simply, "Supergirl." That was where everyone was going.

Jay spotted Ernie and sneaked up behind him.

"I'm from DC Comics," he said in a gruff voice. "Where can I find the owner of this establishment?'

Ernie whirled, wide-eyed, then laughed, "Jay! How goes it?"

He was a plump, stubby man with a plump, stubby cigar jammed into a corner of his mouth. And he was grinning like an idiot.

"You look like a man who just won the Irish Sweepstakes, Ernie. What's going on?"

"Great new attraction. Wanna see?"

Jay tried to appear disinterested, but he'd been hoping for an invitation.

"All right. Maybe there's a story in her.

"Is there ever! See her first, then I'll tell ya."

Jay followed Ernie into the room and stood in the back and watched this Supergirl. She had curly red hair, fair, lightly freckled skin, and she was *built*—not just in her D-cup halter, but in her shoulders, arms, and legs.

Muscles.

The girl was loaded with them. And her skimpy two-piece Supergirl costume showed them all. Not bulging bodybuilder-type muscles, but thick sleek cords running under skin. She'd oiled up like the Mr. Universe guys so the light played off all the highlights when she flexed. She was good, too. Knew how to work the crowd. She'd smile, banter, do her lifts, bend her bars. She'd been around. It could have all been an elaborate scam, but the guys in the crowd didn't seem to mind. Just looking at her was worth the ticket price.

"Here comes the blow-off," Ernie said. "Wait'll ya see this!"

Turned out to be a good blow-off. Supergirl pulled a drape off a pressing bench, got two medium-sized volunteers from the audience and had them sit on each end of an iron bar racked over the bench. When they were set, she lay back—with her crotch toward the audience, natch—and bench-pressed the two guys. As the audience went wild, Ernie pulled Jay outside.

"She terrif or what?"

"She's good, yeah, but not much of a story in a strong-woman act."

"Don't count on that. Wait'll ya hear about her gettin raped tree years ago."

"Raped?" This was getting interesting now. Jay couldn't imagine anyone doing anything to that lady without her permission. "Who did it—Man Mountain Dean?"

"A ghost, she says. An anyways, she weren't muscled-up back then. Maybe ya seen her at Hubert's. She was the snake dancer back in sixty."

"Tell you the truth, Ernie, I didn't get much of a look at her face."

Those muscles had fascinated him. He'd never seen anything like them on a woman before...the way they moved under her skin...

"You an evybody else."

"But what's this about a ghost raping her?"

"What she said back then. Hollered bout it to the cops, then clammed up soon as the papers come sniffin. Quit her job an disappeared. Coupla weeks ago she shows up in my office wit all these muscles and this act. I mean, is she dynamite or what? And if you can give me some good press on her, I can up the ticket price and still be packin em in. And should that come to fruitition, I'd be willing to maybe find a way to—"

Jay held up a hand. "Don't say it, Ernie. Either the story's worth writing or it's not."

Had to keep an eye on the journalistic integrity.

"Okay, okay. Just meet her an talk t'her and see whatcha think."

"Will do. Which way to the dressing room?"

Jay was looking forward to this.

Now that she was swathed in a terry-cloth bathrobe, Jay realized she was kind of pretty. Not beautiful, but pretty in a girlish, nice-smile way. Pushing thirty, maybe a little hard around the edges, but the trace of vulnerability in those blue eyes appealed to Jay. He wanted to get to know her.

"This is Jay," Ernie said. "He's a reporter. Wants a few woids."

She gave Jay an appraising look. "Long as it's only words he wants, otherwise the two of you can take off."

Jay smiled at her. "Just words, I assure you, Miss…" He curved the end of the word up into a question.

"Hansen." She returned the smile. "Olivia Hansen. You can call me Liv."

She seemed interested. Maybe she liked skinny guys.

"I wancha to give Jay a good story, Liv," Ernie said. "About the rape an evyting."

Suddenly the smile disappeared. Liv's expression became fierce. She lifted Ernie off the floor by his lapels and tossed him against the wall.

"I told you never to mention that!" she shouted as Ernie bounced off the wall and cowered away from her. "Didn't I? *Didn't* I?"

"Yeah, Liv, but—"

"No buts!" She turned toward Jay. "What paper you from?"

"*The Light.*"

"Oh, that's great! Just great! 'Flying Saucer Men Stick Needles in Woman's Eyes!' I can't stand it!" She snatched a beige raincoat off a hook and pulled it on over the robe. "You really are low, Ernie."

"Where y'goin?" he said as she headed for the door.

"None of your business!"

"You got a two-o'clock show!"

"I'll be back."

And then she was gone.

"She betta come back," Ernie said, squaring his shoulders inside his rumpled jacket and trying to look like he was really the boss. He smiled wanly at jay. "That all think they're stars."

Jay nodded absently, thinking. He gauged Ernie's weight at a compact 170. Liv had handled him easily.

"Strong girl."

He smoothed his lapels. "Yeah."

"Sure she's coming back?"

"Absotootly. She always goes out between shows." He sighed. "I think the broad's a man-hater. She got her share of stage-door Johnnies, an now an then I see her let one buy her a drink, but she's got no steady. Prolly a dyke."

Jay thought about those muscular arms and legs wrapped around another woman…what a waste.

"But look," Ernie was saying. "Tonight's her early night. She's done at eight. Whyncha come back then and—"

Jay shrugged. "Don't see much of a story here, Ernie. Sorry."

"Maybe I can talk t'her, make her come aroun."

"Sure. Let me know."

Jay waved good-bye and headed down to 42nd Street. Followed it east to the *Daily News* building where he checked the morgue files for stories about a "ghost rape." Sure enough: a little story in the lower left corner of page six. Olivia Hansen's name in print, but no direct quotes. The story looked like it was culled from a police report.

Jay thought of Olivia up on that stage with those sleek, shining muscles and felt a little lead sneaking into his wood. He idly wondered if maybe he had some fruity tendencies that muscles could get to him like this, but reminded himself that they were on a woman. That was the important thing: a *good-looking* woman.

With muscles…

Back to the files: He checked a few more years and found two other similar reports: another "ghost rape" and a "monster rape." Both in the Times Square area.

The juices began flowing as he headed for the street. By the time he reached his office he was psyched. He had his story: Something prowled Times Square at odd intervals, ravaging women. Its victims said it was hideous, ghostlike. What was it? A man? Or something else? Was it perhaps the living excrescence of all the sleaze, disease, perversion, and depravity of Times Square? The embodied concentrate of the lost hopes and shattered dreams of the wretched, wrecked lives of those who haunted the Square?

Oooh, that sounded good.

And not all that farfetched. After all, the White House had been occupied by an Irish Catholic for the past couple of years. What could be more farfetched than that?

Readers would eat it up. All he needed was a final touch, an added ring of authenticity that would enable him to drag it out for two or three issues: personal testimony.

He needed to talk to Olivia Hansen.

———

It hadn't been easy coaxing her out of the cold and into Clancy's. Jay had used every ounce of persuasive skill he owned—and fervent promises of no talk of her past, just her present and immediate future—to cajole her into having one lousy drink with him before she went home. She hadn't removed her raincoat, just sat there opposite him in a rear booth and answered in monosyllables as she sipped her drink.

He'd poured on the charm and pushed the Anthony Perkins boyishness to the limit to stretch one drink into two, and then into three.

She was beginning to loosen up.

"I don't usually drink," she said. He heard a slur growing in her voice as she sipped her screwdriver. Yeah, she was getting very loose. "Bad for the muscles."

Hey, Paula was playing on the juke. The vodka in the screwdrivers had relaxed the anger lines in her face, making her softer, prettier. Jay sensed even more vulnerability in her eyes, and a faint tang of sweat in the air. He found it exciting as all hell.

"Tell me about the muscles."

"What about them?"

"Why have them?"

"I gotta be strong." Her expression was suddenly fierce. "Strong enough to keep any man from doing what he wants with me ever again."

Jay repressed a cheer. She'd opened the door.

He took a deep breath. Here goes nothing.

"You mean the rape?"

"Hey! I thought you weren't going to mention that!"

"I didn't bring it up—you did."

She calmed.

"Want to talk about it?" Jay said softly.

"*No!*" She shook her head violently, then began to do what she said she wouldn't. "It was awful! Horrible! I was in my dressing room at Hubert's, getting ready to go on with my snake dance when he—it—appeared out of nowhere. I mean, one minute I was alone in the room with all the lights on and the next minute he was there and everything went dark and cold."

"What he look like?"

She shuddered and Jay wondered uneasily what it took to get a shudder out of a girl who used to dance wrapped up in a boa constrictor.

"I only got a glance at him before everything went dark but he was old and greasy and unshaven and dirty and his skin wasn't right, like it wasn't human, and he was cold, so goddamn cold, and the things he did to me and the things he made me do, *the things he made me do!*"

She sobbed and Jay thought she was going to lose it.

She took a deep, shuddering breath. "I was powerless, completely powerless. But that'll never happen again." He saw her flexing her muscles under her coat. "No one'll ever do something like that to me again. Ever!"

"But how come you clammed up about it back then? Maybe they could've caught this creep."

She shook her head slowly. "The way he comes and goes? Nobody'll ever catch him. And besides, everyone was looking at me like I was crazy or trying a publicity stunt. Insult on top of injury. I didn't need it."

As the jukebox began *Walk Like a Man*, she glanced at the Schlitz clock on the wall.

"God! I've got to get home! The kid'll be starving!"

Kid?

Jay saw his story fading as she rose to her feet. He had to say something here, and quickly.

"I didn't know you were married."

"I'm not. Never was. Baby's father was...well, we were just talking about him."

Jay was stunned. She got pregnant from the rape and kept the kid! What a headline!

Son of the Times Square Spook!

God, he could run this for months! Make Profumo and Christine Keeler look like the Knights of Columbus!

"Uh..." He didn't know how to phrase it. "Why...?"

"What was I to do? Risk an abortion and maybe die? Besides, it wasn't Baby's fault. He didn't do anything to me. And after carrying him for nine months I... I couldn't give him up. I'm his mother, after all."

Here was one weird lady, but she'd be so *easy* to write about. The quotables just poured out of her. He couldn't let her go. Needed more time to work on her. If he could somehow get a picture of this kid—

"Let me take you home," he blurted.

"I don't need your protection."

Jay smiled, "I was hoping you'd protect me."

She laughed and Jay realized it was the first time she'd done that all night.

"Okay. It's only a few blocks. We can walk."

He used the walk to make contact.

First he took her elbow as they crossed the street, then kept a grip on her arm, then his arm was around her shoulders. By the time they reached her apartment house, she was leaning against him.

This was working out fine, he thought as he followed her up the stairs to the third floor. A little romance here, then handing her a line about helping protect other innocent women from this rapist spook by going public in *The Light,* and she'd come around for sure.

A shotgun apartment—a front room, back room, and a kitchen. Liv went immediately to the back, leaving Jay by the door. The front looked like a gym—barbells and dumbbells all about. A padded pressing bench sat where most people put a couch.

Liv returned from the back.

"Baby's sleeping."

"You leave him alone here all day? How old is he?"

She took off her coat, then loosened the tie on the terry-cloth bathrobe beneath.

"One and a half. He sleeps all day and most of the night. I check on him between shows."

The bathrobe was off now, revealing her Supergirl bikini and her muscles...ah, those muscles. Her breasts bobbed under the fabric as she walked over to him. She put her hands on his chest and looked up at him. He could tell the vodka had worked its magic.

"I need someone tonight. Want to stay?"

Jay ran his fingers up her biceps, over her deltoids and traps, and down to her lats. He pulled her close.

"I couldn't say no even if I wanted to."

He realized with a pang that this was probably the first completely honest statement he'd made all night.

She led him into the dark of the rear room. In the borrowed light from the front he dimly saw a bed against the wall and a crib in the far corner. He heard a rustle from the crib and saw the kid pull himself to his feet and look at them over the rail.

"He's awake, Liv."

"That's okay. We'll be in the dark here and he won't know what we're doing."

Jay glanced at the crib again. He couldn't make out any of the kid's features, just a shadow, craning his head and neck over the rail and staring at them. He didn't like the idea of an audience, even if it was just a one-and-a-half-year-old, but then Liv had his shirt open and was kissing his chest and he forgot all about the kid.

She was crying, sobbing gently under him.

"What's wrong?"

"Nothing. That was so good. Sometimes I just need it. I tell myself I don't, but sometimes I just do. And that was so good."

It *had* been good, Jay thought.

He'd been good. Damn good. At the end there he'd thought she was going to squeeze him to death like a python. Even now, as he lay weak and limp atop her, she still had her arms and legs wrapped around him.

"You don't have to cry."

"Yes, I do. 'Cause I'm sorry."

"Sorry? You kidding? That was wonderful!"

"Oh, good. That makes me feel a little better."

Jay was trying to figure out what she was getting at when he heard a noise over by the crib. He glanced up. The crib was empty.

"I think your baby's out."

He felt her arms and legs tighten about him.

"I know."

He sensed movement along the floor, coming toward the bed, then a little face popped up over the mattress and looked at him from only inches away. He cried out in shock at the huge, dark, staring eyes and wide slit of a mouth crowded with teeth that would have been more at home in a shark. As the kid's teeth angled toward his throat, he struggled to free himself but could barely move, barely breathe.

"Let me go!"

Liv's arms and legs tightened around him even more, locking him helpless against her.

"I'm so sorry," she said through a sob, "but Baby needs you, too."

In 1987 Paul Mikol called and asked me if I'd take the lead for *Night Visions 6*, Dark Harvest's annual showcase anthology in which two established authors and an upandcomer are each given carte blanche to do whatever they wish with 30,000 words: Ten 3,000word short stories or a single 30,000word novella, or anything between—whatever suits you. I'd long admired the *Night Visions* series. And why not? Its list of contributors was a Who's Who of horror fiction.

I decided on three stories and labeled them "The Monroe Triptych" because all were set in the imaginary Long Island north shore Gold Coast town I'd created in 1985 while writing *The Touch*. I'd put a lot of work into The Incorporated Village of Monroe then, going so far as to draw a map of the waterfront and the downtown area. I knew it almost like my own hometown.

"Feelings," the first of those stories, came easily—a simple justdeserts cum voodoo tale, based on a reallife malpractice scam in Florida. And Monroe was a good place for an ambulance chaser to live if he had roots on the Island.

Connections: the very fact that it's set in Monroe ties "Feelings" to The Adversary Cycle; and you'll notice Dr. Walter Johnson mentions his brother, a GP who remained in their home town. You've already met that other Doc Johnson. You'll also notice that Howie's father is Lenny Winter from "The Last 'One Mo' Once Golden Oldies Revival.'"

Writing this one was almost as enjoyable as writing "Cuts."

Feelings

"Five million dollars, Mr. Weinstein? Five million? Where did you come up with such an outrageous figure?"

Howard Weinstein studied his prey across the table in his office conference room. Until today, Dr. Walter Johnson had been little more than a name on a subpoena and interrogatories. His C.V. put his age at fifty-one but he looked a tired old sixty as he sat next to the natty attorney the insurance company had assigned him. His face was lined, haggard, and pale, his movements slow, his voice soft, weak, his shoulders slumped inside a grey suit that looked too big for him. Maybe the strain of the malpractice suit was getting to him. Good. That might spur him to push his insurance company for an early settlement.

"Five *million*?" Dr. Johnson repeated.

Howard hesitated. *I'm* the one who's supposed to be asking the questions, he thought. This is my show. But he had asked his last question and so the deposition was essentially over. He wanted to say, *It's my favorite number,* but this was a legal proceeding and Lydia's fingers were poised over her steno machine's keyboard, awaiting his reply. So he looked Dr. Walter Johnson straight in his watery blue eyes and said,

"That's the compensation my client deserves for the permanent injuries he suffered at your hands due to your gross negligence. He will suffer lifelong impairment—"

"I saved his life!"

"That is hardly clear, Dr. Johnson. It's up to a jury to decide."

"When you sue me within my coverage," Dr. Johnson said, staring at his folded hands where they rested on the table before him, "I can say to myself, 'He's doing business.' But five million dollars? My malpractice coverage doesn't go that high. That will ruin me. That will take everything I own—my house, all the investments I've made over the years, all the money I've put away for my children and future grandchildren—and still leave me millions in debt. You're not just threatening me, you're threatening my family." He looked up at Howard. "Do you have a family, Mr. Weinstein?"

"Is that a threat, Dr. Johnson?" Howard knew the doctor was making no threat, but he reacted instinctively to keep the defendant off balance. He had no children and had divorced his wife three years ago. And anyway, he wouldn't have cared if the doc had been threatening her.

"Oh, no. I was simply wondering if you might have any conception of what this sort of threat does to someone and to his family. My homelife is a shambles. I've had constant stomachaches for months, I'm losing weight, my daughters are worried about me, my wife is a wreck. Do you have any idea what kind of misery you cause?"

"I am more concerned with the misery you caused my client, Dr. Johnson."

The doctor looked him square in the eyes. Howard felt as if the older man's gaze were penetrating to the back of his skull.

"I don't think you feel anything for anyone, Mr. Weinstein. You need a real lesson in empathy. Do you even know what empathy is?"

"I have empathy for my clients, Dr. Johnson."

"I sincerely doubt that. I think the only empathy you know is for your bank account."

"Okay, that's it," Howard said, nodding to Lydia at the steno machine as he closed his case folder and rose from his seat. He had let this go on too long already. "The deposition's over. Thank you for your cooperation, Dr. Johnson. We'll see you in court."

He ushered out the defendant and his attorney, then stepped over to where Lydia was packing up her gear. "Let me see the end of that tape," he said.

"Howie—!"

Ignoring her mild protest, he opened the tape compartment and pulled out the long strip of steno paper. As he scanned through it, looking for where when Dr. Johnson had begun running off at the mouth, Lydia said,

"You're really not going to ruin him, are you? You're really not going to take everything he owns?" She was thin, dark-haired, attractive in a brittle sort of way.

Howard laughed. "Nah! Too much trouble. It's S.O.P.: Ask for an exorbitant amount, then settle for somewhere near the limit of his coverage. Taking all his assets—which I could probably get if we go to court—and going through a long liquidation process would be a big hassle. Best thing to do is to get that big check from the insurance company, take my forty percent, then move on to the next pigeon."

"Is that all he is? A pigeon?"

"Waiting to be plucked."

He knew there was something wrong with the metaphor there, but didn't bother to figure out what. He had found the spot he had been searching for on the tape. He marked it with a pen.

"Stop the transcription here."

"Why?"

"It's where the doc made his closing sob story about threatening his family and—"

"—your empathy for your bank account?" She smiled up at him.

"Yeah. I don't want that part in the deposition."

Her smile took a mischievous twist. "I sort of liked that part."

"Ditch it."

"I can't do that."

"Sure you can, Sis."

Her smile was gone now. "I won't. It's illegal."

In a sudden surge of anger, Howard ripped the offending section from the tape and tore it into tiny pieces. He never would have dared this with any other licensed court stenographer, but Lydia was his sister, and big brothers could take certain liberties with little sisters. Which was the main reason he used her. Her name had been Chambers since her wedding four years ago, so no one was the wiser.

He tossed the remains in the air and they fluttered to the floor in a confetti flurry.

Lydia's lips trembled. "I hate you! You're just like Dad!"

"Don't say that!"

"It's true! You're just a 'Daddy Shoog' with a law degree!"

"Shut *up!*" Howard quickly closed the door to the outer office. "I told you never to mention him around here!"

He prayed none of the secretaries had heard. One of them might get to thinking and might make the connection. She might find out that Lenny Winter, the Fifties DJ known as "Daddy Shoog," was really Leonard Weinstein, Howard's father. And then it wouldn't be long before it was all over Manhattan: Howard Weinstein was the son of that fat balding guy doing the twist and shilling his "One Mo' Once Golden Oldies" albums like Ginsu knives (*But wait! There's more!*") on late night TV commercials.

God! He'd never be able to maintain credibility at another deposition, let alone conduct a court case.

He had made every effort to avoid even a faint resemblance to his father: He'd grown a thick, black mustache, he took care of his hair, combing in a style his father had never used when he had a full head of it, and he kept his body trim and hard. No one would ever guess he was the son of Daddy Shoog.

Had to hand it to the old jerk, though. He was really cleaning up on those doo-wop retreads, especially since he was forgoing the inconvenience of paying royalties to the original artists.

"Too bad you inherited Dad's ethics instead of his personality. The only reason I come around is because I'm family. You've got no friends. Your wife dumped you, you've—"

"*Your* marriage didn't last too long either, Miss Holier Than Thou."

"True, but I'm the one who ended it, not Hal. You got dumped."

"Elise didn't dump me! *I* dumped *her!*"

And did a damn fine job of it, too. Left her without a pot to pee in. God, had he been glad to be rid of her! Three endless years of her nagging, "You're never home! I feel like a widow!" Blah-blah-blah. He'd taught her the folly of suing a lawyer for divorce.

"So what have you got, Howie? You've got your big law practice and that's it!"

"And that's plenty!" She pulled this shit on him every time they argued. Really liked to twist the knife. "I'm just thirty-two and already I'm a legend in this town! A fucking *legend!*"

"And what are you doing after lunch, Mr. Legend? Going down to St. Vincent's to scrape up another client?"

"Hey! My clients are shitbums. You think I don't know that? I know it. *Damn,* do I know it! But they've been injured and they've got a legal right to maximum recovery under the law! It's my duty—"

"Save it for the jury or the newspapers, Howie," Lydia said. Her voice sounded tired, disgusted. She picked up her steno gear and headed for the door. "You and Dad—you make me ashamed."

And then she was gone.

Howard left the files on the desk and went into his private office. He ran a hand through his thick dark hair as he gazed out at Manhattan's midtown spires. What was wrong with Lydia? Didn't she understand? The malpractice field was a gold mine. There were million-dollar clients out there who hadn't the vaguest inkling what they were worth. And if he didn't find them, somebody else would!

He'd come a long way. Started out in general practice, then sniffed the possibilities in liability law. Advertising on TV had brought him a horde of new clients, but all of them combined hadn't equaled the take from his first medical malpractice settlement. He had known then that malpractice was the only way to go.

Especially when you had a method.

It was simple, really. All it took was a few well-compensated contacts in the city's hospitals to let him know when a certain type of patient was being discharged. One of Howard's assistants—Howard used to go himself but he was above that now—would arrange to be there when the potential client left the hospital. He'd take him to lunch and subtly make his pitch.

You couldn't be *too* subtle, though. The prospective client was usually a neurosurgical patient, preferably an indigent sleazo who had shown up in the hospital emergency room with his head bashed in from a mugging or a fight over a bottle or a fix, or who'd fallen down a stairway or stumbled in front of a car during a stupor. Didn't matter what the cause as long as he'd wound up in the ER in bad enough shape for the neurosurgeon on call to be dragged in to put his skull and its contents back in order again.

"But you're not right since the surgery, are you?"

That was the magic question. The answer was almost invariably negative. Of course, the prospect hadn't been "right" before the surgery, either, but that was hard to prove. Nigh on impossible to prove. And even if the potential said he felt pretty good, he usually could find some major complaint when pressed, especially after it was explained to him that a permanent post-surgical deficit could be worth somewhere in the neighborhood of seven figures to him if things went his way.

Yeah, they were druggies and winos and all-purpose sleazos and it was an ordeal to be in conference with one of them for more than just a few minutes, but they were Howard's ticket to the Good Life. They were the perfect malpractice clients. He *loved* to stick them in front of a jury. Their shambling gaits, vacant stares, and disordered thought patterns wrung the hearts of even the most objective jurors. And since they were transients with no steady jobs, friends, or acquaintances, the defense could never prove convincingly that they had been just as shambling, vacant, and disordered before the surgery.

In most cases, the malpractice insurer took one look at the defendant and reached for his checkbook: settlement time.

Yeah, life was sweet when you knew the bushes with the best berries.

Lydia was still fuming when she reached the garage downstairs. She handed in her ticket and found herself waiting next to Dr. Johnson. He nodded to her.

"Can't they find your car?" she said for lack of something better.

He shrugged. "Seems that way. Goes with the rest of the day, I guess." He looked tired, haggard, defeated. He smiled suddenly, obviously forcing it. "How'd I do up there?"

Lydia sensed his desperate need for some hope, some encouragement.

"You did very well, I thought. Especially at the end." She couldn't bring herself to tell him that his final remarks were shredded on the floor of the conference room.

"Do you think I have a snowball's chance in hell of coming out of this with the shirt on my back?"

Lydia couldn't help it. She had to say something to ease this poor man's mind. She put her hand on his arm.

"I see lots of these cases. I'm sure they'll settle within your coverage limits."

He turned to her. "Settle? I'm not going to settle anything!"

His intensity surprised her. "Why not?"

"Because if I agree to settle, it's as much as an admission that I've done something wrong! And I haven't!"

"But you never know what a jury will do, Dr. Johnson."

"So I've been told, over and over and over by the insurance company. 'Settle—settle—settle!' They're scared to death of juries. Better to pay off the bloodsucking lawyer and his client than risk the decision of a jury. Sure! Fine for them! They're only thinking about the bottom line. But I did everything right in this case! I released his subdural hematoma and tied off the leaking artery inside his skull. That man would have died without me! And now he's suing me!"

"I'm sorry," Lydia said.

It sounded lame to her but it was all she could say. She felt somehow partly responsible for Dr. Johnson's misery. After all, Howie was her brother.

"Maybe I should have done what a lot of my fellow neurosurgeons do: Refuse to take emergency room calls. That way you don't leave yourself open to the shyster sharks prowling around for a quick fortune. Maybe I should have gone into general practice with my brother back in our home town. A foggy little place on the coast..."

He rubbed a hand across his eyes. "Looks pretty hopeless, doesn't it. If I go to court, I could lose everything I've worked for during my entire career, and jeopardize my family's whole way of life. If I settle, I'm admitting I'm wrong when I know I'm right." His jaw tightened. "It's that damned greedy bastard lawyer."

Although Lydia knew the doctor was right, the words still stung. Howard might be a lot of things, but he was still her brother.

"Things have got to change," Dr. Johnson said. "This kind of abuse is getting way out of hand. There's got to be a change in the laws to control these...these Hell's Angels in three-piece suits!"

"Don't hold your breath waiting for tort reform," Lydia said. "Ninety-nine percent of state legislators are lawyers, and they're all members of law firms that do a thriving business on liability claims. You don't really think they're going to take some of the bread and butter off their own tables, do you? Talk about conflict of interest!"

Dr. Johnson's expression became bleaker. "Then there's no hope of relief from the Howard Weinsteins of the world, is there? No way to give him a lesson in empathy, in knowing what kind of pain he causes in other people."

Dr. Johnson's car pulled up then, a maroon Jaguar XJ.

"I don't know how to teach him that lesson," he said. "My brother might, but I certainly don't." He sighed heavily. "I honestly don't know what I'm going to do."

"Keep fighting," Lydia told him as she watched him walk around the car and tip the attendant.

He looked at her over the hood of the Jaguar. There was a distant, resigned look in his eyes that made her afraid for him.

"Easy for you to say," he said, then got in and drove off.

Lydia stood there in the garage and watched him go, knowing in some intangible way that she would never see Dr. Walter Johnson again.

"He's dead! God, Howie, he's dead!"

Howard looked up at Lydia's pale, strained features as she leaned over his desk. He thought, Oh, no! It's Dad! It'll be in the papers! Everyone will know!

"Who?" he managed to say.

"Dr. Johnson! The guy you deposed last week in the malpractice case! He killed himself!"

Relief flooded through him. "He killed himself? Did he think that would let him off the hook? The jerk! We'll just take his estate to court!"

"Howard! He was depressed over this suit. You drove him over the edge!"

"I did nothing of the sort! What did he do? Shoot himself?"

Lydia's face got whiter. "No. He...he chopped his hand off. He bled to death."

Howard's mind suddenly went into high gear.

"Wait a minute. Wait. A. Minute! This is great! *Great!* It shows tremendous guilt over his negligence! He cut off the appendage that damaged his patient! No, wait! *Wait!* The act of suicide, especially in such a bizarre manner, points to a deranged mind. This means I can bring the hospital executive committee into the suit for allowing an obviously impaired physician to remain on the staff of their hospital. Maybe include the hospital's entire department of surgery, too! Oh, this is big! *Big!* Thank you, Lydia! You've just made my day! My *year!*"

She stood there with her mouth hanging open, looking stupid. "I don't believe you."

"What? What don't you believe? What?" What the hell was wrong with her, anyway?

"Isn't there a limit, Howard? Isn't there a place where you see a line and say to yourself, 'I can't cross over here? I'll cause too much pain on the other side.'"

He smiled at her. "Of course there is, Sis. And as soon as I find it, I'll let you know."

She didn't smile at the joke. Her face was hard, her eyes icy. "I think Dr. Johnson asked a good question last week. *Do* you have feelings, Howie? Do you ever feel anything for anybody but yourself?"

"Get off the soapbox, Sis."

"Gladly," she said. "Off the soapbox and out of your slimy presence." She turned toward the door, then back again. "Oh, by the way, I think you should know about Dr. Johnson's hand. You know, the one he cut off? They can't find it."

Howard fluttered his hands in the air. "Oooh! I'm scared! Maybe it will come crawling after me in my sleep tonight!"

She spun and slammed out the door. Howard immediately got on the intercom to his receptionist. "Chrissie? Get hold of Brian Jassie down at the coroner's office."

Missing hand? That sounded awful weird. He wanted the straight dope on it. And Brian Jassie could get it for him.

———

Brian had all the details by 4:00 p.m.

"This is what we got so far," he told Howard over the phone. "It's a strange one, I tell you."

"Just tell me what happened, Brian."

"Okay. Here's how they think it went down. About ten o'clock last night, at his Fifth Avenue office, this Dr. Johnson ties a tight tourniquet just above his right wrist with neat little pads to put extra pressure over the main arteries, and whacks off his hand. Records show he was a southpaw. There's evidence that he used local anesthesia. Well, he must have, right? I mean, sawing through your own wrist—"

"Brian!"

"Okay, okay. After the hand is off, there seems to be an interval of about half an hour during which we have no idea what he does, maybe some ritual or something, then he sits down, lowers his stump into a bucket, and loosens the tourniquet. Exsanguinates in a couple of minutes. Very neat, very considerate. No mess for anybody to clean up."

A real nut case, Howard thought. "Why do you say he was involved in some ritual?"

"Just a guess. There were candles all around the room and the histology department says the hand was off for around thirty minutes before he died."

"Then you have the hand."

"Uh, no, we don't."

Howard felt a little knot form in his stomach. "You're kidding."

"'Fraid not. The forensic team looked everywhere in the office and around the building. No hand."

So Lydia hadn't been pulling his chain. The hand really was missing. Well, that would only reinforce his contention that Dr. Johnson was mentally unbalanced and shouldn't have been allowed to practice. Yes, he would definitely bring the hospital executive committee into the suit.

Still, he wondered about that missing hand. He sat there smoothing his mustache and wondering where it could be.

The package arrived the next day.

Chrissie brought it to his desk unopened. It had come by Federal Express and was marked "Personal and Confidential." Howard had her stand by as he opened it, figuring it would have to be shoved into somebody's file—most of the "Personal and Confidential" mail he received was anything but.

Chrissie began to scream when the hand fell out onto his desk. She kept on screaming all the way down the hall to the reception area. Howard stared at the hand. It lay palm up on his desk blotter, a deathly, bled-out white except at the ragged, beefy red wrist stump. The skin was moist, glistening in the fluorescent glare. He could see the creases that ran along the palm and across the finger joints, could even see fingerprint whorls. A faintly sour smell rose from it.

This had to be a joke, Lydia's way of trying to shake him up. Well, it wasn't going to work. This thing had to be a fake. He'd seen those amazingly lifelike platters of sushi and bowls of sukiyaki in the windows of Japanese restaurants. What was it they called the stuff? *Mihon.*

That was it. This was the same thing: expertly sculpted and colored plastic. A gruesome piece of anatomical *mihon*.

Howard touched it with his index finger and felt a faint pins-and-needles sensation run up his arm and all over his skin. It lasted about the time between eye blinks and then it was gone. But by then he had realized from the texture of the skin and the give of the flesh underneath that this wasn't *mihon*. This was the real thing!

He leapt out of his chair and stood there trembling, repeatedly wiping his finger on his suit coat as he shouted to Chrissie to call the police.

Howard was late getting out of the office that day. The endless questions from the detectives and the forensic people had put him far behind schedule. Then to top everything off, his last call of the day had been from Brian at the coroner's office. According to Brian, the forensic experts downtown said the hand had definitely belonged to the late great Dr. Walter Johnson.

So now he was shook up, grossed out, and just plain tired. Irritable, too. He had snapped at the Rican garage attendant—Jose or Gomez or whatever the hell his name was—to move his ass and get the car up front pronto.

His red Porche 914 squealed down the ramp and screeched to a halt in front of him. As he passed the attendant and handed him a fifty-cent tip—half the usual—he could almost feel the man's animosity toward him.

No, wait…it was more than *almost*. It was as if he were actually experiencing the car jockey's anger and envy. It wormed into his system and for a moment Howard too was angry and envious. But at whom? Himself?

And just as suddenly as it came it was gone. He was once again just tired, irritable, and anxious to get himself out to the Island and home where he could have himself a stiff drink and relax.

Traffic wasn't bad. That was one advantage of leaving late. He cruised the LIE to Glen Cove Road, then headed north. He stopped at the MacDonald's drive-thru just this side of the sign that declared the southern limit of "The Incorporated Village of Monroe." He ordered up a Big Mac and fries. As he handed his money to the pimple-faced red-headed girl in the window, a wave of euphoria rolled over him. He felt slightly giddy. He looked up at the girl in her blue uniform and noticed her fixed grin and glazed eyes.

She's stoned! he thought. And damned if I don't feel stoned, too!

He took his bagged order from her and gunned away. The feeling faded almost immediately. But not his puzzlement. First the lot attendant and now the kid at Mickey-D's. What was going on here?

He pulled into his spot in the Soundview Condominiums lot and entered his townhouse. It was a three-storied job with a good view of Monroe Harbor. He'd done some legal work on the land sale and so had been able to get in on a pre-construction purchase. The price: one hundred and sixty-nine large. They were going for twice that now.

Yeah, if you knew the right people and had the wherewithal to take advantage of situations when they presented themselves, your net worth could only go one way: Up.

Howard pulled a Bud from the fridge and opened up the Styrofoam Big Mac container. As he ate, he stared out over the still waters of the Long Island Sound at the lights along the Connecticut shore on the far side. Much as he tried not to, he couldn't help thinking about that severed hand in the mail today. Which led his thoughts around to Dr. Johnson. What was it he had said about empathy last week?

I don't think you feel anything for anyone, Mr. Weinstein. You need a real lesson in empathy.

Something like that. And then a week later he had sat down in his office and cut off his hand, and then had somehow got it into a Federal Express overnight envelope and sent it to Howard. *Personal and Confidential.* And then he had let himself die.

...a lesson in empathy...

Then the hand had arrived and Howard had touched it, felt that tingle, and now he seemed to be able to sense what others were feeling.

...empathy...

Yeah, right. And any moment now, he'd hear Rod Serling's voice fill the room.

He finished the beer and went for another.

But let's not be too quick to laugh everything off, he told himself as he nibbled on some fries. Law school had taught him how to organize his thoughts and present cogent arguments. So far, there was a good case for his being the victim of some sort of curse. That would have been laughable yesterday, but this morning there had been a real live—no, strike that, make that *dead*—a dead human hand lying on his desk. A hand that had once belonged to a defendant in a very juicy malpractice case. A man who had said that Howard Weinstein needed a lesson in how other people felt.

And now Howard Weinstein had encountered two instances in which he had experienced another person's feelings.

Or thought he had.

That was the question. Had Dr. Johnson done a number on Howard's head? Had he planted some sort of suggestion in his subconscious and then reinforced it by sending him a severed hand?

Or was this the real thing? A dead man's curse?

Howard decided to take a scientific approach. The only way to prove a hypothesis was to test it in the field. He tossed off the second beer. Time to hit the town.

As he gathered up the MacDonald's debris, he noticed a dull ache all along his right arm. He rubbed it but that didn't help. He wondered how he could have strained it. Maybe it was a result of jerking away after touching that hand this morning. No, he didn't remember any pain then. He shrugged it off, pulled on a sweater, and stepped out into the spring night.

The air was cool and tangy with salt from the Sound. Too beautiful a night to squeeze back into the Porche, so he decided to walk the few blocks west down to the waterfront nightspots. He had only gone a few steps when he noticed that the ache in his arm was gone.

Canterbury's was the first place he came to along the newly renovated waterfront. He stopped in here occasionally with some of his local clients. Not a bad place for lunch, but after five it turned into a meat market. If AIDS had put a damper on the swinging singles scene, you couldn't tell it here. The space around Canterbury's oval bar was smoky, noisy, and packed with yuppie types.

Howard squeezed up to the bar and suddenly felt his knees get rubbery. He leaned against the mahogany edge and glanced at the fellow rubbing elbows with him to his right. He was downing a straight shot of something and chasing it with a few generous chugs of draft beer. There were four other shot glasses on the bar in front of him, all empty.

Howard lurched away toward the booths at the rear of the room and felt better immediately.

God, it's happening! It's true!

As he moved through the crowd, he was assaulted with a complex mixture of lust, boredom, fatigue, and inebriation. It was a relief to reach the relative sanctuary of the last booth in the rear. The emotions and feelings of the room became background noise, a sensory muzak.

But they were still there. On the way out from the city it had seemed he needed physical contact—from the garage attendant, the girl at Mickey D's—to get the sensory input. Now the feelings seemed to waft through the air.

Howard shut his eyes and rubbed his hands over his temples. This couldn't be happening, couldn't be real. This was the stuff of *Twilight Zone* and *Outer Limits* and *Tales from the Darkside*. This sort of thing did not happen to Howard Weinstein in little old Monroe, Long Island.

But he could not deny his own experience. He had felt drunk before noticing that the guy next to him was doing boilermakers.

Or had he?

Maybe he had unconsciously noticed the guy with the ball and the beer as he had stepped up to the bar and his mind had done the rest.

It was all so confusing. How could he know for sure?

"Can I get you something, Mr. Weinstein?"

Howard looked up. A well-stacked blonde stood over him with a tray under her arm and her order pad ready. She was thirtyish with too much make-up and too-blonde hair, but on the whole not someone he'd kick out of bed. She was dressed in the standard Canterbury cocktail waitress uniform of short skirt, black stockings, and low-cut Elizabethan barmaid blouse, and she was smiling.

"How do you know my name?"

"Why shouldn't I? You're one of the more important men in Monroe, aren't you?"

She was interested in him. Howard couldn't read her thoughts, but he sensed her excited response to his presence. She was probably attracted to money and power and apparently he represented a modicum of both to her. There was a trace of sexual arousal and an undercurrent of anxiety as well.

Anxiety over what? That he'd give her the cold shoulder? He tried to see if he could affect that.

"Nice to be recognized," he said, "especially by such an attractive woman"...he craned his neck to see the name tag centered on her cleavage..."Molly."

The anxiety all but vanished and the sexual arousal rose two notches.

Bingo!

He ordered a Chivas and soda. He was ready for her when she returned with the drink.

"Looks like you'll be working late tonight, huh?"

He could feel her excitement swell. "Not necessarily. It's still the off season so it's not really crazy yet. When the tables are kinda slow like tonight I can usually get off early if I ask."

"Why don't you ask? I've got no plans for the evening. Maybe we could think of something to do together."

Her sexual arousal zoomed.

"Sounds good to me," she said with a smile and a wink.

Howard leaned back and sipped his scotch as he watched the gentle sway of her retreating butt.

So easy! Like having all the answers to a test before you sat down to take it.

This was a curse?

What a night!

Howard walked along the waterfront through the morning mist. He was still a little weak-kneed. He'd had loads of women over the years, plenty of one-night stands, even an all-nighter with a couple of pros. But never, *never* anything like what he had experienced last night.

As soon as they had got to Molly's apartment and begun the foreplay, he had found himself tapped into her feelings. He could sense her excitement, her pleasure—he was more than just aware of it, he was actually experiencing it himself. He could tell when he was going too fast or not fast enough. He found he could toy with her, tantalize her, bring her to peaks but keep her from going over the top. Finally he brought her to an Everest and leaped off with her. Her climax fused into his and the results were shattering. She was left gasping but he was utterly speechless.

And that had only been the first time.

Molly had finally fallen asleep telling him he was the greatest lover in the world, really meaning it. Howard had drifted off with her, thinking it wouldn't be bad if that message got around to all the attractive single women in town. Not bad at all.

He had awakened early and Molly had wanted him to stay but he had begged off. He was catching a new emotion from her: She was starting to get lovey-dovey feelings for him—or at least thought she was. And why not? Decent looks, money, power, and a great lover to boot.

What's not to love?

Those feelings tripped off sirens and red lights for Howard. Uh-uh. No love. Just good times and fun and stay loose. Love meant trouble.

Women started thinking of marriage then.

He felt her hurt and disappointment as he left, trailing vague promises of getting together again real soon. But he couldn't go home just
yet. He was too excited, too exhilarated. This was great! This was fantastic! The possibilities were endless. He walked on, exploring them in
his mind.

A siren broke into his thoughts. He looked around and found he
was in front of Monroe Community Hospital. An ambulance was racing up the road. As it neared, he felt a growing pressure in his chest.
His breath clogged in his throat as the pain became a great lead weight,
crushing his sternum. Then, as the ambulance passed and pulled into
the approach to the emergency entrance, the pain receded.

Whoever was in that ambulance was having a heart attack. Howard
was sure of it. He watched as the ambulance attendants carried someone into the emergency room on a stretcher. Heart attack. No doubt
about it. Just one more bit of proof on the side of this so-called curse Dr.
Johnson had laid on him. And it would be so easy to confirm. Just go
up to the reception desk and ask: *Did the ambulance get here with my uncle
yet? The man with the chest pain?*

He started across the lawn toward the four-story brick structure.
As he neared it however, he began to feel nauseous and weak. His head
pounded, his abdomen burned, ached, cramped, and just plain hurt.
Every joint, every bone in his body hurt. He began to wheeze, his vision
blurred. It all got worse with each step closer to the hospital but he
forced himself on until he reached the emergency entrance and opened
the door.

*...pain... fear... pain... hope... pain... grief... pain... rage... pain...
despair... pain... joy... pain... pain... pain... pain...*

Like a physical assault from a Mongolian horde, like a massive torrent from a sundered dam, like ground zero at Hiroshima, the mental and physical agony flooded over Howard, sending him reeling and
stumbling back across the driveway to the grass where he crumbled
to his knees and crawled as fast as he could away from the hospital.
Anyone watching him would have assumed he was drunk but he didn't
care. He had to get away from that building.

He felt almost himself again by the time he reached the sidewalk.
He sat on the curb, weak and nauseous, swearing he would never go
near another hospital again.

It seemed there were drawbacks to this little power of his after
all. But nothing he couldn't handle, nothing he couldn't ovecome. The
advantages were too enormous!

He had to talk this out with somebody. Brainstorm it. But with whom. Suddenly, he smiled.

Lydia lived in the garden apartments on the downtown fringe, a short walk from here.

Of course!

————

Howard had looked like he was on drugs when Lydia opened the door to her apartment. She had been in the middle of a nice little dream of being married with two kids and no money problem when the pounding on the door had awakened her. Her brother's face had loomed large in the fish-eye peephole so she had opened up and let him in.

That proved a mistake. Howie was absolutely manic. While she made coffee he stalked around her tiny kitchen waving his arms and talking a mile a minute. Watching him, she thought he might be on speed; listening to him, she thought he might be on acid.

But Howie didn't do drugs.

Which meant he had gone crazy.

"Do you see what this means, Sis? Do you *see!* The possibilities are endless! Can you imagine what this will let me do at a deposition? If my questions are getting into a sensitive area, I'll know! I'll sense the defendant's fear, his anxiety, and I'll keep hitting those sore spots, pushing those secret buttons until he comes across with what I want. And even if he doesn't, I'll know where to look for the dirt. Same's true with cross-examinations in the court room. I'll know when I've hit a nerve. And speaking of court rooms, I thought of something that's even better—even better!" He stopped and pointed a finger at her. "Juries! Jury selection!"

Lydia stirred the boiling water into the instant coffee—decaf, for sure. She didn't want to hype him up even the tiniest bit more. "Right, Howie," she said softly. "That's a good point."

"Can you imagine how I'll be able to stack the jury box? I mean, I'll *know* how each juror feels about the case because I'll ask them point blank. I'll say, 'Mrs. So-and-so, how do you feel about the medical profession in general?' If I get some sort of warm glow from her, she's out, no matter what she says. But if I get anger or envy or plain old spitefulness, she's in. I can pack a jury with doctor-haters on all my malpractice cases!" He giggled. "The settlements will be *astronomical!*"

"Whatever makes you happy, Howie," Lydia said. "Now why don't you sit down and drink your coffee and take it easy." She had heard about Dr. Johnson's hand winding up on his desk yesterday. The shock must have got to him. "You can lie down on my bed if you want to."

He was staring at her.

"You think I'm nuts, don't you?"

"No, Howie. I just think you're feeling the strain of—"

"Right now I'm feeling what you're feeling. Which is a lot of disbelief, a little anxiety, a little fatigue, and a little compassion. Very little compassion."

"You don't need a crystal ball or a voodoo-hoodoo curse to figure that one out."

"And you've got a low backache, too. Right?"

Lydia felt a chill. Her low back did hurt. Her period was due tomorrow and her back always ached the day before.

"Half the world's got backaches, Howie."

"You've got to believe me, Lydia. There's got to be a way I can—" His eyes lit. "Wait a minute. I've got an idea." He began yanking the kitchen drawers open until he got to the utensils. He pulled out a paring knife and handed it to her.

"What's this for?" she said.

"I want you to poke yourself here and there on your body with the point—"

"Howie, are you nuts?"

"Not hard enough to break the skin; just enough to cause a little pain." He took the pen from the message pad by the phone and pointed to the kitchen door. "I'll be on the other side of the door there and I'll mark the spots and number them on myself with this pen."

"This is crazy!"

"I've got to convince you, Lydia. You're the only one in this world I trust."

Damn him! It had been like this all their lives. He always knew what to say to get her to go along.

"Okay."

He got on the other side of the swinging door. Lydia put her back to it and poked the knife point at the center of her left palm. It hurt, but certainly nothing she couldn't bear.

"That's one," said Howie from the other side of the door.

Lydia turned her hand over and jabbed the back of her hand.

"That's two," Howie said.

Lucky guesses, Lydia told herself uneasily. For variety, she poked the point gently against her cheek.

"Very funny," Howie said, "but I'm not writing on my face."

The words so startled her that the knife slipped from her grasp. As she grabbed for it, the blade sliced into her index finger.

"Hey!" Howie said, pushing through the door. "You weren't supposed to cut yourself!"

"It was an acc—" And then she realized. "My God, you knew!" She sucked her bleeding finger. He knew!

"Of course I knew. As a matter of fact, for an instant in there I actually *saw* the cut on my finger. Look here. Even drew it for you. See?"

Lydia did see: A half-inch crescent was drawn in ink across the pad of Howie's right index finger, perfectly matching the bloody one on her own.

Suddenly Lydia was weak. She lowered herself into a chair. "My God, Howie, it's really true, isn't it?"

"Sure is." He stood over her, beaming. "And I'm going to milk it dry." He turned and started toward the door.

"Where are you going?"

"Back to the condo. I need some sleep, and I've got a lot of thinking to do. Don't make any plans for dinner tonight. I'm treating. Lobster and champagne at Memison's."

"Aren't we generous."

"Make reservations for two."

And then he was gone. Lydia sat there trying to accept the fact that something that simply didn't happen in real life was happening in hers.

On the way home, Howard kept well away from the hospital. As he walked he realized that the courtroom was small potatoes, just a springboard into politics. *United States Senator Howard Weinstein.* He liked the sound of that. He'd know who to trust and who to boot. And after he'd built up his power base, maybe he'd go for the White House.

Hey, why the hell not?

He was tempted to stop by his father's place out on Shore Drive and see what he was up to. He hadn't heard from the old man in a couple of weeks. Might be interesting to see how Dad really felt about him. And then again, it might not.

He went straight home.

His right arm started bothering him at the front door. The ache was worse than he remembered from last night. Just to test a theory, he walked back outside again. The pain disappeared by the time he got to the parking lot. It recurred when he returned to the condo.

Which mean that someone nearby had a bad case of bursitis or something. So why the hell didn't the jerk do something about it?

Howard was too tired to worry about that now. He downed a couple of shots of scotch to calm his nerves and crawled under the covers. As he closed his eyes and tried to ignore the throb in his arm, he realized that he felt a little sad. Why? Or did the emotion even originate with him? Maybe somebody else nearby was unhappy or depressed about something. Was he getting more sensitive or what? This could get confusing.

He pushed it all away and wrapped himself in dreams of dazzling courtroom prowess and political glory.

The pain awoke him at four in the afternoon. The aching throb in his right arm was worse than ever. He wondered if it had anything to do with touching the hand. Maybe Dr. Johnson was getting even with him after all.

That was not a pleasant thought.

But then why would the pain stop as soon as he left the condo? He couldn't figure this out.

He phoned Lydia. "How about an early dinner, Sis?"

"How early?"

"As early as possible."

"I made reservations for 7:30."

"We'll change them."

"Is something wrong, Howie?" There was a hint of real concern in her voice.

He told her about the pain in his arm. "I've got to get out of here. That's the only time it stops."

"Okay. Meet you there at 5:30."

That was when the peasants ate, but the pain wouldn't allow Howard to be snooty. He took a quick shower and hurried outside before his hair had dried. Blessed relief from the pain came at the far end of the parking lot.

"I'll take that one," Howard said, pointing out a big-tailed two-pounder in Memison's live lobster tank.

"Excellent choice, sir," the waiter said, then turned to Lydia. "And you, Miss?"

"I'll have the fish dinner, please."

Howard was surprised. He sensed a skittish reluctance in her. "No lobster? I thought you loved lobster!"

She was staring at the tank. "I do. But standing here and pointing out the one I'm going to eat...somehow it's not the same. Makes me feel like some sort of executioner."

Howard couldn't help laughing. "I swear to God you're from Mars, Sis. From *Mars!*"

When they returned to the table, Howard refilled their tall, slim champagne glasses from the bottle in the bucket. He watched a fly buzz angrily against the window that ran alongside their table. Outside at the marina, the boats rocked gently at their moorings. He savored the peace.

"You're awful quiet, Howie," Lydia said after a moment.

"Am I?"

"Compared to this morning, you're a sphinx."

Howard didn't know what to tell her, how to say it. Maybe the best thing to do was to lay it all out. Maybe she could help him sort it out.

"I think I'm having second thoughts about this special 'empathy' I've developed," he said finally. "Maybe it really is a curse. I seem to be getting increasingly sensitive. I mean, as I walked over here I got rushes of feelings from everyone I passed. There was this little kid crying on the corner. He had lost his mom and I found myself—*me*—utterly terrified. I couldn't move, I was so scared. Thank God his mother found him just then or I don't know what I'd have done. And when she whacked him on the backside for running off, I felt it. It hurt! The kid was the worst, but I was picking up all sorts of conflicting emotions. It was almost a relief to get in here. Good thing we're so early and it's almost deserted."

"Why'd you have our table moved? To get away from that fat guy?"

Howard nodded. "Yeah. He must have stuffed himself from the buffet. I thought my stomach was going to burst. I couldn't enjoy my dinner feeling like that. And if he's going to have a gallbladder attack, I don't want to be near him."

The fly's buzzing continued. It was beginning to annoy him.

"Howard," Lydia said, looking at him intently. She only called him Howard when she was mad or really serious about something. "Can this really be happening?"

"Don't you think I've asked myself that a thousand times since last night? But yes, it's real, and it's happening to me."

He signaled their waiter as he passed. "Could you do something about that fly?"

"Of course."

The waiter returned in a moment with a fly swatter. He swung it as Howard was pouring more champagne.

Pain like Howard had never known in his life flashed through his entire body as his ears roared and his vision went stark white. It was gone in an instant, over as soon as it had begun.

"My God, Howard, what's the matter!"

Lydia was staring at him, wide-eyed and ashen-faced. He glanced around. So were the other people in the place. He felt their disapproval, their annoyance. The waiter began sopping up the champagne he had spilled when he had dropped the bottle.

"Wh-what happened?"

"You screamed and spasmed like you were having a seizure! Howard, what's wrong with you?"

"When he swatted that fly," he said, nodding his head in the direction of the retreating waiter, "I...I think I felt it."

Her disbelief stung him. "Oh, Howard—"

"It's true, Sis. It hurt so much for that one tiny second there I thought I was going to die."

"But a fly, Howard? A *fly*?" She stared at him. "What's wrong?"

Suddenly he was very hot. Terribly hot. His skin felt like it was on fire. He looked down at his bare arms and watched the skin turn red, rise up in blisters, burst open. He felt as if he were being boiled alive.

...boiled...

His lobster! The kitchen was only a few feet away. They'd be cooking it now—dropping it live into a pot of boiling water!

Screaming with the pain, he leaped up from the table and ran for the door.

Outside...coolness. He leaned against the outer wall of Memison's, gasping and sweating, oblivious to the stares of the passers-by but too well aware of their curiosity.

"Howard, are you going crazy?" It was Lydia. She had followed him out.

"Didn't you see me? I was burning up in there!" He looked down at his arms. The skin was perfect, unblemished.

"All I saw was my brother acting like a crazy man!"

He felt her concern, her fear for him, and her embarrassment because of him.

"When they started boiling my lobster, they started boiling me! I could feel myself being boiled alive!"

"Howard, this has got to stop!"

"Damn right it does." He pushed himself off the wall and began walking down the street, back toward his condo. "I've got some thinking to do. See you."

Lydia was having her first cup of coffee when Howard called the next morning.

"Can I come over, Sis?" His voice was hoarse, strained. "I've got to get out of here."

"Sure, Howie. Is it the arm again?"

"Yeah! Feels like it's being crushed!"

Crushed. That rang a bell somewhere in the back of her mind. "Come right over. I'll leave the door unlocked. If I'm not here, make yourself at home. I'll be back soon. I've got an errand to run."

She hung up, pulled on jeans and a blouse, and hurried down to the Monroe Public Library. A crushed arm...she remembered something about that, something to do with the Soundview Condos.

It took her awhile, but she finally tracked it down in a microfilm spool of the Monroe *Express* from two years ago last summer...

Howard looked like hell. He looked distracted. He wasn't paying attention.

"Listen to me, Howard! It happened two years ago! They were pouring the basement slab in your section of condos. As the cement truck was backing up, a construction worker slipped in some mud and the truck's rear wheels rolled right over his arm. Crushed it so bad even Columbia Presbyterian couldn't save it."

He looked at her dully. "So?"

"So don't you see? You're not just tuned in to the feelings and sensations of people and even lobsters and bugs around you. You're picking up the *residuals* of old pains and hurts."

"Is that why it's so noisy in here?"

"'Noisy'?"

"Yeah. Emotional noise. This place is crowded, I mean *jammed* with emotions, some faint, some strong, some up, some down, some really mean ones. So confusing."

Lydia remembered that these garden apartments had been put up shortly after the war—World War II. If Howard could actually feel forty-plus years of emotion—

"I wish they'd go away and let me sleep. I'd give anything for just a moment's peace."

Lydia went to the medicine cabinet in the bathroom and found the bottle of Valium her doctor had prescribed for her when she was divorcing Harry. She shook two of the yellow tablets into her palm and gave them to Howard with a cup of water.

"Take these and go lie down on my bed. They'll help you sleep."

He did as he was told and shuffled off to the next room, moving like a zombie. Lydia's heart went out to him. She called a friend and begged her to take the steno job she had lined up for this afternoon, then settled down to watch over her big brother.

He slept fitfully through the day. Around dark she took a shower to ease her tension-knotted muscles. It helped some. Wrapped in her terrycloth robe, she returned to the kitchen and found him standing there looking worse than ever.

"I can't stand it!" he said in a voice that sounded as if it were going to break into a million jagged pieces. "It's making me crazy. It's even in my dreams! All those feelings! *I'm going nuts!*"

His wild eyes frightened her. "Just calm down, Howie. I'll make you something to eat and then we can—"

"I've gotta get outta here! I can't take it any longer!"

He started for the door. Lydia tried to stop him.

"Howard—!"

He pushed her aside. "Got to get *out!*"

By the time she threw on enough clothing to follow him, he was nowhere to be seen.

The night was alive with fear and joy and lust and pain and pleasure and love, emotionally and physically strobing Howard with heat and light. He needed relief, he needed quiet, he needed peace.

And there, up ahead, he saw it... a cool and dark place... almost empty of emotions, of feelings of any sort.

He headed for it.

———

She got the call the next morning.

"Are you Lydia Chambers, sister of Howard Weinstein?" said an official sounding voice.

Oh, God!

"Yes."

"Would you come down to the Crosby Marina, please, ma'am?"

"Oh, no! He's not—"

"He's okay," the voice said quickly. "Physically, at least."

———

Lt. Donaldson drove her out to the buoy in a Marine Police outboard. Howard sat in a rowboat tied to the bobbing red channel marker in the center of Monroe Harbor.

"Seems he stole the boat last night," said the lieutenant, who had curly blond hair and looked to be in his mid-thirties. "But he seems to have gone off the deep end. He won't untie from the buoy and he starts screaming and swinging an oar at anyone who comes near. He asked for you."

He cut the engine and let the outboard drift toward Howard and the rowboat.

"Tell them to leave me alone, Sis!" Howard said when they got to within a couple of dozen feet of him.

He looked wild—unshaven, his clothes smudged and wrinkled, his hair standing up at crazy angles. And in his eyes, a dangerous, cornered look.

He looks insane, she thought.

"Come ashore, Howard," she said, trying to exude friendliness and calm confidence. "Come home now."

"I can't, Sis! You can explain it to them. Make them understand. This is the only place where it's quiet, where I can find peace. Oh, I know the fish are eating and being eaten below, but it's sporadic and it's far away and I can handle that. I just can't be in town anymore!"

Lt. Donaldson whispered out of the side of his mouth. "He's been talking crazy like that since we found him out here this morning."

Lydia wondered what she could tell the lieutenant: That her brother wasn't crazy, that he was suffering from a curse? Start talking like that and they'd be measuring her for a straitjacket, too.

"You can't stay out here, Howard."

"I have to. There's a gull's nest in the buoy and the little birds were hungry this morning and it made me hungry, too. But then the mother came and fed them and now their bellies are full and they're content"... he began to sob... "and so am I and I just want to stay here near them where it's quiet and peaceful."

She heard the lieutenant growl. "All right. That does it!"

He stood up and signaled to shore. Another larger boat roared out from the marina. There were men in white jackets aboard, and they were carrying something that looked like a net.

"He'll be asleep for a while yet, Mrs. Chambers," said Dr. Gold. "We had to inject him with a pretty stiff dose of Thorazine to quiet him down."

It had been horrifying to watch them throw a net over her own brother and haul him into the bigger boat like a giant fish, but there had been no other way. Howard would have died out on the water if they had left him there.

She had spent most of the morning signing papers and answering countless questions on Howard's medical and emotional history, family history, current stresses and strains. She had told Dr. Gold everything, including Howard's receiving the hand in the mail two days ago. *God, was it only two days ago?* Everything...except the part about feeling the pain and emotions of other people...and animals and even insects. She couldn't bring herself to risk trying to explain that to Dr. Gold. He might think she was sharing her brother's psychosis.

"When can he leave?" she asked.

"Not for twenty-eight days at least. That's how long he's committed.

Don't worry too much. This appears to be an acute psychosis precipitated by that grisly incident with the severed hand. We'll start his psychotherapy immediately, find an appropriate medication, and do what we can to get him on his psychological feet again as soon as possible. I think he'll do just fine."

Lydia wasn't too sure of that, but all she could do was hope. At least the Monroe Neuropsychiatric Institute was brand new. It had opened only last winter. She had heard about it, but since she never came to this part of town, she hadn't seen it until now. It seemed pleasant enough. And since most of the patients here were probably sedated to some degree, their emotions wouldn't be too strong. Maybe Howard had a chance here.

Dr. Gold walked her to the door.

"In a way it's sort of ironic that your brother should wind up here."

"Why is that?"

"Well, he's one of the limited partners that developed this little hospital. All of the limited partners got a certified historic rehabilitation tax credit for investing, one of the few goodies remaining after tax overhaul."

"Rehabilitation?" A warning bell sounded in a far corner of her mind. "You mean it isn't a new building?"

"Oh, my goodness, no. We've cleaned it up to look spanking new, but in reality it's a hundred and fifty years old."

"A hundred and fifty—!"

"Yes. It was abandoned for such a long time. I understand it was being used for dogfights before we took it over. Even used it as a place to train young fighting pit bulls. Trained them with kittens. A sick, sick—" He stared at her. "Are you all right?"

"Dog fights?" Oh, God, what would that do to Howard? Wouldn't the residual from something like that send him right up the wall?

"I'm sorry if I upset you."

"I'm okay," she said, steeling herself to ask the next question. "What was the building originally?"

"Originally? Why I thought everybody knew that, but I guess you're too young to remember. Up until the early 1960s it was the Monroe Slaughterhouse. One of the busiest in the—"

He stopped as the sound came down the hall—a long, hoarse, agonized scream that echoed off the freshly painted walls and tore into Lydia's soul.

Howard was awake.

The idea for "Tenants" had been wandering through the back of my mind for years. A simple little story about an escaped killer who thinks he's found the perfect hideout from the law in a remote house at the end of a road through a salt marsh. The old coot who lives there is crazy: He keeps talking about his tenants, but he's alone in the shack. Or is he?

I could have set it anywhere, but I chose Monroe—not only because I'd set "Feelings" there, but because I was squeezing out these stories while writing *Reborn*, also set in Monroe, and I saw a connection. I'd envisioned *Reborn* as the first part of a long roman fleuve that would unite *The Keep*, *The Tomb*, and *The Touch*. Why were all these strange things happening in Monroe? Why had the *Dat-tay-vao* been drawn to Monroe in *The Touch*? Was it all random, or was there a reason? I realized *Reborn* contained that reason.

So if the old guy in "Tenants" has some strange boarders, maybe they too wound up in Monroe for a reason. The locale had no direct effect on the novelette itself, but it gave me a little extra kick to know I was connecting it to the cycle.

Gus and his tenants appear again briefly in *Nightworld*.

Tenants

The mail truck was coming.

Gilroy Connors, shoes full of water and shirt still wet from the morning's heavy dew, crouched in the tall grass and punk-topped reeds. He ached all over; his thighs particularly were cramped from holding his present position. But he didn't dare move for fear of giving his presence away.

So he stayed hunkered down across the road from the battered old shack that looked deserted but wasn't—there had been lights on in the place last night. With its single pitched roof and rotting cedar shake siding, it looked more like an overgrown outhouse that a home. A peeling propane tank squatted on the north side; a crumbling brick chimney supported a canted TV antenna. Beyond the shack, glittering in the morning sunlight, lay the northeast end of Monroe Harbor and the Long Island Sound. The place gave new meaning to the word *isolated*. As if a few lifetimes ago someone had brought a couple of tandems of fill out to the end of the hard-packed dirt road, dumped them, and built a shack. Except for a rickety old dock with a sodden rowboat tethered to it, there was not another structure in sight in either direction. Only a slender umbilical cord of insulated wire connected it to the rest of the world via a long column of utility poles marching out from town. All around was empty marsh.

Yeah. Isolated as all hell.

It was perfect.

As Gil watched, the shack's front door opened and a grizzled old man stumbled out, a cigarette in his mouth and a fistful of envelopes in his hand. Tall and lanky with an unruly shock of gray hair standing off his head, he scratched his slightly protruding belly as he squinted in the morning sunlight. He wore a torn undershirt that had probably been white once and a pair of faded green work pants held up by suspenders, He looked as rundown as his home, and as much in need of a shave and a bath as Gil felt. With timing so perfect that it could only be the result of daily practice, the old guy reached the mailbox at exactly the same time as the white jeep-like mail truck.

Must have been watching from the window.

Not an encouraging thought. Had the old guy seen Gil out here? If he had, he gave no sign. Which meant Gil was still safe.

He fingered the handle of the knife inside his shirt.

Lucky for him.

While the old guy and the mailman jawed, Gil studied the shack again. The place was a sign that his recent run of good luck hadn't deserted him yet. He had come out to the marshes to hide until things cooled down in and around Monroe and had been expecting to spend a few real uncomfortable nights out here. The shack would make things a lot easier.

Not much of a place. At most it looked big enough for two rooms and no more. Barely enough space for an ancient couple who didn't move around much—who ate, slept, crapped, watched TV and nothing more. Hopefully, it wasn't a couple. Just the old guy. That would make it simple. A wife, even a real sickly one, could complicate matters.

Gil wanted to know how many were living there before he invited himself in. Not that it would matter much. Either way, he was going in and staying for a while. He just liked to know what he was getting into before he made his move.

One thing was sure: He wasn't going to find any money in there. The old guy had to be next to destitute. But even ten bucks would have made him richer than Gil. He looked at the rusting blue late-sixties Ford Torino with the peeling vinyl roof and hoped it would run. But of course it ran. The old guy had to get into town to cash his Social Security check and buy groceries, didn't he?

Damn well better run.

It had been a long and sloppy trek into these marshes. He intended to drive out.

Finally the mail truck clinked into gear, did a U-turn, and headed back the way it had come. The old guy shoved a couple of envelopes into his back pocket, picked up a rake that had been leaning against the Ford, and began scratching at the dirt on the south side of the house.

Gil decided it was now or never. He straightened up and walked toward the shack. As his feet crunched on the gravel of the yard, the old man wheeled and stared at him with wide, startled eyes.

"Didn't mean to scare you," Gil said in his friendliest voice.

"Well, you sure as hell did, poppin' outta nowhere like that!" the old man said in a deep, gravelly voice. The cigarette between his lips bobbed up and down like a conductor's baton. "We don't exactly get much drop-in company out here. What happen? Boat run outta gas?"

Gil noticed the *we* with annoyance but played along. A stalled boat was as good an excuse as any for being out here in the middle of nowhere.

"Yeah. Had to paddle it into shore way back over there," he said, jerking a thumb over his shoulder.

"Well, I ain't got no phone for you to call anybody—"

No phone! It was all Gil could do to keep from cheering.

"—but I can drive you down to the marina and back so you can get some gas."

"No hurry." He moved closer and leaned against the old Torino's fender. "You live out here all by yourself?"

The old man squinted at him, as if trying to recognize him. "I don't believe we've been introduced, son."

"Oh, right." Gil stuck out his hand. "Rick... Rick Summers."

"And I'm George Haskins," he said, giving Gil's hand a firm shake. "What're you growing there?"

"Carrots. I hear fresh carrots are good for your eyes. Mine are so bad I try to eat as many as I can."

Half blind and no phone. This was sounding better every minute. Now, if he could just find out who the rest of the *we* was, he'd be golden.

He glanced around. Even though he was out in the middle of nowhere at the end of a dirt road that no one but the mailman and this old fart knew existed, he felt exposed. Naked, even. He wanted to get inside.

"Say, I sure could use a cup of coffee, Mr. Haskins. You think you might spare me some?"

George hesitated. Making coffee for the stranger would mean bringing him inside. He didn't like that idea at all. He hadn't had anybody into the house since the late sixties when he took in his tenants. And he'd had damn few visitors before that. People didn't like coming this far out, and George was just as glad. Most people pried. They wanted to know what you did way out here all by yourself. Couldn't believe anybody sane would prefer his own company to theirs.

And of course, there was the matter of the tenants.

He studied this young man who had popped out of nowhere. George's eyes weren't getting any better—"Cataracts only get worse," the doctor had told him—but he could plainly see that the stranger wasn't dressed for boating, what with that blue work shirt and gray denims he was wearing. And those leather shoes! Nobody who knew boats ever wore leather shoes on board. But they were selling boats to anybody with cash these days. This landlubber probably didn't know the first thing about boating. That no doubt was why he was standing here on land instead of chugging about the harbor.

He seemed pleasant enough, though. Good-looking, too, with his muscular build and wavy dark hair. Bet he had an easy time with the girls. *Especially* easy, since from what George understood of the world today, *all* the girls were easy.

Maybe he could risk spotting him a cup of coffee before driving him down to the marina. What harm could there be in that? The tenants were late risers and had the good sense to keep quiet if they heard a strange voice overhead.

He smiled. "Coffee? Sure. Come on inside. And call me George. Everybody else does." He dropped his cigarette into the sandy soil and stomped on it, then turned toward the house.

Just a quick cup of coffee and George would send him off. The longer he stayed, the greater the chances of him finding out about the tenants. And George couldn't risk that. He was more than their landlord.

He had sworn to protect them.

Gil followed close on the old guy's back up the two steps to the door. Inside was dark and stale, reeking of years of cigarette smoke. He wondered when was the last time George had left a window open.

But being indoors was good. Out of sight and inside—even if it stank, it was better than good. It was super. He felt as if a great weight had been lifted from him.

Now to find out who made up the rest of the *we.*

"Got this place all to yourself, ay?" he said, glancing quickly about. They were standing in a rectangular space that passed for a living room/dining room/kitchen. The furniture consisted of an old card table, a rocker, a tilted easy chair, and a dilapidated couch. Shapeless piles of junk cluttered every corner. An ancient Motorola television set with a huge chassis and a tiny screen stood on the far side of the room diagonally across from the door. The screen was lit and a black chick was reading some news into the camera:

"...*eriously injuring an orderly in a daring escape from the Monroe Neuropsychiatric Institute. He was last reported in Glen Cove—*"

Gil whooped. "Glen Cove! Awright!" That was the wrong direction! He was safe for the moment. "Fan*tas*tic!" he yelled, stomping his foot on the floor.

"Hey! Hold it down!" George said as he filled a greasy, dented aluminum kettle with water and put it on the gas stove.

Gil felt the customary flash of anger at being told what he could or couldn't do, but cooled it. He stepped between George and the TV set as he saw his most recent mug shot appear on the screen. The black chick was saying:

"*If you see this man, do not approach him. He might be armed and is considered dangerous.*"

Gil said, "Sorry. It's just that sometimes I get excited by the news."

"Yeah?" George said, lighting another cigarette. "Don't follow it much myself. But you got to keep quiet. You might disturb the tenants and they—"

"Tenants?" Gil said a—lot more loudly than he intended. "You've got *tenants?*"

The old guy was biting his upper lip with what few teeth he had left and saying nothing.

Gil stepped down the short hall, gripping the handle of the knife inside his shirt as he moved. Two doors: The one on the left was open, revealing a tiny bathroom with a toilet, sink, and mildewy shower stall; the one on the right was closed. He gave it a gentle push. Empty: dirty, wrinkled sheets on a narrow bed, dresser, mirror, clothes thrown all around, but nobody there.

"Where are they?" he said, returning to the larger room.

George laughed—a little too loudly, Gil thought—and said, "No tenants. Just a joke. Creepy-crawlies in the crawlspace is all. You know, snapping turtles and frogs and snakes and crickets."

"You keep things like that under your house?" This was turning out to be one weird guy.

"In a manner of speaking, yes. You see, a zillion years ago when I built this place, a big family of crickets took up residence"—he pointed down—"in the crawl space. Drove me crazy at night. So one day I get the bright idea of catching some frogs and throwing them in there to eat the crickets. Worked great. Within two days, there wasn't a chirp to be heard down there."

"Smart."

"Yeah. So I thought. Until the frogs started croaking all night. They were worse than the crickets!"

Gil laughed. "I get it. So you put the snakes down there to catch the frogs!"

"Right. Snakes are quiet. They eat crickets, too. Should've thought of them in the first place. Except I wasn't crazy about living over a nest of snakes."

This was getting to sound like the old lady who swallowed the fly.

Gill said, "And so the next step was to put the turtles down there to eat the snakes."

"Yeah." As George spooned instant coffee into a couple of stained mugs, Gil tried not to think about when they last might have had a good washing. "But I don't think they ate them all, just like I don't think the snakes ate all the frogs, or the frogs ate all the crickets. I still hear an occasional chirp and croak once in a while. Anyway, they've all been down there for years. I ain't for adding anything else to the stew, or even looking down there."

"Don't blame you."

George poured boiling water into the mugs and handed him one.

"So if you hear something moving underfoot, it's just one of my tenants."

"Yeah. Okay. Sure."

This old guy was fruitcake city. As crazy as—

...*Crazy.* That was what that college chick had called him that night when he had tried to pick her up along the road. She was cute. There were a lot of cute girls at Monroe Community College, and he'd always made it a point to drive by every chance he could. She'd said he was crazy to think she'd take a ride from a stranger at that hour of the night. That had made him mad. All these college broads thought they were better and smarter than everybody else. And she'd started to scream when he grabbed her, so he'd hit her to make her stop but she wouldn't stop. She kept on screaming so he kept on hitting her and hitting her and hitting and hitting...

"You're spilling your coffee," George said.

Gil looked down. So he was. It was dripping over the edge of his tilted mug and splashing onto the floor. As he slurped some off the top and sat on the creaking couch, he realized how tired he was. No sleep in the past twenty-four hours. Maybe the coffee would boost him.

"So how come you live out here all by yourself?" Gil asked, hoping to get the conversation on a saner topic than snakes and snapping turtles in the crawlspace.

"I *like* being by myself."

"You must. But whatever rent you pay on this place, it's too much."

"Don't pay no rent at all. I own it."

"Yeah, but the land—"

"My land."

Gil almost dropped his coffee mug. "*Your* land! That's impossible!"

"Nope. All twenty acres been in my family for a zillion and two years."

Gil's brain whirled as he tried to calculate the value of twenty acres of real estate fronting on Monroe Harbor and Long Island Sound.

"You're a fucking millionaire!"

George laughed. "I wish! I'm what you call 'land poor', son. I've got to pay taxes on all this land if I want to keep it, and the damn bastards down at City Hall keep raising my rates and my assessed value so that I've got to come up with more and more money every year just to stay here. Trying to force me out, that's what they're up to."

"So sell, for Christ sake! There must be developers chomping at the bit to get ahold of this land. You could make 'em pay through the nose for a piece of waterfront and all your money worries would be over!"

George shook his head. "Naw. Once you sell one little piece, it's like a leak in a dam. It softens you, weakens you. Soon you're selling another piece, and then another. Pretty soon, I'll be living on this little postage stamp surrounded by big ugly condos, listening to cars and mopeds racing up and down the road with engines roaring and rock and roll blasting. No thanks. I've lived here in peace, and I want to die here in peace."

"Yeah, but—"

"Besides, lots of animals make their homes on my land. They've been pushed out of everywhere else in Monroe. All the trees have been cut down back there, all the hollows and gullies filled in and paved over. There's no place else for them to go. This is their world, too, you know. I'm their last resort. It's my duty to keep this place wild as long as I can. As long as I live...which probably won't be too much longer."

Oh, yes...crazy as a loon. Gil wondered if there might be some way he could get the old guy to will him the property and then cork him off. He stuffed the idea away in the To-Be-Developed file.

"Makes me glad I don't have a phone," George was saying.

Right...no phone and no visitors.

Gil knew this was the perfect hiding place for him. Just a few days was all he needed. But he had to stay here *with* the old guy's coopera-tion. He couldn't risk anything forceful—not if George met the mail-man at the box every day.

And from a few things the old man had said, he thought he knew just what buttons to push to convince George to let him stay.

George noted that his guest's coffee mug was empty. Good. Time to get him moving on. He never had company, didn't like it, and wasn't used to it. Made him itchy. Besides, he wanted this guy on his way before another remark about the tenants slipped out. That had been a close call before.

He stood up.

"Well, guess it's about time to be running you down to the marina for that tank of gas."

The stranger didn't move.

"George," he said in a low voice, "I've got a confession to make."

"Don't want to hear it!" George said. "I ain't no priest! Tell it some-where else. I just want to help get you where you're going!"

"I'm on the run, George."

Oh, hell, George thought. At least that explained why he was acting so skittish. "You mean there's no boat waiting for gas somewhere?"

"I..." His voice faltered. "I lied about the boat."

"Well ain't that just swell? And who, may I ask,"—George wasn't so sure he wanted the answer to this, but he had to ask—"are you on the run from?"

"The Feds."

Double hell. "What for?"

"Income tax evasion."

"No kidding?" George was suddenly interested. "How much you take them for?"

"It's not so much 'how much' as 'how long.'"

"All right: How long?"

"Nine years. I haven't filed a return since I turned eighteen."

"No shit! Is that because you're stupid or because you've got balls?"

"Mr. Haskins," the stranger said, looking at him levelly and speak-ing with what struck George as bone-deep conviction, "I don't believe any government's got the right to tax what a working man earns with the sweat of his brow."

"Couldn't of said it better myself!" George cried. He thought his heart was going to burst. This boy was talking like he'd have wanted his son to talk, if he'd ever had one. "The sonsabitches'll bleed you dry if you let 'em! Look what they've been doin' to me!"

The young stranger stared at the floor. "I was hoping you'd understand."

"Understand? Of course I understand! I've been fighting the IRS for years but never had the guts to actually *resist*! My hat's off to you!"

"Can I stay the night?"

That brought George up short. He wanted to help this courageous young man, but what was he going to do about the tenants?

"What's going to happen to you if they catch you? What kind of sentence you facing?"

"Twenty."

George's stomach turned. A young guy like this in the hole for twenty years just for not paying taxes. He felt his blood begin to boil.

"Bastards!"

He'd have to chance it. Tenants or not, he felt obligated to give this guy a place to stay for the night. It would be okay. The tenants could take the day off and just rest up. They'd been working hard lately. He'd just have to watch his mouth so he didn't make another slip about them.

"Well, George? What do you say?"

"I can let you stay one night and one night only," George said. "After that—"

The young fellow leaped forward and shook his hand. "Thanks a million, George!"

"Hear me out now. Only tonight. Come tomorrow morning, I'll drive you down to the train station, get you a ticket, and put you on board for New York with all the commuters. Once in the city, you can get lost real easy."

George thought he saw tears in the young man's eyes. "I don't know how to thank you."

"Never mind that. You just hit the sack in my room. You look bushed. Get some rest. No one'll know you're here."

He nodded, then went to the window and gazed out at the land. "Beautiful here," he said.

George realized it would probably look even more beautiful if the window were cleaner, but his eyes weren't good enough to notice much difference.

"If this were mine," the young fellow said passionately, "I'd sure as hell find a way to keep it out of the hands of the developers *and* the tax men. Maybe make it into a wildlife preserve or bird sanctuary or something. *Anything* to keep it wild and free."

Shaking his head, he turned and headed for the back room. George watched him in wonder. A wildlife preserve! Why hadn't he thought of that? It would be untaxable and unsubdividable! What a perfect solution!

But it was too late to start the wheels turning on something like that now. It would take years to submit all the proposals and wade through all the red tape to get it approved. And he didn't have years. He didn't need a doctor to tell him that his body was breaking down. He couldn't see right, he couldn't breathe right, and Christ Almighty, he couldn't even pee right. The parts were wearing out and there were no replacements available.

And what would happen when he finally cashed in his chips? What would happen to his land? And the tenants? Where would *they* go?

Maybe this young fellow was the answer. Maybe George could find a way to leave the land to him. He'd respect it, preserve it, just as George would if he could go on living. Maybe that was the solution.

But that meant he'd have to tell him the real truth about the tenants.

He didn't know if the guy was ready for that.

He sat down in the sun on the front steps and lit another cigarette. He had a lot of thinking to do.

———

The five o'clock news was on.

George had kept himself busy all day, what with tending to the carrot patch outside and cleaning up a bit inside. Having company made him realize how long it had been since he'd given the place a good sweeping.

But before he'd done any of that, he'd waited until the young fellow had fallen asleep, then he'd lifted the trapdoor under the rug in the corner of the main room and told the tenants to lay low for the day. They'd understood and said they'd be quiet.

Now he was sitting in front of the TV watching *Eyewitness News* and going through today's mail: Three small checks from the greeting card companies—not much, but it would help pay this quarter's taxes. He looked up at the screen when he heard "the Long Island town of Monroe" mentioned. Some pretty Oriental girl was sitting across from a scholarly looking fellow in a blue suit. She was saying,

"…explain to our viewers just what it is that makes Gilroy Connors so dangerous, Dr. Kline."

"He's a sociopath."

"And just what is that?"

"Simply put, it is a personality disorder in which the individual has no sense of 'mine' and 'not-mine,' no sense of right or wrong in the traditional sense."

"No conscience, so to speak."

"Exactly."

"Are they all murderers like Connors?"

"No. History's most notorious criminals and serial killers are sociopaths, but violence isn't a necessary facet of their make-up. The confidence men who rip off the pensions of widows or steal from a handicapped person are just as sociopathic as the Charles Mansons of the world. The key element in the sociopathic character is his or her complete lack of guilt. They will do whatever is necessary to get what they want and will feel no remorse over anyone they have to harm along the way."

"Gilroy Connors was convicted in the Dorothy Akers murder. Do you think he'll kill again?"

"He has to be considered dangerous. He's a sociopathic personality with a particularly low frustration threshold. But he is also a very glib liar. Since the truth means nothing to him, he can take any side of a question, any moral stance, and speak on it with utter conviction."

A voice—George recognized it as belonging to one of the anchormen—called from off-camera: "Sounds like he'd make a great politician!"

Everyone had a good laugh, and then the Oriental woman said, "But all kidding aside, what should our viewers do if one of them should spot him?"

Dr. Kline's expression was suddenly grim. "Lock the doors and call the police immediately."

The camera closed in on the Asian girl. "There you have it. We've been speaking to Dr. Edward Kline, a Long Island psychiatrist who examined Gilroy Connors and testified for the state at the Dorothy Akers murder trial.

"In case you've been asleep or out of the country during the last twenty-four hours, all of Long Island is being combed for Gilroy Connors, convicted killer of nineteen-year-old college coed Dorothy Akers. Connors escaped custody last night when, due to an error in paperwork, he was accidentally transferred to the Monroe Neuropsychiatric Institute instead of a maximum security facility as ordered by the court. The victim's father, publisher Jeffrey Akers, is offering a fifty thousand dollar reward for information leading to his recapture."

Fifty thousand! George thought. What I could do with that!

"You've heard Dr. Kline," she continued. "If you see this man, call the police immediately."

A blow-up of a mug shot appeared on the screen. George gasped. He knew that man! Even with his rotten vision, he could see that the face on the TV belonged to the man now sleeping in his bed! He turned around to look toward the bedroom and saw his house guest standing behind him, a knife in his hand.

"Don't even think about that reward, old man," Connors said in a chillingly soft voice. "Don't even *dream* about it."

"You're hurtin' my hands!" the old fart whined as Gil knotted the cord around his wrists.

"I'm putting you down for the night, old man, and you're staying down!"

He pulled the rope tighter and the old man yelped.

Gil said, "There—that ought to hold you."

George rolled over onto his back and stared up at him. "What are you going to do with me?"

"Haven't figured that out yet."

"You're gonna kill me, aren't you?" There was more concern than fear in his eyes.

"Maybe. Maybe not. Depends on how you behave."

Truthfully, he didn't know what to do. It would be less of a hassle to kill him now and get it over with, but there was the problem of the mailman. If George wasn't waiting curbside at the box tomorrow morning, the USPS might come knocking on the door. So Gil had to figure out a way to pressure George into acting as if everything was nice and normal tomorrow. Maybe he'd have George stand at the door and wave to the mailman. That might work. He'd have to spend some time figuring this out.

"All that stuff you said about dodging the tax man was just lies, wasn't it?"

Gil smiled at the memory. "Yeah. Pretty good, wasn't it? I mean, I made that up right off the top of my head. Sucked you in like smoke, didn't I?"

"Nothing to be proud of."

"Why not?"

"You heard what they called you on the TV: a 'socialpath'. Means you're crazy."

"You watch your mouth, old man!" Gil could feel the rage surging up in him like a giant wave. He hated that word. "I'm not crazy! And I don't ever want to hear that word out of your mouth again!"

"Doesn't matter anyway," George said. "Soon as you're out of here, my tenants will untie me."

Gil laughed. "Now who's crazy?"

"It's true. They'll free me."

"That's enough of that," Gil said. It wasn't funny anymore. He didn't like being called crazy any more than he liked being near crazy people. And this old man was talking crazy now. "No more of that kind of talk out of you!"

"You'll see. I'm their protector. Soon as you're—"

"Stop that!" Gil yanked George off the bed by his shirt front. He was losing it—he could feel it going. "God *damn* that makes me mad!"

He shoved the old man back against the wall with force enough to rattle the whole house. George's eyes rolled up as he slumped back onto the bed. A small red trickle crawled along his scalp and mixed with the gray of his hair at the back of his head.

"Sleep tight, Pops," Gils said.

He left George on the bed and returned to the other room. He turned the antique TV back on. After what seemed like an inordinately long warm-up time, the picture came in, flipped a few times, then held steady. He hoped there wasn't another psychiatrist on talking about him.

He hated psychiatrists. *Hated* them! Since he'd been picked up for killing that college chick, he'd seen enough of their kind to last a couple of lifetimes. Why'd she have to go and die? It wasn't fair. He hadn't meant to kill her. If only she'd been a little more cooperative. But no— she'd had to go and laugh in his face. He'd just got mad, that was all. He wasn't crazy. He just had a bad temper.

Psychiatrists! What'd they know about him? Labeling him, pigeon-holing him, saying he had no conscience and never felt sorry for anything he did. What'd they know? Did they know how he'd cried after Mom had burnt up in that fire in Dad's car? He'd cried for days. Mom wasn't supposed to be anywhere near that car when it caught fire. Only Dad.

He had *loads* of feelings, and nobody had better tell him any different!

He watched the tube for a while, caught a couple of news broadcasts, but there was only passing mention of his escape and the reward the girl's old man had posted for him. Then came a report that he had been sighted on Staten Island and the search was being concentrated there.

He smiled. They were getting further and further away from where he really was.

He shut off the set at eleven-thirty. Time for some more sleep. Before he made himself comfortable on the couch, he checked out the old man's room. He was there, snoring comfortably under the covers. Gil turned away and then spun back again.

How'd he get under the covers?

Two strides took him to the bedside. His foot kicked against something that skittered across the floor. He found what it was: the old guy's shoes. They'd been on his feet when he'd tied him up! He yanked back the covers and stared in open-mouthed shock at the old man.

George's hands and feet were free. The cords were nowhere in sight.

Just then he thought he caught a blur of movement by the doorway. He swung around but there was nothing there. He turned back to George.

"Hey, you old fart!" He shook George's shoulder roughly until his eyes opened. "Wake up!"

George's eyes slowly came into focus. "Wha—?"

"How'd you do it?"

"Go 'way!"

George rolled onto his other side and Gil saw a patch of white gauze where he had been bleeding earlier. He flipped him onto his back again.

"How'd you untie yourself, goddammit?"

"Didn't. My tenants—"

"You stop talking that shit to me, old man!" Gil said, cocking his right arm.

George flinched away but kept his mouth shut. Maybe he was finally learning.

"You stay right there!"

Gil tore through the drawers and piles of junk in the other room until he found some more cord. During the course of the search he came across a check book and some uncashed checks. He returned to the bedroom and began tying up George again.

"Don't know how you did it the first time, but you ain't doing it again!"

He spread-eagled George on the sheet and tied each skinny limb to a separate corner of the bed, looping the cord down and around on the legs of the frame. Each knot was triple-tied.

"There! See if you can get out of that!"

As George opened his mouth to speak, Gil glared at him and the old man shut it with an almost audible snap.

"That's the spirit," Gil said softly.

He pulled the knife out of his shirt and held its six inch blade up before George. The old man's eyes widened.

"Nice, isn't it? I snatched it from the kitchen of that wimpy Monroe Neuropsychiatric Institute. Would've preferred getting myself a gun, but none of the guards there were armed. Still, I can do a whole lot of damage with something like this and still not kill you. Understand what I'm saying to you, old man?"

George nodded vigorously.

"Good. Now what we're going to have here tonight is a nice quiet little house. No noise, no talk. Just a good night's sleep for both of us. Then we'll see what tomorrow brings."

He gave George one last hard look straight in the eye, then turned and headed back to the couch.

Before sacking out for the night, Gil went through George's check book. Not a whole lot of money in it. Most of the checks went out to cash or to the township for quarterly taxes. He noticed one good-sized regular monthly deposit that was probably his Social Security check, and lots of smaller sporadic additions.

He looked through the three undeposited checks. They were all made out to George Haskins, each from a different greeting card company. The attached invoices indicated they were in payment for varying numbers of verses.

Verses?

You mean old George back there tied up to the bed was a poet? He wrote greeting card verse?

Gil looked around the room. Where? There was no desk in the shack. Hell, he hadn't seen a piece of paper since he got here! Where did George write this stuff?

He went back to the bedroom. He did his best not to show the relief he felt when he saw that old George was still tied up nice and tight.

"Hey, old man," he said, waving the checks in the air. "How come you never told me you were a poet?"

George glared at him. "Those checks are mine! I need them to pay my taxes!"

"Yeah? Well, right now I need them a lot more than you do. I think tomorrow morning we'll make a little trip down to the bank so you can cash these." He checked the balance in the account. "And I think you just might make a cash withdrawal, too."

"I'll lose my land if I don't pay those taxes on time!"

"Well then, I guess you'll just have to come up with some more romantic 'verses' for these card companies. Like, 'George is a poet /

And nobody know it.' See? It's easy!"

Gil laughed as he thought of all the broads who get those flowery, syrupy birthday and anniversary cards and sit mooning over the romantic poems inside, never knowing they were written by this dirty old man in a falling down shack on Long Island!

"I love it!" he said, heading back to the couch. "I just love it!"

He turned out all the lights, shoved the knife between two of the cushions, and bedded down on the dusty old couch for the night. As he drifted off to sleep, he thought he heard rustling movements from under the floorboards. George's 'tenants', no doubt. He shuddered at the thought. The sooner he was out of here, the better.

———

What time is it?

Gil was rubbing the sleep from his eyes and peering around in the mineshaft blackness that surrounded him. Something had awakened him. But what? He sat perfectly still and listened.

A few crickets, maybe a frog—the noises seemed to come from outside instead of from the crawlspace—but nothing more than that.

Still, his senses were tingling with the feeling that something was wrong. He stood up and stepped over toward the light switch. As he moved, his foot caught on something and he fell forward. On the way down his ribs slammed against something else, something hard, like a chair. He hit the floor with his left shoulder. Groaning, he got to his knees and crawled until his fingers found the wall. He fumbled around for the light switch and flipped it.

When his eyes had adjusted to the glare, he glanced at the clock over the kitchen sink—going on 4:00 a.m. He thought he saw something move by the sink but when he squinted for a better look, it was just some junk George had left there. Then he turned back toward the couch to see what had tripped him up.

It was the little hassock that had been over by the rocking chair when he had turned the lights out. At least he was pretty sure it had been there. He *knew* it hadn't been next to the couch where it was now. And the chair he had hit on his way down—that had been over against the wall.

In fact, as he looked around he noticed that not a single piece of furniture in the whole room was where it had been when he had turned out the lights and gone to sleep three or four hours ago. It had all been moved closer to the couch.

Someone was playing games. And Gil only knew of one possible someone.

Retrieving his knife from the couch, he hurried to the bedroom and stopped dead at the door. George was tied hand and foot to the corners of the bed, snoring loudly.

A chill rippled over Gil's skin.

"How the hell...?"

He went back to the main room and checked the door and windows—all were locked from the inside. He looked again at the furniture, clustered around the couch as if the pieces had crept up and watched him as he slept.

Gil didn't believe in ghosts but he was beginning to believe this little shack was haunted.

And he wanted out.

He had seen the keys to the old Torino in one of the drawers. He found them again and hurried outside to the car. He hoped the damn thing started. He wasn't happy about hitting the road so soon, but he preferred taking his chances with the cops out in the open to being cooped up with whatever was haunting that shack.

As he slipped behind the wheel, he noticed a sliver of light shining out from inside the shack's foundation. That was *weird*. Really weird. Nobody kept a light on in a crawlspace. He was about to turn the ignition key but held up. He knew it was going to drive him nuts if he left without seeing what was down there.

Cursing himself for a jerk, he turned on the Ford's headlamps and got out for a closer look.

The light was leaking around a piece of plywood fitted into an opening in the foundation cinder blocks. It was hinged at the bottom and held closed by a short length of one-by-two shoved through the handle at the top. He pulled out the one-by-two and hesitated.

Connors, you are an asshole, he told himself, but he had to see what was in there. If it was snakes and snapping turtles, fine. That would be bad enough. But if it was something worse, he had to know.

Gripping the knife tightly in one hand, he yanked the board toward him with the other and quickly peered in, readying himself to slam it shut in an instant. But what he saw within so shocked him he almost dropped the knife.

There was a furnished apartment inside.

The floor of the crawlspace was carpeted. It was worn, industrial grade carpet, but it was *carpet*. There were chairs, tables, bunk beds, the works. A fully furnished apartment...with a ceiling two feet high.

Everything was doll size except the typewriter. That was a portable electric model that looked huge in contrast to everything else.

Maybe George wasn't really crazy after all. One thing was certain: The old fart had been lying to him. There were no snakes and snapping turtles living down here in his crawlspace.

But just what the hell *was* living down here?

Gil headed back inside to ask the only man who really knew.

As he strode through the big room, his foot caught on something and he went down again, landing square on his belly. It took him a moment to catch his breath, then he rolled over and looked to see what had tripped him.

It wasn't the hassock this time. A length of slim cord was stretched between the leg of the couch and an eye-hook that had been screwed into the wall.

"Son of a bitch!"

He got up and continued on his way—carefully now, scanning the path for more trip ropes. There were none. He made it to the bedroom without falling again—

—and found George sitting on the edge of the bed, massaging his wrists.

Dammit! Every time he turned around it was something else! He could feel the anger and frustration begin to bubble up toward the overflow levels.

"Who the hell untied you?"

"I ain't talking to you."

Gil pointed the knife at him. "You'll talk, old man, or I'll skin you alive!"

"Leave him alone and leave our home!"

It was a little voice, high-pitched without being squeaky, and it came from directly behind him. Gil whirled and saw a fully dressed little man—or something squat, hairy, and bullnecked that came pretty close to looking like a little man—no more than a foot and a half high, standing outside the bedroom door. By the time Gil realized what he was looking at, the creature had started to run.

Gil's first thought was, I'm going crazy! But suddenly he had an explanation for that two-foot high furnished apartment in the crawl-space, and for the moving furniture and trip cords.

He bolted after it. Here was what had been tormenting him tonight! He'd get the little sucker and—

He tripped again. A cord that hadn't been there a moment ago was stretched across the narrow hall. Gil went down on one knee and bounded up again. He'd been half ready for that one. They weren't going to—

Something caught him across the chin and his feet went out from under him. He landed flat on his back and felt a sharp, searing pain in his right thigh. He looked down and saw he had jabbed himself in the leg with his own knife during the fall.

Gil leapt to his feet, the pain a distant cry amid the blood rage that hammered though his brain. He roared and slashed at the rope that had damn near taken his head off and charged into the big room. There he saw not one but two of the little bastards. A chant filled the air:

"Leave him alone and leave our home! Leave him alone and leave our home!"

Over and over, from a good deal more than two voices. He couldn't see any others. How many of the little runts were there? No matter. He'd deal with these two first, then hunt down the others and get to the bottom of this.

The pair split, one darting to the left, the other to the right. Gil wasn't going to let them both escape. He took a single step and launched himself through the air at the one fleeing leftward. He landed with a bone-jarring crash on the floor but his outstretched free hand caught the leg of the fleeing creature. It was hairier than he had realized—furry, really—and it struggled in his grasp, screeching and thrashing like a wild animal as he pulled it toward him. He squeezed it harder and it bit his thumb. Hard. He howled with the pain, hauled the thing back, and flung it against the nearest wall.

Its screeching stopped as it landed against the wall with an audible crunch and fell to the floor, but the chant went on:

"...our home! Leave him alone, and leave our home! Leave him..."

"God damn it!" Gil said, sucking on his bleeding thumb. It hurt like hell.

Then he saw the thing start to move. Mewling in pain, it had begun a slow crawl toward one of the piles of junk in the corner.

"No, you don't!" Gil shouted.

The pain, the rage, that goddamn chant, they all came together in a black cloud of fury that engulfed him. No way was he going to let that little shit get away and set more booby traps for him. Through that cloud, he charged across the room, lifted the thing up with his left hand, and raised the knife in his right. Dimly he heard a voice shouting somewhere behind him but he ignored it.

He rammed the knife through the damned thing, pinning it to the wall.

The chant stopped abruptly, cut off in mid verse. All he could hear was George's wail.

"Oh, no! Oh, Lord, no!"

George stood in the hall and stared at the tiny figure impaled on the wall, watched it squirm as dark fluid flowed down the peeling wallpaper. Then it went slack. He didn't know the little guy's name—they all looked pretty much the same through his cataracts—but he felt like he'd lost an old friend. His anguish was a knife lodged in his own chest.

"You've killed him! Oh, God!"

Gil glared at him, his eyes wild, his breathing ragged. Saliva dripped from a corner of his mouth. He was far over the edge.

"Right, old man. And I'm gonna get the other one and do the same to him!"

George couldn't let that happen. The little guys were his responsibility. He was their protector. He couldn't just stand here like a useless scarecrow.

He launched himself at Gil, his long, nicotine-stained fingernails extended like claws, raking for the younger man's eyes. But Gil pushed him aside easily, knocking him to the floor with a casual swipe if his arm. Pain blazed through George's left hip as he landed, shooting down his leg like a bolt of white hot lightning.

"You're next, you worthless old shit!" Gil screamed. "Soon as I finish with the other little squirt!"

George sobbed as he lay on the floor. If only he were younger, stronger. Even ten years ago he probably could have kicked this punk out on his ass. Now all he could do was lie here on the floor like the worthless old half-blind cripple he was. He pounded the floor helplessly. Might as well be dead!

Suddenly he saw another of the little guys dash across the floor toward the couch, saw the punk spot him and leap after him.

"Run!" George screamed. "*Run!*"

Gil rammed his shoulder against the back of the couch as he shoved his arm far beneath it, slashing back and forth with the knife, trying to get a piece of the second runt. But the blade cut only air and dust bunnies.

As he began to withdraw his arm, he felt something snake over his hand and tighten on his wrist. He tried to yank away but the cord—he was sure it was a cord like the one he had used to truss George—tightened viciously.

A slip knot!

The other end must have been tied to one of the couch legs. He tried to slash at the cord with the knife but he couldn't get the right angle. He reached under with his free left hand to get the knife and realized too late that they must have been waiting for him to do that very thing. He felt another noose tighten over that wrist—

—and still another over his right ankle.

The first cold trickles of fear ran down Gil's spine.

In desperation he tried to tip the couch over to give him some room to maneuver but it wouldn't budge. Just then something bit deeply into his right hand. He tried to shake it off and in doing so he loosened his grip on the knife. It was immediately snatched from his grasp.

At that moment the fourth noose tightened around his left ankle, and he knew he was in deep shit.

They let him lay there for what must have been an hour. He strained at the ropes, trying to break them, trying to untie the knots. All he accomplished was to sink their coils more deeply into his flesh. He wanted to scream out his rage—and his fear—but he wouldn't give them the satisfaction. He heard George moving around somewhere behind him, groaning with pain, heard little voices—How many of the little fuckers were there, anyway?—talking in high-pitched whispers. There seemed to be an argument going on. Finally, it was resolved.

Then came a tugging on the cords as new ones were tied around his wrists and ankles and old ones released. Suddenly he was flipped over onto his back.

He saw George sitting in the rocker holding an ice pack to his left hip. And on the floor there were ten—*Jesus*, ten of them!—foot-and-a-half tall furry little men standing in a semi-circle, staring at him.

One of them stepped forward. He was dressed in doll clothes: a dark blue pullover—it even had an Izod alligator on the left breast—and tan slacks. He had the face of a sixty-year-old man with a barrel chest and furry arms and legs. He pointed at Gil's face and spoke in a high-pitched voice:

"C'ham is dead and it's on your head."

Gil started to laugh. It was like landing in Munchkinland, but then he saw the look in the little man's eyes and knew this was not one of the Lollipop Kids. The laugh died in his throat.

He glanced up at the wall where he'd pinned the first little runt like a bug on a board and saw only a dark stain.

The talking runt gestured two others forward and they approached Gil, dragging his knife. He tried the squirm away from them but the ropes didn't allow for much movement.

"Hey, now, wait a minute! What're you—?"

"The decision's made: You'll make the trade."

Gill was beginning to know terror. "Forget the goddamn rhymes! What's going on here?"

"Hold your nose," the talking runt said to the pair with the knife, "and cut off his clothes. Best be cautious lest he make you nauseous."

Gil winced as the blade began to slice along the seams of his shirt, waiting for the sharp edge to cut him. But it never touched him.

———

George watched as the little guys stripped Connors. He had no idea what they were up to and he didn't care. He felt like more of a failure than ever. He'd never done much with his life, but at least since the end of the Sixties he had been able to tell himself that he had provided a safe harbor for the last of the world's Little People.

When had it been—Sixty-nine, maybe—when all eleven of them had first shown up at his door looking for shelter. They'd said they were waiting for "when time is unfurled and we're called by the world." He hadn't the vaguest notion what that meant but he'd experienced an immediate rapport with them. They were Outsiders, just like he was. And when they offered to pay rent, the deal was sealed.

He smiled. That rhymed. If you listened to them enough, you began to sound like them. Since they spoke in rhyme all the time—there was another one—it was nothing for them to crank out verse for the greeting card companies. Some of the stuff was pretty sappy, but it paid the taxes.

But what next? One of the little guys had been murdered by this psycho who now knew their secret. Soon all the world would know about these Little People. George had doubly failed at his job: He hadn't protected them and hadn't kept their secret. He was just what the punk had called him: a worthless old shit.

He heard Connors groan and looked up. He was nude as a jaybird and the little guys had tied him with new ropes looped through rings fastened high on the walls at each end of the room. They were hauling him off the floor, stringing him across the room like laundry hung out to dry.

George suddenly realized that although he wasn't too pleased with being George Haskins, at this particular moment he preferred it by far to being Gilroy Connors.

Gil felt as if his arms and legs were going to come out of their sockets as the runts hauled him off the floor and stretched him out in the air. For a moment he feared that might be their plan, but when he got half way between the floor and the ceiling, they stopped pulling on the ropes.

He couldn't ever remember feeling so damn helpless in all his life.

The lights went out and he heard a lot of shuffling below him but he couldn't see what they were doing. Then came the sound, a new chant, high-pitched and staccato in a language he had never heard before, a language that didn't seem at home on the human tongue.

A soft glow began to rise from below him. He wished he could see what they were doing. All he could do was watch their weird shadows on the ceiling. So far they hadn't caused him too much pain, but he was beginning to feel weak and dizzy. His back got warm while his front grew cold and numb, like there was a cool wind coming from the ceiling and passing right through him, carrying his energy with it. All of his juice seemed to be flowing downward and collecting in his back.

So tired...and his back felt so heavy. What were they doing below him?

They were glowing.

George had watched them carry C'ham, their dead member, to a spot directly below Connor's suspended body. They had placed one of George's coffee mugs at C'ham's feet, then they stripped off their clothes and gathered in a circle around him. They had started to chant. After a while, a faint yellow light began to shimmer around their furry little bodies.

George found the ceremony fascinating in a weird sort of way—until the glow brightened and flowed up to illuminate the suspended punk. Then even George's lousy eyes could see the horror of what was happening to Gilroy Connors.

His legs, arms, and belly were a cold dead white, but his back was a deep red-purple color, like a gigantic bruise, and it bulged like the belly of a mother-to-be carrying triplets. George could not imagine how the skin was holding together, it was stretched so tight. Looked like it would rupture any minute. George shielded his face, waiting for the splatter. But when it didn't come, he chanced another peek.

It was raining on the Little People.

The skin hadn't ruptured as George had feared. No, a fine red mist was falling from Connors' body. Red microdroplets were slipping from the pores in the purpled swelling on his back and falling through the yellow glow, turning it orange. The scene was as beautiful as it was horrifying.

The bloody dew fell for something like half an hour, then the glow faded and one of the little guys boosted another up to the wall switch and the lights came on. George did not have to strain his eyes to know that Gilroy Connors was dead.

As the circle dissolved, he noticed that the dead little guy was gone. Only the mug remained under Conners.

George found his mouth dry when he tried to speak.

"What happened to... to the one he stabbed?"

"C'ham?" said the leader. George knew this one; his name was Kob. "He's over there."

Sure enough. There were ten little guys standing over by the couch, one of them looking weak and being supported by the others.

"But I thought—"

"Yes. C'ham was dead, but now he's back because of the Crimson Dew."

"And the other one?"

Kob glanced over his shoulder at Connors. "I understand there's a reward for his capture. You should have it. And there's something else you should have."

The little man stepped under Connors' suspended body and

returned with the coffee mug.

"This is for you," he said, holding it up.

George took the mug and saw that it was half-filled with a thin red-dish liquid.

"What am I supposed to do with this?"

"Drink it."

George's stomach turned. "But it's... from him."

"Of course. From him to you." Kob gave George's calf a gentle slap. "We need you George. You're our shield from the world—"

"Some shield!" George said.

"It's true. You've protected us from prying eyes and we need you to go on doing that for some time to come."

"I don't think I've got much time left."

"That's why you should drain that cup."

"What do you mean?"

"Think of it as extending your lease," Kob said.

George looked over at C'ham who'd surely been dead half an hour ago and now was up and walking about. He looked down into the cup again.

...extending your lease.

Well, after what he'd just seen, he guessed anything might be possible.

Tightening his throat against an incipient gag, George raised the cup to his lips and sipped. The fluid was lukewarm and salty—like a bouillon that had been allowed to cool too long. Not good, but not awful, either. He squeezed his eyes shut and chugged the rest. It went down and stayed down, thank the Lord.

"Good!" Kob shouted, and the ten other Little People applauded.

"Now you can help us cut him down and carry him outside."

"So what're you going to do with all that money, George?" Bill said as he handed George the day's mail.

"I ain't got it yet."

George leaned against the roof of the mail truck and dragged on his cigarette. He felt good. His morning backache was pretty much a thing of the past, and he could pee with the best of them—hit a wall from six feet away, he bet. His breathing was better than it had been in thirty years. And best of all, he could stand here and see all the way south along the length of the harbor to downtown Monroe. He didn't like to think about what had been in that mug Kob had handed him, but in the ten days since he had swallowed it down he had come to feel decades younger.

He wished he had some more of it.

"Still can't get over how lucky you were to find him laying in the grass over there," Bill said, glancing across the road. "Especially lucky he wasn't alive from what I heard about him."

"Guess so," George said.

"I understand they still can't explain how he died or why he was all dried up like a mummy."

"Yeah, it's a mystery, all right."

"So when you do get the fifty thou—what are you going to spend it on?"

"Make a few improvements on the old place, I guess. Get me some legal help to see if somehow I can get this area declared off-limits to developers. But mostly set up some sort of fund to keep paying the taxes until that comes to pass."

Bill laughed and let up on the mail truck's brake. "Not ready for the old folks' home yet?" he said as he lurched away.

"Not by a long shot!"

I've got responsibilities, he thought. And tenants to keep happy.

He shuddered.

Yes, he certainly wanted to keep those little fellows happy.

I'd planned on writing three 10,000word novelettes for *Night Visions* 6. I wound up doing four.

Sometime in November I sent Paul Mikol three stories adding up to the 30,000 words of new fiction I'd promised. He called back a few weeks later to say that the third story, "Ethics," was a little too light-hearted and too much like "Feelings." Could I do another in its place? My immediate reaction was, *He's nuts.* But I said I'd think about it. I went back to the two stories in question and reread them back to back.

He was right. I'd written "Feelings" and the other piece months apart and hadn't seen the similarities.

So here it was almost December and I needed 10K words of new fiction. I'd been perking a story about a serial killer (this was 1987, before *The Silence of the Lambs* and the serial killer glut) but one with a differ-ence. This one would be female (they're almost always male), hideously deformed and... sympathetic. I felt if I could tell you about the forces driving Carly to these murderous acts—her childhood, her needs, her emotional hungers—you might understand her. You might even find some sort of love for her.

Years later I happened to reread Richard Matheson's "Born of Man and Woman" and realized what a significant—though unconscious—influence it had on my story. I now believe Carly is Matheson's little girl all grown up.

To date, "Faces" is my most reprinted story and remains one of my favorites.

Connections: Carly Baker and Annie Harrison were part of what would come to be known as "the Monroe cluster," all conceived just about the same time Carol Stevens conceived her child in *Reborn*. (More members of the cluster appear in *Conspiracies*.)

Faces

Bite her face off.

No pain. Her dead already. Kill her quick like others. Not want make pain. Not her fault.

The boyfriend groan but not move. Face way on ground now. Got from behind. Got quick. Never see. He can live.

Girl look me after the boyfriend go down. Gasp first. When see face start scream. Two claws not cut short rip her throat before sound get loud.

Her sick-scared look just like all others. Hate that look. Hate it terrible.

Sorry, girl. Not your fault.

Chew her face skin. Chew all. Chew hard and swallow. Warm wet redness make sickish but chew and chew. Must eat face. Must get all down. Keep down.

Leave the eyes.

The boyfriend groan again. Move arm. Must leave quick. Take last look blood and teeth and stare-eyes that once pretty girlface.

Sorry, girl. Not your fault.

Got go. Get way hurry. First take money. Girl money. Take the boyfriend wallet, also too. Always take money. Need money.

Go now. Not too far. Climb wall of near building. Find dark spot where can see and not be seen. Where can wait. Soon the Detective Harrison arrive.

In downbelow can see the boyfriend roll over. Get to knees. Sway. See him look the girlfriend.

The boyfriend scream terrible. Bad to hear. Make so sad. Make cry.

Kevin Harrison heard Jacobi's voice on the other end of the line and wanted to be sick.

"Don't say it," he groaned.

"Sorry," said Jacobi. "It's another one."

"Where?"

"West Forty-ninth, right near—"

"I'll find it." All he had to do was look for the flashing red lights.

"I'm on my way. Shouldn't take me too long to get in from Monroe at this hour."

"We've got all night, lieutenant." Unsaid, but well understood, was an admonishing, *You're the one who wants to live on Long Island.*

Beside him in the bed, Martha spoke from deep in her pillow as he hung up.

"Not another one?"

"Yeah."

"Oh, God! When is it going to stop?"

"When I catch the guy."

Her hand touched his arm, gently. "I know all this responsibility's not easy. I'm here when you need me."

"I know." He leaned over and kissed her. "Thanks."

He left the warm bed and skipped the shower. No time for that. A fresh shirt, yesterday's rumpled suit, a tie shoved into his pocket, and he was off into the winter night.

With his secure little ranch house falling away behind him, Harrison felt naked and vulnerable out here in the dark. As he headed south on Glen Cove Road toward the LIE, he realized that Martha and the kids were all that were holding him together these days. His family had become an island of sanity and stability in a world gone mad.

Everything else was in flux. For reasons he still could not comprehend, he had volunteered to head up the search for this killer. Now his whole future in the department had come to hinge on his success in finding him.

The papers had named the maniac "the Facelift Killer." As apt a name as the tabloids could want, but Harrison resented it. The moniker was callous, trivializing the mutilations perpetrated on the victims. But it had caught on with the public and they were stuck with it, especially with all the ink the story was getting.

Six killings, one a week for six weeks in a row, and eight million people in a panic. Then, for almost two weeks, the city had gone without a new slaying.

Until tonight.

Harrison's stomach pitched and rolled at the thought of having to look at one of those faceless corpses again.

"That's enough," Harrison said, averting his eyes from the faceless corpse.

The raw, gouged, bloody flesh, the exposed muscle and bone were bad enough, but it was the eyes—those naked, lidless, staring eyes were the worst.

"This makes seven," Jacobi said at his side. Squat, dark, jowly, the sergeant was chewing a big wad of gum, noisily, aggressively, as if he had a grudge against it.

"I can count. Anything new?"

"Nah. Same M.O. as ever—throat slashed, money stolen, face gnawed off."

Harrison shuddered. He had come in as Special Investigator after the third Facelift killing. He had inspected the first three via coroner's photos. Those had been awful. But nothing could match the effect of the real thing up close and still warm and oozing. This was the fourth fresh victim he had seen. There was no getting used to this kind of mutilation, no matter how many he saw. Jacobi put on a good show, but Harrison sensed the revulsion under the sergeant's armor.

And yet...

Beneath all the horror, Harrison sensed something. There was anger here, sick anger and hatred of spectacular proportions. But beyond that, something else, an indefinable something that had drawn him to this case. Whatever it was, that something called to him, and still held him captive.

If he could identify it, maybe he could solve this case and wrap it up. And save his ass.

If he did solve it, it would be all on his own. Because he wasn't getting much help from Jacobi, and even less from his assigned staff. He knew what they all thought—that he had taken the job as a glory grab, a shortcut to the top. Sure, they wanted to see this thing wrapped up, too, but they weren't shedding any tears over the shit he was taking in the press and on TV and from City Hall.

Their attitude was clear: *If you want the spotlight, Harrison, you gotta take the heat that goes with it.*

They were right, of course. He could have been working on a quieter case, like where all the winos were disappearing to. He'd chosen this instead. But he wasn't after the spotlight, dammit! It was this case—something about this case!

He suddenly realized that there was no one around him. The body had been carted off, Jacobi had wandered back to his car. He had been left standing alone at the far end of the alley.

And yet not alone.

Someone was watching him. He could feel it. The realization sent a little chill—one completely unrelated to the cold February wind—trickling down his back. A quick glance around showed no one paying him the slightest bit of attention. He looked up.

There!

Somewhere in the darkness above, someone was watching him. Probably from the roof. He could sense the piercing scrutiny and it made him a little weak. That was no ghoulish neighborhood voyeur, up there. That was the Facelift Killer.

He had to get to Jacobi, have him seal off the building. But he couldn't act spooked. He had to act calm, casual.

See the Detective Harrison's eyes. See from way up in dark. Tall-thin. Hair brown. Nice eyes. Soft brown eyes. Not hard like many-many eyes. Look here. Even from here see eyes make wide. Him know it me.

Watch the Detective Harrison turn slow. Walk slow. Tell inside him want to run. Must leave here. Leave quick.

Bend low. Run cross roof. Jump to next. And next. Again till most block away. Then down wall. Wrap scarf round head. Hide bad-face. Hunch inside big-big coat. Walk through lighted spots.

Hate light. Hate crowds. Theatres here. Movies and plays. Like them. Some night sneak in and see. See one with man in mask. Hang from wall behind big drapes. Make cry.

Wish there mask for me.

Follow street long way to river. See many light across river. Far past there is place where grew. Never want go back to there. Never.

Catch back of truck. Ride home.

Home. Bright bulb hang ceiling. Not care. The Old Jessi waiting. The Jessi friend. Only friend. The Jessi's eyes not see. Ever. When the Jessi look me, her face not wear sick-scared look. Hate that look.

Come in kitchen window. The Jessi's face wrinkle-black. Smile when hear me come. TV on. Always on. The Jessi cannot watch. Say it company for her.

"You're so late tonight."

"Hard work. Get moneys tonight."

Feel sick. Want cry. Hate kill. Wish stop.

"That's nice. Are you going to put it in the drawer?"

"Doing now."

Empty wallets. Put moneys in slots. Ones first slot. Fives next slot. Then tens and twenties. So the Jessi can pay when boy bring foods. Sometimes eat stolen foods. Mostly the Jessi call for foods.

The Old Jessi hardly walk. Good. Do not want her go out. Bad peoples round here. Many. Hurt one who not see. One bad man try hurt Jessi once. Push through door. Thought only the blind Old Jessi live here.

Lucky the Jessi not alone that day.

Not lucky bad man. Hit the Jessi. Laugh hard. Then look me. Get sick-scared look. Hate that look. Kill him quick. Put in tub. Bleed there. Bad man friend come soon after. Kill him also too. Late at night take both dead bad men out. Go through window. Carry down wall. Throw in river.

No bad men come again. Ever.

"I've been waiting all night for my bath. Do you think you can help me a little?"

Always help. But the Old Jessi always ask. The Jessi very polite.

Sponge the Old Jessi back in tub. Rinse her hair. Think of the Detective Harrison. His kind eyes. Must talk him. Want stop this. Stop now. Maybe will understand. Will. Can feel.

Seven grisly murders in eight weeks.

Kevin Harrison studied a photo of the latest victim, taken before she was mutilated. A nice eight by ten glossy furnished by her agent. A real beauty. A dancer with Broadway dreams.

He tossed the photo aside and pulled the stack of files toward him. The remnants of six lives in this pile. Somewhere within had to be an answer, the thread that linked each of them to the Facelift Killer.

But what if there was no common link? What if all the killings were at random, linked only by the fact that they were beautiful? Seven deaths, all over the city. All with their faces gnawed off. *Gnawed.*

He flipped through the victims one by one and studied their photos. He had begun to feel he knew each one of them personally:

Mary Detrick, 20, a junior at N.Y.U., killed in Washington Square Park on January 5. She was the first.

Mia Chandler, 25, a secretary at Merrill Lynch, killed January 13 in Battery Park.

Ellen Beasley, 22, a photographer's assistant, killed in an alley in Chelsea on January 22.

Hazel Hauge, 30, artist agent, killed in her Soho loft on January 27.

Elisabeth Paine, 28, housewife, killed on February 2 while jogging late in Central Park.

Joan Perrin, 25, a model from Brooklyn, pulled from her car while stopped at a light on the Upper East Side on February 8.

He picked up the eight by ten again. And the last: Liza Lee, 21. Dancer. Lived across the river in Jersey City. Ducked into an alley for a toot with her boyfriend tonight and never came out.

Three blondes, three brunettes, one redhead. Some stacked, some on the flat side. All caucs except for Perrin. All lookers. But besides that, how in the world could these women be linked? They came from all over town, and they met their respective ends all over town. What could—

"Well, you sure hit the bullseye about that roof!" Jacobi said as he burst into the office.

Harrison straightened in his chair. "What you find?"

"Blood."

"Whose?"

"The victim's."

"No prints? No hairs? No fibers?"

"We're working on it. But how'd you figure to check the roof top?"

"Lucky guess."

Harrison didn't want to provide Jacobi with more grist for the departmental gossip mill by mentioning his feeling of being watched from up there.

But the killer *had* been watching, hadn't he?

"Any prelims from pathology?"

Jacobi shrugged and stuffed three sticks of gum into his mouth. Then he tried to talk.

"Same as ever. Money gone, throat ripped open by a pair of sharp pointed instruments, not knives, the bite marks on the face are the usual: the teeth that made them aren't human, but the saliva is."

The "non-human" teeth part—more teeth, bigger and sharper teeth that found in any human mouth—had baffled them all from the start. Early on someone remembered a horror novel or movie where the killer used some weird sort of false teeth to bite his victims. That had sent them off on a wild goose chase to all the dental labs looking for records of bizarre bite prostheses. No dice. No one had seen or even heard of teeth that could gnaw off a person's face.

Harrison shuddered. What could explain wounds like that? What were they dealing with here?

The irritating pops, snaps, and cracks of Jacobi's gum filled the office.

"I liked you better when you smoked."

Jacobi's reply was cut off by the phone. The sergeant picked it up.

"Detective Harrison's office!" he said, listened a moment, then, with his hand over the mouthpiece, passed the receiver to Harrison. "Some fairy wantsh to shpeak to you," he said with an evil grin.

"Fairy?"

"Hey," he said, getting up and walking toward the door. "I don't mind. I'm a liberal kinda guy, y'know?"

Harrison shook his head with disgust. Jacobi was getting less likable every day.

"Hello. Harrison here."

"Shorry dishturb you, Detective Harrishon."

The voice was soft, pitched somewhere between a man's and a woman's, and sounded as if the speaker had half a mouthful of saliva. Harrison had never heard anything like it. Who could be—?

And then it struck him: It was three a.m. Only a handful of people knew he was here.

"Do I know you?"

"No. Watch you tonight. You almosht shee me in dark."

That same chill from earlier tonight ran down Harrison's back again.

"Are...are you who I think you are?"

There was a pause, then one soft word, more sobbed than spoken: *"Yesh."*

If the reply had been cocky—something along the line of *And just who do you think I am?*—Harrison would have looked for much more in the way of corroboration. But that single word, and the soul deep heartbreak that propelled it, banished all doubt.

My God! He looked around frantically. No one in sight. Where the fuck was Jacobi now when he needed him? This was the Facelift Killer! He needed a trace!

Got to keep him on the line!

"I have to ask you something to be sure you are who you say you are."

"Yesh?"

"Do you take anything from the victims—I mean, besides their faces?"

"Money. Take money."

This is him! The department had withheld the money part from the papers. Only the real Facelift Killer could know!

"Can I ask you something else?"

"Yesh."

Harrison was asking this one for himself.

"What do you do with the faces?"

He had to know. The question drove him crazy at night. He dreamed about those faces. Did the killer tack them on the wall, or press them in a book, or freeze them, or did he wear them around the house like that Leatherface character from that chainsaw movie?

On the other end of the line he sensed sudden agitation and panic: *"No! Cannot shay! Can not!"*

"Okay, okay. Take it easy."

"You will help shtop?"

"Oh, yes! Oh, God, yes, I'll help you stop!" He prayed his genuine heartfelt desire to end this was coming through. "I'll help you any way I can!"

A long pause, then:

"You hate? Hate me?"

Harrison didn't trust himself to answer that right away. He searched his feelings quickly, but carefully.

"No," he said finally. "I think you have done some awful, horrible things but, strangely enough, I don't hate you."

And that was true. Why didn't he hate this murdering maniac? Oh, he wanted to stop him more than anything in the world, and wouldn't hesitate to shoot him dead if the situation required it, but there was no personal hatred for the Facelift Killer.

What is it in you that speaks to me? he wondered.

"Shank you," said the voice, couched once more in a sob.

And then the killer hung up.

Harrison shouted into the dead phone, banged it on his desk, but the line was dead.

"What the hell's the matter with you?" Jacobi said from the office door.

"That so-called 'fairy' on the phone was the Facelift Killer, you idiot! We could have had a trace if you'd stuck around!"

"Bullshit!"

"He knew about taking the money!"

"So why'd he talk like that? That's a dumb-ass way to try to disguise your voice."

And then it suddenly hit Harrison like a sucker punch to the gut. He swallowed hard and said:

"Jacobi, how do you think your voice would sound if you had a mouth crammed full of teeth much larger and sharper than the kind found in the typical human mouth?"

Harrison took genuine pleasure in the way Jacobi's face blanched slowly to yellow-white.

———

He didn't get home again until after seven the following night. The whole department had been in an uproar all day. This was the first break they had had in the case. It wasn't much, but contact had been made. That was the important part. And although Harrison had done nothing he could think of to deserve any credit, he had accepted the commissioner's compliments and encouragement on the phone shortly before he had left the office tonight.

But what was most important to Harrison was the evidence from the call—Damn! he wished it had been taped—that the killer wanted to stop. They didn't have one more goddam clue tonight than they'd had yesterday, but the call offered hope that soon there might be an end to this horror.

Martha had dinner waiting. The kids were scrubbed and pajamaed and waiting for their goodnight kiss. He gave them each a hug and poured himself a stiff scotch while Martha put them in the sack.

"Do you feel as tired as you look?" she said as she returned from the bedroom wing.

She was a big woman with bright blue eyes and natural dark blond hair. Harrison toasted her with his glass.

"The expression 'dead on his feet' has taken on a whole new meaning for me."

She kissed him, then they sat down to eat.

He had spoken to Martha a couple of times since he had left the house twenty hours ago. She knew about the phone call from the Facelift Killer, about the new hope in the department about the case, but he was glad she didn't bring it up now. He was sick of talking about it. Instead, he sat in front of his cooling meatloaf and wrestled with the images that had been nibbling at the edges of his consciousness all day.

"What are you daydreaming about?" Martha said.

Without thinking, Harrison said, "Annie."

"Annie who?"

"My sister."

Martha put her fork down. "Your sister? Kevin, you don't have a sister."

"Not any more. But I did."

Her expression was alarmed now. "Kevin, are you all right? I've known your family for ten years. You mother has never once mentioned—"

"We don't talk about Annie, Mar. We try not to even think about her. She died when she was five."

"Oh. I'm sorry."

"Don't be. Annie was...deformed. Terribly deformed. She never really had a chance."

Open trunk from inside. Get out. The Detective Harrison's house here. Cold night. Cold feel good. Trunk air make sick, dizzy.

Light here. Hurry round side of house.

Darker here. No one see. Look in window. Dark but see good. Two little ones there. Sleeping. Move away. Not want them cry.

Go more round. The Detective Harrison with lady. Sit table near window. Must be wife. Pretty but not oh-so-beauty. Not have mom-face. Not like ones who die.

Watch behind tree. Hungry. They not eat food. Talk-talk-talk. Cannot hear.

The Detective Harrison do most talk. Kind face. Kind eyes. Some terrible sad there. Hides. Him understands. Heard in phone voice. Understands. Him one can stop kills.

Spent day watch the Detective Harrison car. All day watch at police house. Saw him come-go many times. Soon dark, open trunk with claw. Ride with him. Ride long. Wonder what town this?

The Detective Harrison look this way. Stare like last night. Must not see me! Must *not!*

Harrison stopped in mid-sentence and stared out the window as his skin prickled.

That *watched* feeling again.

It was the same as last night. Something was out in the backyard watching them. He strained to see through the wooded darkness outside the window but saw only shadows within shadows.

But something was there! He could feel it!

He got up and turned on the outside spotlights, hoping, praying that the backyard would be empty.

It was.

He smiled to hide his relief and glanced at Martha.

"Thought that raccoon was back."

He left the spots on and settled back into his place at the table. But the thoughts racing through his mind made eating unthinkable.

What if that maniac had followed him out here? What if the call had been a ploy to get him off-guard so the Facelife Killer could do to Martha what he had done to the other women?

My God...

First thing tomorrow morning he was going to call the local alarm boys and put in a security system. Cost be damned, he had to have it. Immediately!

As for tonight...

Tonight he'd keep the .38 under the pillow.

————

Run way. Run low and fast. Get bushes before light come. Must stay way now. Not come back.

The Detective Harrison *feel* me. Know when watched. Him the one, sure.

Walk in dark, in woods. See back many houses. Come park. Feel strange. See this park before. Cannot be—

Then know.

Monroe! This Monroe! Born here! Live here! Hate Monroe! Monroe bad place, bad people! House, home, old home near here! There! Cross park! Old home! New color but same house.

Hate house!

Sit on froze park grass. Cry. Why Monroe? Do not want be in Monroe. The Mom gone. The Sissy gone. The Jimmy very gone. House here.

Dry tears. Watch old home long time till light go out. Wait more. Go to windows. See new folks inside. The Mom must took the Sissy and go. Where? How long?

Go to back. Push cellar window. Crawl in. See good in dark. New folks make nice cellar. Wood on walls. Rug on floor. No chain.

Sit floor. Remember...

Remember hanging on wall. Look little window near ceiling. Watch kids play in park cross street. Want go with kids. Want play there with kids. Want have friends.

But the Mom won't let. Never leave basement. Too strong. Break everything. Have TV. Broke it. Have toys. Broke them. Stay in basement. Chain round waist hold to center pole. Cannot leave.

Remember terrible bad things happen.

Run. Run way Monroe. Never come back.

Till now.

Now back. Still hate house! Want hurt house. See cigarettes. With matches. Light all. Burn now!

Watch rug burn. Chair burn. So hot. Run back to cold park. Watch house burn. See new folks run out. Trucks come throw water. House burn and burn.

Glad but tears come anyway.

Hate house. Now house gone. Hate Monroe.

Wonder where the Mom and the Sissy live now.

Leave Monroe for new home and the Old Jessi.

The second call came the next day. And this time they were ready for it. The tape recorders were set, the computers were waiting to begin the tracing protocol. As soon as Harrison recognized the voice, he gave the signal. On the other side of the desk, Jacobi put on a headset and people started running in all directions. Off to the races.

"I'm glad you called," Harrison said. "I've been thinking about you."

"You undershtand?" said the soft voice.

"I'm not sure."

"*Musht help shtop.*"

"I will! I will! Tell me how!"

"*Not know.*"

Harrison paused, not sure what to say next. He didn't want to push, but he had to keep him on the line.

"Did you...hurt anyone last night?"

"*No. Shaw houshes. Your houshe. Your wife.*"

Harrison's blood froze. Last night—in the back yard. That had been the Facelift Killer in the dark. He looked up and saw genuine concern in Jacobi's eyes. He forced himself to speak.

"You were at my house? Why didn't you talk to me?"

"*No-no! Cannot let shee! Run way your house. Go mine!*"

"Yours? You live in Monroe?"

"*No! Hate Monroe! Once lived. Gone long! Burn old houshe. Never go back!*"

This could be important. Harrison phrased the next question carefully.

"You burned your old house? When was that?"

If he could just get a date, a year...

"*Lasht night.*"

"Last night?" Harrison remembered hearing the sirens and fire horns in the early morning darkness.

"*Yesh! Hate houshe!*"

And then the line went dead.

———

He looked at Jacobi who had picked up another line.

"Did we get the trace?"

"Waiting to hear. Christ, he sounds retarded, doesn't he?"

Retarded. The word sent ripples across the surface of his brain. Non-human teeth...Monroe...retarded...a picture was forming in the settling sediment, a picture he felt he should avoid.

"Maybe he is."

"You'd think that would make him easy to—"

Jacobi stopped, listened to the receiver, then shook his head disgustedly.

"What?"

"Got as far as the Lower East Side. He was probably calling from somewhere in one of the projects. If we'd had another thirty seconds—"

"We've got something better than a trace to some lousy pay phone," Harrison said. "We've got his old address!" He picked up his suit coat and headed for the door.

"Where we goin'?"

"Not 'we.' Me. I'm going out to Monroe."

Once he reached the town, it took Harrison less than an hour to find the Facelift Killer's last name.

He first checked with the Monroe Fire Department to find the address of last night's house fire. Then he went down to the brick fronted Town Hall and found the lot and block number. After that it was easy to look up its history of ownership. Mr. and Mrs. Elwood Scott were the current owners of the land and the charred shell of a three-bedroom ranch that sat upon it.

There had only been one other set of owners: Mr. and Mrs. Thomas Baker. He had lived most of his life in Monroe but knew nothing about the Baker family. But he knew where to find out: Captain Jeremy Hall, Chief of Police in the Incorporated Village of Monroe.

Captain Hall hadn't changed much over the years. Still had a big belly, long sideburns, and hair cut bristly short on the sides. That was the "in" look these days, but Hall had been wearing his hair like that for at least thirty years. If not for his Bronx accent, he could have played a redneck sheriff in any one of those southern chain gang movies.

After pleasantries and local-boy-leaves-home-to-become-big-city-cop-and-now-comes-to-question-small-town-cop banter, they got down to business.

"The Bakers from North Park Drive?" Hall said after he had noisily sucked the top layer off his steaming coffee. "Who could forget them? There was the mother, divorced, I believe, and the three kids—two girls and the boy."

Harrison pulled out his note pad. "The boy's name—what was it?"

"Tommy, I believe. Yeah—Tommy. I'm sure of it."

"He's the one I want."

Hall's eyes narrowed. "He is, is he? You're working on that Facelift case aren't you?"

"Right."

"And you think Tommy Baker might be your man?"

"It's a possibility. What do you know about him?"

"I know he's dead."

Harrison froze. "Dead? That can't be!"

"It sure as hell *can* be!" Without rising from his seat, he shouted through his office door. "Murph! Pull out that old file on the Baker case! Nineteen eighty-four, I believe!"

"Eighty-four?" Harrison said. He and Martha had been living in Queens then. They hadn't moved back to Monroe yet.

"Right. A real messy affair. Tommy Baker was thirteen years old when he bought it. And he bought it. Believe me, he bought it!"

Harrison sat in glum silence, watching his whole theory go up in smoke.

The Old Jessi sleeps. Stand by mirror near tub. Only mirror have. No like them. The Jessi not need one.

Stare face. Bad face. Teeth, teeth, teeth. And hair. Arms too thin, too long. Claws. None have claws like my. None have face like my.

Face not better. Ate pretty faces but face still same. Still cause sick-scared look. Just like at home.

Remember home. Do not want but thoughts will not go.

Faces.

The Sissy get the Mom-face. Beauty face. The Tommy get the Dad-face. Not see the Dad. Never come home anymore. Who my face? Never see where come. Where my face come? My hands come?

Remember home cellar. Hate home! Hate cellar more! Pull on chain round waist. Pull and pull. Want out. Want play. Please. No one let.

One day when the Mom and the Sissy go, the Tommy bring friends. Come down cellar. Bunch on stairs. Stare. First time see sick-scared look. Not understand.

Friends! Play! Throw ball them. They run. Come back with rocks and sticks. Still sick-scared look. Throw me, hit me.

Make cry. Make the Tommy laugh.

Whenever the Mom and the Sissy go, the Tommy come with boys and sticks. Poke and hit. Hurt. Little hurt on skin. Big hurt inside. Sick-scared look hurt most of all. Hate look. Hate hurt. Hate them.

Most hate the Tommy.

One night chain breaks. Wait on wall for the Tommy. Hurt him. Hurt the Tommy outside. Hurt the Tommy inside. Know because pull inside outside. The Tommy quiet. Quiet, wet, red. The Mom and the Sissy get sick-scared look and scream.

Hate that look. Run way. Hide. Never come back. Till last night.

Cry more now. Cry quiet. In tub. So the Jessi not hear.

Harrison flipped through the slim file on the Tommy Baker murder.

"This is it?"

"We didn't need to collect much paper," Captain Hall said. "I mean, the mother and sister were witnesses. There's some photos in that manila envelope at the back."

Harrison pulled it free and slipped out some large black and whites. His stomach lurched immediately.

"My God!"

"Yeah, he was a mess. Gutted by his older sister."

"His sister?"

"Yeah. Apparently she was some sort of freak of nature."

Harrison felt the floor tilt under him, felt as if he were going to slide off the chair.

"Freak?" he said, hoping Hall wouldn't notice the tremor in his voice. "What did she look like?"

"Never saw her. She took off after she killed the brother. No one's seen hide nor hair of her since. But there's a picture of the rest of the family in there."

Harrison shuffled through the file until he came to a large color family portrait. He held it up. Four people: two adults seated in chairs, a boy and a girl, about ten and eight, kneeling on the floor in front of them. A perfectly normal American family. Four smiling faces.

But where's your oldest child. Where's your big sister? Where did you hide that fifth face while posing for this?

"What was her name? The one who's not here?"

"Not sure. Carla, maybe? Look at the front sheet under Suspect."

Harrison did: "Carla Baker—called 'Carly.'"

Hall grinned. "Right. Carly. Not bad for a guy getting ready for retirement."

Harrison didn't answer. An ineluctable sadness filled him as he stared at the incomplete family portrait.

Carly Baker...poor Carly... where did they hide you away? In the cellar? Locked in the attic? How did your brother treat you? Bad enough to deserve killing?

Probably.

"No pictures of Carly, I suppose."

"Not a one."

That figured.

"How about a description?"

"The mother gave us one but it sounded so weird, we threw it out. I mean, the girl sounded like she was half spider or something!" He drained his cup. "Then later on I got into a discussion with Doc Alberts about it. He told me he was doing deliveries back about the time this kid was born. Said they had a whole rash of monsters, all delivered within a few weeks of each other."

The room started to tilt under Harrison again.

"Early December, 1968, by chance?"

"Yeah! How'd you know?"

He felt queasy. "Lucky guess."

"Huh. Anyway, Doc Alberts said they kept it quiet while they looked into a cause, but that little group of freaks—'cluster,' he called them—was all there was. They figured that a bunch of mothers had been exposed to something nine months before, but whatever it had been was long gone. No monsters since. I understand most of them died shortly after birth, anyway."

"Not all of them."

"Not that it matters," Hall said, getting up and pouring himself a refill from the coffee pot. "Someday someone will find her skeleton, probably somewhere out in Haskins' marshes."

"Maybe." But I wouldn't count on it. He held up the file. "Can I get a Xerox of this?"

———————

"You mean the Facelift Killer is a twenty-year-old girl?"

Martha's face clearly registered her disbelief.

"Not just any girl. A freak. Someone so deformed she really doesn't look human. Completely uneducated and probably mentally retarded to boot."

Harrison hadn't returned to Manhattan. Instead, he'd headed straight for home, less than a mile from Town Hall. He knew the kids were at school and that Martha would be there alone. That was what he had wanted. He needed to talk this out with someone a lot more sensitive than Jacobi.

Besides, what he had learned from Captain Hall and the Baker file had dredged up the most painful memories of his entire life.

"A monster," Martha said.

"Yeah. Born one on the outside, made one on the inside. But there's another child monster I want to talk about. Not Carly Baker. Annie... Ann Harrison."

Martha gasped. "That sister you told me about last night?"

Harrison nodded. He knew this was going to hurt, but he had to do it, had to get it out. He was going to explode into a thousand twitching bloody pieces if he didn't.

"I was nine when she was born. December 2, 1968—a week after Carly Baker. Seven pounds, four ounces of horror. She looked more fish than human."

His sister's image was imprinted on the rear wall of his brain. And it should have been after all those hours he had spent studying her loathsome face. Only her eyes looked human. The rest of her was awful. A lipless mouth, flattened nose, sloping forehead, fingers and toes fused so that they looked more like flippers than hands and feet, a bloated body covered with shiny skin that was a dusky gray-blue. The doctors said she was that color because her heart was bad, had a defect that caused mixing of blue blood and red blood.

A repulsed nine-year-old Kevin Harrison had dubbed her The Tuna—but never within earshot of his parents.

"She wasn't supposed to live long. A few months, they said, and she'd be dead. But she didn't die. Annie lived on and on. One year. Two. My father and the doctors tried to get my mother to put her into some sort of institution, but Mom wouldn't hear of it. She kept Annie in the third bedroom and talked to her and cooed over her and cleaned up her shit and just hung over her all the time. All the time, Martha!"

Martha gripped his hand and nodded for him to go on.

"After a while, it got so there was nothing else in Mom's life. She wouldn't leave Annie. Family trips became a thing of the past. Christ, if she and Dad went out to a movie, *I* had to stay with Annie. No babysitter was trustworthy enough. Our whole lives seemed to center around that freak in the back bedroom. And me? I was forgotten.

"After a while I began to hate my sister."

"Kevin, you don't have to—".

"Yes, I do! I've got to tell you how it was! By the time I was four-teen—just about Tommy Baker's age when he bought it—I thought I was going to go crazy. I was getting all B's in school but did that matter? Hell, no! 'Annie rolled halfway over today. Isn't that wonderful?' Big deal! She was five years old, for Christ sake! I was starting point guard on the high school junior varsity basketball team as a goddam fresh-man, but did anyone come to my games? Hell no!

"I tell you, Martha, after five years of caring for Annie, our house was a powder keg. Looking back now I can see it was my mother's fault for becoming so obsessed. But back then, at age fourteen, I blamed it all on Annie. I really hated her for being born a freak."

He paused before going on. This was the really hard part.

"One night, when my dad had managed to drag my mother out to some company banquet that he had to attend, I was left alone to baby-sit Annie. On those rare occasions, my mother would always tell me to keep Annie company—you know, read her stories and such. But I never did. I'd let her lie back there alone with our old black and white TV while I sat in the living room watching the family set. This time, however, I went into her room."

He remembered the sight of her, lying there with the covers half way up her fat little tuna body that couldn't have been much more than a yard in length. It was winter, like now, and his mother had dressed her in a flannel nightshirt. The coarse hair that grew off the back of her head had been wound into two braids and fastened with pink bows.

"Annie's eyes brightened as I came into the room. She had never spoken. Couldn't, it seemed. Her face could do virtually nothing in the way of expression, and her flipper-like arms weren't good for much, either. You had to read her eyes, and that wasn't easy. None of us knew how much of a brain Annie had, or how much she understood of what was going on around her. My mother said she was bright, but I think Mom was a little whacko on the subject of Annie.

"Anyway, I stood over her crib and started shouting at her. She quivered at the sound. I called her every dirty name in the book. And as I said each one, I poked her with my fingers—not enough to leave a bruise, but enough to let out some of the violence in me. I called her a lousy goddam tunafish with feet. I told her how much I hated her and how I wished she had never been born. I told her everybody hated her and the only thing she was good for was a freak show. Then I said, 'I wish you were dead! Why don't you die? You were supposed to die years ago! Why don't you do everyone a favor and do it now!'

"When I ran out of breath, she looked at me with those big eyes of hers and I could see the tears in them and I knew she had understood me. She rolled over and faced the wall. I ran from the room.

"I cried myself to sleep that night. I'd thought I'd feel good telling her off, but all I kept seeing in my mind's eye was this fourteen-year-old bully shouting at a helpless five-year-old. I felt awful. I promised myself that the first opportunity I had to be alone with her the next day I'd apologize, tell her I really didn't mean the hateful things I'd said, promise to read to her and be her best friend, anything to make it up to her.

"I awoke next morning to the sound of my mother screaming. Annie was dead."

"Oh, my God!" Martha said, her fingers digging into his arm.

"Naturally, I blamed myself."

"But you said she had a heart defect!"

"Yeah. I know. And the autopsy showed that's what killed her—her heart finally gave out. But I've never been able to get it out of my head that my words were what made her heart give up. Sounds sappy and melodramatic, I know, but I've always felt that she was just hanging on to life by the slimmest margin and that I pushed her over the edge."

"Kevin, you shouldn't have to carry that around with you! Nobody should!"

The old grief and guilt were like a slowly expanding balloon in his chest. It was getting hard to breathe.

"In my coolest, calmest, most dispassionate moments I convince myself that it was all a terrible coincidence, that she would have died that night anyway and that I had nothing to do with it."

"That's probably true, so—"

"But that doesn't change that fact that the last memory of her life was of her big brother—the guy she probably thought was the neatest kid on earth, who could run and play basketball, one of the three human beings who made up her whole world, who should have been her champion, her defender against a world that could only greet her with revulsion and rejection—standing over her crib telling her how much he hated her and how he wished she was dead!"

He felt the sobs begin to quake in his chest. He hadn't cried in over a dozen years and he had no intention of allowing himself to start now, but there didn't seem to be any stopping it. It was like running downhill at top speed—if he tried to stop before he reached bottom, he'd go head over heels and break his neck.

"Kevin, you were only fourteen," Martha said soothingly.

"Yeah, I know. But if I could go back in time for just a few seconds,

I'd go back to that night and rap that rotten hateful fourteen-year-old in the mouth before he got a chance to say a single word. But I can't. I can't even say I'm sorry to Annie! I never got a chance to take it back, Martha! I never got a chance to make it up to her!"

And then he was blubbering like a goddam wimp, letting loose half a lifetime's worth of grief and guilt, and Martha's arms were around him and she was telling him everything would be all right, all right, all right...

———

The Detective Harrison understand. Can tell. Want to go kill another face now. Must not. The Detective Harrison not like. Must stop. The Detective Harrison help stop.

Stop for good.

Best way. Only one way stop for good. Not jail. No chain, no little window. Not ever again. Never!

Only one way stop for good. The Detective Harrison will know. Will understand. Will do.

Must call. Call now. Before dark. Before pretty faces come out in night.

———

Harrison had pulled himself together by the time the kids came home from school. He felt strangely buoyant inside, like he'd been purged in some way. Maybe all those shrinks were right after all: sharing old hurts did help.

He played with the kids for a while, then went into the kitchen to see if Martha needed any help with slicing and dicing. He felt as close to her now as he ever had.

"You okay?" she said with a smile.

"Fine."

She had just started slicing a red pepper for the salad. He took over for her.

"Have you decided what to do?" she asked.

He had been thinking about it a lot, and had come to a decision.

"Well, I've got to inform the department about Carly Baker, but I'm going to keep her out of the papers for a while."

"Why? I'd think if she's that freakish looking, the publicity might turn up someone who's seen her."

"Possibly it will come to that. But this case is sensational enough without tabloids like the *Post* and *The Light* turning it into a circus. Besides, I'm afraid of panic leading to some poor deformed innocent getting lynched. I think I can bring her in. She wants to come in."

"You're sure of that?"

"She so much as told me so. Besides, I can sense it in her." He saw Martha giving him a dubious look. "I'm serious. We're somehow connected, like there's an invisible wire between us. Maybe it's because the same thing that deformed her and those other kids deformed Annie, too. And Annie was my sister. Maybe that link is why I volunteered for this case in the first place."

He finished slicing the pepper, then moved on to the mushrooms.

"And after I bring her in, I'm going to track down her mother and start prying into what went on in Monroe in February and March of sixty-eight to cause that so-called 'cluster' of freaks nine months later."

He would do that for Annie. It would be his way of saying good-bye and I'm sorry to his sister.

"But why does she take their faces?" Martha said.

"I don't know. Maybe because theirs were beautiful and hers is no doubt hideous."

"But what does she do with them?"

"Who knows? I'm not all that sure I want to know. But right now—"

The phone rang. Even before he picked it up, he had an inkling of who it was. The first sibilant syllable left no doubt.

"*Ish thish the Detective Harrishon?*"

"Yes."

Harrison stretched the coiled cord around the corner from the kitchen into the dining room, out of Martha's hearing.

"*Will you shtop me tonight?*"

"You want to give yourself up?"

"*Yesh. Pleashe, yesh.*"

"Can you meet me at the precinct house?"

"*No!*"

"Okay! Okay!" God, he didn't want to spook her now. "Where? Anywhere you say."

"*Jusht you.*"

"All right."

"*Midnight. Pleashe where lasht fashe took. Bring gun but not more cop.*"

"All right."

He was automatically agreeing to everything. He'd work out the details later.

"You undershtand, Detective Harrishon?"

"Oh, Carly, Carly, I understand more than you know!"

A sharp intake of breath and then silence at the other end of the line. Finally:

"You know Carly?"

"Yes, Carly. I know you." The sadness welled up in him again and it was all he could do to keep his voice from breaking. "I had a sister like you once. And you... you had a brother like me."

"Yesh," said that soft, breathy voice. "You undershtand. Come tonight, Detective Harrishon."

The line went dead.

———

Wait in shadows. The Detective Harrison will come. Will bring lots cop. Always see on TV show. Always bring lots. Protect him. Many guns.

No need. Only one gun. The Detective Harrison's gun. Him's will shoot. Stop kills. Stop forever.

The Detective Harrison must do. No one else. The Carly cannot. Must be the Detective Harrison. Smart. Know the Carly. Understand.

After stop, no more ugly Carly. No more sick-scared look. Bad face will go way. Forever and ever.

———

Harrison had decided to go it alone.

Not completely alone. He had a van waiting a block and a half away on Seventh Avenue and a walkie-talkie clipped to his belt, but he hadn't told anyone who he was meeting or why. He knew if he did, they'd swarm all over the area and scare Carly off completely. So he had told Jacobi he was meeting an informant and that the van was just a safety measure.

He was on his own here and wanted it that way. Carly Baker wanted to surrender to him and him alone. He understood that. It was part of that strange tenuous bond between them. No one else would do. After he had cuffed her, he would call in the wagon.

After that he would be a hero for a while. He didn't want to be a hero. All he wanted was to end this thing, end the nightmare for the city and for poor Carly Baker. She'd get help, the kind she needed, and he'd use the publicity to springboard an investigation into what had made Annie and Carly and the others in their 'cluster' what they were.

It's all going to work out fine, he told himself as he entered the alley.

He walked half its length and stood in the darkness. The brick walls of the buildings on either side soared up into the night. The ceaseless roar of the city echoed dimly behind him. The alley itself was quiet—no sound, no movement. He took out his flashlight and flicked it on.

"Carly?"

No answer.

"Carly Baker—are you here?"

More silence, then, ahead to his left, the sound of a garbage can scraping along the stony floor of the alley. He swung the light that way, and gasped.

A looming figure stood a dozen feet in front of him. It could only be Carly Baker. She stood easily as tall as he—a good six foot two—and looked like a homeless street person, one of those animated rag-piles that live on subway grates in the winter. Her head was wrapped in a dirty scarf, leaving only her glittery dark eyes showing. The rest of her was muffled in a huge, shapeless overcoat, baggy old polyester slacks with dragging cuffs, and torn sneakers.

"Where the Detective Harrishon's gun?" said the voice.

Harrison's mouth was dry but he managed to get his tongue working.

"In its holster."

"Take out. Pleashe."

Harrison didn't argue with her. The grip of his heavy Chief Special felt damn good in his hand.

The figure spread its arms; within the folds of her coat those arms seem to bend the wrong way. And were those black hooked claws protruding from the cuffs of the sleeves?

She said, "Shoot."

Harrison gaped in shock.

The Detective Harrison not shoot. Eyes wide. Hands with gun and light shake.

Say again: "Shoot!"

"Carly, no! I'm not here to kill you. I'm here to take you in, just as we agreed."

"No!"

Wrong! The Detective Harrison not understand! Must shoot the Carly! Kill the Carly!

"Not jail! Shoot! Shtop the kills! Shtop the Carly!"

"No! I can get you help, Carly. Really, I can! You'll go to a place where no one will hurt you. You'll get medicine to make you feel better!"

Thought him understand! Not understand! Move closer. Put claw out. Him back way. Back to wall.

"Shoot! Kill! Now!"

"No, Annie, please!"

"Not Annie! Carly! Carly!"

"Right. Carly! Don't make me do this!"

Only inches way now. Still not shoot. Other cops hiding not shoot. Why not protect?

"Shoot!" Pull scarf off face. Point claw at face. "End! End! *Pleashe!*"

The Detective Harrison face go white. Mouth hang open. Say, "Oh, my *God!*"

Get sick-scared look. Hate that look! Thought him understand! Say he know the Carly! Not! Stop look! *Stop!*

Not think. Claw go out. Rip throat of the Detective Harrison. Blood fly just like others.

No - No - No! Not want hurt!

The Detective Harrison gurgle. Drop gun and light. Fall. Stare.

Wait other cops shoot. Please kill the Carly. Wait.

No shoot. Then know. No cops. Only the poor Detective Harrison. Cry for the Detective Harrison. Then run. Run and climb. Up and down. Back to new home with the Old Jessi.

The Jessi glad hear Carly come. The Jessi try talk. Carly go sit tub. Close door. Cry for the Detective Harrison. Cry long time. Break mirror million piece. Not see face again. Not ever. Never.

The Jessi say, "Carly, I want my bath. Will you scrub my back?"

Stop cry. Do the Old Jessi's black back. Comb the Jessi's hair.

Feel very sad. None ever comb the Carly's hair. Ever.

"Ethics" was the name of the story I replaced with "Faces" for *Night Visions 6*. This is what happened to it. It became "The Tenth Toe."

The metamorphosis began on November 14, 1988 at the annual SFWA EditorPublisher reception SFWA in New York (which I was overseeing for the fifth time) when Pat LoBrutto asked me if I'd be interested in contributing to this anthology he and Joe Lansdale were editing for Dark Harvest. They were calling it *Razored Saddles*. The story could be sf, horror, fantasy, alternate history, anything my little heart desired... as long as it had something to do with the West.

In a word, cowpunk.

I said, Seriously, Pat—what's it *really* about? He said it wasn't a joke. Could I contribute? I said something like, Gee, that sounds really neat, Pat, but I'm awfully busy. Thanks a million for asking, though.

Avoiding any sudden moves, I backed away, thinking somehow both Pat's and Joe's belts were no longer going through all the loops.

Cowpunk. Sheesh.

I forgot all about it, but Pat called me in February while I was working on a story for *Stalkers* to prod me for that cowpunk piece. Joe Lansdale called in March. Same (cattle) prod. I was going strong on *Sibs* then but promised to do my best to write them a story.

I was wrung out after finishing *Sibs*, but I started wondering if maybe some of the plot elements in "Ethics" could be transposed to the West. I've always found Doc Holiday a weird, wild, and enigmatic figure (this is long before Val Kilmer's portrayal in "Tombstone"). You can't make up a character like that. Why not use him as the protagonist? It would require a complete rewrite but, approached with tongue firmly in cheek, it just might work.

Pat and Joe agreed that it did.

The Tenth Toe (or: The Beginning of My End)

by
Doc Holliday

(transcribed by F. Paul Wilson)

I am thirty-five years old and will not see thirty-six.

I was not always the weak, wheezing, crumbling sack of bones you see before you, a man whose days can be numbered on the fingers of one hand. Nor was I always the hard drinking gambler and shootist you read of in the penny dreadfuls. I started out a much more genteel man, a professional man, even a bit of a milquetoast, one might say. But a flawed milquetoast.

I attended medical school but did not succeed there, so I became a matriculant at a nearby dental school, from which I managed to graduate. I was then a professional man, and proud of it. But I remained flawed—cursed with a larcenous heart. No amount of schooling, be it of the medical, dental, or (I dare say) divinity sort, can extract that stubborn worm. You are born with it, and you die with it, if not from it.

I am dying from it. That young professional man with the larcenous heart led me to notoriety, and to this premature death from consumption.

Allow me to explain…

The first inkling I had of the curse was in the spring of 1878 while I was examining Mrs. Duluth.

Mrs. Duluth's husband owned the Dodge City General Store and it was obvious (at least to me) that food was not in short supply on her supper table. She was fat. Truthfully, I have been in outhouses smaller than this woman. Everything about her was fat. Her face was fat and round like a huge honeydew melon. Her lips were thick and fat. Even her nose and ears were fat.

"Will this hurt?" she said as she lay back, overflowing my relatively new reclining dental chair. I hoped she wouldn't break its lift mechanism.

"Not a bit," I told her. "After all, this is 1878, not the Dark Ages. We are now blessed with the modern methods of painless dentistry."

"What do you plan to do?"

"I'm going to administer some sulfuric ether," I heard myself say.

"And when you're unconscious, I'm going to rob you."

I saw her eyes widen and she must have seen mine do the same. I hadn't meant to say that. True, I had been thinking it, but I'd had no intention of verbalizing it.

"What...what did you say, Doctor Holliday?"

"I said I'm going to rob you. Just a little. I'll go through your purse and take some of your money. Not all of it. Just enough to make this exercise worth my while."

"I really don't think that's very funny, Doctor," she said.

I gulped and steadied myself with an effort. "Neither do I, Mrs. Duluth." And I meant it. What was coming over me? Why was I saying these things? "A joke. A dentist's joke. Sorry."

"I should hope so." She seemed somewhat mollified. "Now, about this tooth—"

"Who cares about that tooth? I'm interested in the third molar there with the big gold filling. I'm going to pop that beauty out and replace it with some garbage metal that looks like gold."

(What was I *saying*?)

"That is quite enough!" she said, rolling out of the chair. She straightened her enormous gingham dress and headed for the door.

"Mrs. Duluth! Wait! I—"

"Never mind! I'll find myself another dentist! One I can trust. Like that new fellow across the street!"

As she went down the steps, she slapped at my shingle, knocking it off one of its hooks. It swung and twisted at a crazy angle until I stepped out and rehung it.

JOHN HENRY HOLLIDAY, DDS
Painless Dentistry

I loved that sign. It was making me rich. I could have made a good living just from the usual drilling, filling, and pulling of my patient's teeth, but that was not enough for my larcenous heart. I had to be *rich!* And I was getting rich quickly from the gold I was mining—literally— from my patients' teeth. I'd found an excellent gold-like compound that I substituted for the real thing while they were out cold in the chair. It was nowhere near as good as gold, but no one had caught on yet. I had another couple of years before the replacement fillings started to fall apart.

Of course, my practice wouldn't last that couple of years if I treated all my patients like Mrs. Duluth. Luckily the waiting room had been empty. I closed the door behind her and stood there thinking. I admit I was somewhat shaken. What was wrong with me? I hadn't meant to say any of those things.

A short while later the widow Porter arrived with her daughter, Bonnie, who had a toothache.

Bonnie was sixteen and extremely buxom for her age. Her bosom was apparently growing at such a rate that the bodice of her dress could not keep pace. She was fairly bursting from it. The tortured seams appeared ready to split. From the way she carried herself, proudly erect with her bust thrust out at the world, I assumed that she was well aware of (and reveled in) the male gender's reaction to her proportions.

Bonnie had a cavity in her second lower left molar. As I leaned over her to examine the tooth more closely, she arched her back so that her breasts brushed against my arm. I straightened and looked at her. She stared back and smiled boldly. This was one of the most brazen young females I'd ever met! I was becoming (I hesitate to say it) aroused.

Teenage girls were never my style. They tend to fall in love, which can be most inconvenient. But for a young thing of Bonnie's proportions, I realized that I might make an exception.

"She'll need a filling," I told her mother.

"Oh, dear!" the widow Porter said. "You mean you'll have to use the drill?"

"The drill?" Bonnie said, the simper suddenly gone out of her. "The drill?"

"Yes." I lifted the instrument from its hook and pumped the pedal to show her how the bit spun.

Her expression was horrified. "You're going to put *that* in my mouth?"

"Yes. But I'd really—"

I could feel my tongue starting to run off without me, but I refused to let it get away this time. I bit down to hold it in place but it broke free.

"—like to put something else in your mouth, if you know what I mean."

Not again! I seemed utterly helpless against this!

"Really?" Bonnie said, smiling again and thrusting her breasts out even further. "Like what?"

I wanted to shove my fist down my throat. Bonnie's mother, I could see, was thinking along similar lines.

The widow Porter shot to her feet and thrust her face to within an inch of mine.

"*What* did you say?"

I tried to pacify her.

"I'm sorry, Mrs. Porter. Perhaps you misunderstood me. Sometimes I don't make myself clear."

She backed off a little. Good. She was listening—even better. I knew I could smooth this over if my mouth would only let me. Just as her face began to soften, I felt my lips begin to move. I could do nothing but listen.

"What I really meant to say was that I'd like to drill her with a special tool I keep buttoned in my pants. As a matter of fact, I'd like to use it on both of you."

"Scoundrel!" she cried, and swung her heavy purse at me, missing my face by a fraction of an inch. "Bounder!"

She grabbed Bonnie by the hand and yanked her from the room. The girl flashed me a smile and a lascivious wink on the way out.

Sweating and gasping, I slumped against the door. I had lost control of my voice! Every thought that flashed into my brain was going straight out my mouth! What was wrong with me?

I was glad it was a slow day. I went to my office and poured two fingers of bourbon from the bottle I kept in the bottom drawer I downed it in a single swallow. I looked at my framed degree from dental school hanging on the wall. I had counted on becoming wealthy here in Dodge. Now I was ruining it.

When I heard the front door open, I hesitated going out. It was frightening not to be able to control your words. But I had to defeat this malady. I had to overcome it by sheer force of will. I forced myself into the anteroom.

It was empty. I went into the drilling room and found a familiar figure sitting in the chair. We played draw poker most nights over at the Forty-Niner Saloon. I wouldn't say we were friends in the truest sense of the word, but I was the closest thing he had to a friend besides his brother.

Wyatt Earp slouched in the chair, helping himself to my nitrous oxide.

Wyatt giggled. "Got a toothache, Doc!"

"Don't overdue that sweet air, Wyatt," I said. "I have to send all the way to Chicago for more."

The smile wavered off and on again. "You'll be going to Chicago and staying there if you try anymore funny business with Miss Bonnie Porter."

I remembered then that Wyatt had been keeping company with the Widow Porter lately.

"I never touched her!"

"But you said some lewd and obscene things that I'd jail you for if you weren't a friend. She's a fine example of young Kansas womanhood and should not be exposed to such behavior."

"She's a tease waiting to blossom into a tart," I said.

Wyatt looked at me with a strange expression. He wanted to frown but the nitrous oxide wouldn't let him.

"I won't have you speak that way about the daughter of a woman for whom I harbor deep feelings."

"You harbor deep feelings for her daughter and you don't want anyone to get to Bonnie before you! And as for the widow Porter, your only deep feelings are for her bank account!"

His half-smile finally disappeared. "Hey, now wait a minute, Doc. I really love that woman!"

I laughed. "You must think I'm as stupid as you are!"

(What was I *saying*? Wyatt had four inches and a good hundred pounds over me! I wanted to vomit!)

"I think you might be a stupid dead man, Doc, if you don't watch what you're saying," he said menacingly as he straightened up from the chair.

I tried to stop myself but couldn't. My mouth ran on.

"Come on, Wyatt. You're fleecing her."

"It's true that I'm allowing her to invest in a couple of the mines that I own, but as a peace officer, I resent your implication that I'm involved in anything illegal."

"You're a disgrace to the badge, Wyatt. People laugh at you—behind your back, of course, because they know if they get on your wrong side they'll wind up in jail on some trumped-up charge, or backshot by your brother Virgil!"

He was stepping toward me, his right hand balled into a fist. I broke out in a cold sweat and felt my bladder try to empty. I probably could have stopped him there with a few rational words, or even a quick confession of abject fear. I actually felt the words forming in my mouth as he raised his arm to punch me—

—and that was when the odor hit me.

Standing helpless before him as he loomed over me, I listened in horror as my voice said:

"God! You smell, too! Did it ever occur to you take a bath before—"

When I woke up on the floor, Wyatt was gone. I staggered to my feet. My jaw ached and my upper lip was swelling. When the room stopped tilting back and forth, I stumbled into the waiting room.

This was a nightmare! If I kept insulting everyone who came to my office, I'd have to close my practice. What would I do? I was already twenty-six and not good for much else besides gambling and shooting. I wasn't a bad shot. Maybe I could take over Earp's job when he left for Tombstone next year.

An odd-looking figure entered then. A skinny old squaw with a hooked nose and dark, piercing eyes set in a face wrinkled like a raisin. That was all I could see of her. The rest of her was swathed in a dusty serape. There was a small red kerchief around her head.

I knew her. Everybody in town knew her: Squaw Jones. She'd been married to an old white man, Aaron Jones, until he got drunk and trampled by a stagecoach a few years ago. Now she wandered in and out of town, selling charms and potions.

"I see Doctor Holliday has bad times," Squaw Jones said. "What is problem?"

"That's what *I'm* supposed to say!" I shouted. "I'm the doctor here!"

"Is your words? You say what wish to hide inside?"

I was shocked. "Yes! How did you know?"

"Squaw smell bad medicine when she pass."

"Bad medicine?"

"You have curse."

"I am well aware of that!"

"Squaw Jones can help. Know of these things. You victim of curse of Untethered Tongue. Very bad medicine."

"You're serious? You're talking about a *curse* curse, like the evil eye or something like that?"

"Much worse."

"I feel bad enough already. Don't try to make me feel stupid, too!"

"You will see, Dr. Holliday," she said, reaching for the door handle. "You will see. And then you will come to Squaw Jones."

"I sincerely doubt it."

"Remember these words. When find man with missing piece, you find enemy."

"I haven't got any enemies!"

"It could be friend."

"I haven't got many of those, either! At least not after this morning!"

"Remember Squaw Jones," she said as she shuffled out the door. "You will need her."

That'll be the day, I thought. I didn't need an Indian. I needed another drink!

———

The next few days recapitulated the events of that morning: I insulted and alienated each member of a steadily dwindling flow of patients. But at least no one punched me.

As I sat and looked out the front window of my empty waiting room, I noticed Mrs. Duluth waddling along the boardwalk. She turned into the doorway of the new dentist who had come into town a few months ago. Dr. James Elliot. He had been starving. Now he had Mrs. Duluth. Glumly, I wondered how many other patients I was driving to him.

The waiting room door opened and there was Squaw Jones again.

"Squaw can come in?"

I motioned her forward. Why not? I had plenty of time on my hands.

Squaw Jones looked the same as she had days ago—a stick figure swathed in a dirty serape. Her bright, beady eyes swept the barren waiting room. I thought I detected a hint of a smile at the corners of her mouth, but it was hard to be sure amid all her wrinkles.

"Curse of Untethered Tongue continue, yes?"

"It's not a curse," I said. "Just a little problem I have to resolve. I don't believe in curses."

She looked me in the eye. There was no doubt about the smile now.

"You could have sent squaw away," she said. "But you chose to see her."

I knew right then I was dealing with a sly old squaw.

"I'm a man of science," I told her. "A dentist. What do you want from me?"

"Squaw wants only to help."

"For a price, I'm sure."

Her shrug was elaborate. "Must clothe this body. Must eat."

"This wouldn't be blackmail, would it?"

"Doctor Holliday!" she said, puffing herself up. "Squaw is like you. Have medicine to sell—like you. Have honor."

"That's not the point. Even granting the existence of such a thing as a curse, I can't imagine anyone who dislikes me enough—before this week, that is—to place a curse on me."

"Unhappy patient, maybe?"

That was all too possible, what with all the gold fillings I'd yanked from people's mouths while they were unconscious in the chair. But someone like that would go to Wyatt first.

"I can't imagine what complaint a patient of mine could have." (I almost choked on that one.)

"Enemy?"

"None whatsoever."

"Someone want to steal your medicine?"

"You mean a competitor? Well, there is one of those. There seems to be an increasing flow of new dentists from the East."

"Who win from Doctor Holliday bad medicine?"

"Well, Dr. Elliot is benefiting now, but..." I laughed. "No. It's too absurd!"

"May be him."

"Jim Elliot? Putting a curse on me so I'll say things I don't want to? Ridiculous!"

"Curse of Untethered Tongue say what in heart. Perhaps Doctor Holliday not like his patients?"

I said, "Look, I'm very busy right now—"

"Bad medicine always help someone."

I felt the first twinges of uneasiness. This whole idea was absurd! And yet...

I turned and found Squaw Jones grinning at me with crooked yellow teeth. She said, "Find man with missing piece."

"You could use a good dentist," I said.

Around suppertime, I was at my usual table in the Forty-Niner, alone, nursing a whiskey, shuffling a deck of cards. I dared not play for fear that I would tell everyone what was in my hand at any moment. My fingers froze in mid-shuffle when Dr. Elliot walked in.

I watched him for a few moments. As much as my mind rebelled against the concept of such a thing as a curse, I couldn't get the thought out of my head. Could this mild-looking fellow dentist have actually placed a curse on my practice? The more I thought about it here amid the smells and laughter of the cow hands, the stage drivers, the gamblers, and the plain old riffraff, the more laughable it became.

I wandered over to where he stood. He had a round face made wider.

by bushy sideburns. He looked tired. Why not? He had been drilling the teeth of my former patients all day.

I was about to say hello when I noticed that he was missing a part of his left fifth digit—the terminal phalanx was gone! As I gaped at the shiny pink dome of fresh scar tissue where his first knuckle should have been, I heard Squaw Jones's voice in my head:

...Find man with missing piece...

I was too shocked for subtlety.

"Your finger! What happened to it?"

He jumped at the sound of my voice and his complexion faded a couple of shades as he looked at me.

"Hello, John. My finger? Why... why nothing happened to it. Why do you ask?"

"I never noticed that you had a... piece missing before now. When did it happen?"

He smiled, regaining his composure. "Oh, that. An old accident when I was in school back east. An industrial accident, you might say. I caught it in a defective drilling machine."

I couldn't take my eyes from that foreshortened digit. "The scar tissue doesn't look that old."

"An old injury, do you hear?" He was becoming agitated. "Very old. Very, very old!"

The obvious freshness of the scar and Dr. Elliot's overwrought behavior sent a stream of ice water running through my arteries.

...When find man with missing piece, you find enemy...

"Yes, of course," I said. "Very old. Of course."

He thrust his hand into his pocket.

I fled the saloon and ran to the stable. I saddled my horse and rode out to where Squaw Jones made her camp.

———

"So now Doctor Holliday believe in curse of Untethered Tongue," she said, nodding and smiling with smug satisfaction.

"Not completely," I said. "Let's just say I disbelieve in it less than I did this afternoon."

Her tent was dim, the air inside steamy and layered with reminders of past meals, strangely spiced.

"But I just can't believe," I said, "that one of my colleagues, a fellow dental practitioner, would be so unethical as to use such scurrilous means to build his practice at my expense!"

"You would never do such thing?"

"Never! I am an ethical practitioner!"

"And what is your wish, Dr. Holliday?"

"To have the curse—if that's what it is—lifted."

"By this squaw?"

"Of course. That's why I'm here."

"Want thirteen ounces gold for ending Untethered Tongue."

"Thirteen oun—?"

"This squaw know it very small price for saving Doctor Holliday's honor, but her heart is touched by his misfortune." She cleared her throat. "Please pay in metal, not bills."

I'd hidden away significantly more than that amount of gold from the fillings I'd removed over the years. But thirteen ounces!

"I'd want a guarantee."

"Nothing sure in magic, Doctor Holliday."

I rose from my seat and started for the door. "I'm sorry. I can't allow myself to be made into a fool." I was bluffing. I bluffed well in poker, even back then, and had little doubt I could get her to back down. But she kept quiet, waiting until my hand closed on the doorknob before she spoke. She did not, however, say the words I was hoping for.

"For three more ounces, maybe this squaw can turn bad medicine back on one who start it."

As I said before: A sly old bird. I had taken the bait, now she set the hook. A gamble of sixteen ounces, but suddenly I didn't care. I wanted to get even.

I returned to my chair.

"Can you really do that?"

She nodded. "If Doctor Holliday make sacrifice."

"Sacrifice? Wait a second here. I—"

"Must have no fear."

"I'll have no fear as long as I have my revenge."

She smiled and rubbed her hands together. "This is good."

"What do I have to do?"

"Doctor Holliday must give three things. First thing closely touches maker of Untethered Tongue. You know who he is?"

"Dr. Elliot," I said. "No doubt about it. But just how 'closely' must this thing touch?"

"Very close. Underclothes. Pen."

I considered that for a moment. How on Earth was I going to handle that? How was I going to get a hold of a pair of Elliot's underwear? Maybe a sock would do.

No matter. I'd find away.

"What else do you need?"

"Need small amount of Doctor Holliday's liquid."

"Liquid?" This was getting more clichéd by the minute. "You mean blood?"

She shook her head. She seemed embarrassed. "Fluid that only man can give."

"I don't understand—" I began. And then I did. "What kind of magic is this?"

"Very, very old."

"Really. And what if I were a woman?"

"We wait for your time of month."

"I see." I found it difficult to believe that I was sitting here having a serious conversation about this.

She cleared her throat again. "The sample—you can give soon?"

I squared my shoulders. "Of course. And the third thing?"

"This squaw will tell when you bring first two."

I wasn't sure I liked the sound of that, but I couldn't turn back now. I had stepped over the edge and had left the safe and sane world behind; I was now adrift in the world of the magical and the irrational. Squaw Jones's world. I had to trust her as a guide.

———

Early the next morning I was at the hotel next to my office eating eggs and potatoes. I've never liked eggs and potatoes, but I was there because Elliot was there. I raged silently as I watched him storing up on his nourishment before a busy day of drilling the teeth of my patients.

I was in a black mood. I had been by his rooming house earlier but had found none of his laundry around. I'd been tempted to break into his quarters but was afraid I'd get caught. I couldn't risk that, with Wyatt still mad at me.

As I watched him, he stirred his coffee and licked the spoon dry before placing it on the tablecloth. A neat man. A fastidious man. I felt like running over and wringing his—

The spoon.

I almost shouted out loud. That's it! The spoon! It had been in his mouth! What contact could be more "close" than being in someone's mouth?

I waited until he finished his meal and departed, then hurried over to his table, just beating the serving girl to it. She gave me a strange look as I darted in front of her and grabbed his spoon off the tray, but I simply continued on my way without a backward glance, as if this were the most natural thing in the world.

The hard part was over. I headed across the street to the back rooms at the Forty-Niner. Miss Lily would be waking up just about now. For a nominal fee, she'd help me obtain the second ingredient. This was the easy part.

"Now what?" I said as I held out the spoon and a small cup of cloudy liquid to Squaw Jones.

She made no move to take them from me. "You have gold?"

"Yes." I pulled a leather pouch from my coat pocket. "Sixteen ounces, as agreed."

I held my breath as she loosened the drawstring and looked inside. My larcenous heart had prevailed on me to cheat her of her payment. No gold for Squaw Jones. Instead I'd made nuggets of lead and coated them with the gold colored material I used for my fake gold fillings. They wouldn't stand close inspection.

She looked inside, gauged the weight of the bag in her hand, then nodded.

"Is good." The pouch disappeared inside her serape and then she took the two ingredients from me. "Now this squaw make mix. Doctor Holliday wait outside."

"What about the third ingredient?"

She smiled. "Soon, Doctor Holliday. Must be patient."

I stepped outside her tent. It was difficult to be patient knowing that Dr. Elliot was busy in his office working on my patients while my office door was locked.

After what seemed like hours, Squaw Jones called me back in. I found her sitting there with a cup of steaming liquid.

"Now time for third ingredient. The sacrifice."

"What sort of sacrifice?" I didn't like the sound of this one bit.

"Small part of you. Something Doctor Holliday will not miss, but something that will not grow back."

"Wait just a minute!" I said. I'd heard about deals like this where you make a trade for "something you'll never miss" and I didn't want to fall into that trap! "We're not talking about my soul, are we?"

She laughed. "No! Only small piece of flesh. Token for gods. Dr. Elliot gave finger."

"How did you know that?"

"You told this squaw last night."

"Did I? I don't remember."

"You did. Doctor Holliday must make same sacrifice if he wish bad medicine go away."

Something that won't grow back. That left out hair and fingernail clippings. I certainly didn't want to lose a part of a finger—I didn't approve of public deformity.

"Maybe this isn't such a good idea."

She shrugged. "Without sacrifice, Dr. Elliot will not feel curse of Unhindered Hands."

"'Unhindered Hands'? Just what is that?"

"Like Untethered Tongue. As Doctor Holliday's lips now speak what he wish kept hidden in heart, Doctor Elliot's hands will do things he only wish to do."

The thought of Dr. Elliot's hands acting upon whatever physical desires occurred to him, to be no more able to restrain his hands than I had been able to restrain my tongue delighted me.

Then I thought of something neither I nor anyone else would miss—

"How about my little toe?"

"It is good," she said.

"How do we do this?"

Following her directions, I removed the boot and sock from my left foot and held it over the steaming liquid.

"Dip toe."

Feeling like a fool for going through this hocus-pocus, yet hating myself for not having the nerve to call the whole thing off and take my chances with my unruly tongue, I dipped my little toe into the cup.

"Enough," she said after a moment. She withdrew the cup and handed me a dirty cloth. "Dry toe."

I scrutinized my left fifth toe. It looked just like the others, only wet.

"Something's wrong!" I said. "I thought I was supposed to 'sacrifice' this toe! Nothing happened!"

"Patience, Doctor Holliday. Patience."

I was convinced now that I was being hoodwinked. I quickly

rubbed my toe dry and rose to my feet.

"This is a farce! I'm glad I didn't give you any real gold!"

Her head snapped around. She stared at me. "Gold not real?"

"No. So you can call off this whole charade."

"Too late. Medicine is made. Curse begins."

"But my toe—"

I looked down at my left foot. There were only four toes. All that remained of my tenth toe was a small pink bulge of fresh scar tissue.

"Where—?"

I opened the cloth and there was my toe. As I watched, it fumed and melted into a pink fluid that was absorbed by the cloth. The odor made me want to gag.

Squaw Jones was pawing through the bag of fake gold nuggets. "Doctor Holliday trick this squaw?"

"Why not? You're probably the one who got me in this fix in the first place. You're playing both sides of street."

She approached me, menace in her eyes. I kept watch on her hands, making sure both were in sight. They were: clutching the pouch of fake gold. Her face came within inches of mine. She stared at me.

Then she coughed. Once.

"Return to your office, Doctor Holliday. Curse of Untethered Tongue is broken; curse of Unhampered Hands begin. Squaw Jones cannot change that now."

I glanced down at my four-toed foot again and realized I was rapidly becoming a believer. With boot and sock in hand, I hurried from Squaw Jones's tent.

"But you will pay another way!" she called after me.

———

The first patient to show up was Mr. O'Toole. My private name for him was "Mr. O'Stool"—he had a bowel fixation which he blamed on his bad teeth. He spent most office visits describing his movements. He was a bore but he came every two weeks for new filling.

But I got through the visit with no problem. I'd had an urge to tell him that I thought he was suffering from a fecal impaction that had backed up to his brain but the remark remained within my mind while my mouth offered bland reassurances.

I drilled his latest imaginary cavity and fairly danced out of the examining room.

I've done it! I've broken the curse!

I went to the front window in my waiting room and looked across the street at Dr. Elliot's office. I whispered:

"I've beaten you, Elliot! Beaten you at your own game!"

As I watched, I saw Bonnie Pontiac come racing out of Dr. Elliot's office, trying to cover her bobbing, exposed breasts with one hand while holding up her ripped skirt with the other. In close pursuit, with a piece of Bonnie's torn bodice clutched in his teeth, was Dr. Elliot. And right behind the two of them was the widow Porter, swinging her handbag. She caught Dr. Elliot full force in the back of the head with a swing and he went down. Then she stood over him and began pounding him with the bag.

I watched until Wyatt ran up. He pulled his pistol and just stood there, his eyes captured by the pink-tipped whiteness of Bonnie's breasts. I knew though that as soon as she covered herself, Wyatt would be on Dr. Elliot like a lynch mob. He wasn't going to take at all kindly to someone going after Bonnie Porter before he'd had firsts.

Poor Dr. Elliot. Couldn't control his hands. Such a shame.

As I turned away I felt a twinge behind my sternum. I began to cough. I'd never coughed like this before in my life. Spasms racked my chest. I pulled out my handkerchief and buried my face in it, trying to muffle the coughs, perhaps suppress them by trapping them inside. Suddenly I felt something tear free in my chest and fill my throat. I gagged it out.

Blood stained my handkerchief.

Hemoptysis—a bloody cough. A sure sign of consumption, or what they were now calling tuberculosis.

But how could I have tuberculosis? I hadn't been visiting anyone in a sanitarium, and the only people in these parts who had any tuberculosis were...

...Indians.

Squaw Jones had coughed in my face, but only once, and that had been just a few hours ago. I couldn't have developed tuberculosis in that short time. It was impossible.

I glanced out the window again. Wyatt was leading Dr. Elliot off toward the jail, and being none too gentle about it. In the crowd that had gathered, all heads were turned to watch them go. All except one. Squaw Jones was there, staring directly at me.

I coughed again.

I remember some highly offended comments about this story in the London *Times* from a pro-abortion reviewer. And then, on the flip side, came angry letters from the goofier Right-to-Life types who decried the story's Halloween connection because they thought it smacked of Satanism.

Like the man says, it ain't easy being me.

But I guess I asked for it.

I knew when I wrote "Buckets" that it would raise hackles. Sometimes you write things for just that reason—to tick people off, or rub their noses in something they refuse to notice. Sometimes a whack upside the head is the only way you can get some folks' attention.

"Buckets" didn't come about that way. "Buckets" was written to order, so to speak. I never would have written it at all if Alan Ryan hadn't been editing *Halloween Horrors II*.

At the 1985 World Fantasy Convention in Tucson, at the Friday night autograph party, Alan Ryan tapped me on the shoulder and said, "I need a story for an anthology. Doctors and Halloween: see if you can write me something around that." And then he was off.

But his idea stayed. The juxtaposition of those two disparate elements intrigued me. So I paged through the notebook where I store my scraps of ideas (it's digital now) and found an old entry scribbled at the height of the Atlanta child murders: "Child-killer faced with ghosts of his victims." No juice there, no second tier. I substituted Negligent Doctor for Child-killer, and Dead Patients for Victims, but the result excited me no more than the original. All right, how about a Child-killer/Doctor? Nah. Still no second tier. I was about to move on when it flashed through my mind that an abortionist could be considered a child-killer. So how about a physician abortionist faced with the shades of all the kids who were never born because of him?

What if...?

What if one day a year those shredded fetuses were allowed to return to the world as the children they would have become had they not been aborted? Who would they most want to visit that day? Their mothers? Maybe. The guy who'd turned them into fetal soup? *Definitely.* And what if that one day were Halloween?

Got it.

The story demanded to be written. Not later—*now.* And once I'd put myself in the position of those kids, allowed myself to tap into their feelings, sample their grief, their sense of loss, their rage—oh yes, their screeching, eye-clawing rage—the story consumed me. I wrote it in a wild rush. Actually, it wrote itself. Given the premise, I could see only one way to bring it all home, only one way to provide the catharsis that the story—and the characters—demanded.

I took the opportunity to offer a different perspective on a touchy problem and did as much as I could with it. I never worried about its political correctness, but I knew from the start that "Buckets" would be extremely unpopular with a fair number, perhaps even a majority of readers. I won't kid you: That made me hesitate. But I decided to go ahead anyway. Besides offering the reader our best, and staying true to our craft, writers have few obligations. So when an opportunity arises to provide a voice for those who have none, we shouldn't turn away.

I'm sorry the London *Times* reviewer so loathed "Buckets," but I'm not the least bit sorry it upset her or the women she pretends to speak for. Nor do I care that the supernatural element disturbs the religious Right-to-Lifers. It's not their story. It's mine. If you don't want to be disturbed by your reading material, don't read horror fiction. We don't write it to make nice-nice. Disturbing the peace is our job. That's what we're paid to do. You don't like it, go buy a cozy, or a Harlequin.

And surely some of the blame should go to Alan Ryan. After all, "Buckets" never would have been written if he hadn't asked me for it.

As you will see, "Buckets" leaves no room for a neutral stance. But given the premise, how else could it be written? (I don't know why, but *Halloween Horrors II* was never published. I saved the story for my first collection, *Soft & Others.*)

Later on, Kris Rusch at Pulphouse pubbed it as a stand-alone paperback.

Buckets

Halloween - 1985

"My, aren't you an early bird!"

Dr. Edward Cantrell looked down at the doe-eyed child in the five-and-dime Princess Leia costume on his front doorstep and tried to guess her age. A beautiful child of about seven or eight, with flaxen hair and scrawny little shoulders drawn up as if she were afraid of him, as if he might bite her. It occurred to him that today was Wednesday and it was not yet noon. Why wasn't she in school? Never mind. It was Halloween and it was none of his business why she was getting a jump on the rest of the kids in the trick-or-treat routine.

"Are you looking for a treat?" he asked her.

She nodded slowly, shyly.

"Okay! You got it!" He went to the bowl behind him on the hall table and picked out a big Snickers. Then he added a dime to the package. He wanted it to become a Halloween tradition over the years that Dr. Cantrell's place was where you got dimes when you trick-or-treated.

He thrust his hand through the open space where the screen used to be. He liked to remove the storm door screen on Halloween; it saved him the inconvenience of repeatedly opening the door against the kids pressing against it for their treats; and besides, he worried about one of the little ones being pushed backward off the front steps. A lawsuit could easily follow something like that.

The little girl lifted her silver bucket.

He took a closer look. No, not silver—shiny stainless steel, reflecting the dull gray overcast sky. It reminded him of something, but he couldn't place it at the moment. Strange sort of thing to be collecting Halloween treats in. Probably some new fad. Whatever became of the old pillowcase or the shopping bag, or even the plastic jack-o-lantern?

He poised his hand over the bucket, then let the candy bar and dime drop. They landed with a soft <u>squish</u>.

Not exactly the sound he had expected. He leaned forward to see what else was in the bucket but the child had swung around and was making her way down the steps.

Out on the sidewalk, some hundred feet away along the maple-lined driveway, two older children waited for her. A stainless-steel bucket dangled from each of their hands.

Edward shivered as he closed the front door. A new chill seemed to fill the air. Maybe he should put on a sweater. But what color? He checked himself over in the hall mirror. Not bad for a guy looking fifty-two in the eye. That was Erica's doing. Trading in the old wife for a new model twenty years younger had had a rejuvenating effect. Also it made him work at staying young looking—like three trips a week to the Short Hills Nautilus Club and watching his diet. He decided to forego the sweater for now.

He almost made it back to his recliner and the unfinished New York Times when the front bell rang again. Sighing resignedly, he turned and went back to the front door. He didn't mind tending to the trick-or-treaters, but he wished Erica were here to share door duty. Why did she have to pick today for her monthly spending spree at the Mall? He knew she loved Bloomingdale's—in fact, she had once told him that after she died she wanted her ashes placed in an urn in the lingerie department there—but she could have waited until tomorrow.

Two boys this time, both about eleven, both made up like punkers with orange and green spiked hair, ripped clothes, and crude tattoos, obviously done with a Bic instead of a real tattooer's pen. They stood restlessly in the chill breeze, shifting from one foot to the other, looking up and down the block, stainless steel buckets in hand.

He threw up his hands. "Whoa! Tough guys, ay? I'd better not mess around with the likes of—!"

One of the boys glanced at him briefly, and in his eyes Edward caught a flash of such rage and hatred—not just for him, but for the whole world—that his voice dried away to a whisper. And then the look was gone as if it had never been and the boy was just another kid again. He hastily grabbed a pair of Three Musketeers and two dimes, leaned through the opening in the door, and dropped one of each into their buckets.

The one on the right went *squish* and the one on the left went *plop*.

He managed to catch just a glimpse of the bottom of the bucket on the right as the kid turned. He couldn't tell what was in there, but it was red.

He was glad to see them go. Surly pair, he thought. Not a word out of either of them. And what was in the bottom of that bucket? Didn't look like any candy he knew, and he considered himself an expert on candy. He patted the belly that he had been trying to flatten for months. More than an expert—an *aficionado* of candy.

Further speculation was forestalled by a call from the hospital. One of his postpartum patients needed a laxative. He okayed a couple of ounces of milk of mag. Then the nurse double-checked his pre-op orders on the hysterectomy tomorrow.

He managed to suffer through it all with dignity. It was Wednesday and he always took Wednesdays off. Jeff Sewell was supposed to be taking his calls today, but all the floors at the hospital had the Cantrell home phone number and they habitually tried here first before they went hunting for whoever was covering him.

Edward was used to it. He had learned ages ago that there was no such thing as a day off in OB-Gyn.

The bell rang again, and for half a second Edward found himself hesitant to answer it. He shrugged off the reluctance and pulled open the door.

Two mothers and two children. He sucked in his gut when he recognized the mothers as long-time patients.

This is more like it!

"Hi, Doctor Cantrell!" the red-haired woman said with a big smile. She put a hand atop the red-haired child's head. "You remember Shana, don't you? You delivered her five years ago next month."

"I remember you, Gloria," he said, noting her flash of pleasure at having her first name remembered. He never forgot a face. "But Shana here looks a little bit different from when I last saw her."

As both women laughed, he scanned his mind for the other's name. Then it came to him:

"Yours looks a little bigger, too, Diane."

"She sure does. What do you say to Doctor Cantrell, Susan?"

The child mumbled something that sounded like "Ricky Meat" and held up an orange plastic jack-o-lantern with a black plastic strap.

"That's what I like to see!" he said. "A real Halloweeny treat holder. Better than those stainless-steel buckets the other kids have been carrying!"

Gloria and Diane looked at each other. "Stainless steel buckets?"

"Can you believe it?" he said as he got the two little girls each a Milky Way and a dime. "My first three Halloween customers this morning carried steel buckets for their treats. Never seen anything like it."

"Neither have we," Diane said.

"You haven't? You should have passed a couple of boys out on the street."

"No. We're the only ones around."

Strange. But maybe they'd cut back to the street through the trees as this group entered the driveway.

He dropped identical candy and coins into the identical jack-o-lanterns and heard them strike the other treats with a reassuring rustle.

He watched the retreating forms of the two young mothers and their two happy kids until they were out of sight. This is the way Halloween should be, he thought. Much better than strange hostile kids with metal buckets.

And just as he completed the thought, he saw three small, white-sheeted forms of indeterminate age and sex round the hedge and head down the driveway. Each had a shiny metal bucket in hand.

He wished Erica were here.

He got the candy bars and coins and waited at the door for them. He had decided that before he parted with the goodies he was going to find out who these kids were and what they had in their little buckets. Fair was fair.

The trio climbed to the top step of the stoop and stood there waiting, silently watching him through the eyeholes of their sheets.

Their silence got under his skin.

Doesn't anybody say "Trick or treat" anymore?

"Well, what have we here?" he said with all the joviality he could muster. "Three little ghosts! The Ghostly Trio!"

One of them, he couldn't tell which, lisped a timid, "Yeth."

"Good! I like ghosts on Halloween! You want a treat?"

They nodded as one.

"Okay! But first you're gonna have to earn it! Show me what you've got in those buckets and I'll give you each a dime and a box of Milk Duds! How's that for a deal?"

The kids looked at each other. Some wordless communication seemed to pass between them, then they turned and started back down the steps.

"Hey, kids! Hey, wait!" he said quickly, forcing a laugh. "I was only kidding! You don't have to show me anything. Here! Just take the candy."

They paused on the second step, obviously confused.

Ever so gently, he coaxed them back. "C'mon, kids. I'm just curious about those buckets, is all. I've been seeing them all day and I've been wondering where they came from. But if I frightened you, well, hey, I'll ask somebody else later on." He held up the candy and the coins and extended his hand through the door. "Here you go."

One little ghost stepped forward but raised an open hand—a little girl's hand—instead of a bucket.

He could not bear to be denied any longer. He pushed open the storm door and stepped out, looming over the child, craning his neck to see into that damn little bucket. The child squealed in fright and turned away, crouching over the bucket as if to protect it from him.

What are they trying to hide? What's the matter with them? And what's the matter with me?

Really. Who *cared* what was in those buckets?

He cared. It was becoming an obsession with him. He'd go crazy if he didn't find out.

Hoping nobody was watching—nobody who'd think he was some sort of child molester—he grabbed the little ghost by the shoulders and twisted her toward him. She couldn't hide the bucket from him now. In the clear light of day he got a good look into it.

Blood.

Blood with some floating bits of tissue and membrane lay maybe an inch and a half deep in the bottom.

Startled and sickened, he could only stand there and stare at the red, swirling liquid. As the child tried to pull the bucket away from him, it tipped, spilling its contents over the front of her white sheet. She screamed—more in dismay than terror, it seemed.

"Let her go!" said a little boy's voice from beside him. Edward turned to see one of the other ghosts hurling the contents of its bucket at him. As if in slow motion, he saw the sheet of red liquid and debris float toward him through the air, spreading as it neared. The warm spray splattered him up and down and he reeled back in revulsion.

By the time he had wiped his eyes clear, the kids were half way down the driveway. He wanted to chase after them but had to get out of these bloody clothes first. He'd look like a homicidal maniac if someone saw him running after three little kids looking like this.

Arms akimbo, he hurried to the utility room and threw his shirt into the sink.

Why? his mind cried as he tried to remember whether hot or cold water set a stain. He tried cold and began rubbing at the blood in the blue oxford cloth.

He scrubbed hard and fast to offset the shaking of his hands. What a horrible thing for anyone to do, but especially children! Questions tumbled over each other in confusion: What could be going through their sick little minds? And where had they gotten the blood?

But most of all, Why me?

Slowly, the red color began to thin and run, but the bits of tissue clung. He looked at them more closely. Damn if that doesn't look like...

Recognition triggered an epiphany. He suddenly understood everything. He now knew who those children were—or at least who had put them up to it—and he understood why. He sighed with relief as anger flooded through him like a cleansing flame. He much preferred being angry to being afraid.

He dried his arms with a paper towel and went to call the cops.

———

"Right-to-Lifers, Joe! Has to be them!"

Sgt. Joe Morelli scratched his head. "You sure, Doc?"

Edward had known the Morelli family since Joe's days as a security guard at the Mall, waiting for a spot to open up on the Short Hills police force. He'd delivered all three of Joe's kids.

"Who else could it be? Those little stainless steel buckets they carry—the ones I told you about—they're the same kind we use in D-and-C's, and get this: We use suction now, but used to use those buckets in abortions. The scrapings from the uterus slid down through a weighted speculum into a bucket just like those."

And it was those bloody scrapings that had been splattered all over him.

"But why you, Doc? I know you do abortions now and then—all you guys do—but you're not an abortionist per se, if you know what I'm saying."

Edward nodded, not mentioning Sandy. He knew Joe's youngest daughter's pregnancy two years ago was still a touchy subject. She'd been only fifteen but Edward had taken care of everything for Joe with the utmost discretion. He now had a devoted friend on the police force.

A thought suddenly flashed through Edward's mind:

They must know about the women's center! But how could they?

It was due to open tomorrow, the first of the month. He had been so careful to avoid any overt connection with it, situating it down in Newark and going so far as to set it up through a corporate front. Abortions might be legal, but it still didn't sit well with a lot of people to know that their neighbor ran an abortion mill.

Maybe that was it. Maybe a bunch of sicko right-to-lifers had connected him with the new center.

"What gets me," Joe was saying, "is that if this is real abortion material like you say, where'd they get it?"

"I wish I knew." The question had plagued him since he had called the police.

"Well, don't you worry, Doc," Joe said, slipping his hat over his thinning hair. "Whatever's going on, it's gonna stop. I'll cruise the neighborhood. If I see any kids, or even adults with any of these buckets, I'll I-D them and find out what's up."

"Thanks, Joe," he said, meaning it. It was comforting to know a cop was looking out for him. "I appreciate that. I'd especially like to get this ugly business cleared up before the wife and I get home from dinner tonight."

"I don't blame you," he said, shaking his head. "I know I wouldn't want Marie to see no buckets of blood."

The trick-or-treaters swelled in numbers as the afternoon progressed. They flowed to the door in motley hordes of all shapes, sizes, and colors. A steady stream of Spocks, Skywalkers, Vaders, Indiana Joneses, Madonnas, Motley Crues, Twisted Sisters, and even a few ghosts, goblins, and witches.

And always among them were one or two kids with steel buckets.

Edward bit his lip and repressed his anger when he saw them. He said nothing, did not try to look into their buckets, gave no sign that their presence meant anything to him, pretended they were no different from the other kids as he dropped candies and coins into the steel buckets among the paper sacks and pillow cases and jack-o-lanterns, all the while praying that Morelli would catch one of the little bastards crossing the street and find out who was behind this bullshit.

He saw the patrol car pull into the drive around 4:00. Morelli finally must have nailed one of them. About time! He had to leave for the women's center soon and wanted this thing settled and done with.

"No luck, Doc," Joe said, rolling down his window. "You must have scared them off."

"Are you crazy?" His anger exploded as he trotted down the walk to the driveway. "They've been through here all afternoon!"

"Hey, take it easy, Doc. If they're around, they must be hiding those buckets when they're on the street, because I've been by here about fifty times and I haven't seen one steel bucket."

Edward reined in his anger. It would do no good to alienate Joe. He wanted the police force on his side.

"Sorry. It's just that this is very upsetting."

"I can imagine. Look, Doc. Why don't I do this: Why don't I just park the car right out at the curb and watch the kids as they come in. Maybe I'll catch one in the act. At the very least, it might keep them away."

"I appreciate that, Joe, but it won't be necessary. I'm going out in a few minutes and won't be back until much later tonight. However, I do wish you'd keep an eye on the place—vandals, you know."

"Sure thing, Doc. No problem."

Edward watched the police car pull out of the driveway, then he set the house alarm and hurried to the garage to make his getaway before the doorbell rang again.

THE
MIDTOWN WOMEN'S
MEDICAL CENTER

Edward savored the effect of the westering sun glinting off the thick brass letters over the entrance as he walked by. Red letters on a white placard proclaimed "Grand Opening Tomorrow" from the front door. He slipped around the side of the building into the alley, unlocked the private entrance, and stepped inside.

Dark, quiet, deserted. Damn! He'd hoped to catch the contractor for one last check of the trim. He wanted everything perfect for the opening tomorrow.

He flipped on the lights and checked his watch. Erica would be meeting him here in about an hour, then they would pick up the Klines and have drinks and dinner at the club. He had just enough time for a quick inspection tour.

So clean, he thought as he walked through the waiting room—the floors shiny and unscuffed, the carpet pile unmatted, the wall surfaces unmarred by chips or finger smudges. Even the air smelled new.

This center—his center—had been in the planning stages for three years. Countless hours of meetings with lawyers, bankers, planning boards, architects and contractors had gone into it. But at last it was ready to go. He planned to work here himself in the beginning, just to keep overhead down, but once the operation got rolling he'd hire other doctors and have them do the work while he ran the show from a distance.

He stepped into Procedure Room One and looked over the equipment. Dominating the room was the Rappaport 206, a state-of-the-art procedure table with thigh and calf supports on the stirrups, three breakaway sections, and fully motorized tilts in all planes—Trendelenburg, reverse Trendelenburg, left and right lateral.

Close by, the Zarick suction extractor—the most efficient abortion device on the market—hung gleaming on its chrome stand. He pressed the ON button to check the power but nothing happened.

"It won't work tonight," said a child's voice behind him, making him almost scream with fright.

He spun around. Fifteen or twenty kids stood there staring at him. Most were costumed, and they all carried those goddamn steel buckets.

"All right!" he said. "This does it! I've had just about enough! I'm getting the police!"

He turned to reach for the phone but stopped after one step. More kids were coming in from the hall. They streamed in slowly and silently, their eyes fixed on him, piercing him. They filled the room, occupying every square foot except for the small circle of space they left around him and the equipment. And behind them he could see more, filling the hall and the waiting room beyond. A sea of faces, all staring at him.

He was frightened now. They were just kids, but there were so damn many of them. A few looked fifteen or so, and one looked to be in her early twenties, but by far most of them appeared to be twelve and under. Some were even toddlers! What sort of sick mind would involve such tiny children in this?

And how did they get in? All the doors were locked.

"Get out of here," he said, forcing his voice into calm, measured tones.

They said nothing, merely continued to stare at him.

"All right, then. If you won't leave, I will! And when I return—" He tried to push by a five-year-old girl in a gypsy costume. Without warning she jabbed her open hand into his abdomen with stunning force, driving him back against the table.

"Who are you?" This time his voice was less calm, his tones less measured.

"You mean you don't recognize us?" a mocking voice said from the crowd.

"I've never seen any of you before today."

"Not true," said another voice. "After our fathers, you're the second most important man in our lives."

This was insane! "I don't know *any* of you!"

"You should." Another voice—were they trying to confuse him by talking from different spots in the room?

"*Why?*"

"Because you killed us."

The absurdity of the statement made him laugh. He straightened from the table and stepped forward. "Okay. That's it. This isn't the least bit funny."

A little boy shoved him back, roughly, violently. His strength was hideous.

"M-my wife will be here s-soon." He was ashamed of the stammer in his voice, but he couldn't help it. "She'll call the police."

"Sergeant Morelli, perhaps?" This voice was more mature than the others—more womanly. He found her and looked her in the eye. She was the tall one in her early twenties, dressed in a sweater and skirt. He had a sudden crazy thought that maybe she was a young teacher and these were her students on a class trip. But these kids looked like they spanned all grades from pre-school to junior high.

"Who are you?"

"I don't have a name," she said, facing him squarely. "Very few of us do. But this one does." She indicated a little girl at her side, a toddler made up like a hobo in raggedy clothes with burnt cork rubbed on her face for a beard. An Emmett Kelly dwarf. "Here Laura," she said to the child as she urged her forward. "Show Dr. Cantrell what you looked like last time he saw you."

Laura stepped up to him. Behind the make-up he could see that she was a beautiful child with short dark hair, a pudgy face, and big brown eyes. She held her bucket out to him.

"She was eleven weeks old," the woman said, "three inches long, and weighed fourteen grams when you ripped her from her mother's uterus. She was no match for you and your suction tube."

Blood and tissue swirled in the bottom of her bucket.

"You don't expect me to buy this, do you?"

"I don't care what you buy, Doctor. But this is Sandra Morelli's child—or at least what her child would look like now if she'd been allowed to be born. But she wasn't born. Her mother had names all picked out—Adam for a boy, Laura for a girl—but her grandfather bullied Laura's mother into an abortion and you were oh-so-willing to see that there were no problems along the way."

"This is absurd!" he said.

"Really?" the woman said. "Then go ahead and call Sergeant Morelli. Maybe he'd like to drive down and meet his granddaughter. The one you killed."

"I killed no one!" he shouted. "No one! Abortion has been legal since 1974! Absolutely legal! And besides—she wasn't really alive!"

What's the matter with me? he asked himself. I'm talking to them as if I believe them!

"Oh, yes," the woman said. "I forgot. Some political appointees decided that we weren't people and that was that. Pretty much like what happened to East European Jews back in World War Two. We're not even afforded the grace of being called embryos or fetuses. We're known as 'products of conception.' What a neat, dehumanizing little phrase. So much easier to scrape the 'products of conception' into a bucket than a person."

"I've had just about enough of this!" he said.

"So?" a young belligerent voice said. "What're y'gonna do?"

He knew he was going to do nothing. He didn't want to have another primary grade kid shove him back against the table again. No kid that size should be that strong. It wasn't natural.

"You can't hold me responsible!" he said. "They came to me, asking for help. They were pregnant and they didn't want to be. My God! *I didn't make them pregnant!*"

Another voice: "No, but you sure gave them a convenient solution!"

"So blame your mothers! They're the ones who spread their legs and didn't want to take responsibility for it! How about *them*?"

"They are not absolved," the woman said. "They shirked their responsibilities to us, but the vast majority of them are each responsible for only one of us. You, Doctor Cantrell, are responsible for all of us. Most of them were scared teenagers, like Laura's mother, who were bullied and badgered into 'terminating' us. Others were too afraid of what their parents would say so they snuck off to women's medical centers like this and lied about their age and put us out of their misery."

"Not all of them, sweetheart!" he said. He was beginning to feel he was on firmer ground now. "Many a time I've done three or four on the same woman! Don't tell me they were poor, scared teenagers. Abortion was their idea of birth control!"

"We know," a number of voices chorused, and something in their tone made him shiver. "We'll see them later."

"The point is," the woman said, "that you were always there, always ready with a gentle smile, a helpful hand, an easy solution, a simple way to get them off the hook by getting rid of us. And a bill, of course."

"If it hadn't been me, it would have been someone else!"

"You can't dilute your own blame. Or your own responsibility," said a voice from behind his chair. "Plenty of doctors refuse to do abortions."

"If you were one of those," said another from his left, "we wouldn't be here tonight."

"The *law* lets me do it. The Supreme Court. So don't blame me. Blame those Supreme Court justices."

"That's politics. We don't care about politics."

"But I believe in a woman's right to control her own life, to make decisions about her own body!"

"We don't care what you believe. Do you think the beliefs of a terrorist matter to the victims of his bombs? Don't you understand? This is *personal*!"

A little girl's voice said, "I could have been adopted, you know. I would've made someone a good kid. But I never had the chance!"

They all began shouting at once, about never getting Christmas gifts or birthday presents or hugs or tucked in at night or playing with matches or playing catch or playing house or even playing doctor—

It seemed to go on endlessly. Finally the woman held up her bucket. "All their possibilities ended in here."

"Wait a goddam minute!" he said. He had just discovered a significant flaw in their little show. "Only a few of them ended up in buckets! If you were up on your facts, you'd know that no one uses those old D-and-C buckets for abortions anymore." He pointed to the glass trap on the Zarick suction extractor. "This is where the products of conception wind up."

The woman stepped forward with her bucket. "They carry this in honor of me. I have the dubious distinction of being your first victim."

"You're not *my* victims!" he shouted. "The law—"

She spat in his face. Shocked and humiliated, Edward wiped away the saliva with his shirt sleeve and pressed himself back against the table. The rage in her face was utterly terrifying.

"The *law*?" she hissed. "Don't speak of legalities to me! Look at me! I'd be twenty-two now and this is how I'd look if you hadn't murdered me. Do a little subtraction, doctor: 1974 was a lot less than *twenty*-two years ago. I'm Ellen Benedict's daughter—or at least I would have been if you hadn't agreed to do that 'D-and-C' on her when she couldn't find a way to explain her pregnancy to her impotent husband!"

Ellen Benedict! God! How did they know about Ellen Benedict? Even *he* had forgotten about her!

The woman stepped forward and grabbed his wrist. He was helpless against her strength as she pressed his hand over her left breast. He might have found the softness beneath her sweater exciting under different circumstances, but now it elicited only dread.

"Feel my heart beating? It was beating when your curette ripped me to pieces. I was only six weeks old. And I'm not the only one here you killed before 1974—I was just your first. So you can't get off the hook by naming the Supreme Court as an accomplice. And even if we allowed you that cop-out, other things you've done since '74 are utterly abominable!" She looked around and pointed into the crowd. "There's one! Come here, honey, and show your bucket to the doctor."

A five- or six-year-old boy came forward. He had blond bangs and the biggest, saddest blue eyes the doctor had ever seen. The boy held out his bucket.

Edward covered his face with his hands. "I don't want to see!"

Suddenly he felt his hands yanked downward with numbing force and found the woman's face scant inches from his own.

"*Look*, damn you! You've seen it before!"

He looked into the upheld bucket. A fully formed male fetus lay curled in the blood, its blue eyes open, its head turned at an unnatural angle.

"This is Rachel Walraven's baby as you last saw him."

The Walraven baby! Oh, God, not that one! How could they know?

"This little boy is how he'd look now if you hadn't broken his neck after the abortifacient you gave his mother made her uterus dump him out."

"He couldn't have survived!" he shouted. He could hear the hysteria edging into his voice. "He was pre-viable! Too immature to survive! The best neonatal ICU in the world couldn't have saved him!"

"Then why'd you break my neck?" the little boy asked.

Edward could only sob—a single harsh sound that seemed to rip itself from the tissues inside his chest and burst free into the air. What could he say? How could he tell them that he had miscalculated the length of gestation and that no one had been more shocked than he at the size of the infant that had dropped into his gloved hands? And then it had opened its eyes and stared at him and my God it had looked like it was trying to breathe! He'd done late terminations before where the fetus had squirmed around awhile in the bucket before finally dying, but this one—!

Christ! he remembered thinking, what if the damn thing lets out a cry? He'd get sued by the patient and be the laughingstock of the staff. Poor Ed Cantrell—can't tell the difference between an abortion and a delivery! He'd look like a jerk!

So he did the only thing he could do. He gave its neck a sharp twist as he lowered it into the bucket. The neck didn't even crack when he broke it.

"Why have you come to me?" he said.

"Answer us first," a child's voice said. "Why do you do it? You don't need the money. Why did you kill us?"

"I told you! I believe in every woman's right to—"

They began to boo him, drowning him out. Then the boos changed to a chant: "*Why? Why? Why? Why?*"

"Stop that! Listen to me! I told you why!"

But still they chanted, sounding like a crowd at a football game: "*Why? Why? Why? Why?*"

Finally he could stand no more. He raised his fists and screamed. "All right! Because I can! Is what you want to hear? I do it because I *can!*"

The room was suddenly dead silent.

The answer startled him. He had never asked himself why before. "Because I can," he said softly.

"Yes," the woman said with equal softness. "The ultimate power."

He suddenly felt very old, very tired. "What do you want of me?"

No one answered.

"Why have you come?"

They all spoke as one: "Because today, this Halloween, this night… *we* can."

"And we don't want this place to open," the woman said.

So that was it. They wanted to kill the women's center before it got started—*abort it*, so to speak. He almost smiled at the pun. He looked at their faces, their staring eyes. They mean business, he thought. And he knew they wouldn't take no for an answer.

Well, this was no time to stand on principle. Promise them anything, then get the hell out of here to safety.

"Okay," he said, in what he hoped was a meek voice. "You've convinced me. I'll turn this into a general medical center. No abortions. Just family practice for the community."

They watched him silently. Finally a voice said, "He's lying."

The woman nodded. "I know." She turned to the children. "Do it," she said.

Pure chaos erupted as the children went wild. They were like a berserk mob, surging in all directions. But silent. So silent.

Edward felt himself shoved aside as the children tore into the procedure table and the Zarick extractor. The table was ripped from the floor and all its upholstery shredded. Its sections were torn free and hurled against the walls with such force that they punctured through the plasterboard.

The rage in the children's eyes seemed to leak out into the room, filling it, thickening the air like an onrushing storm, making his skin ripple with fear at its ferocity.

As he saw the Zarick start to topple, he forced himself forward to try to save it but was casually slammed against the wall with stunning force. In a semi-daze, he watched the Zarick raised into the air; he ducked flying glass as it was slammed onto the floor, not just once, but over and over until it was nothing more than a twisted wreck of wire, plastic hose, and ruptured circuitry.

And from down the hall he could hear similar carnage in the other procedure rooms. Finally the noise stopped and room one was packed with children again.

He began to weep. He hated himself for it, but couldn't help it. He simply broke down and cried in front of them. He was frightened. And all the money, all the plans...destroyed.

He pulled himself together and straightened his spine. He would rebuild. All this destruction was covered by insurance. He would blame it on vandalism, collect his money, and have the place brand new inside of a month. These vicious little bastards weren't going to stop him. But he couldn't let them know that.

"Get out, all of you," he said softly. "You've had your fun. You've ruined me. Now leave me alone."

"We'll leave you alone," said the woman who would have been Ellen Benedict's child. "But not yet."

Suddenly, they began to empty their buckets on him, hurling the contents at him in a continuous wave, turning the air red with flying blood and tissue, engulfing him from all sides, choking him, clogging his mouth and nostrils.

And then they reached for him...

Erica knocked on the front door of the center for the third time and still got no answer.

Now where can he be? she thought as she walked around to the private entrance. She tried the door and found it unlocked. She pushed in but stopped on the threshold.

The waiting room was lit and looked normal enough.

"Ed?" she called, but he didn't answer.

Odd. His car was out front. She was supposed to meet him here at five. She'd taken a cab from the mall—after all, she didn't want Ginger dropping her off here; there would be too many questions. The silence was beginning to make her uneasy.

She glanced down the hallway. Dark and quiet.

Almost quiet.

She heard tiny little scraping noises, tiny movements, so soft that she would have missed them if there had been any other sound in the building. It seemed to come from the first procedure room. She stepped up to the door and listened to the dark. Yes, they were definitely coming from in there.

She flipped on the light...and felt her knees buckle.

The room was red—the walls, the ceiling, the remnants of the shattered fixtures, all dripping with red. The clots and the coppery odor that saturated the air left no doubt in Erica's reeling mind that she was looking at blood. But on the floor—the blood-puddled linoleum was littered with countless shiny, silvery buckets. The little rustling sounds were coming from them. She saw something that looked like hair in a nearby bucket and took a staggering step over to see what was inside.

It was Edward's head, floating in a pool of blood, his eyes wide and mad, looking at her. She wanted to scream but the air clogged in her throat as she saw Ed's lips begin to move. They were forming words but there was no sound, for there were no lungs to push air through his larynx. Yet still his lips kept moving in what seemed to be silent pleas. But pleas for what?

And then he opened his mouth wide and screamed—silently.

Copyrights

The Secret History of the World

The preponderance of my work deals with a history of the world that remains undiscovered, unexplored, and unknown to most of humanity. Some of this secret history has been revealed in the Adversary Cycle, some in the Repairman Jack novels, and bits and pieces in other, seemingly unconnected works. Taken together, even these millions of words barely scratch the surface of what has been going on behind the scenes, hidden from the workaday world. I've listed them below in chronological order. (NB: "Year Zero" is the end of civilization as we know it; "Year Zero Minus One" is the year preceding it, etc.)

Scenes from the Secret History is FREE on Smashwords

The Past
"Demonsong" (prehistory)*
"The Compendium of Srem" (1498)
"Wardenclyffe" (1903-1906)
"Aryans and Absinthe" (1923-1924)*
Black Wind (1926-1945)
The Keep (1941)
Reborn (February-March 1968)
"Dat Tay Vao"* (March 1968)
Jack: Secret Histories (1983)
Jack: Secret Circles (1983)
"Piney Power" (1983)+
Jack: Secret Vengeance (1983)
"Faces"* (1988)
Cold City (1990)
Dark City (1991)
Fear City (1993)
"Fix"** (2004) with Joe Konrath and Ann Voss Peterson

Year Zero Minus Three
Sibs (February)
The Tomb (summer)
"The Barrens"* (ends in September)
"A Day in the Life" (October)+
"The Long Way Home"+
Legacies (December)

Year Zero Minus Two
"Interlude at Duane's" (April)+
Conspiracies (April) (includes "Home Repairs"+)
All the Rage (May) (includes "The Last Rakosh"+)
Hosts (June)
The Haunted Air (August)
Scar-Lip Redux (August)
The Upwelling (August)
Lexie (September)
Gateways (September)
Crisscross (November)
Infernal (December)

Year Zero Minus One
Harbingers (January)
"Infernal Night" (with Heather Graham)+
Bloodline (April)
The Fifth Harmonic (April)
Panacea (April)
The God Gene (May)
By the Sword (May)
Ground Zero (July)
The Touch (ends in August)
The Void Protocol (September)
The Peabody-Ozymandias Traveling Circus & Oddity Emporium (September)
  "Tenants"*
The Last Christmas (December)

Year Zero
"Pelts"*
Reprisal (ends in February)
Fatal Error (February) (includes "The Wringer"+)
Double Threat (February-March)
Double Dose (March)
The Dark at the End (March)
Signalz (May)
Nightworld (May)
* available in *Secret Stories*
** available in *Other Sandboxes*
+ available in Quick Fixes—*Tales of Repairman Jack*

The Teen Trilogy*
Jack: Secret Histories
Jack: Secret Circles
Jack: Secret Vengeance

The Early Years Trilogy*
Cold City
Dark City
Fear City

The Adversary Cycle*
The Keep
The Tomb
The Touch
Reborn
Reprisal
Signalz
Nightworld

The ICE Trilogy*
Panacea
The God Gene
The Void Protocol

Graphic Novels
The Keep
Scar-Lip Redux

The LaNague Federation
Healer
Wheels within Wheels
An Enemy of the State
Dydeetown World
The Tery

Collaborations

Mirage (with Matthew J. Costello)
Nightkill (with Steven Spruill)
Masque (with Matthew J. Costello)
Draculas (with Crouch, Konrath, Strand)
The Proteus Cure (with Tracy L. Carbone)
A Necessary End (with Sarah Pinborough)
"Fix"* (with J. A. Konrath & Ann Voss Peterson)
Three Films and a Play (with Matthew J. Costello)
Faster Than Light—Vols. 1 & 2 (with Matthew J. Costello)

The Nocturnia Chronicles (with Thomas F. Monteleone)

Definitely Not Kansas
Family Secrets
The Silent Ones

Short Fiction

Soft & Others
Ad Statum Perspicuum
The Barrens & Others
Aftershock & Others

A Little Beige Book *of Nondescript Stories*
The Christmas Thingy
*Quick Fixes—Tales of Repairman Jack**
Sex Slaves of the Dragon Tong
*The Compendium of Srem**
Ephemerata
*Secret Stories**
Other Sandboxes
The Compendium of F—50 Years of F. Paul Wilson (Vols. 1-3)

Editor

Freak Show
Diagnosis: Terminal
The Hogben Chronicles (with Pierce Watters)

Omnibus Editions
The Complete LaNague
Calling Dr. Death (3 medical thrillers)
*Scenes from the Secret History**
Ephemerata
Three Films and a Play (with Matthew J. Costello)

About the Author

F. PAUL WILSON is the award-winning, *New York Times* bestselling author of eighty-plus books and nearly one hundred short stories spanning science fiction, horror, adventure, medical thrillers, and virtually everything between. *The Tomb* received the Porgie Award from *The West Coast Review of Books*; *Wheels Within Wheels* won the first Prometheus Award. His novella "Aftershock" won a Stoker Award. He was voted Grand Master by the World Horror Convention, received the Lifetime Achievement Award from the Horror Writers of America, and the Thriller Lifetime Achievement Award from the editors of *Romantic Times*. He also received the prestigious Inkpot Award from San Diego ComiCon and is listed in the 50th anniversary edition of *Who's Who in America*.

In 1983 Paramount rendered his novel *The Keep* into a visually striking but otherwise incomprehensible movie with screenplay and direction by Michael Mann. *The Tomb* has spent 25 years in development hell at Beacon Films. Dario Argento adapted his story "Pelts" for *Masters of Horror*.

Over nine million copies of his books are in print in the US and his work has been translated into twenty-four languages. He also has written for the stage, screen, and interactive media.

Curious about other Crossroad Press books?
Stop by our site:
https://www.crossroadpress.com
We offer quality writing
in digital, audio, and print formats.

Made in the USA
Monee, IL
01 February 2025

11310534R00267